DEADLY
Desire

BRENDA JOYCE

St. Martin's Paperbacks

DEADLY DESIRE

Copyright © 2002 by Brenda Joyce Dreams Unlimited, Inc.
Excerpts from *Deadly Pleasure* and *Deadly Affairs* copyright © 2002 by Brenda Joyce Dreams Unlimited, Inc.

ISBN: 0-312-98263-1

Printed in the United States of America

St. Martin's Paperbacks edition / May 2002

St. Martin's Paperbacks are published by St. Martin's Press, 175 Fifth Avenue, New York, NY 10010.

10 9 8 7 6 5 4 3 2 1

One

Francesca Cahill began to plot how to steal out of the house the moment she awoke. She was in the habit of arising at an unfashionable hour, or so her mother accused, but then, Julia Van Wyck Cahill was as fashionable as one of the city's reigning social matriarchs could be. Francesca never deceived herself—not only was she a bluestocking and a radical reformer through and through; she felt rather certain that, behind her back, she was also sometimes labeled an eccentric. No mind. She did not give a whit for fashion anyway, or parties or shopping or teas. She had secretly enrolled at Barnard College, hoping to attain her degree and follow in the footsteps of her idol, the journalist and reformer Jacob Riis. But in the past month, since January 18 to be exact, her plans had somehow, fatefully, changed.

It had all begun with the abduction of her neighbor's six-year-old-boy. Francesca Cahill had discovered the odd, not-quite-a-ransom note and, more important, had been crucial to the city's police department in investigating and then solving the case. In fact, she had worked very closely with the city's new police commissioner, Rick Bragg.

She smiled as she paused in the huge front hall of the house that had been built eight years ago and dubbed "the Marble Palace" by the press. She directed her smile at the new doorman, who she thought was named Jonathon. He was her own age, and, as blond and blue-eyed as she, he smiled back.

The note had arrived fifteen minutes ago. It had been in a sealed and unmarked envelope, which in itself was some cause for alarm. The scripted contents had been a nearly indecipherable scrawl. It read:

Dearest Francesca,

we are in dire need of your help! Do come immediately.

Your friend,
Mrs. Richard Wyeth Channing

The note had been written by Mrs. Channing, her brother's fiancée's mother. And apparently it had been written in extreme haste, as the handwriting was so poor it might have been executed by a child in grade school, not to mention the fact that the envelope had not carried Abigail Channing's name or address. Francesca had not a doubt that the Channings were in trouble.

But how?

She smiled bravely at the doorman. "Jonathon, if you do see my mother, is there any chance you might not mention that you have seen me go out?" As she spoke, she glanced guiltily down the hall, where huge Corinthian pillars were set at intervals until a wide white alabaster staircase led to the three floors above. She had badly burned her right hand while saving the life of Maggie Kennedy—a poor seamstress with whom she was starting to have something of a friendship. Now it was thoroughly bandaged, and she had been ordered to remain in her bed—or close to it—for an entire week. As much as she had no wish to gain an infection, the doctor had told her two hours ago that she was healing quite nicely. In fact, her hand no longer hurt her at all.

And how could she refuse a call for help from the woman who would one day be her brother's mother-in-law and, by familial extension, a second mother to her?

Francesca was very glad now that she had refused to take laudanum that morning, which she had instead discreetly thrown away. Francesca suspected that her mother was hoping to do far more than merely obey Dr. Finney's instructions to keep her at home for an entire week. She thought, but could not prove, that Julia wished to dull her own daughter's personality with the laudanum, in the hope of keeping her out of further jeopardy and any more criminal investigations. Her entire family had been thoroughly undone by this latest incident; in fact, almost everyone she knew was quite upset that she had been so badly hurt while attempting to protect Mrs. Kennedy.

Jonathon had turned white, apparently rather fearful of her mother. "Miss Cahill, er, if she does ask—"

"You have not seen me," she instructed with a cheerful smile, as she was simply thrilled to have a new case on her hands. "I promise you, Jonathon, no harm will come of it. My mother is quite used to my headstrong and independent ways."

Jonathon looked very unhappy indeed.

Taking a big breath, Francesca stepped outside into the frigidly cold air, the huge front door closing behind her. Her right hand was bandaged and so she wore only one glove on her left. She began to smile, a bit exultant. It was a rare day indeed that one outwitted Julia Van Wyck Cahill.

Of course, she must not gloat. There was serious business ahead, if her instincts served her.

The sweeping front lawns were crusted with hard, white snow. Francesca paused below the front steps, sighing with relief. Her gaze swept past the circular drive, the wrought-iron gates, and the light vehicular traffic on Fifth Avenue. A four-in-hand was coming down the street, as were two hansoms and a very elegant brougham. Even from this distance, she could see past the trees bordering Central Park, and several horseback riders were on the riding path, while a woman and two children strolled beside it. It was actually, in spite of the cold, a beautiful day.

And then a man she had quickly come to despise—and fear—spoke into her ear.

"Good afternoon, Miss Cahill. It is a beautiful day, is it not?"

Francesca nearly jumped out of her skin as she whirled to find Arthur Kurland, the dastardly reporter from *The Sun*, standing behind her. He had been hiding behind two man-size Greek urns just below the mansion's front steps.

Francesca was breathless. This man was extremely skilled at uncovering secrets, and she certainly had a secret or two that she wished to hide. She tried to smile. "Mr. Kurland. Were you about to call on someone in my family—or were you lurking about the hedges trespassing?"

He smiled and stepped forward. He was in his thirties, dark-haired, and of a medium build. His appearance was nondescript. But there was nothing nondescript about the articles he wrote for *The Sun* or his perceptiveness and acuity. The man missed nothing—unfortunately. "I suppose I am guilty as charged." He grinned. "I am waiting for you, Miss Cahill."

"Then you are wasting your time, as I have had a touch of the flu and I have nothing interesting to report to you." She started walking briskly down the drive toward the avenue. Her intention was to hail a cab, as her father, Andrew Cahill, had his coach and Julia would be out to lunch shortly in the other Cahill vehicle.

"Surely the police commissioner brought you some interesting news for me to scoop," he said, falling into step beside her. He smiled. "I do believe he has called on you every day since the Cross Murderer was apprehended. What happened to your hand?"

Francesca halted in midstride, facing him with a dreadful feeling. Was he insinuating something? He had seen her and Bragg together too many times to count—they had investigated three politically sensitive cases together, starting with the Burton Abduction.

"Miss Cahill?" Arthur Kurland gripped her arm. "It is so interesting—but hardly newsworthy—that Commissioner Bragg has been calling on you every day since the Cross Murderer was incarcerated. Or is it newsworthy?" He grinned.

"If the commissioner's social life is newsworthy, then you are in dire trouble, indeed, as a newsman," she said tartly. "Bragg goes way back with my father, in case you did not know."

"I know all about your father's political associations. He is even closer to Bragg's father, Rathe Bragg, who has just returned to the city, by the way."

Francesca started. Bragg hadn't said a word about his father returning to the city.

Kurland grinned. "An exchange of information, Miss Cahill. You do recall how we work? I give you something, and you give me something."

She had been conned by this man once before, with the terrible consequence of betraying Bragg's brother Calder Hart. She fought to recover from her surprise. "I truly have no information for you."

"Somehow, I doubt that," he said as she began walking even more briskly toward Fifth Avenue. He kept pace with her. "I think Bragg has been making condolence calls. Did you know that the Cross Murderer is in Bellevue Hospital, with second-degree burns?"

"Really?" Francesca was cool, hardly feigning surprise.

He smiled again. "What happened to your hand, Miss Cahill?"

"I broke it," she snapped, but her anger was only a mask for her fear.

"Why do I always get the most distinct impression that you are hiding something from me?" he asked, with obvious delight. "Why do I have the strongest feeling that you and Bragg are hiding something from me—from the city?"

She didn't have to look at him to know that he was grinning. "You are like a gnat," she said very rudely. "No one is hiding anything."

"Not really. But I do have a sting, my dear, one that can be fatal."

She froze in midstep and faced him. Real fear seized her. This man was a prize-winning journalist. And he had no compunctions, no morals. It was only a matter of time before he pieced together the puzzle of all of their lives. And then what?

Her heart beat hard. "What do you want?"

"Tell me something important, something that I do not know." His eyes were suddenly hard.

"I have nothing to tell," she said tersely.

"Really? Then why is guilt written all over your face?" Kurland asked.

If she gave him what he wanted, he would be satisfied and go—at least for now. "Very well. You win. But you shall owe me for this."

He whipped out a small notepad and a lead pencil. "Yes?" he asked eagerly.

"I stopped the Cross Murderer from striking again. I am the one who set the fire, and that is why my hand is burned."

He began to smile at her. "I knew you were involved, Miss Cahill. I simply knew it."

"How clever of you," she said, feeling ill. She would make the news yet again, and her family would not be happy about it.

"You see, a street urchin was handing these out yesterday not far from Union Square." He reached into his pocket and handed her a calling card.

Of course she recognized it. After all, it was hers.

It read:

Francesca Cahill
Crime-Solver Extraordinaire
No. 810 Fifth Avenue, New York City
All Cases Accepted, No Crime Too Small

The Channings daringly lived on the West Side, which residents like Francesca felt was akin to Texas or the moon, as it was so distant and remote from the rest of the city. Francesca had been shaken from her encounter with Kurland but resolutely dismissed it from her mind. Sarah Channing had become a good friend since her engagement to Francesca's brother, Evan. Although they were nothing at all alike in appearance or manner, Sarah and Francesca were actually quite alike. Sarah was a passionate artist and, in fact, a bohemian at heart. Like Francesca, she had no use for society, its rules, displays, and etiquette. In fact, quite shockingly,

Francesca had heard Sarah say she wished to never marry. Francesca had recently decided that she would never marry, either, never mind her mother's plans. If Sarah's mother was in trouble, Francesca was determined to help. And it never crossed her mind that she might not be able to do so.

Francesca paid her cab fare and approached the mansion, which was quite new and horrendously Gothic, not to mention huge. The horse trotted away as a trolley approached, its bells clanging. Francesca paused on the top step before a pair of wooden doors that would have been beautiful had they not had gargoyle heads in each center. When Sarah's father had died, her mother, a rather frivolous and harmless socialite, had inherited his millions and promptly built their new house. Mrs. Channing was not known for her elegance or good taste.

Francesca's knock was promptly answered, and she was told by the doorman that neither Miss nor Mrs. Channing was receiving visitors. "Would you care to leave your card?" the liveried doorman asked. His uniform was red and gold.

Francesca realized with dismay that Sarah must be at work in her studio. Although one would never know it to look at her, given her plain appearance and shy demeanor, she was a brilliant, even passionate and bold painter. "Actually, I received a note from Mrs. Channing, and I do believe that she will see me."

"I am afraid that she is in her rooms and has said that she will not come down," the doorman said gravely.

A butler sailed into the entry hall. "Goodard? Who is it?"

"A Miss Francesca Cahill."

The butler sailed to a stop before her. "Mrs. Channing will see Miss Cahill, Goodard." He gave the doorman a significant look. "Due to the Crisis," he said.

"There is a crisis?" Francesca asked quickly.

"I shall inform Mrs. Channing that you are here," the heavyset butler intoned gravely.

"Harold? Who is it?"

Francesca stepped forward at the sound of Mrs. Channing's voice. A not-quite pretty woman with reddish blond hair who was extremely well-dressed, yet overdressed, and who somehow reminded one of a flighty and mindless bird was entering the foyer, her slippers clicking on the marble floors. "Francesca! Thank God!" She clapped her hands together, but tears filled her wide eyes. One of her rings was a diamond the size of an acorn.

Francesca smiled. "Hello, Mrs. Channing. I received your note. Are you all right?"

Abigail Channing shook her head wordlessly. She rushed to Francesca, her teal skirts billowing about her. "Thank the Lord you are here!" she cried. "I have been praying that you would come!"

Francesca looked into her widened eyes—as there was little else to do, with the other woman's face a mere two inches from her own. "Is everything all right, Mrs. Channing? You seem upset."

"I am hardly upset—I am at my wits' end, at a complete loss."

"What has happened, Mrs. Channing?"

"We are in the midst of a disaster," Mrs. Channing said, tears coming to her dark eyes. "I *told* Sarah we should call for you! But she *refused*, saying you were recovering from that horrid encounter with that Cross Killer, that we must *not* disturb you! But you are a sleuth, and we do need a sleuth now, so I sent you that note! You see, the police were here, but I do not think they care at all to help us."

"What has happened?" Francesca repeated, thinking there must have been a crime. A familiar tingle was now running up and down her spine.

"Come with me!" Mrs. Channing exclaimed hoarsely. "This is something that words cannot do justice to, that words cannot describe." And she slipped free of Francesca's arm and began hurrying into the hall.

Francesca started and followed, not bothering to hand off her coat, hat, and single glove. What could have possibly happened? Had a bedchamber sneak been at his work? This was the most common kind of crime in the homes of the rich. She quickly realized, as they moved down one hall and then another, that they were not heading in the direction of a bedroom, as all bedrooms would be on the second floor. They were moving toward Sarah's studio. She was perplexed.

If not a burglar, then what else had transpired?

Suddenly Mrs. Channing turned and placed her back against the door of Sarah's studio, as if to bar the way. "Prepare yourself," she warned rather theatrically. But her eyes were huge with dismay.

Francesca nodded, more than intrigued now—she was worried. Apprehension filled her. "Is Sarah all right?"

"Sarah has taken to her rooms, and she will not come out," Mrs. Channing said.

Francesca stared.

Mrs. Channing gave her an abrupt nod as if to say, "Oh yes, this is grave indeed," and she thrust open the door.

Francesca stepped inside. The room was all windows, a true artist's studio, so it was brilliantly lit. She cried out.

Someone had been on a rampage in the large, airy room.

At a glance, it appeared to have been ransacked.

Canvases, palettes, paints, and jars were overturned. Two windows were broken, as if someone had smashed them with an ax or thrown an object through them. Glass covered the floor by them. Paint in the primary hues had been splattered across the floor and walls, the effect vivid, brilliant, disturbing. Because amid the yellows, blues, and greens there was dark, dark red and slashes of black. It was almost as if another artist had formed an abstract collage of colors upon the floor.

And for one instant, Francesca thought the red was blood.

She rushed forward, kneeling, dabbing her finger into one drying pool of dark red. It was paint, not blood. Relief flooded her instantly.

Then she saw the canvas lying faceup on the floor.

Whatever that canvas had once been, it was now unrecognizable. It had been saturated with the same dark red paint that looked exactly like blood, and then it had been slashed into ribbons.

Two

"Sarah! I cannot believe what happened!" Francesca cried. She had been pacing in a gilded salon, which was as overdone as the outside of the house. A bear rug with a growling head and vicious fangs competed with the Orientals on the floor; chairs had hooves and claws for feet, and one lamp had a tusk for a pull cord. Mr. Channing, God rest his soul, had been a hunter and a collector of strange and exotic objects. Apparently his widow was continuing his hobby.

Sarah had just entered the room. Today she was wearing a drab blue dress covered with splotches of paint. Francesca had never seen her with her dark hair down—today it rioted down her back to her waist in Pre-Raphaelite curls. It quite made Sarah appear ethereal—like a tiny angel. She appeared very pale, her nose and eyes red. Clearly she had been weeping. "Francesca? What are you doing here?" she asked softly—brokenly.

Francesca forgot all about her own problems. She rushed forward and embraced her friend. "You poor dear! Your mother sent for me. Who would do such a thing?"

Sarah trembled in her arms. "I told Mother not to call you! An inspector was already here. You have a badly burned hand and you are recuperating, and not just physically!"

Francesca took Sarah's hand with her own good one. "How could you *not* call me? I am your friend! Sarah, we must catch this miserable culprit! Who could have done such a thing?"

"Yes, that is the question, is it not?" Sarah returned hoarsely. She had big brown eyes, the color of chocolate, now tear-filled. "I am so devastated, I cannot think clearly.

Every time I try to consider who might have done such a thing, my mind becomes useless, racing in incoherent circles. I just found out this morning at five-fifteen, when I usually begin work," Sarah said, and she was shaking visibly.

"I cannot even imagine how you must feel," Francesca returned softly. And it was the truth. She tried to imagine how she would feel if someone had gone into her room and destroyed her notes, her journal, her books. It was an impossible stretch of the imagination, and she was not a brilliant artist, merely an intellectual woman. She knew it would be awful, but she did not think it would be the same as what Sarah was going through.

Besides, every instinct told her that there was a terrible symbolism to the blood-red paint.

Sarah turned her liquid brown eyes upon Francesca. She had a way of looking so directly at a person that one almost wished to run and hide. "Francesca, how can you take my case now—when you are hurt? Besides, didn't you promise to cease all investigative work for a few weeks?"

Francesca had, and clearly she had mentioned her resolve to Sarah in the past two days—and just as clearly, she had been under the influence of laudanum when she had spoken. "Never you mind, my hand is healing very well; Finney said so himself. I would never let down a friend in need, Sarah. These are extenuating circumstances."

Sarah seemed too distressed and miserable to debate. Francesca smiled and guided her to a couch, where they both sat down. She leaned forward eagerly. She had every intention of solving Sarah's case and bringing the ruffian who had done this to justice. "Tell me everything about last night, Sarah."

"We had an early evening last night, and I was at work— on your portrait, actually—around half past ten. At midnight I felt somewhat satisfied with several different compositions, and I left and went to bed. Actually, it was ten past midnight," she added. Her face collapsed. "I was so excited to begin your portrait for Mr. Hart. Now, now . . ." She could not continue.

Francesca took Sarah's hand, tensing terribly. Calder Hart was one of the city's wealthiest and most infamous citizens. He was infamous because he did not follow any of society's rules of etiquette; in fact, he openly flaunted his absolute disregard for polite society. Because he was so rich, he could get away with it, and he remained on everyone's party list in spite of his shocking manners and his penchant for speaking as he pleased. He was also notorious for being a ladies' man and would be the first to admit it.

But most important, he was also a fervent, if not fanatical, world-famous art collector. Francesca could commit murder herself for his insistence that Sarah paint her portrait. Of course, he would soon lose interest in her portrait, as he had only suggested it to annoy her when he had found her in a rather disheveled and sensual state at the Channing ball.

But then, that was Hart—he enjoyed shocking society, causing trouble, creating a sensation. And recently, there had been moments when they had been at odds. Francesca sighed. "As soon as the police are finished with the studio, which is now officially a crime scene, we can have it cleaned up and made as good as ever." She then smiled brightly, encouragingly—not adding that the studio might be off-limits and in an investigative limbo for some time.

"This is my chance to become an artist of some repute," Sarah whispered. "To have Mr. Hart commission your portrait was like having God whisper in my ear that I would be famous."

Francesca was not surprised that Sarah would be sacrilegious, not since she had come to realize her soul was a bohemian one, even if she did appear conventional.

"Mr. Hart has asked for delivery as soon as possible—I assured him I would complete the portrait by April the first. And he assured me he would hang it in his front hall! I have heard he hangs his favorite, more irreplaceable pieces there!" Tears flooded her eyes. "How will I ever paint now? How?"

Francesca had already known that she would have to go through with the portrait, as it was Sarah's chance to gain real recognition in the art world. "You need a few days to recover from what has happened, and I am sure Calder will understand if you deliver the painting at another, later date." Hart's dark, handsome image came to mind. "In fact, I know he will be very understanding, as there is nothing the man cares more about than his art." That wasn't quite true. Hart had once told her that his life was about wealth, art, and women, in that order. She had been shocked, but only briefly—he had grown up terribly poor, and had he not attained his wealth, he would not be the collector that he was . . . and he would not have the most beautiful women in the world as his lovers. In fact, every time she ran into him socially, he was with a different woman, and they were all married ladies.

"I don't know if he will understand. He is a very hard man. He frightens me," Sarah said. Now she faced Francesca, wide-eyed and fervent. "He is very fond of you. Please tell him what has happened, Francesca. Make him understand there will be a delay." Several tears slid down her cheeks.

"Sarah, I know Calder will be more than understanding, and you do not have to be frightened of him," Francesca said, meaning it. "I will gladly speak with him, as soon as I can." It had already crossed her mind that he might be able to help in this particular investigation, as he was so immersed in the city's art world.

"Thank you," Sarah whispered, collapsing on the couch.

Francesca stood, not really hearing Sarah's frightened whisper. Then she decided she must dismiss Hart from her mind, as he had the knack of annoying her even when he was not present. It was his problem if he wished to waste his money on her portrait and hang it next to his sacrilegious Caravaggio. "We have a case to solve. In fact, I shall go home, fetch Joel, and see if there is any word out on the street about the who or the why of this. And then I shall go down to police headquarters to report this crime. It will be far better if I speak with Bragg directly instead of Mrs. Channing having to deal with a pair of roundsmen and then an inspector. First, however, I wish to interview Harris, the doorman." She did want a head start on the case before the

police became involved. She simply could not help herself—
this was *her* case. Mrs. Channing had made that abundantly
clear.

Sarah nodded. "I can see that, in spite of the unhappy
circumstances, you are thrilled to be back at what you love
most—sleuthing."

Francesca smiled a little. "I cannot seem to help myself,
I guess. We are very alike, Sarah, you and I."

"I realize that. Although no one would ever know it to
look at us, as you are so beautiful and so full of life, while
I am drab and shy."

"You are not drab! You are not shy!" Francesca rushed to
her and hugged her. "In fact, with your hair down and your
big brown eyes, you are beautiful, Sarah, but most important,
you are so unique."

"I do not mind being drab and I hardly care if everyone
thinks me a timid little mouse. You know I do not care what
others think. I only care about my art." Her eyes changed,
and suddenly there was the heat of anger within them. "Why,
Francesca? Why?"

"I don't know. But I shall find out. I will not let you down,
Sarah." And it was a vow.

Police headquarters was at 300 Mulberry Street. It was a
slumlike neighborhood of hooks and crooks, pickpockets,
whores, and thieves. Francesca was quite accustomed now
to the sight of drunks loitering across the street from the
police department's front steps. She did not bat an eye as she
walked past a young gentleman handing several silver dollars
to a woman with a garishly rouged face and flaming red hair.
Francesca did smile, though, as she passed Bragg's very
handsome black motorcar, which was parked right in front
of the brownstone that housed police headquarters. Two
roundsmen in their blue serge uniforms and leather helmets
and carrying nightsticks were keeping an eye upon it. They
did not bat an eye upon seeing her as she walked past, as
she was now a familiar figure at police headquarters.

An undeniable tension filled her. And it had far less to do

with the bloodlike red paint that had been spilled everywhere in Sarah's studio than it did with the anticipation rising so strongly within her.

She and Bragg had spent days and days together, solving three gruesome crimes. They had traveled throughout the city, into some of its worst and most dangerous wards. There had been interrogations; there had been violent confrontations—and she had been with him through it all. They had engaged in hours of debate and problem-solving; and recently, there had been more than one earth-shattering kiss, including their last one, at the Channing ball.

Francesca shivered, pausing before going into the front lobby of headquarters. How could she have not fallen in love with Rick Bragg? she thought, but helplessly.

She had fallen in love with him the moment they had met, at her own home during a party. He had been resplendent in a tuxedo, with his darkly golden skin and eyes, his tawny, sun-streaked hair, and his high, high cheekbones. And she had recognized him instantly before any introductions, having seen his caricature in most of the city's newspapers. His appointment as police commissioner had been widely speculated upon, as he was expected to reform the city's notoriously corrupt police department. Rick Bragg was a rather public figure. And as soon as her father introduced them, they had instantly become engaged in a thrilling and highly charged debate.

Briefly, Francesca closed her eyes, suddenly afraid. The Countess Bartolla Benevente had discovered them in a moment of passion at the Channing ball. She had assured Francesca that her secret was safe. But the countess was not the only one to know of Rick and Francesca's misguided feelings for each other—Francesca had confided in her sister, Connie, the Lady Montrose, and Calder Hart had instantly surmised the situation. And then there was that dastardly Arthur Kurland—he had even spied upon Francesca as she had been leaving Bragg's home at No. 11 Madison Square, unchaperoned and at an unusual hour. And perhaps this last bit frightened her more than anything.

Kurland could be so dangerous. For what he did not know—what very few knew—was the fact that Bragg was a married man who had been and remained separated for four long years.

In fact, he had not seen his wife even once since she had left him, all those years ago.

It still hurt, thinking about the terrible fact that he did have a wife, even if he despised her. Francesca had only learned this fact a few weeks ago, shortly after they had first met. It was undeniably tragic. His wife had left him when he had decided to represent the poor and the indigent, the insane, the criminally accused, after graduating from law school. She had been furious that he had not accepted an offer to join a large and prestigious law firm in Washington, D.C. She had spent the past four years flaunting her lovers throughout Europe while spending all of his hard-earned money, careless of how moderate the income of a determined public servant was.

And Francesca understood the need for discretion now. Bragg was in public office. He was the city's police commissioner. A marital separation was not acceptable to society. They would tar and feather him and chase him out of office, and he was the best thing that had happened to the city since Teddy Roosevelt. More important, his political aspirations were vast. Bragg might be the city's police commissioner now, but he aspired to even greater offices in the future, and those reform activists around him and the Citizen's Union party had the very same ambitions for him. Francesca knew his greatest dream was to run for the Senate. She knew he would succeed. It was her dream for him as well. He was, she had no doubt, destined for greatness.

She took a huge breath, in order to compose herself. She must not think about his life now, as there was a madman on the loose yet again—of that she had no doubt. She had come downtown for legitimate reasons. And as Sarah Channing was a family friend, she knew Bragg would personally involve himself in the case.

She pushed through the precinct's front doors, which were

slightly ajar. Summoning up a friendly smile, she waved at Captain Shea, who was behind the front desk. Several gentlemen were there arguing loudly, with a bored-looking Sergeant O'Malley standing over them. An unshaven man was seated on the wood bench before the front desk, his hands in cuffs, a roundsman beside him. As always, there was a good bit of raucous conversation in the lobby, to which was added the background noise of the constantly pinging telegraph. It was the telegraph that connected all of the police stations in the city. And every now and then, a typewriter or a telephone could be heard.

"I am going up!" Francesca called to Shea. "He is in?"

He waved her on. "G'day, Miz Cahill. He most certainly is."

She loved being well-known at headquarters. She loved being waved on up as if she belonged there even more. And in a way, she did belong there now. Bragg had admitted that he could not have solved any of the past three cases without her.

Not to mention the fact that she herself had been the one to bag the Randall Killer and the Cross Murderer, she thought with a satisfaction she simply could not deny.

As usual, she skipped the elevator, although it was present on the ground floor, its iron cage door open. She ran up the stairs to the second floor and realized that Bragg was hardly alone. His frosted glass door was open. Bragg was with an older man and woman, another gorgeous woman hanging on his arm. Two toddlers were on the floor, pulling books out of his bookcase, and a dark boy of about ten or eleven seemed to be watching over them.

Francesca recognized the people present instantly, from photographs she had seen. It was a family reunion, and she was frozen, suddenly, uncharacteristically, shy.

His mother, Grace Bragg, was a handsome older woman with red hair, a pair of spectacles slipping down her nose. She clung to his arm, smiling. Francesca knew she was an extremely politically active woman and that in her day she had been a leading suffragette before the movement became a popular one. His half sister, Lucy, who was perhaps twenty-four or twenty-five, clung to his arm, speaking rapidly and excitedly. He had a good-humored smile upon his face, and he was nodding at everything she said, clearly being patient.

And he looked so much like his father, Rathe Bragg, who stood beside him, that Francesca felt he would mature exactly the same way, into a very handsome older man with silvery blond hair, a dimpled grin, and sparkling amber eyes. Suddenly one of the toddlers howled—the boy, who was as dark as his sister was fair—and Rathe swooped up his grandson.

Bragg suddenly saw her. His gaze widened and his smile vanished.

Suddenly Francesca realized she was intruding upon a very special moment. She felt herself flush and would have signaled to him and quickly backed away, but the room had fallen stunningly silent. His mother, his father, and his half sister all turned to look at her. Then so did the swarthy boy and the two toddlers.

It was an awful and embarrassing moment.

"Gimme!" The gibberish was a feminine shriek.

Francesca blinked and saw the little golden-haired girl on the floor pointing an accusing finger at her brother, who remained in her grandfather's arms. The little boy held a toy horse.

"Mama!" came another ear-shattering cry.

Lucy rushed over, scolding the little girl gently and lifting her quickly up. She turned and stared again at Francesca.

"Francesca." Bragg strode forward and their eyes locked instantly. "Is everything all right?" he asked quietly, pausing before her in the doorway. His gaze was now searching and concerned. He, of course, knew she was under house arrest or, at least, the doctor's arrest.

"Yes. No. I am intruding. . . . I had no idea," she said breathlessly, tearing her gaze from his—never an easy task—and finding herself still the center of all attention. She felt her cheeks flaming. She had so wanted to meet his parents, but not like this, absolutely unprepared and flustered and undone.

But he gripped her arm. "Come in. I want you to meet everyone." His subsequent smile went right through her. It was so warm it could melt a block of Hudson River ice. He sent her another glance, and Francesca knew that he knew she wished to discuss a business matter with him.

But then, it was always this way. He seemed to be able to discern her thoughts so effortlessly.

"Rathe, Grace, I'd like you to meet Miss Francesca Cahill. She has become a good friend of mine. In fact, she is passionately dedicated to reform." He smiled at his stepmother. "You both have a lot in common."

His father was regarding Francesca with open interest, at once curious and kind. She felt certain that Bragg would look exactly like Rathe in thirty years. His mother, however, was not smiling. In fact, she was looking from Bragg to Francesca and back again, her brows knitted.

And Francesca's world seemed to tilt wildly beneath her feet. She desperately wanted his parents to like her. She wished Grace was not looking at her with suspicion. Francesca tried to smile and failed. *Grace knew. Somehow, she knew they were not simply friends and professional partners.*

"Hello," Rathe said amiably, his eyes the same shade of amber as his son's. "It is good to meet you, Miss Cahill. I do believe I have dined with your father on several occasions, most recently in Washington at a fund-raiser for President Roosevelt."

Her interest was piqued. "I remember when Papa went. I begged to join him, as I am a huge supporter of the president." She was rueful. "I was refused."

"Andrew made a mistake; the evening was an interesting one." His smile was identical to his son's. "Are you the woman who helped my son bringing Randall's killer to justice?"

"Yes. How did you know?" Would he—they—approve or disapprove of her sleuthing?

"We read the New York papers even when we are not in New York," Rathe said with an infectious grin and two deep dimples. "Did I not hear something about a fry pan?"

Francesca had apprehended this particular killer with a large iron pan. "There was no other weapon available to me," she managed.

"Francesca is no ordinary debutante. She has been indispensable to several police investigations," Bragg said, sending her a smile.

Francesca's heart turned over and she looked at him, absurdly pleased. "Thank you."

"But it is the truth," he said simply.

"Surely you are not a professional sleuth?" Grace asked quietly.

Francesca started, facing the older woman. She felt like a delinquent schoolgirl. In fact, sleuthing had ceased being a hobby when she had been hired by Lydia Stuart to solve a case. And now Mrs. Channing had requested her services. But her parents were close with the Braggs, and as far as Francesca was concerned, they must never find out about her new profession.

Bragg saved the day. "Francesca has fallen into several investigations, purely by chance," he said.

She sent him a grateful smile. She had no intention of ever lying to either one of his parents.

"And I am Lucy, Lucy Savage." The beautiful redhead put her daughter down and came swiftly forward. She extended her hand. Francesca took it. "Rick is my brother. I am so pleased to meet you!" She smiled widely, but her blue eyes were filled with curiosity. "I am very impressed. I have never met a sleuth before, especially not a female one."

Instantly Francesca liked her. "Are those two adorable children yours?"

Lucy laughed. "Yes, and so is Roberto. But the twins are hardly adorable—they try the patience of everyone who attempts to contain them! They are twin hurricanes, truly. They do take after their father," she added. "Roberto, come meet Miss Cahill."

The dark-skinned boy came forward and politely shook Francesca's hand. He did not seem at all related to the rest

of the family, and Francesca wondered if he was related by
blood and, if not, how he fit in.

"We live in Texas. That is where my wonderfully impossible husband, Shoz, and my grandparents, Derek and Miranda Bragg, are. Paradise, Texas." Lucy grinned. "And
believe me, it is a little piece of paradise, right here on earth!
I am on a bit of a holiday," she said brightly. "At the very
last moment I could not resist a trip to the big city! So tell
me how you solved the murder."

"Lucy, Francesca has just stepped through the door, hardly
expecting to find a Bragg reunion in progress, not to mention
my extremely garrulous little sister. Can you slow down?"
Bragg asked with a fond shake of his head.

"Perhaps I can show you the city," Francesca said, now
glancing at Grace Bragg again. She was watching Francesca
carefully, not missing a single word, as if carefully sizing her
up. Francesca prayed she would like her. She sensed this
woman would not fall for any tricks and that she would not
be easy to impress, either.

"Oh, that would be fun," Lucy said. "Of course, I did
grow up here—before my handsome husband abducted me
and carried me off to Death Valley." She grinned.

Francesca blinked, diverted. "Death Valley? He *abducted*
you?"

"It is a long story," Bragg remarked calmly, before Lucy
could speak.

"But I want to hear about how you caught the man who
murdered Hart's father!" Lucy cried. "When shall we get
together? What about right now?"

"Lucy," this from Rathe, and his tone was fatherly and
stern. But he was smiling, and he said to Francesca, "My
daughter is a whirlwind. She was born that way—and marriage and children have not calmed her down."

Francesca smiled. Lucy sent her a conspiratorial glance
that meant, "ignore him." Then, "What happened to your
hand?" she asked.

Francesca hesitated, instinctively looking at Bragg.

"I can answer that one," a voice from the doorway said.

Francesca froze. The voice had been lazy and sensual in tone. There was only one man who spoke in such a languid and amused drawl.

"Calder!" Lucy shrieked, flying past Francesca. She turned and watched the gorgeous redhead mauling Calder Hart.

And he was grinning—a flash of very white teeth in extremely swarthy skin. He lifted Lucy off of her feet. "I like that greeting," he said, and it was brazenly flirtatious.

Francesca realized in that moment that they were not really related. Bragg and Calder were half brothers, but they shared the same mother, not the same father. Hart did not have one drop of Bragg blood in his veins. She felt paralyzed and oddly annoyed.

"Keep looking at me that way and Shoz will kill you," Lucy breathed, grinning up at him and still in his arms.

"But you like keeping him on his toes," Hart said easily, looking pleased with himself. "And he's an old man now."

"He is very jealous," Lucy said, clearly with satisfaction. "But he isn't so old that he can't teach you a thing or two." She did grin.

"You are probably right." Slowly Hart released Lucy, and finally he looked directly at Francesca.

She flushed.

"So much for bedrest," he said. And then he shrugged, as if it was not his problem, as if he did not give a damn. He looked at Rick. "We should have bet on her. I was going to give her three or four days. Clearly, I would have lost."

"Calder," Bragg said tersely with an abrupt nod of his head. He wasn't thrilled to see his brother and it was obvious.

Hart entered the room, as always a rather devastating sight. He was darkly, dangerously handsome, and he favored brilliant white shirts and pitch-black suits. Only he could carry off such a look and not look like a funeral home manager.

Grace was smiling—and tears sparkled on her lashes behind her spectacles. She had taken both Hart and Bragg in when their mother had died when they were young boys. She cupped Hart's cheek. "Why has it been so long? Why, Calder?"

Hart hesitated. "It is good to see you," he said, and Francesca was startled, as she had never seen Hart unsure of himself before. He was usually terribly—insufferably—arrogant.

"It is wonderful to see you! Are you sure you don't mind all of us staying with you? I hate to inconvenience you," Grace said softly.

He shrugged again, but now he was flushing. "God knows I have plenty of room."

His house was the size of a museum, Francesca thought.

Rathe had clasped Hart's shoulder, as warm as Hart was stiff. "You are looking well. It is good to see you, Son."

Hart nodded, turning away quickly, so no one would see how emotional he was. But Francesca had seen, and she suspected he had a tear or two in his eyes.

She realized that Bragg was watching her. She felt guilty, so she smiled at him, but he did not smile back.

Hart had turned to Lucy. "Francesca fancies herself a sleuth," he said lightly. He gave her a disapproving glance. "She likes to put herself in danger—I imagine the rush is rather similar to that experienced by gamblers . . . or illicit lovers."

Francesca frowned at him. "Please." She did not need this now.

Bragg sighed in exasperation. "Enough, Calder."

He ignored his brother. "Do you not get a rush of adrenaline when you confront a maddened criminal, Francesca?" Hart drawled. "A rush that I imagine is exactly the same as when you are wildly kissing the man of your dreams?" Both dark brows slashed upward. As he had practically caught her in Bragg's arms at the Channing ball a few days ago—the cause of his commissioning her portrait—she knew he was referring to the passion she felt for his brother.

Hart was purposefully putting her on the spot. He was purposefully referring to the fact that she and Bragg were in love—which he thought was lust and nothing more. She felt like slapping him—but she had done that once and would *never* do so again. "The only rush I get is one of fear," she snapped. "Fear, Hart, not excitement, *fear*."

He laughed. "I somehow doubt that." He turned to Lucy, who was wide-eyed. "She enjoys danger. Soon, no doubt, it will become an addiction—if it hasn't already."

"Calder, do you wish to upset Miss Cahill?" Grace finally spoke with quiet censure.

Hart looked at his stepmother. "If my brother can't keep her in line, then someone should."

Francesca found herself rushing to the rescue even though she was angry with Hart. "He hasn't upset me, Mrs. Bragg. I am sure that he doesn't wish to be abrasive. It is just a character defect." She smiled sweetly at Hart. "And do not blame Bragg—Rick—for my actions. That is completely unfair."

He sighed and looked at the ceiling. "Of course you defend *him*."

Bragg stepped between them, but he faced Hart. "This was an extremely pleasant gathering until you arrived, Calder. As always, you enter a room and do your best to cause trouble."

But Hart was speaking. "Oh, so now the fact that you allow her to engage in police work is my fault?" Hart shook his head.

"That's enough," Rathe said firmly. "Company is present—and the two of you haven't changed at all. It's like watching you both when you were boys. What's next? Fists and blows?"

Grace looked at her, Francesca. The older woman's eyes were wide and intent and. . . . accusing? But just what could she be accusing her of?

"I'm sorry," Bragg said instantly, to his father. "And you're right. We're acting like children."

"I apologize." Hart actually seemed sincere. "In fact, I give up." He looked directly at Francesca. "If you wish to endanger yourself, it is not my affair." He shrugged. "If you and Rick wish to rush around the city together, chasing murderers, so be it." He did not smile. His eyes had become black. "Who knows? Next time instead of a mere burn, perhaps one of these madmen will place a bullet in you." His gaze locked with hers.

"I think I had better go," Francesca said tersely.

"I'll walk you down," Lucy said quickly, rushing to her side. "Mother, please watch the children for me, just for a moment."

"I think Francesca can find her way downstairs," Bragg said firmly. Then he gave her an odd look. And there was a question in his eyes.

"I did want to speak with you, but it can wait until later," Francesca said. She truly wanted to escape, and as much as she liked Lucy, she wasn't ready for a tête-à-tête with his sister. Perhaps she would call Bragg later on the telephone and fill him in on what had happened at the Channings'.

"Rick will lend you his Daimler," Lucy said, whipping her coat off a wall peg. "Isn't that right, Rick?"

"Peter will take you home." Peter was his man, and Francesca had come to realize that he was a jack-of-all-trades. "Lucy, Francesca has a burned hand. My understanding is that she is supposed to be at home for the entire week." He spoke quite calmly. "Do not try and subvert her good intentions."

"And to think I was under the impression that she was to remain in bed," Hart murmured.

Francesca flushed, even though his meaning had to have been innocent.

"I am merely walking her to the roadster," Lucy said demurely. "At least we can chat a bit."

Bragg capitulated. "Fine. But mind your manners, Lucy."

She shook her head. "I am a grown woman, Rick, not a child."

"I know." His smile was an affectionate one. "Mind your manners," he repeated.

She groaned and rolled her eyes.

Francesca turned toward his parents. "It was so nice to meet you." Then she glanced at Hart. He wasn't even looking at her. He was studying his fingernails, as if an insect had appeared upon them, making them a fascinating sight indeed.

"It was a pleasure, Francesca," Rathe said, smiling. Grace also smiled at her.

Lucy grabbed her arm and dragged her into the hall. "Well, you survived, and admirably, I think." She grinned.

Francesca was now weak-kneed. She realized she had been perspiring. And she might never forgive Hart for trying to humiliate her in front of the Braggs. "Do you think so? I mean, do you think your parents like me?" She and Lucy entered the elevator cage.

"What's not to like?" Lucy asked, hauling the cage door shut. She faced her. "So? What *is* going on?" she demanded, her hands on her hips.

"What?" Francesca had not a clue as to what Lucy was speaking about, but her tone caused no small amount of apprehension.

"Are you in love with my brother?" she cried.

The question was like a blow—right between the eyes. "What?"

Lucy grabbed her arm. "Are you in love with my brother?" she repeated. "And if so . . . *which one?*"

Three

The elevator began to descend. Francesca was certain she had misheard. "I beg your pardon?"

Lucy was staring, her eyes eager and wide. "Are you in love with Rick . . . or Calder?"

Francesca could not believe her ears. *What was she talking about?*

Lucy shook her head, suddenly amused. "Wait—you don't know?"

"What are you talking about?" *Was* she mad? Yes, Francesca was in love with Bragg—for she hadn't known he was married when they had met and begun working together on the Burton Abduction. He had been a perfect gentleman, but she had fallen hopelessly in love with him as they tried to decipher clue after puzzling clue. For he was everything she admired in a man. In fact, even now, those who knew him and his marital status had to admit that if he were eligible, he and Francesca would be perfect for each other.

Hart had said that, too.

What was Lucy thinking? Hart was only a friend, and often an insufferable one, at that—as he had just proven moments ago.

"I am talking about the fact that Rick clearly admires you in a way that is not platonic. But Hart obviously cares about you, too, which is something I have never seen before. And while you clearly adore Rick, I see the way that you look at Calder. But, of course, most women are mesmerized by Calder." She shrugged. "I know I am being very blunt—"

"You are!" Francesca cried, suddenly panic-stricken. The elevator had stopped, but she did not notice. All she could

recall now was the way Hart had looked at her at the Channing ball when she had been wearing that horrid and provocative red dress. She was the least fashionable woman that
she could think of, as she preferred navy blue skirts and
white shirtwaists or a tailored ensemble. When Hart had seen
her in her new and extremely daring red gown, a gown that
had not suited her at all, as she was *not* a siren, he had looked
at her the way a man looks at a woman that he wants. It was
precisely then that he had, finally, found her alluring. It was
in that single moment that a dangerous and ugly beast had
raised its head between them—one that would not now go
away.

Francesca wished the moment had never happened.

She regretted ever wearing that red dress.

"We can get out now," Lucy said very quietly.

Francesca was jerked out of her thoughts. Her gaze met
the other woman's and quickly skidded away. Lucy was
wrong. She was wrong about *everything*.

"I have upset you. I am sorry." Lucy took her hand and
led her out of the elevator. "I didn't mean to. I should have
kept my thoughts to myself. I apologize. I just never expected this."

Francesca managed to nod. She said, "Rick is married and
Hart is a terrible ladies' man. Neither one is for me."

Lucy opened her mouth, clearly to refute Francesca's
words. But then she smiled and closed it. "Are you free for
lunch tomorrow? Or perhaps a glass of champagne? We
could stop by at the Fifth Avenue Hotel—it is one of Rick's
favorites. I do so want to get to know you better before I
return to Paradise."

Francesca wanted to hug her for changing the topic, but
within herself she remained aghast, no, horrified. "Either one
would be lovely," she said, barely relieved to be discussing
something as simple as a social engagement. They stepped
outside.

"There's Peter. Isn't he a sweetheart?" Lucy was speaking
of Bragg's man. The huge six-foot, six-inch Swede had seen
them. "Peter!" She waved. "Miss Cahill needs a ride!"

Peter nodded and walked over to the front of the Daimler to crank it up. Lucy smiled at Francesca and gave her an impulsive hug. "I am so glad I decided to bring the children to New York," she said.

"I have been hoping to meet you—and your parents," Francesca admitted.

Lucy grinned, as if she truly knew why. "Have a wonderful day. And, Francesca? I really did not mean to upset you."

Francesca smiled weakly and got into the car. Peter had the motor started, and he climbed into the driver's seat beside her, handing her a pair of goggles. Francesca put them on, then turned to glance back at police headquarters.

Lucy was exchanging words with a very disreputable- and dangerous-looking man who was clearly a thug of sorts. She seemed angry—he seemed amused. Actually, he seemed more than amused, for his grin was lascivious and even cruel. What was this?

Flushed, Lucy whirled away.

The hoodlum seized her by the arm, whirling her back around.

Lucy cried out, trying to shake him free.

Francesca ripped off her goggles and pushed open her car door just as Peter started to drive the Daimler forward. The roadster was braked, and Francesca stumbled out. "Lucy!"

Lucy and the brawny shaggy-haired thug both turned toward her. He released Lucy and fled down the block.

For one moment, Francesca hesitated, torn over whether to chase the thug or go to her new friend. In the end, her better judgment won out, and she hurried to Lucy. "Are you all right?" she gasped.

Lucy jerked away from her, smiling—and it was forced. "Oh, I am fine!"

Francesca was disbelieving. "Who was that? What did he want? Did he hurt you?"

"What—what are you talking about?" Lucy asked, wide-eyed.

"What am I talking about?" Francesca echoed. "That lout

in the heavy brown tweed jacket. He grabbed you; you seemed to be arguing—"

"I don't know what you are talking about," Lucy said abruptly—coldly. "Now, I am afraid I must go, as the twins and Roberto are waiting."

Francesca recoiled.

Lucy seemed to realize how cool she had become. She smiled and touched Francesca's sleeve. "I mean, I've never seen that man before. He must have mistaken me for someone else." She smiled, but it seemed forced. "So, until tomorrow?"

"Tomorrow, then," Francesca managed, but she knew a liar when she saw one, and Lucy was lying through her teeth.

Not only that, but there had been fear in her wide blue eyes, real, raw fear.

Francesca slipped into the house and found the front hall empty, with the exception of Jonathon, the new doorman.

"May I take your coat?" he said.

"Where is everyone? Has anyone noticed that I have not been at home?" Francesca asked quickly, speaking in a very low tone as she handed him her hat, gloves, and coat. He had not batted an eye earlier when she had left, her manner rather furtive. However, she had been gone most of the afternoon. Francesca felt that she was doomed.

His eyes wide and serious, he said, "There has been a bit of a fuss. I do believe Mrs. Cahill requested your presence some time ago, upon returning from her luncheon."

Francesca moaned.

He managed to keep a very straight face, although his blue eyes were fascinated.

There would be no avoiding her mother now. However, a confrontation could be delayed—perhaps even until the morrow. Francesca dashed across the hall. It was a large room with black-and-white marble floors, high ceilings, and huge Corinthian columns, spaced at intervals. The staircase was alabaster, wide and graceful, carpeted in red. She raced up it, not at all in a manner that was ladylike or dignified.

The family rooms were on the third floor. All of the rooms used for entertaining were on the first two floors. Francesca saw no one as she rushed up the corridor and toward her bedroom. She hurried through the door, sighing with relief.

And then she saw her mother sitting on the sofa in front of the fireplace.

"Francesca, I would like to speak with you." Julia did not turn.

Briefly Francesca closed her eyes. Then, with some despair, she started forward. "Hello, Mama. I only went out to take some air."

"I do not recall taking air being a part of Dr. Finney's instructions," Julia Van Wyck Cahill said far too calmly, finally turning to look at her. "I am dismissing the new doorman."

Francesca hurried forward. "Mama, that's not fair! You certainly did not intend for him to be some sort of gaoler, did you?" She reached for the back of the couch.

"He is smitten with you. You will have him so thoroughly wrapped around your finger that you will soon be roaming about this city in the middle of the night—while in the midst of another criminal investigation!" Julia was not angry. Tears sparkled on her dark lashes. Francesca blinked. Julia was never emotionally out of control.

Then Francesca took a steadying breath, sitting on the velvet sofa beside her mother. "Please do not fire Jonathon on my account."

Julia looked at her and sighed.

Eagerly Francesca said, "I am just fine, Mama. Really. You don't have to worry so." But silently she thanked God that her mother was completely unaware of the several times she had been sleuthing in the middle of the night—although Bragg and her brother had caught her out and about.

"You have been gone for hours, Francesca." Julia faced her grimly. "What am I supposed to do with you?"

Francesca saw how worried her mother was and did not know what to say or do. When Julia was her forceful, dominant self, it was much easier to wage a futile battle for her cause. Now she felt terrible. "I did need some air," she said. "Everything will be fine, Mama; please don't worry about me."

"How can I not worry about you? You have been involved in three, *three*, criminal investigations! I just cannot understand what you think you are doing! I am very proud of you, Francesca, as you have turned into a beautiful woman." Julia took Francesca's good hand in both of hers. "I was so pleased to see you in that red gown at the Channing ball. You were stunning and elegant and you turned every male head there."

She became uneasy. She did not want to discuss the Channing ball now, for several reasons. "I am not comfortable in that dress."

"And then," Julia said, as if she had not heard her, "you disappear! You leave your table and simply disappear, and the next thing I know, I come home to find Maggie stabbed and Dr. Finney tending your burned hand, with policemen all about the house and a paddy wagon outside!"

"I am sorry," Francesca said simply. There wasn't anything else that she could say.

"I know you are sorry. But I also know you believe you were right in lying to us, in sneaking about, all in the cause of saving Maggie Kennedy's life."

Francesca stared. "Should I have let her die? Been murdered?"

"The case was in the hands of the police!" Julia cried. "You should have left it to them! And I am very angry with Rick Bragg for allowing you to become involved! I intend to give him a piece of my mind."

Francesca saw that Julia meant her every word. She cringed inwardly. "He isn't very happy with me, either," she managed. "He doesn't want me involved, Mama."

"What am I supposed to do? You are too old to punish. This is my house, but you do not respect my rules. Should I toss you out? Disown you? That is what other parents might do!"

Francesca froze. Then, "Mama, you're not serious!" She adored her family, no matter the problems, most of which were caused by her mother's desire for her to be a conventional young lady.

"If only you could be more like your sister!" Julia despaired. Then, "I will not toss you out, because then you would truly have the freedom to continue this insane sleuthing of yours. Not to mention that your father would toss me out. Francesca, do you respect me?" Julia asked.

She was already tense, or she would have stiffened. "You know that I do."

"Then will you respect my rules?" Julia asked simply.

Francesca hesitated. "Mama, if someone is in trouble—or danger—how can I turn my back on him or her? How? It is not in my nature to ignore a man or a woman in trouble!"

"And that is the real problem," Julia said with a sigh. "Your passionate, compassionate nature. Compassion is a wonderful thing. So is charity. We give thousands of dollars every year to dozens of different causes. You know that. We are compassionate people. But your version of charity is to help some desperately troubled man or woman with your own two hands. I am desperately afraid." She stood. "Can you blame me?"

"No." Francesca also stood.

"Why did you really go out? Where were you?" Julia asked.

Francesca hated lying to her parents. And because of Evan's engagement, they would quickly learn of the vandalism that had occurred at Sarah's studio. Suddenly Francesca thought of the ruffian who had so frightened Lucy Savage. What was Lucy hiding? "I decided to visit Sarah." She wet her lips and sighed. "Someone broke into her studio and did their best to destroy it, Mama."

Julia stared. Then, "Is Sarah all right? How is Mrs. Channing?"

"They are both terribly upset but, other than that, fine."

Suddenly Julia looked at her daughter with utter suspicion. "What happened at the Channings' is a police matter," she said firmly.

Francesca hoped her mother could not see her cringe. She

hadn't told Bragg about the crime, and she had told the Channings that she would report it. But then, his family reunion had interfered with her better intentions.

She did not want to use the telephone. It was awkward, and sometimes one could not hear the other party clearly. Perhaps, if she rested now, she could steal out of the house a bit later and catch him at home. To change the subject, she said, "Bragg's family is in town."

Julia was surprised. "Rathe and Grace Bragg are back?" She suddenly smiled. "It will be so good to see them again! Why, I had heard they might be returning to the city. This is wonderful news."

"Do you know them well, Mama?"

"Both he and Andrew worked very hard on Grover Cleveland's reelection," Julia said. "He is as fervent a reformist as your father and as fervent a Republican."

"He served in Cleveland's first administration," Francesca remarked. "I cannot wait to hear all about it."

"Yes, I imagine you will find that conversation fascinating. I shall have them over for dinner." She smiled at the thought. "Perhaps on Sunday. It will round out the table nicely."

Francesca's heart dropped. She could think of nothing worse! "Mama, about Sunday dinner," she began.

"Absolutely not!" Julia exclaimed. "Do not think to weasel out of it. Calder Hart accepted the invitation, as you well know—you were right there."

Francesca was overcome with dismay and unease. She refused to recall Lucy's absurd question of which brother she was in love with. Francesca knew why Julia had invited Hart to dine with them on Sunday—she was determined to marry Francesca off and had foolishly set her cap for Hart. That was insane, because Hart had no intention of marrying, and he was quite open about it. He never even looked at available young women, and Francesca knew that for a fact. His only interest was married women and shady ladies whom he might take pleasure with. God only knew why he had accepted the invitation to dine with them.

"Why are you scowling?" Julia peered closely at her. "We

ave an agreement, and I know you have not forgotten it."

"I have not forgotten."

Julia smiled, and it was a pleased smile. "While Maggie Kennedy's life was in danger, I agreed to allow her *and* her four children to remain here, under my roof, placing everyone in this house in danger." She looked pointedly at Francesca's bandaged hand. "In return, you agreed to let me choose the suitor of *my* choice, and you said you would allow im to court you.

"Perhaps, in the end, you will turn out like Connie," Julia continued. "Sociable, charitable, and happily married, with a child or two."

Francesca's heart lurched wildly and then sank. "Mama, please cease and desist with this ludicrous matchmaking. I know you are entirely aware of Hart's reputation. You will never snag him, and I would never accept him anyway."

Julia smiled as if she were a fat old cat who had just eaten a mouse or two. "My dear, every rake has his day. Now, where can I reach the Braggs so I may invite them to dinner?"

Francesca felt faint. "Mama, please don't invite them on Sunday. It will simply be too much—really." She tried to force a smile and failed. She could think of no worse situation than Julia forcing Calder upon her in front of Rathe and Grace Bragg, and now Lucy's comments were haunting her.

"Why will it be too much, Francesca? Because Rathe Bragg is the police commissioner's father?"

Francesca felt her world spin out of control. "What does that mean?" she asked carefully.

"It means I am not a fool and I am not blind." Julia smiled firmly. "Your infatuation has become obvious, but I am certain you will get over it, now that you know he is married. Even you, the most stubborn person I can think of, could not be so foolish as to cling to a hopeless situation involving a married man. I shall send up a dinner tray."

Francesca was on her feet. Her mother *knew?* In that moment, *she* knew that she was doomed.

"Francesca! What is this? Shouldn't you be at home?" Montrose cried sternly.

Francesca smiled breathlessly at her brother-in-law as she entered the house. Not only had she not been able to inform Bragg of the Channing Incident the night before; she also had fallen asleep right after her conversation with her mother and slept as if comatose until just an hour ago. Clearly her burned hand was sapping some of her usual strength.

But the full night's rest had done wonders for her. She had so much to do! She must continue the Channing investigation, and as soon as she spoke with her sister, she would go downtown to inform Bragg of the Channing Incident.

"Please, do not chase me away, as I am in dire need of Connie's advice right now," she said. Upon awakening, her first thought had been that she must weasel out of Sunday's dinner. She was now dreading the evening with all of her being. Surely Connie would have some advice for her, as not attending the event did not seem like a possibility.

Connie and Montrose lived right around the corner from Francesca, on Sixty-second Street just off of Madison Avenue. The house had been a wedding present from Andrew; it had been designed and built during their year-long engagement. It had been a rather typical marriage for New York society: Connie had the wealth, and her husband had the blue blood and titles. What had not been typical was that they had both fallen immediately in love.

But that had been five years ago. "I am afraid to ask why you are in need of Connie's advice." Still, Montrose's smile was affectionate. He was a big, muscular man with dark hair and turquoise eyes, as handsome as he was noble. "Must you always seize the bit between your teeth like a wild filly? What could it be now that has put such a look of anxiety upon your face?"

"So now you compare me to a horse?" But she was smiling. It was good to see Neil in a pleasant mood, as there had simply been too much tension in his house for too long.

"Did I just do that?" He chucked her under her chin. "I meant no disrespect. How is your hand today?"

"Fine. Although Mama hopes to keep me dosed with laudanum, I think."

"I wonder why!" he laughed.

"I cannot help it if I have a life to live."

"Unlike other young ladies, who only wish to shop and wed and do as they are told without question?"

"I take that as a compliment," she said seriously.

"I meant it as one," he returned as sincerely. Then, "My wife is upstairs, and I do not know if she is awake. But you may go up and rouse her, if you wish."

Francesca was surprised. "Connie isn't up?" Her sister was always up with Charlotte and Lucinda, who were three years old and eight months, respectively.

"No, she is not. Not that I know of." His expression closed.

"Is this a new habit of hers?" she asked carefully.

And he seemed to withdraw even more.

"Neil?" And in that moment, she saw the anguish in his eyes, anguish that, for one moment, he did not hide. Her own worries vanished. Clearly things were still not right with Connie and Montrose. Francesca was grim, and she felt responsible, because if she hadn't been the one to discover Neil with his lover, Connie might not have ever learned the truth.

Of course, Connie had suspected something, so maybe she would have learned of his infidelity eventually anyway. Francesca touched his hand. "How is Connie, Neil?"

He avoided her eyes. "Fine."

Francesca stared and, knowing him so well, knew he was lying and that nothing was fine. "How are you?" A few days ago, he had been very angry and very upset. He had told her that his heart was the one that was broken. And that had simply made no sense.

"Why don't you go up?" He now looked at her. "I am going to read the morning papers, and then I have a board meeting." He nodded and walked out.

Francesca was left staring after him feeling rather uneasy. Today he had no wish to confess his feelings to her, but then, he was usually a private man. That slip the other day had been just that, an angry, emotional outburst. Francesca sighed. If Neil did not wish to confide in her, there was nothing she could do about it.

But Connie was her best friend in the entire world. Francesca knew Connie as well as she knew herself. Connie never loitered in bed. She was the busiest woman Francesca knew, a wife, a mother, a socialite. Until recently, she had loved her husband, her children, her life. And she never overslept.

Francesca turned and made her own way through the house and upstairs. Outside of Connie's suite she paused. Not a sound from within could be heard. She knocked, but there was no answer. Stepping inside, she saw that the sitting room was hardly empty. Connie sat at her secretaire, but she was not writing. Instead, she had her chin on her hands and she was gazing down at Madison Avenue through gauzy parted curtains.

"Con?"

She whirled. "Oh, I did not hear you!" As always, even in a peignoir—which was stunning—Connie was breathtaking in her beauty and extremely elegant. Only Francesca's sister could roll out of bed looking as if she were on her way to a ball.

Connie was a platinum blonde with vivid blue eyes, a heart-shaped face, and a perfectly curved figure. Actually, Francesca and Connie were often thought to be twins, as they so resembled each other. The only differences between them in appearance were their height—Francesca was two inches taller—and Francesca's coloring. Her hair was a rich honey gold, her skin as dusky.

And of course, they were not alike at all. Not in character and not by nature or inclination.

"You slept late today," Francesca said softly. The pensive expression she had just witnessed had disappeared. "Are you all right? May I come in?"

Connie nodded, standing. "I don't feel quite myself. I decided not to get up," she said, flushing, but with what emotion? Guilt? Then she smiled, and she seemed quite her normal self. "But I am glad to see you, Fran. Even if you are the one who is supposed to be in bed." She shook her head with disapproval but continued to smile.

"I simply could not stand another moment of confinement," Francesca said, happy to see her sister behaving normally. "Are you going to get dressed?"

"In a moment. So what brings you by?" Connie went to a cord by the door and pulled it; a bell would sound below stairs, alerting a servant that he or she was needed.

"I need advice." Francesca smiled, pulling up an ottoman and sitting upon it.

"From me?" Connie was amused, settling on the sofa. "I do find that hard to believe."

"Why?"

"If you wish my advice, this must be about a social event—or a man."

Francesca winced. "It is about both."

Connie studied her.

Francesca hesitated. "You aren't still flirting with Calder, are you?"

Connie flushed. "No. He suddenly lost interest in our flirtation, I think. I haven't heard from him in a week."

Francesca did not tell her that Hart had ceased chasing her because she, Francesca, had insisted he stop. But it wasn't too long ago that he had ruthlessly been intending to seduce Connie and that Connie had been enjoying a very dangerous flirtation. It still disturbed Francesca no end whenever she recalled the two of them together at the Plaza, flirting so intently that they hadn't even been aware that Francesca was present.

But that was Hart. He could not seem to resist beautiful married women.

"Why are you asking, Francesca?" Connie asked curiously.

"Well, Mama has invited Calder for dinner on Sunday."

Connie merely gazed at her. "So?"

Francesca fidgeted. "Mama is insane, Connie. She thinks to match me with Calder."

Connie almost fell off of the sofa. She had paled. *"What?!"*

"I know. It is absurd. What should I do?"

Connie stared.

"Con?" Francesca's unease grew. Did her sister still have a small fascination for Calder Hart? Was she jealous?

Then Connie said, very thoughtfully, "You know, maybe that is not such an absurd idea, Fran."

Now it was Francesca's turn to almost fall from the ottoman. *"What?!"*

Connie shrugged. "He is the most eligible bachelor in this city. He is, I think, the wealthiest one. He does, eventually, have to marry." She paused, contemplating the scenario. "Why not you?"

Francesca was on her feet. "Because I am in love with someone else."

Connie stood. "You think you are in love!"

"How dare you tell me how I am feeling?"

"Fran! I am on your side, remember? And even if you have fallen truly in love with Rick Bragg, he is married, remember?"

How could she ever forget? Francesca tried to inhale, with extreme difficulty. "Con, believe me, I know he is married. But he is separated—or have you forgotten?"

"It doesn't matter if he is separated or not. He isn't available. You cannot ever marry him. So you cannot remain in love with him—and frankly, Hart is far more interesting, wouldn't you say?" Connie demanded.

Francesca backed up. "What would you say if I told you that Bragg has decided to divorce his wife?"

"I would say that you are dreaming," Connie said slowly. "A divorce would destroy him, his career, and you, because you would immediately become the other woman."

Connie was right. Francesca sat back down again. Bragg had told her that he was going to divorce his wife, but he had been extremely upset when he had said so, as she had ust escaped the Cross Murderer's efforts to murder her. And ven so, Francesca had known the moment he spoke that a divorce was unthinkable, because his political future was more important than their personal one.

"Did he really tell you he wants a divorce, Fran?" Connie asked quietly, seriously.

Francesca nodded and looked up. She felt moisture gathering in her eyes. "I could never allow him to do it. He is destined for greatness, Con."

"Dear God, he really does love you."

Francesca nodded and could not speak. The magnitude of the sacrifice Bragg wished to make was simply incredible.

Connie sat down and took her good hand. "Fran? No good can ever come of your love for Bragg, just as no good can ever come of a man's divorce. I fear for you, Fran. I am afraid there is going to be so much heartbreak."

Francesca hugged her sister, hard. "You are going through your own ordeal, and still you worry about me and my foolish dreams," she whispered.

"Of course I worry about you." Connie broke the embrace. "You are my headstrong little sister who is always leaping in front of trolleys and just barely getting out of the way."

Francesca smiled and wiped away a tear. "I have never jumped in front of a trolley."

"Then a Cross Murderer," Connie amended. "Fran, Mama is very wise. Her matchmaking might not be a terrible idea."

Francesca shuddered. "Calder told me himself. He will never marry."

Connie raised both brows. "Famous last words," she murmured.

"I really am in love with Bragg."

Connie patted her hand. "I know you are. And it frightens me."

Francesca knew the moment would never be more opportune. She stared at her sister.

"Uh-oh. What is it? You look ill."

This was her chance to tell her sister *everything*. "I am in a bit of trouble," Francesca said slowly.

Connie became grim. "You are always in trouble, Fran."

"Not this kind," Francesca whispered.

Connie suddenly started. "You are not . . . *pregnant,* are you?"

"No!" Francesca stood. "No, Con, we have been noble, Bragg and I, even if he is separated, even though he despises his wife, even though she left him and he has not seen her in four years."

"Thank God," Connie said fervently.

Francesca inhaled, meeting her sister's gaze. "You are right. I am ill. I am ill with fear." She opened her purse and withdrew a carefully folded note. She handed it to Connie. "I received this a few days ago. Read it," she said.

Connie unfolded the note and silently read it. It said:

My dear Miss Cahill,
I should be in New York City soon, and I wish to meet you at your convenience. I shall be staying at the Waldorf-Astoria when I arrive. I look forward to making your acquaintance.

Yours Truly
Mrs. Rick Bragg

Slowly Connie looked up. She seemed stunned.

Francesca smiled at her and felt how weak her smile was.

"When did you receive this?" Connie asked.

"It came by hand on Thursday," Francesca said. "I have been telling myself that it is a joke, but the truth is, I know it isn't a joke."

"I thought she was in Europe," Connie said.

"No, she is in Boston. Her father is very ill." Francesca suddenly closed her eyes and laid her forehead on her hands.

She had tried very hard to forget all about the note because it was too terrible to really contemplate.

"Well," Connie said, and Francesca did not look up, "someone has been gossiping."

Yes, that much was clear, Francesca thought. Someone had noticed the attraction she and Bragg shared and had decided to inform Leigh Anne. Someone was deliberately stirring up this particular hornets' nest. "What does she want? Bragg and I have been as virtuous as possible, given the circumstances," Francesca said grimly.

"It's obvious why she wishes to meet you. You are the other woman."

Francesca looked at her. "You are making it sound so sordid."

"It *is* sordid. There is nothing romantic about being the other woman, about being a man's mistress," Connie said firmly.

Francesca stood. "I am not his mistress and that is horribly unfair. You yourself just remarked how much Bragg must love me, to think of throwing his entire life away for us."

"Nothing is going to change the fact that you are the other woman," Connie said firmly.

"Do you have a single romantic bone in your body?"

Connie just looked at her. And as she did, something impossibly sad flitted through her eyes.

In that instant, Francesca forgot about her own troubles—after all, she and Bragg had done their moral best to avoid giving in to their desire, so his wife was, in a way, barking up the wrong tree. But Connie was married, with two children, and what Francesca had just seen in her eyes was a result of Neil's own misbehavior. "Connie, I am sorry; I am being unfair, burdening you with this."

"You are hardly being unfair—I'm your sister, Fran. I think you had better be prepared for a difficult and unpleasant interview. What will you say if she asks you directly about your feelings?"

"I have no idea," Francesca said. Abruptly she sat down. "I do wish I knew who has been whispering tales in her ear.

I wonder if that person seeks to hurt me, Bragg, or Leigh Anne. And how could this have happened so quickly? Bragg and I just met on January the eighteenth. Leigh Anne has been in Boston for what? A week? I am almost thinking that somebody traveled up to Boston to spread his or her gossip!"

"Her gossip," Connie said firmly. "This is the work of another woman, Fran."

"Yes, I think you are right."

"Have you mentioned this to Bragg?"

"No!"

Connie simply looked at her and finally said, "Shouldn't you?"

Francesca could only gaze back at her. "I'm afraid to."

"Why?"

"I don't know. I think I keep hoping this note, and his wife, will simply go away—maybe back to Europe. I'm afraid of how she will affect our lives if she does come to New York."

"I do think she's coming, Fran. The note is rather explicit."

"Thanks."

"Well, if it were me, I would draw a line right in the sand. I am quite certain that is what she intends to do."

"What do you mean?" Francesca asked foolishly.

Connie touched her. "There is no reason for her to want to meet you other than to tell you quite clearly to stay away from her husband. She does have every right," she added gently.

"No, she does not. She abandoned him, Con. She left him shortly after their marriage. She has taken a dozen lovers since. He did not wish for a separation. She has no rights!"

"Actually, separated or not, she has every right, Fran. She is his legal wife."

Francesca sank down into a chair. She could not speak. Dear God, Connie was right.

Leigh Anne Bragg had every right, no matter the state of her marriage, to hate Francesca and demand that she stay away from her husband. She had every right to come to New

York and move right into No. 11 Madison Square! And in
that moment Francesca felt sheer panic.

"What is it?"

"What if she moves in with him?"

"Well, that seems doubtful, if they have been separated
for four years."

Francesca was relieved. Of course Leigh Anne would stay
at the Waldorf!

Connie pulled up the chair from her secretaire and sat
down there. "Francesca, I shall be blunt. Frankly, it is time
for you to give up on Bragg and move on, romantically
speaking." Her tone was firm.

Francesca stared. "Could you stop loving Neil?"

Connie stood. "This conversation is about you, Fran, not
me and Neil. I am glad now that Mama is encouraging a
match with Calder. You must forget about Bragg. In fact, if
you really love him, you will end your friendship with him."

"That is why I cannot end our friendship!" Francesca
cried.

"You are usually so clever," Connie said with a shake of
her head. "She is his wife, he is police commissioner—and
headed for the United States Senate—and *you* are the other
woman. *You* can hurt him terribly, Fran, if you continue this
. . . liaison."

The truth was stunning. Francesca stared in shock. "But
she is his Achilles' heel," she finally whispered. "If the public ever found out about his separation—"

"No," Connie said. She leaped to her feet and grabbed
Francesca by the shoulders. "If the public learns they are
separated, the answer is easy—a reconciliation. All will be
forgiven. *You* are his Achilles' heel, Francesca. He will never
be forgiven for another woman. *You* are the one who can
destroy him. If you love him, you *must* let him go!"

Francesca hesitated. Bragg's office door was open, and he
was inside with the new chief of police, Brendan Farr. Bragg
was listening intently while Farr, a tall, gray-haired man,
seemed to be presenting a point. He spoke quickly and ur-

gently, every now and then punctuating a word with a gesture of his hand.

Bragg looked past Farr and his gaze locked with Francesca's. He smiled.

Farr stopped in midsentence, turning and clearly annoyed at the interruption.

Bragg said, "I don't think it's a good idea, at the moment."

Farr whirled back to Bragg. In spite of the flash of annoyance and maybe anger that Francesca had just seen, he spoke with deference. "Very well." He nodded at Bragg and then crossed the room.

Francesca had not moved from where she stood on the threshold of the office. She was surprised to find herself instinctively tensing as he approached.

He nodded politely. "Good day, Miss Cahill. I hope it is not police business which brings you here." But he smiled, in spite of his inference that she should not be involved in police affairs.

She smiled brightly. "Absolutely not." Of course, they both knew that there was no other valid reason for her to call on Bragg.

His iron-gray eyes held hers, and when he smiled, it did not reach his eyes. And then he was gone. For one moment, Francesca stared after him. She hadn't liked him when they had first met a few days ago, and now she realized that she did not trust him, but then, neither did Bragg.

Farr had been a typically corrupt inspector before Bragg had taken control of the department. Now Bragg felt he would toe the straight and narrow line of virtue in order to please. Choosing which man to promote to the oh-so-important position of chief of police had been a very difficult decision.

"What brings you here?"

Francesca started and met Bragg's smile. Her heart seemed to accelerate its beat. Now she had his wife's terrible note on her mind.

Of course she had to tell him about it.

She was afraid to even guess what his reaction would be.

It had been so much easier to simply forget its very existence.

"I had hoped to speak with you yesterday," Francesca began. "But you were so busy with your family that it was simply impossible."

His gaze was warm and searching. No other man ever looked at her quite the same way. It was as if he wished to know exactly what she was thinking and it was also as if, in a very tender way, he found her amusing.

His smile faded. He moved past her and closed the door.

"Bragg?" She wondered if somehow she had said or done something wrong. He seemed so serious, so intent, now.

"They like you," he said flatly.

"They do? They said so?"

"No one had to say anything," he said. "I could tell."

"I'm not sure Grace likes me," she began.

He silenced her by pulling her close. "Why are you up and about town again? Why aren't you resting? What if your burn becomes infected? I am worried, Francesca."

She stared into his eyes and recalled Connie's last words: *You are his Achilles' heel, Francesca. If you love him, you must let him go!*

"Tell me you are not here on police business, as Farr suggested," Bragg whispered.

It was hard to shove Connie's words far away, to a place where she would not hear them, echoing with a horrible and fatal insistence. Francesca laid her hands on his hard chest. His suit jacket was open, and through his cotton shirt she felt muscle and bone and the pounding of his heart.

"I am guilty as charged," she whispered. And she felt his heart beat faster, harder.

"Why am I not surprised?" he asked in a husky tone. He cupped her face with one large palm. Their gazes locked.

And a little voice inside her head said, *You had better tell him about the note or there will be hell to pay.*

Of course, it was hard to listen to that inner voice, when he held her face and she felt his heart beating beneath her palm. She knew what its acceleration meant.

"What is it? You look so unhappy," he murmured.

She inhaled. *This was her chance to tell him that Leigh Anne knew about their feelings and that she was on her way to New York.* Francesca opened her mouth to begin but somehow could not get a word out.

For she had the most awful sense that when she did, it would change everything. That the entire world as she had known it since he had stepped into her house on January 18 would crumble and vanish forever. Suddenly she was gripping his shirt. "It's nothing," she began.

His eyes told her that he did not believe her, but before she could reaffirm what she had said his arm slid behind her and before she could take a breath she was in his arms, against his chest, and his mouth was on hers.

They hadn't kissed since the Channing ball. Francesca had forgotten how much she wanted to be with this man. But not this way, oh no. She wanted to be in his bed; she wanted to be unclothed; she wanted to consummate their relationship. She wanted to be his lover, desperately so.

You are his Achilles' heel . . . You are the one who can destroy him.

Their hearts thundered as one. His entire hard body fused with hers; his hands moved up and down her back, her bottom; her hands slid over his chest, his abdomen. His arousal ground against her hip. Somehow she was turned so her back was against the wall. He leaned all of his weight against her and she strained back against him. She almost hated her sister in that moment. *Connie was wrong.*

He suddenly ended the kiss, briefly hugging her, hard. In his arms she felt small, safe, and secure, in spite of the blood that continued to run like hot, bubbling lava in her veins. His face was buried against hers. His beard was merely a few hours old, but it was scratchy and delicious.

"I like your beard," she whispered.

"I love you," he returned.

And the echo began. *You are his Achilles' heel . . .*

"What is it?" he asked sharply.

Francesca had stiffened; now she pulled away. "Nothing."

He stared intently. "Something is bothering you."

She had never lied to him. She never would. "Sarah Channing is in trouble, Bragg." That was the truth. Still, there was nagging guilt.

For one moment he was surprised, and then, all business, he said, "What happened?"

Francesca felt a surge of relief. "Someone broke into her studio and went on a rampage. Her work has been destroyed, and in general, the studio is quite unusable now."

His gaze remained on hers. "Is she all right? Was anyone hurt? Has it been reported to the police?"

"Sarah is extremely upset, as is Mrs. Channing. No one was hurt, and Mrs. Channing did report the crime." She hesitated. "An Inspector O'Connor is in charge. Actually, it happened between midnight Thursday and yesterday morning at five-fifteen."

He absorbed that. "So that is why you came by yesterday?"

She nodded.

Then, "Dare I ask how it is that you are involved when you have been told to remain at home and preferably in bed for an entire week?"

"She is my friend! My brother's fiancée!" she exclaimed. "Of course I am involved!"

"Francesca," he began firmly.

"Bragg, stop. You know Sarah. Her life is her work. She is the victim of a strange crime—a strange and angry attack! I cannot sit by and do nothing! The real question is, Why? Why would anyone harbor a grudge or be angry with Sarah Channing?"

Bragg sighed. "It seems very odd, I agree."

"I do have one theory," Francesca added.

He smiled, briefly and reluctantly. "Please."

She told him about the fact that Sarah had become engaged to her brother and that perhaps a jealous young woman had struck out at her.

He gave her an interested and thoughtful look, started to pace toward his desk, and then whirled.

Francesca turned to see what had so captured his interest.

The door was now open and Lucy Savage stood there, wide-eyed and intent.

She smiled quickly, but she was looking from the one to the other. "I knocked, but no one heard me, so I came in." Her glance moved between them again.

Which brother do you love?

That was not a question Francesca wished to recall, not ever and especially not now. But surely Lucy had not been outside that door when Bragg had been kissing her as if it were the end of the world. How much had she seen? How much had she heard?

"Do knock and come in," Bragg remarked calmly.

Lucy flushed and entered. "I did knock, Rick. Aren't you happy to see me?" She moved to him and tugged his arm into hers and kissed his cheek. "I miss you and I thought to drag you to lunch." She smiled at Francesca. "Hello, Fran. So, the two of you are on a new case?" she asked with open eagerness.

Bragg said flatly, "Francesca is not on a case."

Francesca turned to him. "Actually, Mrs. Channing has hired me to find the ruffian who did this, Bragg."

"Do not tell me you are taking this case! You do not even have the use of both hands!"

"I already have, Bragg," Francesca said calmly. "How could I not? Sarah is miserably upset. This is her life and she is a friend of mine! Besides"—she softened and touched his sleeve—"how dangerous could this be? Someone attacked her studio, not her. For all we know, other artists have suffered the same violation. In fact, I think we should find out if there have been any other similar attacks in the city."

"I do not want you on any case, especially not now," Bragg said dangerously.

"I could not refuse. I know I can help. I promise to stay out of harm's way!" Francesca cried.

He stared at her; she stared back.

"I want to help," Lucy said, apparently fascinated.

"Absolutely not." Bragg whirled. Then he glared at Francesca. "She is worse than you. Trouble is her middle name.

Besides, her husband would kill me—Apache style—should anything happen to her."

Lucy grinned. "That means a very slow death with lots of torture," she said happily.

Francesca smiled back at Lucy, although secretly she was intrigued with the notion of having her as a sidekick. "I actually have an assistant. He is a cutpurse who is eleven years old and he has been invaluable to me thus far, as he knows every inch of the city. His name is Joel."

Lucy was wide-eyed. "So you have really made this your work?"

Francesca smiled and opened her purse. Her smile vanished as she stared at the carefully folded white note that was tucked inside beside her tiny derringer, a candle, matches, a notepad, a lead pencil, some cash, and her calling cards.

"Fran?"

She inhaled and reached inside for a calling card. As she handed it to Lucy, she glanced at Bragg, consumed with fresh guilt.

Why was she so afraid to tell him about the note? He was the most understanding man she knew.

"Oh my," Lucy said on a breath. She looked up. "What a wonderful calling card. I should be intrigued if I did not know you! I would hire you instantly, too."

"Thank you," Francesca said, pleased.

Bragg made a sound very much like a groan. "Francesca, I cannot prevent you from taking on Mrs. Channing as a client. But I can ask you not to do so."

She stared. The world seemed to have stopped turning in that moment. "Please do not."

He hesitated. "If I did, what would you say?"

Her heart hurt her now. "I could not turn my back on a friend in need," she managed, stricken. She added silently, *Please, do not make me choose.*

"I see." He turned away from her, but there was no mistaking his expression. It was resigned, hurt, angry, and somehow he had made her make a choice.

She stared. How had their happiness dissolved so quickly?

Should she turn down Sarah and Mrs. Channing? But how could she! Sarah was grief-stricken. Someone, clearly, wanted to hurt her—someone was so angry! "This isn't fair, Bragg," she whispered, agonized, to his back.

"Is life fair?" he asked darkly, whirling to stare at her.

She thought about his wife. "No."

"You must do as you will, Francesca. I do not control you, nor do I wish to," he said.

But he was angry, displeased. Francesca did not know what to do now. "I cannot bear it when I have so upset you," she said softly, in that moment forgetting that they were not alone.

He then sighed as if resigned to the inevitable and looked at his sister. "I have appointments all afternoon. And as you can see, a matter has cropped up which I should personally attend. I am afraid that lunch is not a possibility."

"I understand," Lucy said softly. Then, "Do not be too hard on Fran, Rick. She is an extraordinary woman. You should be proud of her."

His jaw flexed. Clearly he felt that the cat was out of the bag with his sister, for he said, "I *am* proud of her." He turned to Francesca, and he remained unsmiling. "I am going over there now, but in an unofficial capacity. I do not have time right now for another investigation, unless the situation is dire." Their eyes held and she knew he was thinking about the Cross Murders. That had been dire indeed. "Then I shall speak with Inspector O'Connor."

Francesca wasn't pleased with the sound of that. She so wanted to work with Bragg again on this investigation. "Shall I tell you what I have thus far learned?"

He finally smiled, taking his greatcoat off of a wall peg. "Actually, I was going to offer you a lift to wherever it is that you are going. You can tell me what you have discovered as we ride uptown." His regard was once again affectionate. "For I have little doubt you already have a lead or two."

She moved to him and touched his hand. "Thank you, Bragg." Then she turned. "I will accept your lunch invitation," she said.

Their eyes met. Lucy understood, and her expression was amazingly innocent. "How wonderful," she said.

"Where is Peter?" Francesca asked as Bragg drove carefully through the traffic heading uptown on Sixth Avenue. An elevated train thundered past one avenue over as they crept forward, jammed between two omnibuses and a trolley.

"At the house." Bragg looked at her. "The nanny whom your mother found is Mrs. Flowers, and unfortunately, she wears the most absurd and oversize flowers on her hat. That gave me the instant impression that she is rather silly and would be generally ineffective and useless. I asked Peter to remain behind today as I had the feeling he would be very much in demand." He sighed. "I was also afraid to leave Mrs. Flowers alone with the children."

Francesca winced and looked back at Lucy, who rode in the backseat of the Daimler, and had she been a horse, her ears would have been pricked forward. "Bragg is fostering two orphans. Their mother was murdered by a lunatic. My mother just found him a nanny," she explained.

Lucy said, "This is amazing."

Bragg glanced briefly back at her. "Not a word. They are pure mischief, a constant headache, and it is a temporary situation."

"I see," Lucy said, her fine red brows arched. "My brother loves children," she remarked.

"I would have never guessed," Francesca quipped.

Bragg shot her a look. "I was expecting to have my own children in the house, not two orphans, one of whom piddles wherever she pleases, the other who refuses to eat."

"Oh my," Lucy said, smothering a laugh. "How ever did you arrange this?"

"I begged," Francesca said, but she was not smiling, because Bragg was grim and she just knew he was thinking about the fact that he would never have children now. He had told her so himself. He despised his wife that much.

"How did you determine when the attack on Sarah's studio took place?" Bragg asked, finally driving past the trolley and quite obviously changing the topic. Now two horse-drawn carriages blocked their way. Traffic was heavy for a Saturday.

"They returned at half past ten on Thursday from an evening out," Francesca said quickly. "Sarah went back to her studio until ten past midnight." She grimaced a little, thinking about the fact that Sarah had been arranging the composition of her portrait for Calder Hart. "Sarah discovered the disaster this morning at five-fifteen, which is the time she usually begins work. The staff sleep on the fourth floor; a single doorman was on. I have already spoken to Harris, the doorman, who has been with the Channings for six years. He did not fall asleep, and he did not see or hear anything."

"Have you spoken to the rest of the staff?" Bragg asked. The park had appeared on their right. It was brilliantly white with snow, and numerous sleds could be seen on a distant hill where both children and adults were enjoying the afternoon. Two riders were cantering across the Great Lawn, and numerous pedestrians were strolling on the track.

"There was no time," Francesca said. "I thought I should go to you directly."

"Does Sarah have any suspicions as to who the culprit might be?"

"No. She says she has no enemies. There is one other idea I have had."

"Do tell."

"She says she doesn't know the names of most of the staff, as she is always either in her studio or wandering about thinking about her work. Perhaps a servant misinterpreted her manner as being insulting and rude; perhaps a servant was deranged enough to decide to vandalize her studio."

"A servant would certainly have easy access," Lucy remarked.

Bragg and Francesca turned to look at her. She smiled at them both.

Then Lucy said, "But what about a jilted debutante? If your brother is a catch, I would not be surprised if we found out that some spoiled young woman had become furiously angry over such a lost opportunity, enough so to attack Sarah's studio."

He raised a brow at her. "If we found out?"

Lucy grinned. "If the two of you found out."

"You and Evan should put your heads together and see what comes up," Bragg said to Francesca. "Evan could prove very helpful in this instance."

She smiled at him. "I think we shall do just that."

"Perhaps there is a displeased client," Bragg remarked.

Francesca stiffened.

He looked at her, pausing for a group of gay, laughing pedestrians, young men and women, all with skates slung over their shoulders. "Well?"

She hesitated and, oddly, gave Lucy a nervous glance.

"What is it?" he asked, driving forward.

"She really has no clients. Sarah has not sold her art." She wet her lips. "Yet."

He gave her a long look.

She faced him. "Do not be angry!" she cried.

"I shall try not to be. What is it that you are not telling me?"

"I had nothing to do with this," she warned.

Suddenly he pulled over to the curb, a bit forceful on the brake. "Oh, ho. Let me guess. Hart is involved in this!"

Her heart lurched and fell. Then it beat like a drum. "Bragg, he isn't really involved."

"Why are you white?" he demanded.

"All right! He is Sarah's client. Her only one. Recently, he commissioned a painting from her!" she cried, praying he would not ask about the commission, yet knowing he would find out, sooner or later, and she had better tell him the truth.

Bragg stared at her. "That's it?"

She hesitated, licked her lips, and nodded. "Not exactly."

He waited.

She closed her eyes, wishing she could disappear, at least for a moment or two. But then, none of this was her fault. She turned and looked at him. "I had nothing to do with this—really."

"Somehow, I doubt that."

"The painting Hart commissioned? It is a portrait." She swallowed. "Of me."

Francesca trailed behind Bragg as he strode into the same large, overdecorated salon that she had been in earlier. Lucy was at her side. Bragg hadn't said another word since he had learned of Hart's commission, much to Francesca's dismay. He was clearly angry. Lucy had tried to engage him in conversation, and his replies had consisted of monosyllables.

Now Francesca tore her gaze from his rigid shoulders and glanced at Lucy. The redhead gave her a soft, sympathetic smile, then leaned close and whispered, "Don't worry. I am sure things will work out. He is jealous."

Francesca tried to smile back and failed. Bragg had whipped around to glare at them, so she could not tell Lucy that he had nothing to be jealous of.

Mrs. Channing had led the way into the parlor, and now she sank into a huge, thronelike chair, which dwarfed her. She had not stopped talking since they had arrived, and she was going on and on about how distressed Sarah was, how maddened someone must be, and why would anyone do such a thing?

"I do need to speak with Sarah," Bragg said firmly.

Mrs. Channing's hands fluttered nervously. "She is coming down, Commissioner. She has already been sent for." Tears filled her eyes. "My poor dear has been so happy. You know, with the engagement and all. And to have some madman come along and ruin it all this way!"

Francesca turned to Lucy. "The engagement to my brother was a recent one."

"How wonderful," Lucy said. "Shouldn't he be here?"

Francesca hesitated, wondering what to say. "He doesn't know what has happened," she finally said.

Lucy's look told her everything. She knew that the match was not about love.

"Have you employed anyone new recently?" Bragg was asking Mrs. Channing.

"No. We have had no change of staff this year, certainly not that I can remember."

"I should like a list of your entire household. With mailing addresses for everyone," Bragg said. "Both current and previous. I should also like for each servant to list his or her previous employment and spouses, if there are any."

Mrs. Channing blinked. "Oh."

Francesca understood. He wished to determine if any of the staff had suspicious or criminal backgrounds or connections. It would be a laborious task indeed.

"Commissioner?" Sarah said softly, from behind Francesca.

She turned. Sarah was terribly pale, but she had clearly composed herself, as her bearing was ramrod-straight. Her cousin, the Countess Bartolla Benevente, stood beside her, a flamboyantly beautiful auburn-haired woman clad in a gown more suitable for evening than day, with a huge sapphire necklace about her throat. Bartolla had her arm around Sarah. Tall and statuesquoe, the countess dwarfed the petite artist.

Bragg moved to her. "I am terribly sorry about this, Sarah," he said softly.

She nodded, fighting to keep her composure.

Bragg nodded at Bartolla politely. She smiled at him. "Good morning, Commissioner." She was a natural flirt, but Bragg had never seemed to notice. "Hullo, Francesca. I heard you were here earlier. How is your hand?"

Francesca kissed her cheek. "Much better, thank you." She had once thought to dislike Bartolla, but it had proved impossible, as she was a very daring and unusual woman, who courageously defied convention—in the most public manner. However, she had walked in on Francesca and Bragg while they were passionately entwined on the sofa at the Channing ball. She had assured Francesca that her secret was safe. Francesca was face-to-face with the other woman for the first time since that night. It was impossible to decide whether she could trust Bartolla or not. Just then, it was as if Bartolla had never caught her in a compromising position. Could she have forgotten?

Perhaps, Francesca thought, the incident was insignificant to her, as she was a wealthy widow and a woman of the world.

The notion was a comforting one.

However, Francesca had to stare at the auburn-haired woman. She and Leigh Anne Bragg were friends.

The countess had told her so.

But surely Bartolla had not said anything to Leigh Anne, as she was also Francesca's friend.

"Sarah, Bartolla, this is Bragg's sister, Lucy Savage. Bartolla is Sarah's cousin and an Italian countess," Francesca added, feeling rather as if she had been struck by an object right between the eyes.

At the Channing ball, Bragg had commented that Bartolla had not liked the attention Francesca was receiving. He had also said that she was not really a friend.

Francesca realized she must speak with the other woman and attempt to draw her carefully out.

Now Lucy smiled at Sarah, but when she turned to Bartolla her expression changed, closing instantly. Bartolla's smile had also vanished. The two women, both tall, both voluptuous, both impossibly beautiful, the one red-haired, the other auburn, looked at each other as if they had become two female cats, claws out, fur on end, fangs apparent. A silence fell.

Francesca looked from Lucy's cool expression to Bartolla's even colder one and thought, *My God, they are both so stunningly beautiful, and they cannot stand each other because of it*. It was instant sheer dislike, a mutual hatred at first sight.

"Sarah? Have you had any new thoughts on the vandalism of your studio?" Bragg cut into the tension quietly.

Sarah shook her head. "I keep thinking about it. My mind seems to be going round and round in circles. I think of all the servants here, but I find it hard to believe that I have so offended someone in this house that he or she would take such extreme action against me. But now I also keep recalling the reception I have been receiving . . . since my engagement. Before the engagement, I was a bit like wallpaper. People would glance at me and then it was as if I were not even present. Now ladies are falling all over themselves to congratulate me on my good fortune, include me in their conversation, and invite me to too many events to consider. I am beginning to wonder," Sarah said.

Bartolla moved to stand beside her. "She makes no demands. I have never seen anything like it. She fetches her own tea, her own mail; she forgets to ask for help when she is dressing; she gives her clothes to the housemaids. . . . She is always kind; she never loses her temper. The staff adore her, Commissioner."

But Francesca moved to Sarah and slid her arm around her small shoulders. "You wonder what?" she asked softly.

Sarah met her gaze. "It has been unreal. Surreal. A sea of smiles, stretched wide—and tight. Perhaps I am overwrought now, but I wonder if those smiles are merely that, a stretching of the mouth, a purely physical act, that has nothing to do with anything at all."

Francesca stared. "Are you saying that you think everyone around you is false?"

Sarah shrugged. "No one cared about me before; why should they suddenly care now? Perhaps there is a jealously maddened woman out there who is furious with my so-called good fortune."

Francesca looked at Bragg, and he returned her gaze. "I will speak to Evan immediately," she said. He was an incorrigible flirt. Perhaps he *had* misled a too-hopeful debutante.

"Please do. Shall we go down and take a look at your studio, Sarah?"

Sarah hesitated, once again extremely distressed. Finally, she nodded.

Everyone turned to leave the salon. Bragg stopped, facing them all. "I shall go alone with Miss Channing."

Francesca started, about to protest. But Bragg looked at her and said, "Francesca may join us, of course. As the Channings are her clients."

She smiled at him. Then, as they left the others behind in

the salon, she said, "Do you think it is safe to leave Lucy and Bartolla together?"

His jaw firmed, telling her he still had Hart's commission on his mind. "They shall have to work it out."

Sarah was leading the way. She paused outside her studio door. "Bartolla has been a huge comfort to me. I am glad she is here. She is so strong. I wish I were more like her, and more like you, Francesca."

Francesca put her arm around her. "You are the strong one," she said firmly.

"Actually . . ." She hesitated. "I am scared."

Francesca's gaze met hers. Before she could reassure her, Bragg spoke. "You have no reason to be frightened, Sarah. This may be a foolish prank and little else."

Francesca had seen the studio. She had seen the slashed canvas and, worse, all that dark red paint. She did not think this the work of a prankster, oh no. But she would let Bragg decide for himself.

"I hope you are right," Sarah said softly.

Bragg looked over her head at Francesca, and she realized that, even though he had yet to see the studio, he did not think it a prank, not at all. He was merely hoping to calm Sarah.

And of course, it was too much work to be a prank. After all, someone had carefully and deliberately broken into the Channing home in order to carry out his or her vicious night's work.

Sarah pushed open the door. "I am not going in," she said, her breath catching.

Francesca followed Bragg inside. He paused in the center of the room, slowly regarding it all.

Francesca paused beside him. The day was brilliantly sunny now, and the studio was brightly illuminated, the contrast gruesome, of light and shadow, of sunshine falling across overturned paint, the brushes and canvases, the pools of blood-red paint. For the first time, Francesca noticed that the intruder had taken a brush or a stick and begun to write upon the wall. She started, forgetting to breathe.

Was that what she thought it was?

The single crude letter had been interrupted. It began like an *I* or the number 1, but the top curved down. Bragg was staring at it, too. He seemed to have lost some of his coloring.

"Is that an attempt at a letter?" Francesca asked, with the beginnings of real dread.

"I don't know," he said, glancing rigidly at her. "It might be the beginnings of a *p* or a capital *B* Or it might be nothing at all."

She could not speak. Then, "It looks like an *f*, Bragg," she said on a deep breath.

And their eyes met.

Four

They stared at each other. Then Bragg said, "Only one canvas has been slashed."

Francesca tore her gaze from his, to glance around the studio. While a few completed canvases remained stacked upon the walls, all brilliantly colored portraits done in a Post-impressionist style, a half a dozen were strewn about the studio's cement floor. She realized that he was right. Five of the paintings that had been overturned and thrown about were in perfect condition. Two were landscapes, one a scene of a mother and her two children, the other two portraits of young women. Francesca approached the sixth canvas.

She could not make it out. Black and red paint marred the surface, making the work beneath indecipherable. It had also been slashed into ribbons. Slowly she looked up.

Bragg held her gaze for a moment. "I find this rather significant," he said.

"Yes. It seems that this one painting was singled out for destruction."

"I wonder if it is a portrait?"

"And if so, of whom?" Francesca smiled a little.

He began to smile back, then recalled himself. "When were you going to tell me?"

She cringed inwardly and knew exactly what he was speaking about. "That's not fair."

"Why does he want your portrait, Francesca? Or need I bother to ask?" His eyes had turned black.

"You said so yourself! He likes causing trouble!" Francesca exclaimed.

"Yes, he does, but in this case, I feel he has an ulterior motive."

"The only motive he has is to annoy me. You see, he was angry with me when he decided to commission the portrait. This is just a game to him, Bragg. He could not care less about my portrait!"

Bragg's eyes narrowed. "My half brother is pure predator when it comes to beautiful women. You know that. Yet still you defend him. You always defend him!"

"I am hardly defending Hart," she snapped. "And he has not ever preyed upon me—and he never will. For God's sake, you know as well as I do that a marriageable prospect is anathema to him! Trust me. He has no intention of going forward with this ridiculous commission."

Bragg looked ready to explode. "Then why did he give Sarah a deposit for the painting?" he asked dangerously.

She started. "I have no idea, and I am growing tired of this subject. You are treating me as if this is my fault! Believe me, I find Hart as insufferable as you do."

"Then tell him you will not sit for the portrait," Bragg said flatly.

She froze. "I can't do that." She saw his knowing look. "And it is not about him; it is about Sarah! She is thrilled that Hart wishes for her to paint for him. I cannot let her down."

Bragg stared and abruptly turned his back on her. "Sarah? I am sorry, but you must come inside."

Francesca started to gape. She realized what she was doing, and she quickly closed her mouth.

Sarah paused on the threshold of the room. She was very pale now, and she looked ill.

Francesca wanted to kick Bragg in the shin until she realized why he had called Sarah in. He said softly, "We need to identify that canvas, Sarah. Do you know which subject it was?" he asked, pointing at the destroyed canvas on the floor.

Sarah looked at it and cried out. Then her hands went to her midsection and she began to retch.

Francesca rushed to her, helping her remain upright. Sarah gasped for breath, but she fought the urge to heave, and she did not. She finally straightened, panting. Her eyes were wide.

"You know what the canvas was," Bragg said.

Sarah nodded, swallowing. "It was the portrait I did of Bartolla," she said.

"I am so pleased that you girls decided to join us for lunch!" Mrs. Channing cried happily.

They had all taken their seats at the cherrywood table, which seated fifty—in a monstrously huge dining room, where the walls were papered in red and the ceiling was mint green with red starburst moldings. Every time Francesca glanced up—past three grossly large crystal chandeliers with angels sculpted atop them—she thought the starbursts looked like splatters of blood.

Why had Bartolla's portrait been destroyed? Had the act of vandalism been aimed at her and not Sarah?

"It is simply so exciting that you are Derek Bragg's granddaughter and the heiress to his fortune," Mrs. Channing was saying. "I have always wanted to meet him! He is a legend, you know."

"Actually, I have five brothers, not to mention dozens of cousins," Lucy remarked.

"The Bragg heiress is in town! Oh, we must give you a party. Pull out the old welcome wagon." Mrs. Channing winked, not hearing Lucy at all.

Bartolla leaned across the table and met Francesca's gaze. "You are staring. Don't you like my dress?" She was smiling, but her green eyes were probing.

"You are the most stunningly dressed woman I know," Francesca said truthfully. Bartolla was even more outstanding than her own sister, Connie, although Connie was by far the more elegant. Still, Bartolla was the woman one would always notice first in any room.

Bartolla seemed pleased. Francesca smiled, thinking she was the kind of woman who had enemies.

Bartolla turned her smile on Lucy, and it turned to ice. "How wonderful it must be, to grow up a Bragg heiress."

Lucy's smile was superficial. "It was wonderful growing up, period. I have parents I respect, admire, and adore, not to mention my five brothers, my half brother, and Calder, whom I consider a stepbrother. I love each and every one— even if they are all first-rate pranksters. And I have dozens of cousins, aunts and uncles, and, of course, Grandpa Derek and Grandma Miranda. We are a very close family, even if we are scattered about the country and England. I consider myself extremely lucky."

"Your husband probably considers himself lucky as well," Bartolla said far too sweetly. The innuendo was clear—that Lucy's husband was a fortune-hunter. "Did not the two of you somehow inherit the Bragg ranch? I do believe I read about it."

Lucy was all sugar in return. "My husband fell in love with me at first sight. We are still in love. And yes, it was the most amazing wedding gift—my grandparents' entire ranch! Of course, we had to earn their trust. But it is a long story. Are you married, Mrs. er . . . ?" And she cocked her head innocently.

Francesca sighed. She felt like telling them both to sheathe their claws.

"I am a widow, God rest my dear departed husband's soul," Bartolla said with vast sadness, a trembling hand upon her breast. It boasted an extremely large emerald ring.

"How sad," Lucy said, waving her own hand, which boasted a yellow diamond ring, almost as large as Bartolla's emerald. It was questionable which ring was worth more.

"Oh, we are having salads for lunch; how perfect," Francesca interrupted. She was afraid knives would be thrown across the table if the two women were allowed to continue.

But Lucy said, "My, how impressive. You married an Italian count. I have traveled quite extensively in Europe. Benevente. The name is familiar. I wonder if I knew your husband?"

Bartolla's smile was stretched tight. "I doubt it."

"But surely we ran in the same circles—didn't we?" Lucy batted her big blue eyes innocently.

"I am sure we did," Bartolla said, refusing to admit that perhaps she and her husband were not wealthy enough to travel in the same society as the Braggs.

"And there is Scotch salmon," Francesca said. She smiled brightly, then gave Lucy a dark look, which meant, "cease and desist." "What a wonderful lunch."

"I do hope you girls are hungry," Mrs. Channing said. She added to Lucy, "You may not have known the count. He was a dear man, but so much older, of course. These past few years he did not go out often, as he was so ill. Didn't he have a stroke, dear, a few years ago?"

"Actually, he walked a mile every day. Right up until his death," Bartolla said flatly.

Lucy practically snickered. Bartolla's jaw clamped down. Lucy said, "Shoz is a bit older than me, too. He is forty. But he looks exactly the way he did when we first met five years ago." She smiled. "He's incredibly handsome. How old was your husband when he died?"

Bartolla stared.

"Oh, he was in his sixties, I believe. And they were only married eight years! The count was smitten, Lucy, simply smitten with his young American wife," Mrs. Channing supplied eagerly.

Bartolla stabbed her salad with a fork.

"I am sure," Lucy said, gleeful.

"I can't eat."

Sarah had spoken. Everyone looked at her. She sat rigidly, her plate untouched.

"Of course you can't," Francesca said softly. "Mrs. Channing? Would you mind terribly if Sarah and I took a walk? I think some fresh air would do her good."

Mrs. Channing's face had fallen, but she was resigned. "No, Francesca, of course not."

And as Francesca and Sarah got up, Lucy jumped up, too. "I must join you," she said. "I do hope you understand, Mrs.

Channing. But Francesca has allowed me to assist her in this case."

"Sarah?" In the music room, Francesca took her hand. "Perhaps it might be best if we instructed the staff to clean up your studio."

Sarah sighed. "The commissioner said he is sending a detective over and not to touch anything."

"I know; I was there," Francesca said quietly. "But I think it might be best if you got back to work immediately. We could tidy up just a section."

Sarah blinked at her. "I have no urge to work."

Francesca did not like the sound of that. "But—"

Sarah held up both hands. "Do not insist! I am not painting a thing," she said flatly. "Not even your portrait."

Francesca knew she should be relieved, but she was not. She saw how distressed Sarah remained, and even as an image of Hart formed in her mind, and it was rather mocking, she would have preferred that Sarah insist they rush to do the portrait rather than refuse to paint at all. "How can I help?" she finally asked softly.

Sarah fought tears. "Find the hoodlum who did this. Then bring him to me so I may know why!"

Francesca was seeing the side of Sarah so rarely seen by anyone, as a young woman of courage and strength. She wished her brother might see his fiancée now, like this. "I told you I would get to the bottom of this, and you know I will," she said.

"Yes, I know." Sarah sighed again and walked over to a window that looked out on the back lawns. They were blanketed in snow, and beyond them was nothing but undeveloped land. The Palisades were just visible, rising up out of the horizon, a steep and jagged iron-gray line of rock cliffs.

"Sarah? We are having a family dinner tonight at the Plaza. I have a wonderful idea," Lucy said with a smile. "Why don't you and your mother and, of course, your fiancée join us?" She turned to Francesca. "And you, too, Fran. I know it is the last minute, but it will be very festive, I promise you that, and I think it will lift your spirits considerably!"

Francesca hesitated. A part of her instantly wanted to agree, because Bragg would be there. But so would Hart.

"I think Mama has made plans," Sarah said. Then, "Truthfully, I am a bit despondent, and I hope to stay in tonight."

"Posh," Lucy said, taking her hand. "You will adore my family! You will enjoy yourself; trust me!" she cried.

Sarah smiled a little at her. "I am sure Mama will love to have dinner with your family. She is always so impressed by nobility and wealth."

Lucy winced.

"But she means well," Francesca added quickly, surprised by Sarah's comment, which, while truthful, was a bit unkind.

"Yes, she always means well," Sarah said, and she appeared saddened.

Francesca and Lucy exchanged glances.

"And you are coming as well," Lucy said firmly to Francesca.

Francesca hesitated, and her urge to spend the evening with Bragg won out. "Very well." Then she turned to Sarah. "Sarah? Has it occurred to you that the vandal might have a grudge against Bartolla and not yourself?"

Sarah stiffened. She did not speak for a moment. Then, "No, it did not. But perhaps you are right! I have no enemies, but I would not be surprised if Bartolla did."

The three women exchanged glances and then returned to the dining room in search of their prey. Bartolla had just returned to her rooms, and Francesca asked Lucy to wait for her downstairs as she hurried up to conduct a brief and, she hoped, insightful interview.

"My, that was quick," Bartolla said when a maid allowed Francesca into a lavish suite of rooms. Bartolla was trying to decide between three different fur stoles, each with a matching muff. "What do you think?" she asked, holding up the fox. "Or does the mink suit the blue of my dress better?"

"The mink. Bartolla, I am sorry that you and Lucy have not hit it off."

Bartolla laid the stole back on the four-poster bed. "Why?

And whoever said we have not hit it off? I have no problem with her. I think she is jealous of me." She shrugged. "After all, I am a countess. She is only . . . a Bragg."

Francesca decided not to delve into the subject. "I need to ask you a few questions," she said. "It's important."

Bartolla walked over to a huge armoire, which was open. She stared inside, debating hats and gloves. "I know nothing about Sarah's vandal, Francesca."

"And if the vandal is someone you know? Someone who wishes to strike at you and not Sarah?" Francesca asked.

Bartolla turned. "What?"

Francesca said, "Only one canvas was destroyed. It was slashed to shreds and obscured with paint. It was your portrait, Bartolla."

She stared. Then she started to smile. "Oh, please! And you think someone stole into this house in the middle of the night because of me? I hardly think so!" She laughed.

"Bartolla, you are the kind of woman to break hearts. Is there no one you can think of who has recently suffered such a fate?"

Bartolla's smile vanished. "I have only just arrived in town. I have not had time to break any hearts, Francesca."

"Are you certain?"

"I am certain," she said firmly. "And I am also late." She hesitated, then said, "Sarah does not wish to join us, but I am meeting your brother for a bit of window-shopping, as it is such a beautiful day."

Francesca tensed. She knew they were just friends, still, she knew her brother, and his head had been turned the moment he had met Bartolla Benevente.

"Would you care to join us?" Bartolla smiled.

"No, thank you. Do you have enemies, Bartolla?"

Her eyes narrowed. "Yes, I do. But you may trust me on this, Francesca. No enemy of mine would bother to steal into this house and slash up my portrait. An enemy of mine would do far worse."

Francesca absorbed that. "What is far worse?"

Bartolla blinked. "She would hurt me where it counts."

"And that would be how?"

"My, you are so unimaginative! Or is it naive? Francesca, if I were still married, she might do something to damage my relationship with my husband. Does that give you an idea of the kind of game I am talking about?"

Francesca found it interesting that Bartolla referred to such a malicious act as a game.

"Now, if you do not mind? You are going down the wrong path, and I would like to freshen up."

"I'm sorry to keep you. Bartolla, have you seen Leigh Anne recently?"

Bartolla started. "Leigh Anne? You mean the commissioner's wife?" She seemed genuinely surprised.

"Yes."

"How could I see her? Is she in town?"

"I heard she was in Boston."

Bartolla shook her head, smiling. "My dear Francesca, if she is in Boston, how could I see her? The answer is no. Why are you asking such a question?" And she was amused.

"I don't know. I suppose I am expecting her to come to the city, now that she is back in the country," Francesca fabricated smoothly. Still, just speaking about Bragg's wife disturbed her and made her nervous and uneasy.

"You seem so unhappy." Bartolla patted her arm. "Didn't I tell you that you are far too naive to manage a married man?" She gave her a knowing look. Now I really must go."

"May we continue this conversation at another time?" Francesca asked after a pause. "Not about his wife. About the possibility that perhaps this was an enemy of—"

"It was not. Now, if you do not mind?"

Francesca nodded. "If you change your mind—"

"You shall be the first to know."

"You are very quiet," Lucy remarked as they paused outside the Channing house a bit later.

Francesca did not smile. "I feel bad for Sarah." And that was entirely true, but she was also disturbed by the conversations she had had with Bartolla. And she was worried, too, because when Bragg had left they had not resolved their dispute over Hart's absurd commission. She hoped he would have recovered his usually good humor by the time she saw him that night.

"So do I. She is terribly nice, and her art is beautiful." Lucy had peeked in on the studio before they had left. "My bet is that someone hates that countess and this is not a blow against Sarah."

Francesca was grim. "I do happen to like Bartolla, Lucy, but I am inclined to agree with you. She has undoubtedly made a few enemies along the way, and perhaps one of them has now lashed out at her." They started down the block. "I will question her at length, as soon as she gives me another chance."

Lucy shrugged and said, "I'll wager that the enemy in question is a woman."

Francesca sighed. Then she said, "Why are the two of you in a competition?"

"A competition? Why would I ever compete with her?" Lucy asked with a shake of her head. "There is no competition!. True, she is rather attractive and intelligent, but look at her! She is a widow—she must have married that old man at sixteen! Now she is here to find another husband. A rich one. You may trust me on that."

Francesca's eyes widened. "That is rather unfair, don't you think? I mean, you do not even know her! And if anything, perhaps you might feel sorry for her, having had to marry an older man."

"And do you know her? Really?" Lucy asked pointedly.

"I know her a bit. And by the way, she is wealthy, and my understanding is that she wishes to remain independent. She is not husband-hunting."

"Be careful, Francesca. For I understand the two of you have just met."

"We are friends."

"Really? You are a bit too beautiful to be her friend. And you are a Cahill," Lucy said pointedly.

"I hope you are wrong. For in some ways, Bartolla and I are alike."

"You are not alike, except that you both prefer to do as you wish and not as society wishes. Again, be careful. I would not trust her if I were you."

Francesca felt shaken. They started walking again, only to pause at the curb. Lucy said, "I had better return to Hart's, where my mother is watching the twins and Roberto. I shall change the supper reservation. Do you think we should also invite your parents?"

"Please don't!" Francesca said in a rush. "They have plans tonight, anyway."

Lucy smiled. "So where do we go from here in the investigation?"

Francesca hesitated. "Evan is out right now, so I will speak to him later. I need to snoop around the art world, I think."

"Well, you can always start with Calder." Lucy grinned, both brows lifted.

Francesca folded her arms. "He is the obvious choice. I also promised Sarah that I would tell him there will be a delay in delivery of the portrait."

"You mean *your* portrait," Lucy said, laughter in her tone.

Francesca ignored that. "But I do hate to disturb him when his house is full."

"He may not even be home." Lucy leaned close. "Who is his mistress now?"

Francesca lowered her voice. "She is actually very nice, and beautiful in an unearthly way. I believe her background is genteel, but she will not speak of it. Do you want to meet her? I am sure she would love it if we called upon her."

"How about on Monday? I really do have to get back to the twins," Lucy said.

"Monday will be fine," Francesca said, as she preferred attempting to see Calder and continuing the investigation, as there were still plenty of hours left before supper.

Lucy had espied a cab, and she waved at it. "Are you coming, then?"

Francesca hesitated. She could not deny that the thought of seeing Hart made her somewhat uneasy. But Hart could be a fount of useful information. He was her connection to the art world, quite obviously. She could not avoid him now. "Of course." She forced a smile.

Lucy eyed her. "My, you do look as if you are walking to the guillotine."

Francesca did not know what to say, so she said nothing. But the truth was that somehow even approaching Hart for important information made her feel as if she were betraying Bragg.

Suddenly the Channing carriage came up beside them, pausing in the drive before entering the street. Bartolla waved at them.

Francesca smiled at her, although Lucy did not.

Bartolla unlatched and pushed open her window. "Need a lift?" she asked. She was wearing the mink stole and an elaborate and beautiful navy blue hat, one with ostrich feathers. She was frankly breathtaking.

"Yes," Francesca said with a smile, but at the same time Lucy frowned and said, "No."

Bartolla smiled at them both. "Have a good afternoon!" she cried. The carriage pulled away. The cab had also driven past them, and the only other conveyance in sight was a trolley. It was, of course, going downtown.

They looked at each other. "So which lover is she off to meet?" Lucy asked archly.

"She is window-shopping with my brother, and he is not her lover."

Lucy stared. "Is he handsome?"

"Yes—and engaged."

"Oh ho! Evan Cahill is handsome and rich. . . . are you insane? How can you even *like* her!" Lucy cried.

Francesca had stiffened. "Evan is a gentleman. He would never betray Sarah." She did not mention that he hated being engaged, that he did not like Sarah, and that he kept a mistress, a beautiful stage actress, and that he had always preferred stunning and flamboyant women.

"Oh, please! The writing is on the wall. How can you be blind?" Lucy faced her, her eyes flashing. "Let me tell you something, Francesca. She has eyed Rick behind your back— and not in a pólite way. Fortunately, he could not care less about a woman like that, or she'd seduce him away from you, quicker than you could say 'snake.' "

Francesca stared at her new friend and again thought about the fact that Bartolla was a friend of Leigh Anne. Then she recalled far too vividly the wide-eyed and somewhat pleased look on Bartolla's face when she had found Francesca and Bragg in the throes of passion on the couch at the Channing ball. She was suddenly ill at heart—and nervously afraid.

"What is it?" Lucy asked quickly.

Francesca hesitated. "She happens to be Leigh Anne's friend."

Lucy cried out, "I should have known!"

"What does that mean?"

"It means it takes a bitch to be friends with one," Lucy said, and she was red-faced with anger now.

Francesca stared at Lucy, wide-eyed. But why should she be surprised by such a reaction from Bragg's sister? She touched her arm. "I take it you don't like Leigh Anne?"

"That's an understatement. I *hate* her," Lucy hissed. "After all she did to Rick, I hope she dies—now. Apache style!"

Francesca had a feeling that Lucy had not exaggerated her feelings, not in the least. "What did she do?" she whispered, her lips feeling numb.

"What did she do?" Lucy was incredulous—aghast. "Do you have to even ask? She broke my brother's heart," she said.

Five

Hart's mansion, No. 973 Fifth Avenue, was about ten blocks farther uptown than the Cahill residence. The five-story stone mansion was the only house on the block, as the area was sporadically developed and Hart's property apparently *was* the entire block. Behind the house were sweeping lawns, tennis courts, a stable, and a guest "cottage." (The cottage had five bedrooms.) Unsurprisingly, a huge bronze statue of a stag graced the mansion's roof. As soon as Francesca entered Hart's huge mansion, a house that was so vast it was almost impossible to imagine a bachelor residing there alone, there was pandemonium.

The twins came rushing into the huge front hall, which was large enough to host a small ball. They were screeching at their mother, who went wild in turn. Francesca smiled as Lucy knelt to hug both twins at once, asking them a dozen questions all in one breath. Her smile was strained.

Leigh Anne had broken Bragg's heart? That was not possible. He had never been in love with her—he had said so himself.

Roberto had followed the twins into the hall, and he paused beside a life-size statue of a reclining woman, an extremely beautiful nude girl with large breasts who was holding a dove in her cupped hands and in doing so strategically shielding her loins. As Grace entered the hall on Roberto's heels, Francesca started, because she had been at Hart's home several times and this sculpture was a new one. Not surprisingly, its eroticism was shocking, but it was undeniably beautiful. It stood opposite another sculpture that she had seen before. A pair of women, also life-size and nude, were running in great fear.

Francesca quickly glanced around at the rest of the art in the hall, but nothing had changed—the domed ceiling above was a fresco that seemed to be depicting hell, as the men, women, and children being whisked upward were screaming and afraid. Another painting, this one a large oil on the wall, depicted a man on his back, about to be trod upon by his steed. It was titled *The Conversion of St. Paul* and it was as disturbing as it was powerful.

"How are you, *caro*?" Lucy was asking, hugging her ten-year-old son.

He protested but bit back a smile and did not pull away. "Shoz sent a telegram. He wants you to send one back to him immediately," Roberto said seriously.

Lucy's eyes brightened. "What did it say?"

"He misses us," Roberto said simply.

"Did you have a pleasant day?" Grace asked her daughter, having followed Roberto into the hall.

"It was perfect." Lucy grinned. "And we are having guests for dinner—Mrs. Channing and her daughter, Sarah, and her fiancé, Evan, who is Francesca's brother, and Francesca."

Grace smiled and looked at Francesca. "Hello."

Francesca felt flushed. "Mrs. Bragg, I do hope it won't be an imposition," she began.

"Not at all." Grace glanced back over her shoulder.

Francesca stiffened. She suddenly realized that Hart stood at the far end of the hall, as still as any one of his statues. He was staring at them. Or was he staring at her?

She was aware of a new tension and she watched him start slowly forward. He wasn't wearing his jacket. His silver vest was open, his tie undone, his shirt collar unbuttoned, revealing a small swath of dark skin and midnight-black hair. He was actually quite disheveled, but *disheveled* wasn't the right word to describe him. She did not know the right word or words to describe him. There was always something languid and patient about his posture, his movements. There was always something sensual and even dangerous about the way he stood, watching her so carefully. Yet there was also the hint of amusement in his eyes, as if he were in a dangerous game that he very much enjoyed. Hart would always be a predator, she thought. It was his basic nature.

She did not move.

A very faint smile etched his hard mouth as he finally emerged out of the shadows. "You like my new nude," he murmured.

Her heart beat hard. "I think so."

Now he did smile, and his eyes gleamed, holding hers. "I'm glad. I am rather fond of her, myself."

Francesca glanced at the young woman holding the dove. Now she noticed that one tendril of curling hair was entangled with a very erect nipple. "She is too young for you. Besides, she must be a pacifist," she said as tartly as possible, no easy feat when one could not breathe properly. "Which you are not."

His white teeth flashed. "She is probably fourteen or fifteen. And that is rather young, even for me. And that is not a dove which she is holding . . . so carefully. It is a pigeon," he said softly. "And why do you say I am not a pacifist? Only a fool enjoys war."

"But frequently the symbolism is the same," Francesca breathed, not looking at the nude but at him. She didn't exactly want to talk about the fact that the nude was cupping a pigeon against her loins. "So you are a pacifist, Hart?"

"Until prompted to be otherwise." He smiled at her. "I do not think the message this sculptor intends has anything to do with pacifism."

In spite of her unease, she felt a flash of excitement. "Why else use symbolism associated with peace?"

He grinned. "The young lady we are so admiring is holding the pigeon in a certain manner—not for the classic strategic reason. This sculpture was only recently completed. Today artists are not afraid to reveal anatomy, Francesca."

"I am missing your point."

"Take a good look at Lady Brianna," he murmured.

Francesca supposed that was the model's name, and she did.

"No, look at her hands," he suggested far too smoothly. Amusement was in his tone.

Her heart seemed to stop. "She's stroking the bird," she whispered.

Very softly, he said, "At least."

And she thought, *Feathers. How erotic they would be. . . .*

Her heart lurched, far too intensely for comfort. She jerked her gaze back to Hart and found him standing stock-still, staring. His eyes were narrowed and filled with specu-lation now.

It was hard to breathe, much less think clearly. "I have changed my tune. The sculpture is about erotica, not paci-fism."

"I have not been fair," he said, his smile odd now. "I do know this artist's work and background. And yes, it is about erotica, and most galleries refuse to show Monsieur Dubei, considering his work far too scandalous and shocking for public purview. Do you find it too scandalous? Should I hide the lovely Brianna in my master suite?"

She inhaled, fighting for her every breath. "You have chil-dren in the house, but . . ."

"But?" He stared intensely.

"But"—she wet her lips—"she is beautiful. It would be a shame to hide her in a back room." Francesca somehow shrugged.

He smiled widely at her. "You are a bohemian at heart, Francesca. And clearly I agree with you completely. As for the children, the twins and Roberto do not understand."

She couldn't help agreeing with him.

"So? What brings you to my humble home? Let me guess. You are enamored of my stepsister." His gaze was hooded now.

"I have come to see you," she said hoarsely. She tried to clear her throat and succeeded.

His black brows slashed upward. "Really? I am touched."

His fingers brushed over the vicinity where his heart lay.

"It is business, Hart," she said, her brisk and purposeful self once again. But she knew better, she truly did, than to expect to encounter Hart without any turbulence. He loved throwing others off balance.

"And now I am crestfallen," he murmured. "But I do hope you mean anything but sleuthing?"

She shook her head at him, not in response to his last question, but to his pretense at being broken-hearted. Yet annoyance escaped her now. Did he always have to use that tone of voice with her? Did he enjoy provoking her somehow?

"Shall I have Alfred send in refreshments, Calder?"

Francesca almost jumped out of her skin at the sound of Grace's voice behind them. She had forgotten that they were not alone—and she had forgotten it entirely. She felt her cheeks flame as she turned.

Grace wasn't smiling, and she wasn't frowning, either. Her gaze was extremely thoughtful and not necessarily happy.

Lucy was also staring, wide-eyed. She had a twin by each hand, with Chrissy trying to go in one direction and Jack in another, both of them arguing not quite coherently with each other—and clearly Lucy was impervious to the tug-of-war. Roberto was merely waiting patiently with his mother, although he seemed to be trying to give Jack a small toy soldier.

Francesca met Lucy's eyes and was overcome with guilt. *Which brother do you love?* That question remained absurd, but Francesca was not wishing she had never heard it.

"Francesca? Are you hungry?" Hart's black eyes held hers. "Do you have an appetite?"

"No," she said flatly, thinking about the sculpture and the pigeon. She knew she flushed slightly again.

He laughed, his glance a knowing one. Then he shook his head. "We shall be in my study." He gestured for her to precede him inside. "After you, Francesca."

She managed an odd smile at Grace and Lucy. Then she

hurried down the hall as if to escape him, which was absurd. She felt him following at a slower, more leisurely pace. But then, had she ever seen Hart in a hurry? He was one of the most unflappable men she knew.

And the moment she stepped inside his study—a room three times the size of that of the "average" rich man—she faced him, far too nervously for comfort. He had hardly closed the door when she said, "How could you, Calder?"

He was amused, and he strolled toward her slowly. "How could I what?"

"How could you talk about that woman like that, in front of them?"

He laughed. "It is not a woman. We were discussing a work of art and, if anything, one artist's perception of a moment of pleasure." He shrugged. "Miss me?" he asked in a tender drawl.

"Not in a million years!"

He chuckled again, more softly. "Come here, Francesca."

Purposefully doing the opposite, Francesca walked over to a window, but failed to see what was outside. She had to clear her head. She had come to him for a reason, but he always turned every encounter into a battle zone with sexual overtones, no matter the time or place.

Suddenly his hand was on her shoulder. She leaped away. He eyed her. "Why are you so nervous?"

"I am hardly nervous," she lied.

He was amused and it was obvious. "I suppose I should apologize. But I am not really sorry. That mind of yours is so inquisitive, and no subject should be taboo. I cannot help myself. I was very curious as to what you were thinking."

"I am thinking that you are impossible. Why, Calder? Why ask me in front of Grace and Lucy? Why not debate the subject—and merit—of that piece of art at another, more appropriate time?"

He shrugged. "I suppose I do not care if Grace and Lucy see you as you really are."

She froze. Then heatedly, "What does that mean?"

"It means," he said, unsmiling, "that I know you wish to

impress them with being ever so proper—after all, she is Rick's mother, and God forbid she should not like you when you are so in love with her son." He calmly folded his arms over his chest. He had large, muscular arms and a broad chest, which was not noticeable when he wore a suit. His physique was noticeable now. "But you are not a proper little moron. You are an independent woman with a dizzyingly clever mind. Sometimes I think of you as a sponge, Francesca."

She folded *her* arms over *her* chest. "What does that mean?"

"It means you have a thirst for knowledge that is infinite. But most important, your mind is an open one."

She was mollified. Warily she said, "I am here to discuss a case." But speaking about Bragg reminded her of Lucy's angry declaration. Had his heart been broken by his wife?

"Oh, wait. Did I say *love*?" His brows lifted. "I meant lust. You are still lusting after my half brother, aren't you? Or have the two of you consummated your tragic, star-crossed affair?"

She closed her eyes and fought consciously to control herself. "We have been over this before. What Bragg and I do is none of your business. And as I shall never convince you that love exists, why should I bother yet again to defend myself? Do you want to help me solve a case or not?" she snapped.

"If you are on a case, then I might turn you over my knee myself," he said flatly. "As if you were twelve, not twenty."

"What the hell does that mean?" The tension had become unbearable. Her neck felt like it would soon snap.

"Is that, or is it not, a bandage on your hand?" he demanded.

"Have we not been over this before? I am a grown woman and—" She stopped.

He smiled at her, because they had been over this before, and he had been thoroughly insulting. "You are not quite grown up," he said softly.

"Because I am twenty? Or because I have yet to sleep with a man?"

His jaw hardened. "The latter."

She felt like making a comment about how that would change with Bragg, soon, but she decided that was not a good idea. For the expression in Hart's eyes was dangerous. "This is not a dangerous case," she finally said. "I do appreciate your concern, but you need not worry."

"I can't believe this—you! A few days ago you faced an insane killer, and now you are on another case?" His expression was thunderous. He turned abruptly and strode over to a sideboard. His movements were abrupt and hard, and she sensed that he was very angry with her now.

"You cannot control me, Hart." But clearly he was concerned for her welfare, and that was somehow thrilling.

He poured two glasses of whiskey, straight up, not replying or even looking at her.

"I am not drinking whiskey," she warned. As he moved, she could almost visualize the muscles and tendons in his back.

"Really? Then I shall go it alone." He turned, handing her a drink.

She refused to accept it.

He set it back on the sideboard and sipped. He made a sound of pleasure, all the while watching her over the rim of his glass.

She rolled her eyes, truly annoyed, wondering if the whiskey was better than the one he had given her on Wednesday, when she was in pain from her burned hand. It had been her first time ever drinking anything other than wine, sherry, or champagne, and she had truly enjoyed it.

"I brought this back with me from Ireland last year," he remarked calmly. "It is Irish whiskey, which is very different from scotch." His eyes were wide and as innocent as a baby's.

She tore her gaze from those fathomless black orbs, stared at her untouched glass, and looked grimly back at him. "Lucy

wants to meet Daisy. Do you have a problem with that?"
Daisy was his very beautiful mistress.

"Not at all. But I suggest you give Daisy some notice."

She had failed to provoke him. "Perhaps Grace might like
to come along as well?"

He shrugged. "She is a feminist. She would like her, I
think."

Francesca huffed. "How can I annoy you?"

"Easily, in fact. But if you fail to comprehend how, then
I shall not be the one to enlighten you," he said. He sat in a
chair and crossed his strong legs. On other men the gesture
might be effeminate, but not on Hart. "Does my dear brother
know you are on a case?"

She hesitated. "Yes."

"So you apparently control him," he remarked calmly,
clearly enjoying his whiskey.

"I control no one!" She marched over to him, grabbed the
glass he had set down on a table for her, marched back to a
chair, and sat. She took a sip—ignoring his knowing smirk.
She sat up straight. "Ooh," she said. She sipped again. Fire
burned its way down her throat and right to her belly, and
then to her loins. "This is *good*."

He laughed. "A woman after my own heart," he said.

And then the tears came to her eyes, blinding her. "Oh,"
she gasped, choking.

He was up and across the seating area as she coughed,
sitting down beside her, his hand on her shoulder, as if to
steady her. And suddenly it was on her nape, and it was a
very large, very firm, and very warm hand. The tears remained, but Francesca stiffened. The fire had changed. She
wanted to look at him, but she was afraid to move.

His hand had also become still, for he had felt it, too.
That ugly beast that had arisen between them the night of
the ball. Or had it always been there, lying in wait for them
all along?

Slowly Hart dropped his hand and stood up. Then he
looked down at her.

She looked up and did not look away. If only, she thought,

with despair and a rush of something else, he were not so tall. If only he were not so dark, so wealthy, so smug and smart, so damn powerful, so interesting, and so sure of himself!

"Tell me about the case," he said, slamming down his entire drink in a gulp.

She had a brief moment to ogle him without his remarking it. She reminded herself that all women were attracted to him and, thus far, every instance of attraction was fatal. Besides, sexual attraction was not love. She damn well knew the difference. Didn't she?

"The case," he prompted, looking annoyed.

"Someone broke into Sarah Channing's studio and proceeded to cause what wreckage they could. Canvases were overturned, paint spilled everywhere. One canvas was slashed to ribbons, and the vandal began to write in red paint on the wall." She finally met his eyes.

"Is Sarah all right?" he asked.

She softened. He was not the heartless cad he wished the entire world to think him. "She is so upset. She cannot paint. In fact, she asked me to speak with you about that damnable portrait you commissioned." Now she did scowl.

And he did smile. "I am sure it will be lovely. I only wish you were posing nude."

She almost dropped her glass. Whiskey sloshed all over her hand. "Never! Are you mad?"

"No, I am an art collector, remember? Francesca, I have seen hundreds of women unclothed, and I have hundreds of nudes in my collection. The request is hardly an unusual one. If you were unclothed, your portrait would be a magnificent one."

She stood, sloshed more whiskey, then sat. She could only stare.

And she imagined herself nude in a portrait hanging on his wall.

Instantly she shoved the image far away. She didn't want to hang on his wall, dressed or undressed, not in any way, period!

"Francesca, it is only my wish. I would hardly ask you to consider it," he said very softly.

His silky tone washed over her in warm waves. "Good. Because I would refuse."

"But"—he did smile—"I am sure that one day I could entice you to pose for such a portrait."

"Never."

He merely smiled at her and sipped his whiskey, watching her carefully now.

This was the perfect moment to ask him why. Why did he even want her portrait? Instead, she said firmly, "Will there be a problem if there is some delay in Sarah delivering the portrait? Her studio is a shambles, and currently the police will not allow it to be restored."

He sighed. "One can never rush an artist, Francesca, and good things are worth the wait. In this instance, though, I am impatient."

"You are the most patient man I have ever met."

He merely smiled at her.

Suddenly the comprehension was searing—he was the most patient of men, but he was impatient, now. She knew she must not analyze this. "Sarah wants to know who did this, and why."

He paced and stared out of the window. From his library he had views of Fifth Avenue and the park. Then he turned. "If you are asking me if I know who might have done this, the answer is no."

"Have you heard of any other artist suffering a similar attack?"

His gaze locked with hers as he finally sat down. "No. And if there had been such an attack, I would have heard about it."

"Are you sure?"

He smiled and relaxed slightly. "Yes, Francesca, I am sure. A day does not go by that I do not visit an art gallery or museum. I know curators, gallery owners, other collectors and quite a few artists. Vandalism like this would be a heated topic in our small and privileged world of art. It might not make the news, but it would be the topic of conversation amongst our clique."

She nodded. "I do not know whether I am relieved or not that there has been no other instance of vandalism. Hart?"

His gaze moved back to hers. And briefly it settled on her mouth.

She tried to ignore the thought that came instantly to mind. "The canvas which was destroyed was a portrait of Bartolla."

He looked at her and then he laughed. "This is not about Sarah Channing then."

"That's what Lucy thinks."

"Lucy is clever," he agreed.

"So you also despise Bartolla?" She was now very curious, as she knew they had been lovers.

He seemed taken aback. "Why would I despise her?"

She hesitated. "Perhaps because you were lovers and it did not end well?"

He seemed amused. "We spent two nights together—and the entire day in between. Does that satisfy your obvious curiosity, Francesca, or do you wish for a few unsavory details?"

She stiffened, trying not to imagine the two of them in bed together—for two nights and an entire day. It was an easy feat. "I hardly need details," she muttered.

"I would be happy to supply them," he said, laughing. "Bartolla is as bitchy in bed as out. And there you have it. It was over before it even began. Bartolla Benevente is *not* my type of woman."

Francesca knew she flushed, and she was also surprised. "She isn't? But she is so extremely beautiful."

He stared her down. "Is she?"

She grew uneasy. "Oh, come, Hart. She is stunning."

"So are other women, more so, in fact. Take my stepsister, Lucy, or Daisy." He smiled fondly as he said his mistress's name. "And what about your sister?" He eyed her now.

Francesca wondered if he had excluded her on purpose and decided that he had. But she would not complain, oh no.

"They are all extremely beautiful women. And they are all interesting women, as well."

"Yes, they are," he said, his gaze unwavering.

She gave up. "And do I fit somewhere in this scheme of beauty?"

He laughed, with relish. "You are so easy to play! I told you the other day that you are very beautiful, far more so than any other woman. How quickly you forget," he said warmly.

Her heart would not keep still. That wasn't what he had said, oh no. He had said she was more beautiful than her sister—which was absurd—and that her beauty came from within, or something like that. Now had he said that she was more beautiful than any other woman? Had she misheard? Or was he again referring to her spirit or her mind?

Francesca reminded herself that he liked her. She reminded herself of the way he had undressed her with his eyes at the ball. Then she reminded herself that she should not care whether he thought her beautiful on the outside or not.

But she did care.

"What is wrong, Francesca?" Hart asked softly.

She shook her head, not looking at him now. She hated it when he whispered that way. "I have so much on my mind. That is all. I should go."

"Let me guess again. You are torturing yourself with unrequited lust for my brother? Or perhaps now guilt has come into play."

She leaped to her feet. There was guilt, but how could he know?

"You are very easy to read, my dear," he said as softly. "You are as simple to read as an open book—with large, oversize print."

She could not tear her gaze from his. This was not a safe subject, oh no.

"No self-defense?"

"I do not know what you are rambling on and on about," she said, a huge lie. "But do you have any idea who might wish to strike at Bartolla in such an odd way?"

"Not a single one," he said with narrowed eyes. "Be evasive, then. Change the subject."

"Hart, do you wish to help or not?"

"Frankly, Francesca, I do not give a damn what happens to Bartolla. In fact, there are very few people I am concerned about. But I am concerned about your involvement in another case. Leave this one alone. Bartolla can manage her own enemies, my dear." He stood. "Care for another whiskey?"

Francesca sighed, sinking back down on the couch. "I promised Sarah I would find out who did this and why. I do not break my promises, Hart."

He did not comment.

She looked up and caught him staring down at her. It crossed her mind that it would be a pleasurable afternoon indeed to sit in Hart's study with him, sipping Irish whiskey and fencing over indelicate subjects. He immediately turned away from her and to the sideboard. She said lightly, "Are you trying to get me drunk? I am coming to supper, you know."

He seemed surprised, for his shoulders stiffened. "I did not know. How did—let me guess. Dear Lucy invited you."

She nodded and thought about Bragg, with a twinge of worry and another twinge of unwelcome guilt. "Will you be present?"

"Yes, I will. Does that please you—or disturb you?" His gaze was probing as he faced her.

"I'm not certain."

He stared for a long moment. Then, very softly, he said, "At least, this once, you are finally being honest—with both me and yourself."

"What does that mean?" she cried, disturbed.

"I think you know." He moved away.

She leaped up and grabbed his arm from behind. "I don't have a clue."

He turned so quickly that she crashed against his chest. "Only because you refuse to have a clue," he said, his hands somehow closing on her arms as he steadied her.

For one moment, a moment of pure panic, she stared at his full, chiseled mouth, at the cleft in his chin, at the damp olive-colored skin and black hair in the vee of his shirt. His chest was extremely hard and solid against her breasts. She yanked away from him. "I have to go," she managed, but before she could turn—and her intention was to run—he took her wrist, detaining her.

Their gazes locked.

"I think it is time that we were brutally honest with each other," he said harshly.

She tried to back away, but his grip was uncompromising. She did not want to hear this, oh no. For with Hart she never knew what would come next. "Let's not," she gasped.

"I am sick of the hypocrisy here," he said warningly.

"I . . . I do not understand!"

"No? I think you do! You go on and on about my brother—whom you have told yourself that you *love,* as he is a man of virtue and a perfectly respectable choice, except for the fact that he is unhappily married. But you come here, to me, staring at me as if I am a freak show—but we both know that that is not it, now is it, Francesca?"

She cried out, "Let me go!"

"I have had it! You want Rick as your husband, but I am the man you want in your bed. Admit it," he ground out.

"No, that's not it!" she cried, terrified of what might happen next.

"Afraid, Francesca? Afraid of the real woman inside of yourself?" he purred.

"I am afraid of you!" she snapped.

"I don't think so. It is not me you are afraid of. I think you are afraid of the truth; I think you are afraid of yourself." He finally released her. He was panting, and the artery in his neck was pulsing.

She backed away. "You're mad. Vain. Conceited. Arrogant!"

"Do I not get the chance to finish?" Both eyebrows slashed upward, and somehow he looked as innocent as a lamb.

"No, you do not—for I am leaving." She whirled—and his next words stopped her in her tracks.

"You are drawn to me, my dear, the way a woman is drawn to a man."

She trembled. "Please stop," she said desperately.

He stalked around her so that he was facing her. "And it frightens you. I frighten you. What you feel frightens you. Real lust frightens you!"

"I am in love with Bragg."

The most controlled rage she had ever seen crossed his face, but only for a half a second, and then it was gone. "I think you are a storyteller, Francesca, an impossibly adept storyteller."

"Leave me alone," she pleaded.

"No, I will not leave this alone. You came to *me,* my dear. I did not seek you out."

He was right—again. "Let's just leave this be, Hart. We are friends, remember?"

His gaze moved over her features, one by one. To his credit, it never slipped lower. "Yes. We are friends. But there is more, and it is sheer hypocrisy not to admit it."

She shook her head. She would die before admitting that to him.

"What's wrong, Francesca? Are you afraid that the story you have told yourself will blow up in your face?"

She gasped, because his meaning was far crueler than his words or his tone.

He tilted up her chin. When she tried to move, he caught her face in one hand. "You have told yourself that you have found your knight in shining armor, my brother Rick. Isn't that the truth? You met him and he fit the bill, so you have told yourself a wonderful story and, stubborn brat that you are, you have been clinging to it ever since. After all, what could be more appropriate than for Francesca Cahill, re-former extraordinaire, to fall in love with my reform-minded Republican brother? But wait! Being as this is a love story, there has to be an unhappy middle and, lo and behold, the perfect hero isn't quite so perfect after all. For he is *married.*

Oh, wait! It isn't that bad, after all, for as it turns out he *is* a man of virtue, and he really loves you, while he despises his wife! And did I forget to mention that she is vile and evil? So the story can limp along, and true love might survive after all! Does this sound at all familiar, Francesca?"

"I almost hate you," she whispered. And she felt a tear sliding down her cheek.

He froze, having just seen the tear. For one moment he hesitated; then he said coldly, "And in your fairy tale there is no room for real lust, now is there? There is no room for me."

"No. There is not," she managed harshly.

He released her. "You are drawn to me, but you refuse to admit it, because it doesn't fit your worldview to want a man like myself. Wanting my brother works, doesn't it? Wanting me is simply appalling."

"No," she tried, beginning to understand. "No, Calder—"

"So cling to your damn fairy tale! But there will not be a happy ending, Francesca! Even if you become his lover, there will only be ruin, guilt, and shame. And you may trust me on that!" He was shouting. He seemed to realize it, and he seemed surprised and upset. He gave her a pained and disgusted look and turned away.

She watched him pour two whiskeys with a hand that shook.

She felt paralyzed. "You're wrong," she finally said. "I do love Bragg. I really do. Even you have said we are perfect for each other," she managed to his back.

He did not turn. "Yes, you are. And I am sorry for the both of you, that you cannot marry, have children, and ride your white steeds off into the sunset together." He turned and gave her a toast. "I am sorry I will not be at your wedding, the first one to toast the police commissioner and his new, second wife."

Francesca hugged herself. More tears came to her eyes.

The expression on his face—and in his eyes—was extremely hard to decipher. But it was more than pained and more than angry and it was not simple disgust. "Now you shall cry?" He was incredulous.

"No." She took a deep and fortifying breath.

"The truth is often brutal and hurtful," he said, watching her.

"You do not know the truth."

He set his glass down and walked over to her. Somehow, she stood her ground. "I am your friend, Francesca, and never forget it."

"Then, wish me well."

"I already do. I've told you this before; I do not wish to see you hurt."

"I'm not going to get hurt."

His entire expression tightened. "You are a mule."

She made a sound. It was choked.

He took her good hand in his. "Listen closely. I will only discuss this once."

She found herself nodding.

"I have never given my friendship to anyone," he said, his gaze upon her face. "You are the first."

She stared, and she began to shake. "I don't understand."

He leaned close. "Do I need to repeat myself?"

"No." She wet her lips, her heart thundering in her breast. What did this mean? She was too overcome to understand it now. "But what about Lucy? Her brothers—"

"It's not friendship. I am the foster brother, and that is different."

She stared, trying to comprehend him. It was simply impossible, he was far too complicated to ever understand, she thought.

"And now I will tell you why I am angry. I am angry because my brother will only bring you ruin—oh yes, I see the writing on the wall. And I must stand by and watch it all unfold, knowing how the story will end, and as I have already told you, the ending will not be a happy one."

"No, Hart. You are wrong! If you care about me, truly, then—"

"I do! Let me finish. I am angry because you are breathless in my presence and we both know why, but you will not admit it."

She froze. "Please don't."

"Because it ruins the story you have been telling yourself. Am I correct, Francesca?" His grip tightened. "Am I?"

She could not nod. She did not dare.

"But mostly, I am angry because you do not value what I have given you, for if you did, you would trust me and you would not flit about me like some nervous ninny."

She didn't know what to think, say, or do. "What?"

His face darkened and he leaned even closer to her. And when he spoke, his words were so low and soft she had to strain to hear. "I told you once that I never touch, or pursue, innocent virgins like yourself. I meant my every word. I'll never touch you, Francesca. I might want to, I do want to; in fact, I want to take you to my bed very much. But I do not dabble with innocence, as I am not a marrying man. And I am a man who can control himself." He hesitated, then said, "Your friendship is more important to me than sex. Is that clear? Should I be clearer?"

Stunned, she shook her head no.

"And that is the end of this subject. Stare as you will. Pretend my brother is the only man for you—the only man whom you lust for—but do not do so around me." He slammed down his glass. To her amazement, it did not break. "Because, my dear, I am sick of *it, him, the two of you!*"

She wanted to tell him that she was sorry. But she was at a huge loss for words.

"And do *not* play the horrified virgin around me. I will *never* compromise you! He might—but I will not!" With that, his arm lashed out and the empty glass went flying across the room. As it shattered against a small table not far from where she stood, he strode past her, heading out of the room.

She could hardly believe what had just happened. She was reeling; she could not think clearly, much less coherently. And why was he so angry? Hadn't they just resolved every-thing? And why did she wish to bury her head in a pillow and cry? Somehow, she was running after him. "Calder, wait!"

He did not stop. "Good day, Francesca."

She ran faster. "Please, wait! You are so angry. . . . I treasure our friendship, too!"

He halted and faced her. She almost slammed into him again. "Do you? Somehow, I do not think so. I think you treasure your little fairy tale. You may see yourself out." He bowed his head and disappeared around the corner of the hall.

She collapsed against the wall. She felt as if a hurricane had just passed by, one she had barely survived. No, she felt as if it had passed by but had not yet left. As if she remained in the storm's eye and, somehow, the worst was about to come.

A polite cough sounded behind her.

Horror overcame her. Francesca turned.

"I'll escort you out," Rathe Bragg said kindly.

Francesca wanted to die.

Six

Francesca felt as if she had been run over by a lorry. She wondered how she might navigate an evening when Hart would be present—and when Bragg would also be present. Of course, unlike Hart, Bragg did not sulk like a spoiled child and did not hold a grudge. His nature was a sunny one, just as his character was optimistic. He would undoubtedly have forgotten about their argument or realized the cause— Hart's commission—was hardly worth it. Still, his father had seen Hart storming away. How much had he heard and what did he think?

She had so wanted to make a good impression. By now, Rathe had already told Grace about her and Hart. Francesca could not even smile at Jonathon, the young and handsome doorman, as she handed him her coat. "Have you seen my disreputable brother?" she asked. In spite of her own personal feelings, she did have a case to solve.

"I do believe Mr. Cahill is with your father, Miss Cahill. They adjourned to the library some time ago."

Francesca was about to head down the hall, for she wished to speak with Evan about her second theory, that a rejected debutante was insane enough and vicious enough to vandalize Sarah's studio. But before she could do so, she heard two very familiar voices coming from the stairwell. Francesca saw her mother and Maggie Kennedy descending slowly, her mother magnificently dressed in a crimson ball gown, with rubies about her throat and diamond earbobs. The gown was a Poiret. Maggie wore a plain navy blue skirt and a shirt-waist. She was using a cane, which she leaned heavily upon.

The redhead was pale and clearly still weak from the stab wound she had suffered earlier in the week.

Francesca reversed direction and rushed toward the wide alabaster staircase. "Mrs. Kennedy! Should you be up and about?"

"I have asked her the exact same question," Julia said, pulling on elbow-length black gloves. Her hair had been waved with hot tongs, and she was a very elegant and beautiful older woman. Francesca was fully aware that her mother still turned heads.

"I am much better, thank you," Maggie said, rather out of breath. "Dr. Finney said I should walk about a bit now, to gain back my strength."

"But going up and down stairs is another matter indeed," Francesca said bluntly.

Maggie smiled at her. "I do need to get my strength back, Miss Cahill. You see, I was just explaining to Mrs. Cahill that I will go home tomorrow."

Francesca stared in surprise. Maggie Kennedy was the mother of her sidekick, Joel. She was a seamstress who worked at the Moe Levy factory by day while sewing custom garments for private clients at night. Francesca had liked her the first moment they had met, about a month ago. Then, in her last investigation, she had realized that Mrs. Kennedy might be the Cross Murderer's last victim.

Francesca and Bragg had persuaded the pretty seamstress to move into the Cahill mansion with her four young children. And after being stabbed on Tuesday night, she had remained there in order to recuperate.

"That is nonsense," Julia said firmly, now. "My dear Maggie, you are clearly not able to return to your home. You cannot even navigate these stairs!"

"My mother is right," Francesca began, dismayed and concerned.

"I have imposed quite enough," Maggie said, a pink flush now marring her porcelain and perfectly flawless skin. She had been invited to stay at the Cahill mansion when it had become obvious that her life was in dire danger. Francesca had been the one to invite her and her four children to stay with them. Julia had graciously risen to the occasion. "I think your brother has had quite enough of my four little rascals," Maggie said with a slight smile, "and I shall lose my job at Moe Levy if I do not return to the factory on Monday."

"Has Evan said something about the children?" Julia asked with her slender brows arched.

"Evan adores your children," Francesca said. He had been squiring them about the park and to the zoo and even to an indoor bowling lane ever since they had become guests at the house.

"It isn't fair," Maggie said softly. Then she flushed. "I am so worried about my employment, Miss Cahill."

"But Francesca," she said automatically, "the police commissioner spoke to your manager, explaining the circumstances. You will not lose your work."

Maggie simply looked at her. "Are you certain? Because I do not think Mr. Wentz cares whether or not the police commissioner wishes me to be employed."

Francesca hesitated. "Mrs. Kennedy? Let me be singularly bold. Bragg can cause trouble for the factory if you are dismissed."

She stared. Then, "I do not think he would ever do such a thing, Miss Cahill. Not on my account."

"Yes, he would. If I insisted," Francesca said, and then she realized what she had said and how it sounded and turned to face her mother.

Julia wasn't pleased. Her blue eyes said, *We shall talk, and soon, Francesca,* and clearly there would be a lecture involved.

Francesca sighed.

Julia said, surprising everyone, "Maggie, you are not well enough to go back to work, I shall not allow it, but on Monday I shall go down to the factory and speak to your manager myself."

Maggie paled. "Oh, I could not let you do such a thing!"

"Nonsense. And not only shall I go myself; I shall make it clear that I am ordering new uniforms for my entire staff and for the Montrose household as well." She smiled.

Maggie gaped.

Francesca whooped and embraced her mother in a bear hug. "Mama!"

"Francesca, what are you doing?" Julia said sternly, trying to disengage her daughter, but her eyes were smiling, even if her expression remained firm.

"You never cease to surprise me," Francesca said, giving her another huge squeeze. "Now, I am off to speak briefly with Evan, and then I am to supper at the Plaza with the Braggs." She started back down the hall.

"We will speak more later, Maggie," Julia said. Then, "Francesca!"

She turned. "Yes, Mama?"

Julia approached. "We need to speak," she said.

Dismay filled her. "Can't it wait? I must be at the Plaza at seven and I am already going to be late."

"No, this is about your sister," Julia said, her voice low so she could not be overheard. "She and Neil were supposed to join us this evening, but apparently she is in her bed with some kind of migraine—yet she refuses to see Dr. Finney."

Francesca stared. "I saw her this morning."

"I know. What is wrong? Is she ill?"

Francesca hesitated. "The only thing wrong with her is that she has a broken heart. But perhaps she does have a migraine, Mama."

"Since when does your sister have migraines?" Their gazes locked. "I feel like I don't know my own daughter anymore."

Francesca took her hand. "She seemed quite normal this morning. Except for the fact that it was well after nine and she was in her nightgown. Maybe Connie is changing a bit? Maybe she does have a migraine."

"I don't know whether to hope her excuse is truthful or not," Julia said. "You know I have never interfered in your sister's marriage. But I am tempted to do so, now."

Inwardly, Francesca cringed. "She will get through this. I suppose she needs time. She has always loved Neil. I feel

certain that has not changed. And . . . Neil truly loves her.
He regrets all that he has done. Give them some time, Mama,
to sort out things."

A look of anger appeared briefly in Julia's eyes, and then
it was gone. "It is a bit late for him to cry over spilled milk,"
she said.

Francesca was taken aback. Her mother adored Montrose.
In the past, he could do no wrong. But there had been no
mistaking the anger she had just seen.

"I am going to have a bit of a heart-to-heart with your
sister," Julia decided flatly. "The two of them have been at
odds for too long. I shall put my two cents in."

Francesca hesitated. She did not know if this was a good
idea or not. Her entire life, Connie had been pushed and
prodded by Julia to be a perfect child, a perfect debutante,
and now the perfect wife, mother, and socialite. On the other
hand, if Julia could help Connie regain her happiness, if her
relationship could just go back to the way it had been before
his affair, it would be wonderful. "Well, tread gently, then."

Julia gazed at her in surprise. "That is extremely good
advice, Francesca."

Francesca was thrilled with her mother's praise. It was so
rare. "Thank you, Mama."

Julia patted her shoulder. "So why have you been running
about the city all day when you are supposed to rest? And
what is this about a dinner with the Braggs?"

Francesca froze.

Julia sighed. "I am entirely suspicious, Francesca. But
even you would not be involved in police affairs so soon
after your brush with a fiery death."

"Of course not," she managed.

"And I am delighted you shall be dining in such good
company." She kissed her cheek. "Wear your new turquoise
gown. I am sure it will be a wonderful evening."

The door to her father's library was wide open. The room
was Francesca's favorite in the entire house, as it was a warm
room with wood paneling and soft gold tapestry cloth cov-

ering the walls. The windowpanes were stained glass and the same rich, dark oak wood that formed ribs across the ceiling. Her father's desk was also dark oak, but with a leather-inlaid top. They kept their telephone there.

Now there was nothing warm about the library, in spite of a fire that roared in the hearth. Because Evan's face was flushed with fury and he was saying angrily, "And if you do not change your mind, you are the one who shall pay the consequences!"

Andrew was as flushed. "You threaten me?" he gasped.

"Yes, I do," Evan said coldly. He was six foot tall, with the fair Cahill complexion but raven-black hair. His blue eyes were murderous. "After all, it is a tit for a tat, is it not, Father? Doesn't blackmail deserve threats?"

Francesca was aghast. She rushed into the room. "Stop! What is happening! What is this?" she cried, reeling from the utter hatred on her brother's handsome face.

"He dares to threaten me!" Andrew cried, a distinct and unflattering shade of crimson. He was a portly man with a benevolent face and thick whiskers.

"I am simply stating my case. He wishes to ruin the rest of my life by forcing me to marry a woman I will never love—or even like. If he does not change his mind, then rest assured, our relationship as a father and son is over."

Francesca felt as if she had been struck. Clearly Andrew felt the blow as well, for he seemed to be reeling. She ran to his side and grabbed his arm, as if to steady him. "Evan, you do not mean that."

"I mean it. In four months he will have me exchanging vows with Sarah Channing. In four months my life becomes one of manacles and chains, of unhappiness and anguish. And I will not take it." His blue eyes were nearly black.

Andrew Cahill shook Francesca off. "You haven't spoken to me in almost a month. Now you dare to come in here and tell me that you will cease being my son if I do not call off this wedding?"

"Yes. I dare." Evan did not back down.

"I am doing this precisely because you are my son! I am

doing this because you are almost twenty-five and you have no direction in your life except for gambling halls and dens! And cheap women!"

Evan folded his arms across his chest. "We cannot all be like you, Father. We can't all grow up impoverished and illiterate but with such a burning ambition that we shake off those shackles with sheer fortitude and wit. I am truly sorry I have not grown up on a farm, milking cows and plowing fields the way that you have done. I am sorry that I did not go to work for a butcher at the age of twelve and that I did not spend the rest of my childhood working myself to the bone and saving every penny earned so I could buy that damned butcher shop! I am sorry I did not do so, and then continue on to buy my competitors out, one by one, until Cahill Meatpacking was born! I am not you! And I never will be you!" he shouted.

"No one expects you to be exactly like Father," Francesca began.

"You do not have to grow up on a farm on a diet of milk, butter, and bread in order to have some kind of ambition, some sense of direction, and some glimmer of responsibility," Andrew snapped. "Or have you forgotten that the reason you are so currently *shackled* is because you have gaming debts which total almost two hundred thousand dollars?"

Evan's flush increased.

"Papa, don't," Francesca whispered. "He regrets those debts; he truly does!"

"Does he?" Andrew moved behind his desk and almost tore a drawer from it. He held up a handful of papers. "These debts are new and they have just come to my attention. Last week you incurred another eighteen thousand dollars of damned debt!" he shouted.

Francesca turned huge eyes upon her brother. Had he been gambling again? But he had promised that he would never do so again. How could he?

He met her gaze and looked away, with clear guilt. Then he looked up at Andrew. "Do not make me marry this woman. I will pay off my debts, somehow. Over time. But do not shackle me to Sarah Channing."

Francesca looked at Andrew. "Papa? It is the worst match. I adore Sarah, but she is not for Evan. And she doesn't even want to marry, not him or anyone. Please, Papa, let them go their separate ways."

"She is the best thing to ever happen to him!" Andrew cried.

"You are wrong! She is the worst thing to ever happen to me!" Evan cried in return.

"And whom would you have as a wife? That countess Benevente?" Andrew demanded.

Evan stilled. "I hadn't really thought about it, but she is available and we should do nicely indeed."

"Over my dead body," Andrew spat. "That woman would cause you nothing but grief! You are a fool, Evan, a complete fool, ruled by one thing, no, two things. And I do believe you know what those two things are."

Evan's face hardened. "You know what? I am done here. I am truly done." He turned and strode for the door.

"What the hell does that mean?" Andrew cried, not moving from behind his desk.

"Don't," Francesca whispered, ready to cry.

Evan paused in the doorway, his smile ugly. "I am finished. I am finished with all of this. I am sick of being your lackey at the office, and I am not marrying Sarah Channing, and as of this moment, I am no longer your son."

"Please don't!" Francesca cried, rushing to him.

Andrew strode forward.

Evan did not move.

Francesca found herself trapped between the two men, her father, who was about five-foot-nine but stout, and her taller, slim brother. It was not a happy or pleasant place to be.

"Are you saying that you are leaving the company?" Andrew asked, his tone eerily quiet.

"Yes."

"And you will not marry Sarah?"

"Yes."

"Then I am not paying your debts," Andrew said softly.

"I will find a way to pay them myself," Evan said.

Andrew hesitated.

"Papa, don't; enough has been said," Francesca said into the sudden silence, grabbing his hand.

But it was as if he hadn't heard her. "Then you may leave this house, for you are no longer my son," he said.

Francesca followed Evan down the hall. "Go back. Apologize. Don't do this!"

He reached the stairs. When the Cahill mansion had been built, it had been done so in such a way that his house was attached on the other side. The intention was that one day, after marrying, he would live right next door with his wife and children. Evan's house was almost as large and grand as his parents'. There was an outside entrance on Sixty-second Street, but he could also enter from within the Cahill home, on the second floor. That was clearly where he was going, now.

Evan paused and faced his sister, still flushed. "I would not be a man if I meekly did as Father ordered."

She closed her eyes, filled with fear. Then she looked at him. "If you do not pay your debts, you will wind up in debtors' jail."

"That's right," he said grimly. "And that is a risk I have decided to take, because I am not marrying Sarah Channing."

Francesca touched his sleeve. "Wouldn't it be better to pretend to go along with the engagement for now, while raising the money to pay off your debtors?"

He looked at her and sighed. "Leave it to you, Fran, to strike to the heart of common sense. Yes, obviously it would. But I am so furious right now that I think I have come to hate Father."

"Don't say that!"

"Why not? He has been disappointed in me since I was born. I have never done a single thing right, not in his eyes."

"That's not true!"

"Yes, it is. And you know it. And do you want to know something else? This isn't just about Sarah. I hate being his lackey, and that is what I have been my entire life. I hate *the* company. I hate it! I have hated every single day I have worked there, and you know I started working there after school when I was twelve years old."

She bit her lip. "I knew you didn't really like the business, but I never suspected you disliked it so much!"

"I do," he said firmly.

"You will not at least think about retracting some of what you have said?"

He didn't hesitate. "No. I shall take a room at one of the hotels, look for a new job, and eventually let a place of my own."

"Oh God," Francesca said, feeling as if her world were falling apart. "But this is your home." She meant next door. "Mama and Papa built Number Eight-twelve for you. You have been living there since you were eighteen."

"You may have it on your wedding day. I don't want it."

She sensed he didn't really mean it. She sensed that within him there was a part that remained loyal to his family, a part that did not want to leave. Or was it wishful thinking on her part? "Please rethink what you are going to do," she whispered.

"Fran, do you think I have decided to quit Cahill Meat-packing on a whim? Do you think I decided to break off the engagement on a whim? I owe one hundred and ninety-eight thousand dollars! I have some unsavory types breathing down my neck! I am worried that one of these days one of them will *break* my neck! I have been up at nights, debating my options. *I have no choice!*"

"You dislike Sarah that much?"

"No, Fran. In fact, as a friend, I rather like her. This is about me, and this is about Father. Sarah is just an unwitting pawn in a much larger scheme of things."

Tears came to Francesca's eyes. But she understood. "What about Mama?" she asked suddenly, with dread and concern. Mama adored Evan. For her, he could do almost no wrong. Francesca thought that she was going to be heartbroken but could not be sure.

"Mama will cry. And it will break my heart to be the one to make her cry. But I love her dearly, and I will not let my war with Father interfere in our relationship. We will continue on, somehow."

Francesca stared at him. He was dark and grim now. Her brother was, by disposition, kind and friendly; in fact, he had a naturally sunny disposition and he rarely lost his temper. She had never seen him so resolved or determined—or so darkly and deeply angry—before. "I will help you raise the money," she said, meaning it. And instantly Hart's image came to mind.

He was so wealthy. He had given her a $5,000 check for one of her societies, the Ladies Society for the Eradication of Tenements. Thus far, they were the only two members, as she had not had any time to lobby for her latest cause.

He softened. "I knew you would. I could use the help, Fran."

"I know. I will never let you down, Evan."

He smiled then. "I know that, too. I feel the same way."

They smiled at each other.

Suddenly Francesca saw Maggie in the hall, approaching from the other end, clearly having been in the kitchens. She was paler than she had been earlier and leaning far more heavily upon her cane.

Evan heard her and he turned. His eyes went wide. "Mrs. Kennedy! What are you doing downstairs!" He rushed to her, putting his arm about her. "You should not be downstairs," he scolded gently. "What are you thinking?"

Maggie had clearly used up most of her strength, and she leaned against him, two bright pink spots of exertion on her cheeks. "The doctor told me I could move about, but I have suddenly lost all of my strength," she said softly.

"That is obvious, and Finney is a fool," Evan said. "Do not protest. I am going to carry you upstairs."

"No," Maggie said instantly. "I can walk—"

He swept her up into his arms, as easily as if she were a feather. "Where are the children?" he asked, starting up the stairs with boundless agility. Clearly Maggie's slight weight did not affect him at all.

"They are having dinner in the kitchens. Please put me down, Mr. Cahill."

"Mrs. Kennedy, I am merely being a gentleman. Do cease and desist." But his tone was soft and he was smiling down at her.

Francesca's heart had done a quick somersault. She stared thoughtfully after them. It was simply not possible that Evan would find a seamstress romantically interesting, or would he? She knew him so well. He liked flamboyant beauty, and he frequented women like his mistress, Grace Conway, the actress, and Bartolla Benevente. He never fooled with house-maids or barmaids. He was not that sort of man.

He glanced down toward her. "I will be going to dinner, Fran. Shall we ride over together?"

"Yes." She hesitated.

He understood. "Sarah and I have agreed to meet at the Plaza. I will speak with Sarah later tonight, or first thing tomorrow."

She suddenly felt some relief, because the ending of this engagement was a good thing for them both. It was, ulti-mately, in both of their best interests. "I won't say a word," she promised.

And too late, she realized that they had not had a chance to discuss Sarah's case.

The Plaza Hotel was one of the city's most renowned and elegant hotels. Doormen in red livery rushed to intercept their brougham, and Francesca was assisted out. It had begun to snow, rather heavily, but the huge bronze canopy effec-tively shielded her and other guests from the inclement weather. The gaslights of the hotel and those on the street caught the snowflakes as they fell in their halo, and the snow seemed to be dancing in the air.

On the cab ride over, Francesca had told Evan what had happened to Sarah's studio, and he had been concerned. He had been incredulous, though, at the notion that a young lady of his acquaintance might have been so hopeful at the prospect of becoming his bride that she had gone off on a rampage in Sarah's studio. He thought Francesca's theory of a jilted woman absurd.

Now, as Francesca walked up the stairs and into the lobby, with Evan by her side, she was acutely aware of being beset by an extremely nervous anticipation. She felt like checking her appearance in the cloakroom, as she had barely had fifteen minutes to change into an evening gown. Her hair had been hastily swept up and back; there had been no time to wave it with tongs. At the last moment she had seized a small pot of rouge, and she had used it on her lips in the coach. Evan had not been amused.

Now he whispered in her ear, "You are so tense—and so excited. You are worrying me, Fran."

She smiled at him. "I am merely looking forward to what shall be an impossibly interesting evening."

"No, you are looking forward to seeing the police commissioner, even though you know he is married. And the other night when Bartolla mentioned his wife, you were not surprised—you already knew! What are you thinking?" he demanded.

They had entered the lobby. It was a vast room, the ceiling high, huge columns forming a square around an atrium. To Francesca's right were the registration and concierge counters, all gleaming mahogany inlaid with a pale, streaked marble. Directly ahead, but on the other side of the atrium, was the oh-so popular and elegant restaurant. The last time she had been within it had not been to dine. Hart had been pursuing her sister and she had dropped in on them to chaperon them and to prevent Connie from making a drastic mistake.

It felt like ages ago that he had set his sights on her sister. Still, the notion disturbed Francesca no end even if he had backed off—at her insistence.

"Fran? Have you heard a word I said?"

"Not really," she said truthfully, smiling. "There they are." She stopped in midstep.

They had taken a table in the atrium and were being served champagne. She saw Bragg first.

He wore a white dinner jacket and midnight-black trousers; he sat on a small love seat, beside Lucy, looking far too thoughtful and miles away. She knew he was thinking about police affairs or perhaps even the Channing Investigation. Light from the chandelier that was overhead fell upon him, highlighting the streaks in his dark golden hair and accentuating his high cheekbones. An impossibly warm feeling came over her. She so trusted this man.

But there was also a twinge of guilt. Of course, she had to tell him about Leigh Anne's note. She should have told him the very day she had received it. It crossed her mind that if he took her home, she would have the private moment to do so tonight.

He shifted ever so slightly and he saw her and their eyes locked. His expression changed, becoming dark, intent.

And then he was on his feet, smiling. He moved toward her, his strides long and effortless. Francesca was vaguely aware of the rest of his family turning to look her way while she tried to appear calm and unmoved.

But it was a facade. She did not have a calm cell in her entire body.

He paused before her. "Cahill," he murmured to Evan, giving him the barest and most cursory glance. "Francesca." His eyes warmed. "I'll take your coat," he said, his golden gaze skimming over her.

She handed it to him, their hands brushing, touching. She knew at once that he was no longer distressed over her posing for Hart's portrait. She knew he was happy to be spending the evening with her, too. "I thought we might be late, but I see that Sarah is not yet here," she said lightly, hoping everyone would think their conversation innocent, should anyone be observing them, and somehow, everyone was.

"No." His gaze slid over her new turquoise dress again. The vee over her breasts was low, tiny cap sleeves clung to her shoulders, and the gown fell closely over her hips, finally swelling in a pool of lace around her calves and ankles. The dress showed off the best curves of her body, accentuating them, when, in truth, she was a touch too thin. At the very last moment, she had thought to add a necklace with a pearl cameo. "Mrs. Kennedy's work?" he asked with a soft smile.

Francesca nodded, pleased because he clearly liked it. "Any news on the vandal who struck at Sarah's studio?" she asked. From the corner of her eye she glanced at his family. Grace remained calmly seated, as if sipping champagne, but her gaze was steadily upon them. Rathe was standing politely, as was another man whom Francesca had never seen before. As he was almost Bragg's twin, he had to be Rathe's son as well. Like his father and his mother, he was watching them, but unlike the other two, his gaze was hooded and hard to comprehend.

Francesca wondered if Bragg's family cared at all for his wife.

"There has been no other instance of such vandalism in the city in the past three months," Bragg was saying. "But Inspector O'Connor is checking further back."

"If such an attack were not reported to the police, then he will never learn of it."

"That's true," he said with a slight smile. "And a single act of vandalism might not have ever been reported."

She absorbed that. "Have you or your men interviewed Bartolla?"

"She has been elusive," he said, meeting her gaze. "She clearly is amused by the entire event. And I do believe O'Connor is smitten with her." He rolled his eyes. "He has been newly promoted," he added.

Francesca laughed but sobered quickly. "I spoke with her briefly. She had nothing of importance to say and she did seem unperturbed by the entire event."

"I think I will call on her tomorrow myself," he said. "Press her a bit."

Francesca touched his hand. His skin was smooth but not silken or soft. His eyes touched hers. She said, "Let me join you."

He hesitated. "You may join me, but I think I might have

more success, in this one case, with Bartolla if I speak with her alone."

She stared, not liking the implications of his comment. "What does that mean?" How terse her own tone sounded to her ears.

"You do not have to be dismayed, Francesca. The countess adores men. And while I have no intention of flirting with her, I think I can interview her more effectively if you are not present."

She hated the idea.

"Don't scowl," he said with amusement. "When you are old, you shall have scowl lines."

It wasn't funny and she did not laugh, but she hated the extent of her jealousy.

"What is this about?" Evan asked, apparently having been listening to their conversation. "How is the countess involved?"

Francesca started, having forgotten that her brother was standing behind them. She glanced at Bragg. He said, "The single canvas destroyed in the attack upon Sarah's studio was a portrait of Bartolla. Perhaps, and it is a mere perhaps, the vandal struck a blow at the countess and not at your fiancée."

Evan's eyes were wide. "Is she in danger?"

Bragg hesitated, and it was clear that he was uncertain as to which woman Evan referred to. Francesca knew that he referred to Bartolla, as she had previously assured him that Sarah was fine and did not seem to be in any danger. Her words had been automatic, however, as she had only to recall the use of so much dark red paint to shudder and have a terrible sense of foreboding. "Neither Sarah nor Bartolla appears to be in any imminent danger."

Evan was now concerned. Grim, he walked away. "You must be Mr. Bragg," he said, extending his hand toward Rathe. As they shook hands, Lucy jumped up to make the introductions.

Francesca turned to Bragg. "So much has happened," she said in a low voice, thinking about the horrendous falling-out between Evan and her father. "I have to talk to you." And she was thinking about his wife's note.

"Are you all right?"

She shook her head. "Offer to drive me home tonight, after supper," she said. "It will give us a private moment to speak."

His jaw flexed. "That is not a good idea," he said flatly.

She faced him fully. "Please. We won't have a single moment alone otherwise; I feel sure of it. Now that your family is in town, it will be harder than ever to have a decent conversation."

He took her elbow and they stepped away from his family. "It is hard enough being with you when they are present," he said, low. His eyes were dark. "But you are right. We do have to speak."

Alarm filled her. "What does that mean?" she cried softly.

"Just as you wish to speak with me, I wish to speak with you."

"About what?" She was more than alarmed now; she was afraid.

He knew Leigh Anne was on her way to New York. He knew that his wife wanted to meet her. He had heard about her encounter with Hart.

But he knew something, something dire, and she was afraid of what his reaction would be.

He seemed surprised. "Francesca, this is not the time or the place for a real conversation between us."

She grabbed his hand, as he was about to leave. "Is this about us?" she asked in a very low voice.

"Yes," he said. He tugged his hand free and stepped back to the others. But she could not move.

There was a thought in her mind, but it was too terrible to contemplate. Still, it refused to go away. Not too long ago he had claimed that being alone with her was simply too difficult a test of resolve and willpower. *What if he had decided that it was impossible to be mere friends?*

Once, he had suggested that maybe they should not see

each other again. Because it was too dangerous being together.

"I don't believe we've met," a male voice said, cutting into her worst fears.

She started and found herself looking at the man who might have been Rick Bragg's twin. His hair was darker—more brown than blond—and his face was squarer. But the rest was the same—the amber eyes, the dark eyebrows, the high, high cheekbones, the dimples and cleft chin. "I'm Francesca Cahill," she said, and she heard how tremulous her own tone was.

He smiled and it was a smile to melt female hearts. "The infamous sleuth. I'm Rourke, the eldest after my no-good policeman brother." He extended his hand.

She shook it, trying to clear her head. "Rourke? What an unusual name."

"It's my middle name. But I got tired of being beaten up when I was six, trying to defend the worst name a child could have—Brian Bragg. So it's been Rourke ever since." His eyes were warm and kind and he grinned.

"Are you the one in medical school?" she asked with real curiosity. She realized he was probably several years older than she was, and just two years or so younger than Bragg.

"Yes. In Philadelphia. Third year. Excellent grades. My sister is enamored of you."

Francesca smiled and was about to say that she truly liked Lucy as well. But he added, "And apparently, she is not the only one."

She felt her smile vanish. She followed his gaze—and caught Bragg watching them both intently.

For once, she was entirely at a loss for words. She looked at Rourke and could not summon up a coherent reply.

His smile was compassionate. "I'm sorry. I suppose I shouldn't have said that. I have a bad habit; I tend to speak my mind."

Francesca shook her head. "I don't have a clue as to what you are talking about," she said, intending to keep her tone light. But it came out terribly hoarse.

He patted her arm. "We'll strike that ungentlemanly comment right off the record. Friends?" He grinned. But a huge question remained in his eyes.

"Friends," she whispered. And then, beyond Rourke's broad shoulder, she saw the thug who had been standing outside of police headquarters yesterday, who had been so intently watching Lucy.

Francesca felt herself stiffen, and she turned to find Lucy in order to gauge her reaction—and to see if she had remarked the burly man.

"What is it?" Rourke asked quickly.

Lucy had been sipping champagne. Now she turned white and set her flute down abruptly.

Francesca faced Rourke. "Nothing. So, what year are you in?"

"My third," he said quietly, his regard intent and searching. "But I already said that."

With one ear Francesca heard Lucy making an excuse that she must powder her nose. She smiled at Rourke and, out of the corner of her eye, watched Lucy cross the atrium, clearly wishing to hurry and, as clearly, trying not to. In the lobby, the thug had disappeared. Suddenly Bragg was standing beside them.

"I see you have met Miss Cahill," he said to his younger brother, not looking particularly pleased.

"I have, and it is a pleasure indeed." Rourke smiled.

"Do not let my brother's profession delude you," Bragg said. "He is an unrepentant ladies' man."

Rourke chuckled. "We can't all be as noble as you." He winked at Francesca.

"My nobility vanished some time ago," Bragg said tersely, and he turned to Francesca and their gazes locked.

She thought that he meant that he had lost his morals because of her. She stared, instantly dismayed. Surely he did not mean what he had appeared to mean?

Bragg turned back to Rourke, who seemed to be watching them both like a hawk. And he did not seem like the kind of man to miss a thing. "I doubt you have turned from a saint into a devil," he said, but quietly. "However, on a more important note, what is wrong with Lucy?" And Rourke looked right at Francesca.

"I don't know," Bragg said. "But think I shall go find out."

"I'll go," Rourke said. "You can escort Miss Cahill in to supper." And the two brothers exchanged a potent look.

"The Channings haven't arrived," Bragg finally said, a slight flush upon his cheekbones.

"I'll go," Francesca interrupted, and before either one of them could engage her in a debate, she hurried across the atrium, lengthening her stride, as Lucy had turned the corner and vanished from sight.

But the ladies' room was on the far side of the lobby and just around that corner. Of course, Francesca was certain that Lucy had no real interest in the ladies' room and that it was not her destination. Turning the corner, she saw Lucy and darted behind a column so she could watch her.

It shielded her from view, just in case Lucy turned. The redhead had paused beside the ladies' room door, looking back over her shoulder, clearly to see if anyone was watching—or following. As she was wearing a daring crimson gown, she stood out like a sore thumb—the several ladies and gentlemen in the hall were all turning to look at her, with either envy or admiration, as did every bellman and concierge who passed.

Lucy did not notice. She was pale with fear. Giving one last glance to make sure she was not being watched—and Francesca felt certain it was her family she was afraid of now—she hurried down another corridor.

Francesca followed.

She realized Lucy's intention instantly. At the corridor's farthest end were a small door and an EXIT sign. That door was closing behind the strange man. Lucy now hurried through it and outside.

Francesca reached inside her purse, and her left hand closed awkwardly over her tiny gun. *Damn it,* she thought. This was exactly what she had not wanted to happen. She did not want to confront a hoodlum without the use of her right hand.

But she had no choice, because Lucy was frightened and Francesca was certain that she was in danger.

She slipped through the small door and outside. She was on the south side of Central Park. Carriages and a few motorcars were double- and triple-parked up and down the endless block. A few pedestrians were heading her way.

And Lucy stood a few doors down the block, near a service entryway. So did the hoodlum. Francesca stood stock-still, straining to hear them, as a pair of gentlemen walked past her, eyeing her in her bare evening gown as they went.

"Leave me alone!" Lucy cried.

"An' why should I? When you got something I want?" he returned, and his tone was lewd and smug.

"You followed me to New York!"

"Damn right I did!" he laughed and suddenly he grabbed her. "You know what? Maybe we should start over." And he started to kiss her.

Francesca rushed forward, removing the gun from her purse. "Get your hands off of her!" she cried.

The hoodlum froze, but he did not release Lucy. "What the hell?" And then he saw the gun she held and he laughed.

She pointed the gun at him. "Release her," she said.

He laughed harder.

Seven

Lucy turned incredulous eyes upon Francesca. As she did, the thug said with a grin, "What is that?"

"I think you know what it is. Let her go," Francesca said, hoping that her hand was not shaking visibly. But her heart was certainly pounding now. What had Lucy gotten into?

He yanked on Lucy. "We got business to—"

Francesca did not give him a chance to finish. She pointed the gun at his feet and pulled the trigger. The shot rang out loudly in the night.

The thug yelped, releasing Lucy. Francesca thought that she had shot his foot although she had really aimed more at the pavement. He turned disbelieving eyes upon her and their gazes met. His eyes were blue and bloodshot. Then he turned and ran.

Lucy and Francesca looked at each other, stunned. The shot had been surprisingly loud—like the shot from any normally sized gun. Francesca glanced past Lucy. A number of elegant carriages were in the street, moving down it. Window latches were being clicked free, windows pushed out. Heads were popping into sight. Opera glasses were trained upon them.

Francesca and Lucy looked at each other again. As one, they grabbed hands and rushed back into the side entrance of the hotel. They slammed the door closed, then huddled in the doorway. Francesca looked in both directions down the hallway, but it was vacant—thank God.

"Did you hit him?" Lucy cried.

"I'm not sure. I think so. But only in the foot!" Francesca realized that both her hands were shaking now as she hurriedly stuffed the derringer back into her purse. It remained almost impossible to use her bandaged hand. She looked back up the hall, almost expecting to see Bragg coming down it, his expression thunderous. But surely that gunshot had not been heard inside of the hotel and she was merely stricken with paranoia.

"Did anyone see us?" Lucy asked breathlessly.

"I don't think so. Except for those inside the carriages on the street." Their gazes locked with sudden comprehension. They were hardly unremarkable now, not with Lucy in her crimson evening gown and Francesca in her turquoise one.

"Damn it," Lucy breathed.

"What is going on?" Francesca cried.

Lucy's eyes went wide with fear and she backed away, shaking her head. "Nothing."

For one moment, Francesca was disbelieving. "Nothing? I was there! I saw and heard everything. He accosted you. You are in trouble, Lucy!"

Lucy looked ready to cry. "I can't . . ."

This time, Francesca used her bandaged hand as well, taking both of Lucy's hands in hers. "Let me help. You are already a dear friend. Please, let me help!"

Tears welled in Lucy's eyes, but they did not fall. "This is simply a mistake. Nothing is going on! That man has mistaken me for someone else." She stared grimly at Francesca, on the verge of copious tears.

And clearly, she was so afraid. Francesca did not believe a word Lucy had just said—that thug was not mistaking her for someone else. She touched her bare arm. "Lucy, please let me help you."

"There is nothing for you to do!"

Francesca inhaled. "You have the most wonderful family behind you. Your brother is police commissioner, your father one of the wealthiest and most powerful men in the country." She thought about Hart's wealth and power. "And your stepbrother can certainly move a few mountains here in the city. I can see that you are afraid . . . but you do not need to be

in whatever trouble you are in alone. They can help, as can
I, I am sure!"

Lucy pulled away. "I am going to the ladies' room," she
said. "And we are about to be late for supper."

Francesca had not been able to walk away from Lucy in her
distress and had joined her in the ladies' room. There was a
huge bronze clock on one of the bureaus in the lounge, and
Francesca realized as they left that they had been gone almost
a half an hour. Lucy read her mind. She said, "I will tell
everyone I had a coughing fit."

Francesca just looked at her.

Lucy seemed belligerent. "I do not want anyone worrying
needlessly, Francesca. There is no reason to mention that . . .
that *incident* to anyone."

Francesca disagreed but did not say so. Lucy was in trouble, and surely her brother could help. Francesca would
speak to Bragg the moment they were alone.

Lucy gripped her arm as they entered the spacious lobby.
"Do not breathe a word of this to anyone, not even Rick!"

Francesca looked into her eyes, which were steely with
determination. "You know I desperately want to," she finally
said.

"No. Or our friendship is over," she said harshly.

Francesca recoiled. Whatever dilemma Lucy was in,
clearly Francesca must solve it alone; either that or jeopard-
ize their new friendship.

"Can I trust you?" Lucy asked.

Francesca nodded. "Yes. Although it is against my better
judgment."

Lucy sighed, relief flashing in her eyes. "Thank you." She
now smiled. "I will tell them we went up to my rooms to
check on the twins and Roberto."

Francesca nodded, as that was a far more plausible lie.
But it was a lie, and she was acutely uncomfortable now.

Lucy faced her as they crossed the lobby, passing the concierge and registration desks. "I know. I hate lying to those
I love the most!"

"In general, a lie is never a good idea." Francesca glanced ahead. The family had remained in the atrium, but Bragg was standing and looking impatiently at them as they approached. Even from a distance, she could see that Bragg's stare was particularly intent and suspicious.

"Oh, we are lucky; the Channings are just arriving!" Lucy exclaimed softly.

Francesca glanced over her shoulder and saw Sarah and her mother entering through the large front doors at the opposite end of the lobby. Both women were dwarfed by huge sable coats.

Bragg stepped over to them. "Where have you two been?" he asked, his gaze moving carefully from Francesca to Lucy.

"We went up to my rooms to check on the twins and Roberto," Lucy said with a wide smile. "And I decided to show Francesca photographs of the ranch and Shoz."

Francesca smiled at Bragg.

He did not smile back. He knew a lie when he heard one.

Rathe had stood and he came forward, looking closely at his daughter. "Are you all right? Is everything all right with the children?"

"Jack has a bit of an upset stomach, but other than that, we are all as perfect as can be," Lucy said, far too happily.

Her father gave her a long look. A pause that seemed endless ensued. "Good," he finally said.

Francesca sensed that he suspected quite a bit. To make matters worse, Grace had also come over. She said, "Have you been crying?"

"Of course not. I have an allergy." Lucy smiled at her mother. She did not smile back.

Instead, Rathe and Grace exchanged a glance. "We are looking forward to seeing your parents tomorrow night," Rathe remarked, turning to Francesca. "It has been awhile since Andrew and I spent an evening solving all of the world's political and social problems."

Francesca laughed. It felt good to laugh just then, after the past few moments. Then she realized that Rourke had gone up to Lucy and he seemed angry. He pulled her aside.

Francesca pretended not to notice, but she strained to hear. Whatever he whispered to her, Lucy became angry and she pulled defiantly away.

"The Channings are here," Bragg remarked quietly.

"I am so sorry we are so late!" Mrs. Channing replied, handing her sable to the cloakroom clerk who had suddenly materialized. "But that awful detective returned and he just would not leave Sarah and the countess alone. It was an impossible and *endless* interview!" She turned a dark look on Bragg, as if it were his fault. "Sarah, dear, do hand off your *sable*," she said.

"I am sorry, Mrs. Channing, if Inspector O'Connor has disturbed you. I did not realize he would return to interview you and your daughter tonight."

"It was the worst timing," Mrs. Channing said, but she beamed now at Rathe and Grace.

Bragg quickly made introductions all around, and as he did so, Francesca saw Rourke cast a once-over at Sarah. She winced as she saw Sarah's gown, then glanced back at Rourke. She saw him wince as well.

Sarah did not look well to begin with. She was far too pale, yet she had two bright, garish spots on her cheeks, which looked like rouge from an earlier epoch—but they were clearly a natural and agitated flush. And she was wearing a dark emerald green gown that overpowered her small size and delicate features. The color suited her, but the bulky shape and amount of fabric made Sarah look plump, when she was anything but. She was also wearing a ridiculously expensive emerald choker that was absolutely inappropriate for a young unwed girl. Francesca knew Sarah's mother had chosen it for her, just as she now knew that Sarah couldn't care less about the clothes or the jewelry she wore.

Evan had turned to his fiancée. "Sarah," he said, taking her hand and kissing it. "I am so sorry about your studio."

Sarah seemed tense. She pulled away. "Thank you, Evan. But I am sure the culprit will be found." She turned wide eyes upon Francesca. Francesca now winced again—she had to help Lucy, but she also had to find the vandal who had destroyed Sarah's studio.

"Evan dear, how handsome you look!" Mrs. Channing cried, kissing his cheek. "Yes, it has been the worst nightmare, and poor Sarah is beside herself."

Lucy came over and hugged Sarah. "How about a sip of champagne? It will help, I am sure."

"I can't drink. My stomach isn't quite right," Sarah said tersely.

Bragg laid his hand on her shoulder. "Has O'Connor upset you, Miss Channing?"

"No." Her tone was abrupt. "I am glad he is on the case. I just want this solved and over with."

Bragg seemed somewhat unsatisfied with that. His glance met Francesca's with concern.

But she was also concerned. She had never seen Sarah so tense or terse or abrupt.

"What happened to your studio?" Rourke asked.

Sarah turned. "Someone broke into it, apparently last night. They overturned most of my paintings, spilled and threw paint everywhere, and slashed up one particular portrait. And I just cannot think of who would do such a thing, or why." She held her head high. Francesca felt that the effort of being social was costing her dearly and that she wished to be anywhere but at the Plaza.

"Sarah surely has no enemies," Evan said, in an attempt to be gallant. "As she is very kind and everyone thinks so."

Sarah gave him a cursory smile.

"I am sorry," Rourke said, his amber eyes speculative. He glanced at Francesca. "Are you on the case?"

Francesca hesitated. "Mrs. Channing specifically asked me to help."

Rourke seemed amused. "I have never encountered a female sleuth before."

"Are there not female doctors?"

"There is one in the entire medical school. She is extremely unpopular with most of the students and staff."

"What a shame," Francesca said. "Surely you are not so quick to judge?"

"I tried not to, but she goes out of her way to be rude and I have given up." He shrugged.

"I am sure she will be a better doctor than all of her male counterparts combined," Sarah said.

Rourke looked at her.

So did Francesca. Of course, Francesca was less surprised; after all, she knew Sarah, who was actually very bohemian—but one would never guess from looking at her. However, what was surprising was her voicing her thoughts in the mixed company in which they were in.

Sarah's color increased. "Well, when a woman wishes to do something that is reserved exclusively for men, the passion she has usually causes her to excel. Take Francesca. As a sleuth she is superb."

"Ah, not really," Francesca murmured.

Rourke lifted both brows. "I take it you know this from experience?" His gaze moved over her features one by one, as if he were dissecting her in one of his medical classes.

Sarah shrugged, clearly careless and indifferent. She was so out of character tonight, Francesca thought, she could not help but be worried, and her eyes were simply so bright. "I think so."

"Shall we sit down for supper?" Mrs. Channing cried with alarm. "Dear sir, my daughter is the most polite lady, and her painting is a pleasant little hobby, the kind most ladies enjoy. A few simple watercolors here and there, and that is the brunt of it."

Francesca looked at Sarah and felt horrible for her and wished Mrs. Channing would not try to ingratiate herself so much into the present company. She was about to make a quiet remark, but a rebuttal nonetheless, when Lucy said, "I think she is brilliant."

Sarah smiled grimly at her.

Grace turned to Mrs. Channing. "I happen to agree with Sarah. In fact, for a long time I have seen what I only suspected when I was Sarah's age—that women have superior

tellects, when they are allowed to use them. And those
omen who dare to fearlessly go where Man does not wish
er to, why, they are simply superb doctors and lawyers and
rtists." She smiled at Mrs. Channing and then at Sarah. "I
rould love to see your art sometime."

Sarah smiled back. "I should love to show you. I am a
uge admirer of yours, Mrs. Bragg. I have followed your
areer as a suffragette and an agitator for women throughout
re country for years. I am thrilled to meet you. I never
reamed this would actually happen."

"That is very kind of you," Grace said.

Francesca could only blink. Now why hadn't she been
ble to approach Grace Bragg in such a fashion?

"Peas in a pod," Rourke seemed to mutter. He raised his
oice. "So you are an artist?"

Sarah nodded. "Yes."

"And what kind of art do you engage in?" he continued.
Other than simple watercolors, as most ladies prefer?"

"I prefer oils," Sarah said briskly. "In fact, I rarely use
atercolor anymore. I consider myself somewhat of an Im-
ressionism, but I have studied the old masters extensively.
here is a movement in the art world today called Post-
npressionism, but I do not belong in it. In truth, even
rough I am somewhat of an Impressionist, my background
s so solidly Romantic that I might be considered as such.
nd my second preference is charcoal." She did not smile.
here was an odd light in her eyes. She even spoke differ-
ntly, in an impatient way, with a staccato ring to her words.

Rourke's gaze narrowed. "And your choice of subjects?
light I take it landscapes are not a preference?"

"No, they are not. I find landscapes boring. I adore doing
ortraits of women and children," Sarah said flatly, and sud-
enly she smiled and glanced at Francesca. Francesca wanted
o wave frantically at her; instead, she sent her a warning
ook, but Sarah had not seen. She had turned back to Rourke.
Calder Hart has commissioned a portrait of Francesca. I am
o very fortunate."

A silence fell.

And suddenly Francesca realized that Hart was not pres
ent, that he had not come—and in that moment she knew
that he was not joining them for supper. In that moment there
was vast confusion; there was disappointment and there was
relief. And somehow she also knew why he had decided not
to join them. She felt herself still as the conversation swirled
around them. *She* was the reason he had refused to come to
his own family supper.

She amended her thoughts. The *conversation* they had had
earlier was the cause, not she herself.

She refused to entertain any disappointment. Disappoint
ment was absurd.

Rourke smiled slightly. "So, Hart has commissioned Miss
Cahill's portrait. I cannot say that I blame him." He smiled
far too warmly at Francesca, then turned to look directly at
his brother. "Do you blame him, Rick?"

"Hart does as he chooses; he always has," Bragg said
coldly.

"Oh, ho, this is jolly indeed!" Rourke began to chuckle.

"I think Mrs. Channing is right and we should go in to
supper," Rathe said, stepping between the brothers while
clasping each one on the shoulder. But his gaze moved to
Francesca with speculation.

She felt herself flush.

His regard was not as kind as it had been earlier, and there
was a set to his expression that she did not like.

Rathe was about to escort Mrs. Channing, and Bragg had
looped his arm in Grace's, when Inspector Newman appeared
in the lobby, two roundsmen with him. In general, detectives
were obvious in their shabby tweed overcoats and bowler
hats, even if one did not notice the badges pinned to their
jackets, for they simply did not look like gentlemen. Of
course, Francesca recognized Newman from several of the
past cases she had worked on. And the sight of two unifor
mooed policemen in the lobby of the hotel was not a usual
one. Francesca halted in her tracks. The feeling she had was
a distinctly sinking one.

Bragg had seen them, too. "What is this?"

Francesca muttered, beneath her breath, "I have no idea."

"Grace, one moment, please," he said to his stepmother, and he strode away. Newman was at the concierge desk, where a group of hotel staff had congregated, but he saw Bragg and quickly detached himself, coming forward. Francesca was drawn to them like paper clips to a magnet.

"Newman? What's amiss?" Bragg asked.

"Gunshots, C'mish, sir. Or at least one, just outside of the hotel."

"Was anybody hurt?"

"Looks like it. There a trail of blood on Fifty-ninth Street, leading west, between Fifth and Sixth," he said.

Bragg stared.

"Starts just outside of a side entrance to the hotel, too," Newman added. He was a short, beefy man with huge red cheeks that were perpetually flushed. He now saw Francesca and nodded. "G'day, Miz Cahill."

Abruptly Bragg turned. "What the hell is going on, Francesca?"

She inhaled and smiled. "I don't know. This is the first I have heard of this incident."

He stared.

She held his gaze, no easy task, oh no.

"But didn't you and my sister go around the corridor on that side of the lobby—meaning the corridor that leads to Fifty-ninth Street?"

He had watched them too carefully, she realized with a pang. He had seen them bypass the ladies' room and go down the damning corridor that led to the street.

Suddenly Bragg turned to Newman. "I shall go outside in a moment to see the sight," he said. "Please, continue interviewing the staff."

Newman nodded and turned away. The moment he did so, Brag said oh-so calmly, "May I see your gun, Francesca?"

Eight

She had misheard, surely. "I beg your pardon?"

"You and Lucy are up to something. And Lucy is not herself. I suspect she is in trouble—again. A shot was fired outside of this hotel recently. Oddly, I am suspicious," Bragg said flatly.

"Bragg, you will embarrass me in front of your family," she said nervously.

"Did you fire your gun recently?" he asked, looking very displeased.

She hesitated. "I am sworn to a confidence, Bragg."

"Whose? My sister's?"

She closed her eyes and swore silently, to herself. She did not want to be put in this position. Then she looked at him. "Do not make me lie. Please. If I could, I would tell you everything, but I can't. I promised."

He hesitated, glanced around them, and then took her arm and pulled her several more steps into the lobby. "Francesca, if you had a cause to fire your gun, then something is terribly wrong."

"Don't make me lie to you," she begged.

"Did you fire your gun?" he asked.

She inhaled, because he was not going to give her a single inch. "Yes. But I did not mean to shoot anyone."

"So it was a warning shot." He seemed frustrated now. "I am going to have a long talk with my little sister," he said abruptly.

Francesca thought that might be for the best. In spite of Lucy's pleas for secrecy, Francesca's instinct was to make this a family matter. But she could not betray Lucy, either.

"Bragg," she said carefully, "I am in quite the position. I really do not know anything, except that Lucy does not want you or anyone else in her family involved. She was very clear on that." She met his probing regard. "Of course, I cannot stop you from speaking with her. But she trusts me, and I do intend to help her."

He hesitated, at once grim and bewildered. "You are almost frightening me. How badly in trouble is she? Is it dangerous—or need I even ask?"

She spoke again, as carefully. "That's just it. I really don't know anything myself."

"That is hardly a relief," he said sharply.

"I do realize that." Her mind raced. "Could I stop by headquarters tomorrow and look at the Rogues' Gallery?" she asked, referring to a catalog of photographs and drawings of various criminals.

He stared, and then frustration crossed his face. "You may look at the mug book, Francesca."

Their gazes locked. "What are you going to do?" she asked.

His smile was odd. "I suppose I might take a look at that mug book myself when you are done. And Lucy doesn't have to know—now does she?"

She tensed, at once elated and afraid. Clearly Bragg was going to help his sister, no matter the promise Francesca had made, no matter what Lucy wanted.

He stalked away, after Newman, clearly to go outside and look at Francesca's handiwork.

Francesca stared after him, hoping that Lucy would not blame her for his involvement.

SATURDAY, FEBRUARY 15, 1902—11:00 P.M.

"That was such a wonderful evening," Mrs. Channing gushed. "Don't you think so, Grace?"

"It was very enjoyable," Grace said with a polite smile. "I have so missed my son. I am so happy to be back in the city." She turned her smile on Bragg.

He smiled back at her. "The feeling is mutual," he said.

"Are you staying here in New York, then?" Mrs. Channing asked eagerly. "Didn't you sell your home a few years ago?"

"Actually, it has been leased," Rathe said with an easy smile. "My wife thinks we should be moving uptown, and we will soon begin to look for a suitable parcel of land to buy." He took his wife's hand.

Francesca was walking with the group while Sarah and Evan trailed behind, neither one speaking. Sarah had fallen extremely silent through the meal, barely eating a thing. Rourke was behind them, apparently absorbed in thought—his head was down, his hands in his trouser pockets. Now Francesca watched Rathe smile at his wife, and then she saw Grace send him a soft, answering smile.

She had already sensed that they loved each other dearly, but she was surprised now to realize they were still *in* love.

Rourke moved to her side. He said, "Shall I see you home, Miss Cahill?"

Alarm filled her. She looked into his handsome face, a face that was so eerily like his brother's. Worse, she met his eyes and saw the comprehension and amusement there. "I should probably go with my brother," she said swiftly. Bragg was on her other side and she had felt him stiffen.

"But he must escort his fiancée all the way to Dakota," Rourke said dryly. "And if he wishes to linger a bit with his future bride?" He glanced back at the silent couple. Francesca thought, but was not certain, that there was censure in his eyes.

Francesca glanced at Bragg, urging him to come to the rescue. Not that she minded Rourke. He was intelligent and interesting, but far too astute. But she wished to speak with Bragg and, frankly, had no wish to be alone with Rourke, for she had no desire to parry and fend off his innuendos.

Evan said, his eyes sparkling, "My sister tends to do as she pleases. But I should certainly approve were you to take her home, Rourke."

Rourke chuckled.

Bragg said, "Actually, I am taking Francesca home. There

re some significant matters which I wish to discuss with
er." His gaze was cool upon Evan. "And I assure you that
he will be far safer in my hands than my brother's."

"At least I am an eligible bachelor," Rourke murmured.

Alarmed, Francesca said to him, "I am on a case. We
haven't had a chance to discuss it. I really do need Bragg's
dvice."

Rourke gave her a knowing look. "Very well. I shall
gracefully bow out," he said.

Before she could even smile, as he was wryly amusing,
here was a thump behind her.

Francesca turned, as everyone did, to find Sarah on the
floor in what appeared to be a dead faint. Rourke was already
kneeling beside her, and Mrs. Channing screamed.

Rourke lifted Sarah's head onto his knee, his fingers going
to the artery in her neck.

"What is it?" Bragg asked, kneeling beside him.

He did not answer. Francesca saw that Sarah was deathly
white. Then Rourke reached into his pocket, but he swore.
"Smelling salts, anyone? I usually keep them on hand for my
landlord, but I seem to have left them behind tonight."

"Did she faint?" Rathe asked.

Miss Channing was moaning now.

"It seems so, but I would hesitate to say so definitively.
Her pulse is a bit slow. However, she is feverish," Rourke
added, his hand covering her forehead. He laid her head back
down on the floor and began to raise her knees. As he did
so, his brows lifted in surprise. "She is all bones," he remarked.

"She is too busy painting to eat," Mrs. Channing managed, near tears. "Oh, my poor dear Sarah!"

Rourke ignored her. He was fanning the air near Sarah's
face when Evan appeared, having run off to the concierge
desk. "Here," he said, handing Rourke the salts.

"Thanks," Rourke said. "Miss Channing? You have
fainted; do not be alarmed," he said softly, holding the salts
to her nose.

Sarah suddenly cried out, her eyes flying open and tearing.

Rourke slid his hand beneath her head, but he said, "Lie still
for a moment. We wish for the blood to go back to your
head."

Sarah looked at him. It was a moment before she spoke.
"I fainted?"

"I think so. See?" He smiled at her. "Already the color is
returning to that pretty face of yours."

Sarah started to smile, and then she stopped. She said, "I
think I can sit up."

"Slowly, then," he said, a soft command. He helped her
to sit.

Sarah leaned back in his arms, closing her eyes.

"Dizzy?" Rourke asked. Sarah could not see his expression, but Francesca could, and clearly. He was concerned.

She nodded.

"My medical bag is at Hart's. See if there is a doctor in
the house," he said, not glancing up. Evan turned and hurried
off.

"I don't need a doctor," Sarah muttered, opening her eyes
at last.

"You have a bit of a fever." He looked more closely at
her. "I thought so earlier. You did not eat a thing, Miss Channing," he chided.

"I did not notice; I'm surprised you did," she said a bit
tartly. Then she seemed to lean into his arms again. "I'm
sorry. I am so upset. I am not myself tonight."

"It is understandable. Ah, the troops arrive."

A concierge and another gentleman, who introduced himself as the hotel manager, had hurried over. "There is one
doctor in the house, sir, but he is at the opera tonight. We
can send for Dr. Johnson and find the lady a room until he
arrives."

"I think that is a very good idea," Rourke said. He smiled
at his patient. "Sarah? We shall find you a room and you can
rest until the doctor arrives."

"I am fine. Just a bit weak. I should go home." She stared
at him, but she appeared fragile, not mulish or stubborn at
all.

"Absolutely not. It will only be a few moments until Dr. Johnson arrives."

"I am sure it will be more like an hour. I must get home!" She was agitated now. Francesca knelt down beside her and laid her hand on her back. Sarah did not seem to notice.

"What is the rush? I really would prefer that your temperature be taken, your throat looked at, your heart and lungs listened to. It is all normal procedure," he added with a pleasant smile.

"I must work in the morning, Rourke," she said.

"I doubt you will be working in the morning," Rourke returned evenly—patiently.

Sarah regarded him and her flush increased. "You are right!" she suddenly exclaimed weakly. "I am not well. I have no desire to paint. I can't paint! And I haven't felt well all day." Tears suddenly filled her eyes. "What if Hart changes his mind? What if I lose his commission?" she cried. "It is the most important event of my life!"

"My stepbrother will not change his mind. He is many things, but indecisive he is not. If he has commissioned Miss Cahill's portrait, there is a reason, and knowing Hart, neither hell nor high water shall detour him from his course."

Sarah did not seem relieved. "I prefer to go home. Mama? We can send for Dr. Finney."

Mrs. Channing hesitated when Bragg said, "I can stop at Finney's now, on my way to the Cahill residence. By the time you arrive at the Channings', Rourke, Finney will be there, or shortly thereafter. He is a fine doctor," he added.

"A good plan," Rourke said. He smiled at Sarah. "Can you stand up?"

"Of course," she said.

Rourke helped her to her feet. "Cahill? I shall escort you and your fiancée back to her home, if you do not mind."

"Not at all," Evan said, appearing relieved. "I'll go get a cab."

Rathe and Grace had taken off in one cab, their destination Hart's. Rourke had accompanied Evan and the Channings to

the West Side. Lucy had gone to her rooms in the hotel—
Francesca had learned that she had thought it too much of
an imposition to stay at Hart's with three children and her
nanny. Francesca felt certain Calder would not have cared.
Bragg had gone with Lucy, clearly to have a word or two,
while Francesca had waited alone in the lobby. Now, finally,
he appeared, looking grim. "I am sorry to have been so
long," he said, helping her on with her coat, which she had
been holding.

A doorman held open the door for them as they stepped
outside. "How did it go?" Francesca asked worriedly.

"My sister can be a stubborn jackass," Bragg said, his
hand on the small of Francesca's back. They went down the
steps and another doorman understood. He stepped out into
the mostly deserted street to hail a cab. Bragg had apparently
left the sometimes temperamental Daimler at his home.

"Which means?"

He slid his arm around her and she moved against his
side. He looked down at her; she looked up into his eyes.
Warmth spread quickly through her. "It means she denied
everything, even your firing a gun outside of the hotel. Then
she reversed herself and told me to mind my own business,
as her affairs were just that, her own affairs."

Francesca trembled. Even though he wore a heavy greatcoat, his body was hard and strong and male against hers.
"So we have not learned a thing."

"Not a thing. Cold?"

"No." She smiled just a little.

"I didn't think so," he said, finally looking at her mouth.

A wild excitement suddenly flamed and she leaned just a
bit closer to him. It was enough. His hand clasped her hip.
Their gazes locked.

The urgency was sudden and overwhelming. And so many
thoughts went through her mind at once, they were less coherent than a kaleidoscope of feelings and fears. She thought
about how much she loved and admired him, and then in the
same breath she thought about his wife and her note. She
thought about the terrible fight she had witnessed between

her brother and her father. She thought about poor Sarah and the trouble Lucy was in. She thought about Calder Hart, who had promised to never touch her. And she thought about the fact that finally, at long last, they were alone—and moments away from being within the privacy of a hansom.

The realization was stunning. It was simply absurd to deny and control the depths of their feelings for each other.

"Commissioner? Cab's here."

As the doorman spoke, Bragg's hand dropped from her hip. "Thank you," he said gruffly, handing the man a coin.

Francesca climbed into the hansom first, flushing and praying the doorman hadn't noticed any intimacy between her and Bragg. Reality was like ice-cold water. One second before, it had seemed obvious that they should go to his house and become lovers. Now, all she could think of was what if the doorman spoke to a news reporter?

Bragg climbed in after her, closing the door. "We are making two stops, the first at Eight-ten Fifth Avenue," he said.

The driver murmured an affirmative, released the brake, and whipped his gelding on.

Francesca began to look at Bragg with worry when he abruptly pulled her into his arms.

"Bragg!" she began.

His mouth seized hers and her protest died. Their lips locked, her hands found his shoulders, his back, and she fell back onto the swabs of the seat, Bragg on top of her. He opened her mouth, and his tongue became a forceful, thrusting instrument. His hand moved inside her coat, up her side, and over her breast.

She moaned, moving his own coat out of the way, running her hands up and down inside his white dinner jacket, exploring the hard planes and angles of his torso and chest. His mouth moved to her throat. Fiery sensation trailed in the wake of his lips, his tongue. Francesca gripped his head, encouraging him to go lower.

He did.

He rained kisses on her bare chest, and when he reached the edge of her bodice he paused.

"Don't stop," she whispered frantically.

He rubbed his cheek over her breast until the silk of her gown raised her nipple.

Francesca pushed her bodice down.

He inhaled, hard, his lips inches from her nipple, and then she heard herself beg, "Please," and he touched it with his tongue, slowly, deliberately, again and again, until she began to writhe, wildly, on the cab seat.

He sucked it into his mouth.

Francesca cried out, then felt his hand beneath her skirts, sliding up her stockinged knee, her bare thigh. She froze.

He lifted his head and looked at her and she saw passion straining his face. And then she felt his fingers move up her thigh, finally brushing her sex.

She collapsed against the seat, moaning, mindless. He began to kiss her again—her mouth, her face—but his fingers stroked over her and then she felt what had to be an electrical current or a bolt of lightning. Her body arched wildly, stars exploded inside the cab, not once, but many times, and as they began to flutter down through the night sky she began to drift with them, lower and lower still, weightless.

Until suddenly there was a hard piece of wood beneath her neck, a solid seat beneath her back, one leg dangling off, awkwardly, and Bragg's solid body was moving off, away. She looked up at the ceiling of the cab, which was torn, and then she started to sit and she looked at him, stunned.

He stared, his eyes still dark and heated. "Are you all right?"

She realized she was not quite dressed; she pulled up her bodice and rearranged her skirts. "Are you all right?" she asked cautiously.

He made a sound. "Yes. And no. I lost control, Francesca. I didn't mean to ravage you in the cab."

She wanted to touch him but, oddly, was afraid to. "I'm glad that you did."

"I'm not."

His words were a blow. "What?"

"This is too hard."

Fear paralyzed her. It was a moment before she could speak. "I am an independent woman. I am glad we love each other, no matter the circumstances! Bragg, I have no regrets!"

"Are you certain?"

"Yes!"

He suddenly flopped back fully in the seat, his eyes closed, his face upturned to the torn canopy. "God damn it," he said.

She stared at his taut neck, his strained profile, and dared to glimpse the rigid outlines of his entire body. Dismayed, she sank back in her seat. Why couldn't he say to hell with everything and take her as his lover? But then, that was why she loved him so. "I don't care, Bragg, about my virginity," she said somewhat bitterly. "I wish gladly to give it to you."

His eyes flew open. "Don't talk like that!"

"But it's the truth. I have thought about it. You are the one. Nothing will ever change my feelings."

He turned his head to stare but otherwise did not move. The cab continued to rumble through the city. "We've had this conversation before. I am not going to ruin you, Francesca. I love you too much."

"But I don't care!" she cried. "I am never going to marry anyone else, so what difference does it make?"

"You don't know that," he said, sounding bitter now. He faced her more fully, his gaze now oddly intent.

And instantly she became rigid and fearful. "What is it? Why do you want to speak to me?"

"On Thursday I told you I intended to divorce Leigh Anne. Yet you haven't said a word about it, not then, not since then. Granted, we have not really had a moment alone together. But I know you. You would find that moment to discuss our future. Yet you have not," he said grimly. "I know you very well. You aren't happy, are you? Something's changed. Yet I don't know what."

She was so stiff with tension she could hardly breathe. "I know you would never say such a thing on a whim."

"A whim? A man only marries once. This is not about a whim, Francesca."

She found it hard to breathe properly now. A man only marries once. He was giving himself away. And this was what she wanted, but not this way. Not over the carcass of his wife and career. She would never let him destroy himself—she would never be the cause of his destruction.

"I haven't changed my mind. I wrote Leigh Anne a letter telling her that I have decided upon a divorce," he said stiffly.

"Have you really thought this through?" she asked with dread. How had the evening boiled down to this? Just a moment ago they had been in the throes of ecstasy. Now they were on the verge of anger and argument.

"The words—and expression—of an ecstatic woman. I have thought of nothing else in the dark hours between midnight and dawn." He seemed angry now. "But I cannot tell her in a letter. That would be unfair. Later this week I will go up to Boston and tell her in person, myself."

She thought of the note, which she had left at home. *"My dear Miss Cahill, . . . I wish to meet you at your convenience."* Then she recalled Lucy's furious outburst. *"I hate her. After all she did to Rick . . ."*

"What did she do?"

"Do you have to even ask? She broke my brother's heart."

Francesca began to perspire. She knew she should not raise this topic now, but she had to—she had to know. "Lucy said that she broke your heart."

"What?" He was startled.

She wet her lips. A little voice inside her head said, *Don't do this. He loves you, he has proven it; he just made love to you.* "Lucy said Leigh Anne broke your heart."

His jaw tightened. His face hardened. "I don't want you gossiping with her about my marriage."

She flinched as if struck. "Did she break your heart?"

"No."

"Then why would Lucy say such a thing?"

"How would I know?" he exploded.

"Stop." She seized his arm. "Why are you shouting at me? What have I done? I am asking a simple question."

He was furious. "I was young. Naive. I trusted her. And more significantly, the woman I loved did not exist. Did she break my heart? It took me some time to recover from the fact that I had married a whore. Now. Does that answer your question?"

"She broke your heart," Francesca whispered, shocked. And something inside her own heart broke, and while it was only a small spoke, while the other spokes remained intact, the entire wheel was forever changed. It would always wobble now.

"I did not grieve, Francesca," he warned.

"You just said 'the woman I loved,' You loved her." She was reeling.

He slammed his hands down on the seat. "I was in love, yes, but not with Leigh Anne. I was in love with the most beautiful and perfect little angel to set foot on the earth. Except the woman I loved was an illusion. Now—have you finished your interrogation?" he asked tersely.

"You told me it was lust. You lied—to me," she whispered.

"It was lust. Because you can't love a figment of your imagination," he said.

Francesca turned her back to him to stare out her window, gripping the edges of the seat. *The most beautiful and perfect little angel. . . .* how his words hurt. She wanted to vanish, to die.

"Francesca? I am sorry," he said softly now. "But the mere mention of my wife still has the power to upset me. I did not mean to shout at you."

"I think you are still in love with her," Francesca heard herself say slowly. How she hated her own words, but now, oh God, she knew that they were true.

He gripped her arm. "I love *you*," he said flatly. His eyes seemed black. "She is the worst thing to ever have happened to me. You are the best thing to ever have happened to me. I am going to ask her for a divorce. I will give her the shirt off of my back if she will agree, and if not, I will fight her, for as long as it takes. And then I am going to marry you," he said. "Francesca, will you marry me?"

She looked at him and shook her head slowly. "No. I cannot," she said.

Nine

His eyes widened. "What?"

She inhaled and reached for his hand. "I can't let you divorce her," she said.

He pulled his hand away. "Why not?"

"Because your career in politics would be over," she said, frightened now. His face was so hard.

"I see."

"No, I don't think that you do! I can't let you divorce Leigh Anne because it would destroy everything you have dreamed of and worked for your entire life! I could not live with myself, Bragg, if I were so selfish!"

His jaw was tight. "Isn't it my decision to make?"

"I would never forgive myself, and maybe there would come a time when you would hate me!" she cried.

"I could never hate you." He stared at her so intently she wanted to squirm. His gaze narrowed. "Is there someone else you wish to marry?"

"No! The question is absurd!" But she grew uneasy, because she knew exactly where their conversation was now heading.

"Is it? I do believe a very infamous art collector is desperate for your portrait," he said coldly.

"Do not bring Hart into this," she warned. "He has nothing to do with how much I love you."

"Do you love me? You would not be the first woman to marry a divorced man."

"It is because I love you that I cannot accept your offer," Francesca said, feeling ill. The world seemed to be spinning—but in the wrong direction. She was refusing a marriage proposal from the man she loved. How had her life come to this?

He was silent for a moment. "Stay away from Calder," he said coolly.

Francesca could hardly believe her ears. *"What?"* Then, "What does Calder have to do with anything?"

"He has been coming between us ever since his father was murdered," Bragg said flatly. "Which was when you first met him."

She stared, stunned that he had injected Hart into their conversation, now. She was about to tell him that he was wrong and that Hart had not come between them, but she could not speak. Not after the horrible encounter she had had with him earlier that day. Not after he had told her that he wished to take her to bed but would never do so, because he so treasured her as a friend. "He is only a friend," she finally said, and was aghast, because her tone sounded pitifully weak to her own ears.

"Stop. You can tell yourself until you are blue in the face that his intentions are merely platonic. Lie then if you will. But not to me."

"I am not lying," she managed. "Do not accuse me of lying!"

He inhaled. "I am sorry. Clearly you have convinced yourself that that is the truth. I don't want to fight with you, Francesca. But I do not trust my half brother, not one whit. He would love nothing more than to stab me in the back— and steal the woman I love out from under my nose."

"That's not true."

"No? So now you are an expert on Calder?" He gave her a sidelong look. "As always, you defend him blindly. When will you ever learn? He is not to be trusted, Francesca. Not even by you."

Francesca did not answer now. Bragg was wrong. Oddly, she did trust Calder, and she realized now that he had been right—it was herself that she did not trust when they were together. It was a horrible realization to have, especially in that moment.

"Again, will you stay away from him?" Bragg was demanding.

She was, to her amazement, torn. "This is not fair."

"Why can't you simply agree? Sit for that damned portrait if you must, but otherwise, avoid Calder at all costs."

Somehow she knew he was not giving her a choice. "You are strong-arming me."

"Yes, I am."

She closed her eyes, and Hart's image blazed there in her mind, darkly amused yet oddly tender. She sighed and looked at Bragg, then almost recoiled at the fierce and intent look in his eyes. *This would be for the best.* "I will avoid him socially," she said. "But considering that I have promised to uncover the ruffian responsible for the vandalism of Sarah's studio, I may need Hart's insights into the art world."

"I can accept that," he said flatly. "If I asked you to reconsider my proposal, would you?"

She stiffened, surprised at his rapid reversal back to his marriage proposal. She met his dark, disturbed, and even angry eyes. Her mind was made up, but she could not refuse him now. "Of course."

His face hardened. "You are being glib. Do not tell me you will think this over when your mind is firmly set."

"Sometimes it feels like you are inside of my mind," Francesca whispered, shaken and tearful now.

"It is because we are so alike," he said flatly, but the anger remained there in his eyes, flashing and black.

She hesitated. "But how can you be so certain that you would really give up your career for me? How, Bragg?"

And he hesitated. "I don't want to lose you to someone else. I cannot bear the notion," he finally said.

She trembled, wondering if he somehow thought he might lose her to Hart, which was preposterous. And he had hesitated before answering, and somehow his answer did not seem like the right one. Yet she knew that he loved her. What had just happened in the cab proved that, as did all the moments they had shared on the past three criminal investigations they had solved. But she also felt that he still loved his wife—and she felt it very strongly. That love might be perverse, and it might be odd and angry. But somehow, it still was love.

She touched his arm. "Tell me the real truth. Do you *really* want to give up everything you have worked your entire life for?"

He turned and stared at her.

"Bragg?" she prompted. "What if I never married another man? What if I devoted myself to crime-solving and reform, growing old as a spinster? What would your choice be then?"

It was hard to tell in the darkness of the cab, but he seemed to flush. He inhaled harshly. "I do not want to end my own career. How could I? There is so much to be done! The police department in this city is just the beginning. If I lived to be a hundred, I could not accomplish all that I must." He was excessively grim. "But this is not a perfect world, Francesca. One must compromise and make choices. Your scenario is absurd. You are an amazing and unique woman. Perhaps I am the only man to fully understand and appreciate you, but did you not see how many men wished to make your acquaintance at the Channing ball? If I do not come forward, and soon, one of them will. I have made my choice, Francesca."

She looked at him and now he looked away. She sensed then that his choice was not as absolute and firm as he had made it out to be. He was a great man, a natural leader, and a true reformer. He did not want to really give it all up. But he did not want to lose her, either. How could she solve this dilemma? "I am going to make you a promise, Bragg," she said thoughtfully.

His gaze met hers.

She smiled just a little and took his hand in her left one, squeezing it hard. "I will *never* give my heart to another man. My heart will *always* belong to you," she said.

His face softened. "This is why I love you so." He swept her up into his arms, hard, and held her that way briefly. When he released her, he said, "You are twenty years old. I

refuse to accept such a pledge. For God forbid there might
come a day when you regret it."

"I will never regret it, and you have it, now," she whispered. "I am the kind of woman to only love once, Bragg."

"I hate to tell you, Francesca, there are many different
ways to love. Life's paths are surprising. You might be surprised, one day, when you find yourself on a road you never
dreamed of." He was very serious now.

He simply did not understand. "Does this mean you have
realized a divorce is not a good idea?" she asked.

He hesitated. "No."

"You are still going to approach Leigh Anne?" she asked,
alarmed.

"Not immediately. Perhaps I am rushing things." He
smiled just a little and pulled her against his side. "Maybe
if you and I continue this discussion, we can come to terms
that satisfy us both."

She blinked. "What does that mean?"

He smiled. "You realize you cannot live without me and
agree to become my wife while supporting my decision to
divorce."

His tone was light now, so she smiled. But she began to
tremble, with fear. He remained set in his decision, too. There
was, however, one solution to this terrible impasse. It was a
long moment before she could speak.

"There is another solution, here," she said hoarsely. "A
way to navigate through the waters of the present before we
must face the seas of the future."

He met her gaze, mildly perplexed. "Is there?"

"Yes," she cried. "Make me your mistress, Bragg."

His answer was instantaneous. "Absolutely not."

The cab had halted in the snow-dusted driveway before the
front steps of the Cahill mansion. Neither one of them
moved. Francesca sat in the far corner of the backseat, angry
and upset. Bragg was staring out his own window. The driver
coughed.

"One moment," Bragg said. "I wish you to wait for me."

He pushed open his door then and jumped out, slipping a little on the frozen, icy snow. He turned and looked into the cab.

Francesca finally met his gaze. "Why not?" she asked, choked up with tears. "I have thought about this very carefully."

"No, you haven't thought about this at all. Either that, or you do not know me at all," he said grimly. He held out his hand.

She took it reluctantly and allowed him to help her down from the cab. His hand touched the small of her back. It felt so right—it felt so wrong. They started carefully up the short stone walkway to the front steps of the imposing limestone house. "I know you the way I know myself," she said. "Sometimes we think the exact same thoughts, or it is as if you read my mind."

"No. You do not know my thoughts." He clasped her hand hard and pulled her about to face him. "You deserve more than being a man's plaything, Francesca. You deserve to be a man's wife, his partner, the mother of his children. I would be afflicted with guilt every time I looked at you if I took you as a mistress. Do you know how corrosive guilt is?"

Tears began to moisten her eyes. "Yes," she whispered.

"And I also know that sooner or later you would have many conflicting emotions. Most important, sooner or later there would be shame. Because our secret would not last long." He touched her cheek. "How long would you remain in love with me, while filled with shame?"

She pulled away from him and crossed her arms tightly, so tightly it was hard to breathe. Or maybe the air had changed, becoming thick and unpalatable, or maybe it was something else.

"And how would you feel if the day ever came when you came face-to-face with my wife, while you were my mistress?" he asked simply.

"Stop!" His words felt like a knife now, inside her heart.

"I told you once I respect you far too much to treat you the way other men treat women like Georgette de Labouche and Daisy Jones," he said softly. "Don't cry. My respect for you is no less than what you deserve. And what about Andrew? Good God, he is my friend. I respect and admire your father, Francesca. I could never betray him by using his daughter in such a manner."

Everything he said was right, which was why it hurt so much. "So where does that leave us?" she asked. "Where, Bragg? If I cannot let you divorce your wife and you will not make me your lover, then where do we go from here? And how do we get there?"

He stared, dropping her hand. And something impossibly sad crossed his face, filled his eyes. "I don't know. Our friendship is becoming an impossible one."

"No." It was a gasp, a horrified one.

He held her gaze, not speaking.

"Do not even think it!" He had *not* been about to suggest they end their friendship. "The one thing I refuse to do is lose you as a friend. It is simply not a possibility, Bragg!" she cried desperately.

"We shouldn't be alone," he said bluntly. "And you know it."

She stared, but he was not in focus. She realized that her vision was blurred from all her tears. "I had better go inside," she said stiffly. "Thank you for seeing me home."

He nodded and walked her to the front door, this time not touching her.

And when he was gone, Francesca stared blindly out a window at the deserted and snowy avenue, in the throes of sheer fear.

This could not be happening.

SUNDAY, FEBRUARY 16, 1902 — 9:00 A.M.

"Nuthin's changed," Joel Kennedy said with a scowl. "Ain't been no flood or hurricane."

They had just alighted from a cab and now stood in front of police headquarters, a squat brownstone building that Joel was clearly unhappy to see still standing. Mulberry Street was eerily deserted, but then, it was quite early on a Sunday morning and Francesca suspected that most hooks and crooks had been up into the wee hours of the morning the night before. Bragg's motorcar was not parked in front of the brownstone building. She was relieved.

What had happened between them the night before was terrifying. She could not face him just yet. It was still hard to think clearly; she only knew that she did love him and they would, somehow, find a solution to the terrible impasse they now found themselves in.

It *was* cold. Last night the temperature had apparently dropped to eight degrees above zero; today it remained about the same. "Let's get inside," Francesca said, shivering. "How do you like your new gloves and hat?" she asked.

As they walked past two uniformed policemen who seemed oblivious to them, Joel grinned. "Real leather an' lined with wool. I like 'em a lot, Miz Cahill. Thanks."

She smiled at him. "They're lined with cashmere," she said. Joel had been wearing rags on his hands. She'd sent one of the housemen out to buy him the hat and gloves.

"Cashmere?" His eyes widened to impossible dimensions. "No kiddin'? I thought cashmere was only for rich folk!"

"There's no law that I know of which bars you from wearing cashmere," Francesca said, smiling.

Inside the precinct station, it was as quiet as outside. Captain Shea was at the front desk, but he was reading a newspaper and sipping a mug of steaming coffee. Another officer whom she recognized but did not know was actually snoring as he dozed, sitting in a chair behind the front desk. Francesca realized she had never been down to headquarters this early on a Sunday. It was so *quiet*. Not only were no complaints being lodged, but there were no fisticuffs or disgruntled felons about, and the constant pinging of the telegraph was absent. She realized she had come to like the sound.

Shea saw her and put down his paper. "G'morning, Miz Cahill. What brings you downtown this early?" He was a black-haired fellow with graying temples and a pleasant smile. Francesca knew from her conversations with Bragg that Shea was actually honest. At one point, Bragg had considered promoting him—and appointing him chief of police. That would have been unheard of. In the end, he hadn't done so, admitting that Shea was just not strong enough for the job.

"I am on a case," Francesca said, walking up to the front desk. Actually, she was on two cases—Lucy's and Sarah's. Lucy's predicament seemed the more pressing, however, and that was where she would start. She wanted to dispatch the character who had accosted her as swiftly as possible, before any real harm was done.

"I thought so. Hey, Tom! Sleepyhead, wake up! C'mish's friend is here." He jabbed Tom in the ribs but smiled at Francesca. "Police c'missioner isn't here, Miz Cahill. But can we help?"

"I do hope so," she said, disappointed in spite of herself. An image of Bragg's hard expression the night before swept through her mind. She shoved it aside, as she simply had too much to do.

Besides, some people went to their graves without ever having found what she had found—which was the other half of her soul, a man who could complete her and make her whole.

"Is there any chance I can take at look at the Rogues' Gallery?" she asked, referring to the infamous mug book begun by an even more infamous—and crooked—earlier police chief, Thomas Byrnes. "I am afraid I can't divulge any information, as the relationship between myself and my client is a confidential one, but Bragg has said that he does not mind." She added for effect, "I had dinner with him and his entire family last night."

"Why don't I set you up somewhere nice an' private, say the conference room? An' you can take all the time you need to look at the book."

Francesca thanked him, then winked at Joel when Shea wasn't looking. Thank God there was a case to solve; otherwise she might be in bed, brooding.

A few moments later, Francesca and Joel were seated at

a long conference table in the room opposite Bragg's office. His door was solidly closed. The upper half was a heavy frosted glass. Francesca knew he wasn't there; still, she found herself staring at his door, as if expecting him to walk out at any moment.

Shea entered, the mug book in his hands. "Here it is," he said cheerfully. "Hope this helps. You need anything, just holler."

"Thank you," Francesca said. When he was gone, she opened the book, Joel standing by her shoulder.

"What did you say he looked like?" Joel asked. Francesca had already filled him in on most, but not all, of the details of what had happened. He did not know, however, that Lucy Savage had been accosted and that she was Bragg's sister.

"He is of medium build, but quite husky. His hair is dark and long; his eyes are blue. And there is a small scar on his right cheek." Small, but it had been ugly.

"Don't ring no bells," Joel remarked cheerfully, for he was also happy to be back at work again. They began carefully studying each page of the book. Each photograph was accompanied by the culprit's name and a brief description of his or her vice. There were cutpurses and sandbaggers, cracksmen and moll buzzers, and almost every woman identified by the book was a shoplifter. They were all shady characters indeed. Francesca turned the page—and froze.

There he was.

" 'Joseph Craddock, rowdy, sharper, and rounder,' " Francesca read aloud on a long breath.

"That's him? That's the thug?" Joel asked with excitement.

"It most certainly is, only here he does not have his scar," Francesca said, equally excited.

"Should I put the word out on the streets?"

"Absolutely." Francesca faced him, leaving the book open. "Let's offer a small reward for anyone who has information as to where he can be located. Say fifty dollars?"

Joel's eyes widened. "That ain't no small reward!" he exclaimed.

She patted his dark head. "I do want results. I must speak

with this crook, sooner rather than later. I am sure he will approach my client again, Joel, but what if it isn't for a few days? Then we shall lose valuable time."

He shook his head, grimacing. "I can't let you throw away good money like that. Offer twenty, lady. It'll do just as good."

"Just as fine," she corrected gently. Still, she remained thrilled. Then she sobered. "Joel, what exactly is a rowdy, sharper, and rounder?"

He laughed. "A rowdy's lots of trouble. Probably been busted for fightin', drinkin', bullyin', an' all that. Sharper is a real crook, someone good at the swindle and the con. As for a rounder, that just means he's been at it again and again."

"A repeat offender," Francesca murmured. "Let's find out if he has been in jail more than the one time that I know of." She stood.

Joel followed her downstairs. "Someone like that been in the calaboose more 'n once, I'd bet."

"I think so, too. I hope there is a big fat juicy file on him." She smiled at the thought as she hurried to the front desk, the book tucked under her arm. "I do hope you can help, Captain," she said with a wide smile. "For we have found our man."

"Let's see what you got," Shea said amiably, setting the paperwork he was now involved in aside.

Francesca laid the mug book on the counter and opened it to the page with Craddock's picture. The sergeant, Tom, came over curiously. "That's the culprit. Craddock. Joseph Craddock. Do you know of him? Can I see if there is a file upon him?"

"Hmm, he looks somewhat familiar, but after a few years on the job, they all start to look alike, don't they, Tom?"

"He's as mean as the rest," Tom agreed. "Name is familiar, though. I'll bet we got a file on him a mile wide."

"Could you check?" Francesca asked eagerly.

Tom looked at Shea, who nodded. Then the taller police officer left—only to return within a moment, a folder in hand. "We got him, all right." He laid the folder on the desk and said, "I glanced at it. He got sent up to Kendall for extortion. But he's been in and out of the Tombs a dozen times. Drunk 'n' disorderly, fistfighting, mostly. Still, he was charged with murder once. See?" He pointed at the page and Francesca did see. Someone named Lester Parridy had been strangled to death, and there had been a trial—the charges had been dropped.

"Lots of civvy complaints against him, too. Some ladies been scared by him, it seems. Here's one, Mrs. Van Arke. But she dropped her complaint an' we dropped the charges then, too."

"The complaint was blackmail," Francesca breathed. Extortion, blackmail, murder. She shivered. Was Lucy's plight far worse than it seemed?

"Yep. Just two years ago."

Francesca saw that the Van Arke file had been opened in April of 1900 and closed the following month. The woman's address glared up at her—No. 250 Fifth Avenue. That would be an older home, far downtown, now swallowed up by a neighborhood of department stores and specialty shops. "When was Craddock released from Fort Kendall?" Francesca asked.

"Looks like he got out in '96." Shea blinked. "He didn't go in until '88. They sendin' them up for six years now for extortion, Tom?"

"Musta been a lot more than extortion."

"Either that or he was a real bad boy up there in the hold," Shea said, shaking his head.

"Can I copy this file?" Francesca asked. There was just too much valuable information. "And is that his last known address? Eighteen Allen Street?"

Shea had opened his mouth, as if to agree, when he blinked, stiffened, and became oddly still.

Francesca felt a breath on her neck, and she quickly turned.

Brendan Farr, New York City's newest chief of police, smiled at her. It did not reach his iron-gray eyes.

"Chief," she heard herself gasp, taking a step back, as he

stood so closely to her. And then she smiled, but inwardly she tensed. "Goood morning," she somehow said.

Farr continued to smile, his gaze moving slowly, leisurely, past her. It fell on the open mug book and then on the equally open file. "Good morning, Miss Cahill. My, it is a surprise to see you here at headquarters on such a beautiful Sabbath morning." He now gave her the same slow and careful scrutiny, but this time it was insulting, the once-over a man who is not a gentleman gives to a woman who is not a lady.

She swallowed and told herself that she could manage this man and that she did not need to be intimidated. Nevertheless, he unnerved her. "I am waiting for the commissioner," she lied. "And I was chatting with your men." She tried out another false smile.

It had no effect. "I see that." He was a very tall man, in his late forties, with a strong, solid build and hair as gray as his eyes. He walked past her and looked at the mug book and then at the file. "I do believe you are studying police files, Miss Cahill."

Francesca glanced nervously at Shea. "I am on a case, and I have asked for some help. I hope that was all right?" She smiled yet again. How ingratiating could she be?

He snapped the book closed and then the folder. "I am afraid it is not all right, Miss Cahill. Police affairs are exactly that—police affairs."

She was so stiff, a pain began going up and down her neck. "My business is not police affairs. I have a client who has requested my services."

He smiled at her—it was not pleasant. "And I have a police force to run. There are rules. Rules and regulations. In any case, police files are confidential and not available to the public." He stared. "Do I make myself clear?"

She nodded. "I am sorry if I have overstepped my bounds. I did not know."

"Now you do know." He smiled at her, the same mirthless smile that failed to reach his eyes. "Perhaps your client might better direct his or her requests to the police," he said softly.

Francesca could not think of a good reply. "I shall suggest it."

"Good."

"Sir?" Shea said nervously. "She's a close friend of the c'mish, an' he lets her do as she wants around here."

Francesca winced. Oh, how bad did that sound!

"I am well aware of just how close Miss Cahill is to our commissioner," Farr remarked suavely. Was there an innuendo there? Francesca thought so. Worse, she did not think Farr the kind of man to miss a single trick. "Nevertheless, rules are rules, and we do not share our information with civilians, Shea."

"Yes, sir. I'm sorry, sir," Shea said, as if he were in the military.

"Do not let it happen again." Farr gave him a chilling look before sending an identical glance at Tom. "Suspensions will be in order next time." He nodded at Francesca. "Good day, Miss Cahill."

There was no mistake about it; he was suggesting—strongly—that she leave.

"Good day," she said, and then she tensed again as he took the folder and tucked it under his arm and walked away. She glanced at Joel, unhappily surprised, then looked at Shea and Tom with real dismay. "I am so sorry," she said.

Shea flushed now. "Don't worry about it, Miz Cahill. I got work to do." He turned away.

She felt like a pariah. And then she felt eyes on her from behind.

She knew and she slowly turned around.

Bragg stood in his dark brown greatcoat by the double front doors, unmoving. She wondered how long he had been standing there and how much he had heard. She was vastly relieved to see him, in spite of the terrible night before. But she did not smile, as she could not.

He started forward, unsmiling as well. "Good morning."

"Good morning. Bragg, I may have gotten Shea and Tom in some trouble." She searched his eyes for a sign that he had had a change of heart—that he loved her far too much to ever consider ending their friendship. But he was too grim. Her heart sank with dismay.

He also looked as if he had been up most of the night, tossing and turning.

"So I heard," he said quietly.

"But you will protect them, won't you?" she asked quietly, quickly.

"I am not intending to be Farr's nanny. He runs this department; I oversee it," Bragg said. "It is important that he rule and regulate the men."

Francesca understood but was dismayed and appalled. "I don't trust him."

"It's not your place to trust him or mistrust him," Bragg said. "And frankly, he is right. No other civilian could walk in here and charm my men in order to gain access to our files." He did not look very happy now, and Francesca knew he was blaming himself.

"I didn't realize you would mind."

"There are rules, Francesca," he said tiredly.

She felt like she was losing him. But surely that could not be! "I'm sorry." She hesitated, then said, "But this hasn't been all bad. We got Randall's killer and the Cross Murderer. Not to mention the fact that we found Jonny Burton alive."

"I know," he said, softening, and his gaze moved slowly over her face. "But there are rules—and we have both been breaking them," he said. He lowered his voice, so only Joel could overhear. "A consequence of our *friendship*."

She stared, dismayed.

He stared back. And as softly, he said, "How are you?"

"Not all that well," she whispered. "And you?"

"I have hardly slept," he said, sending her a potent glance. "Sleep eludes me now. I hate fighting with you, Francesca."

"Then let's never fight again," she whispered.

He smiled just a little and finally turned to Joel. "Hey, kid," he said.

Joel did not even attempt to smile at him. He sent him a black look.

"I will not always be a copper, you know," Bragg said.

"But you're the king of them now, ain't you?" Joel glared. Having been in trouble with the police for most of his life, he was hardly fond of anyone associated with the leather-heads.

Francesca sighed. "One day, I will tell you about the kind of lawyer Bragg was before he became police commissioner," she said. "And you might change your opinion of him."

Joel shrugged.

Bragg was regarding her. "So you are after one Joseph Craddock," he said flatly. "A man who spent eight years in prison here in New York State."

"You heard?"

He nodded. "He doesn't sound like a savory sort, Francesca."

"I'm afraid he isn't," she said. "But he is most definitely the man I saw accosting Lucy last night."

Bragg walked over to the desk. "When Farr is finished with the Craddock file, put it on my desk," he said.

"Aye-aye, C'mish," Shea said instantly.

When Shea had walked away, they stepped closer to each other. "Craddock may have blackmailed a woman two years ago," Francesca said in a low, hushed tone.

"Is this what you think? That he is blackmailing my sister?" Bragg returned as quietly.

She considered the question. "I don't know. But your family *is* very wealthy, and it is no secret."

Their gazes met. After a moment, Bragg spoke. "So that does beg the question—what is Lucy hiding?"

Francesca looked at him. "I don't know. But perhaps that is what we must find out."

Francesca arrived at the West Side Channing home alone. She had sent Joel off to spread word of the reward she was offering, while she had gone to Wells Fargo to send a telegram to the warden at Fort Kendall. She fervently hoped that she would hear from him later that day or early on Monday. And if he did not reply, then she would have to go to the

Kendall prison herself and meet him directly. She had already learned it was about eight hours north of the city by train, on the Albany route.

Evan's coach was parked outside the house in the drive. As Francesca paid her cabbie, she was surprised. Then she thought about the fact that last night her brother had not been able to tell Sarah that he wished to end their engagement. She wondered if Sarah would be up to receiving him now.

Francesca was ushered into the house immediately, and she saw her brother pacing in a salon adjacent to the hall—the one with the bear head rugs and gilded furniture. "Evan?"

He halted upon seeing her. "Good morning, Fran."

Her brief smile faded; he was so grim. She walked over to him, lowering her voice. "Have you seen Sarah? How is she? What happened last night?"

He sighed, his hands in the pockets of his brown tweed sack jacket. He appeared tired. "She seemed very weak last night, Fran," he said with genuine concern. "Rourke wound up carrying her into the house and up to her bed. I stayed, of course, and Finney arrived. Her fever was a hundred and one."

Francesca went rigid with worry and surprise. "That is very high!"

"I know. Finney said it is probably a severe case of the flu."

"And what did Rourke say?"

"Not much. Which worries me, I confess."

She plucked his sleeve. "You do care about Sarah."

"Not that way, Fran. She is a nice girl, and the kind that would not even harm a fly. I hope she is not seriously ill."

Their gazes locked. The flu could kill its victims, especially the very young or the aged or infirm. Francesca hadn't thought of Sarah as being infirm, but now she recalled Rourke exclaiming that she was far too thin, that she was all bones.

"What brings you here?" Evan asked.

"The case," Francesca returned. "Let's talk for a moment, please."

He nodded and they sat down in a pair of facing chairs.

"Can you think of any young woman who, before your engagement, seemed especially enamored of you? Was any particular young lady trying harder than the others to win your heart—and your hand?"

He sighed. "Actually, after you asked me this last night, I have been thinking about it. I cannot imagine any young lady in our set doing such a thing. If you want to know the truth, I think it is far more likely that the vandal was striking out at Bartolla. She is simply the most beautiful and fascinating woman in the city, and I see the way all men hope to attain her notice and admiration. She is not a young virginal lady, looking for marriage. Someone, perhaps another woman, might have been jilted because of her, and decided now to strike back. Or maybe an old lover of hers has just realized she is in town? There are many possibilities here," Evan said.

"Yes, there are," Francesca agreed. "I suppose I must speak with Bartolla, again, although she hardly seems interested in helping solve this case. And of course, I do wish to see Sarah." Francesca got to her feet. "Evan? Have you changed your mind about leaving the company and moving out of the house?" she asked hopefully.

His expression hardened. "I did not sleep last night. That is, I packed most of my bags, and they are in my front hall. After I leave here, I am picking them up and taking a room at the Fifth Avenue Hotel," he said. "So, no, I have hardly changed my mind."

In a way, a terrible way, she was proud of him, because what Andrew was doing—and the way he was doing it— was so wrong. But she hated thinking ill in any way of her father, for he was her favorite person in the world, or at least, he had been—until Bragg. She sighed, resigned, when footsteps sounded on the stairs.

As one, brother and sister turned. Rourke was trotting down the stairs, looking somewhat disheveled, as if he had had a restless night. His tie was askew, his suit jacket open, and he had a day's growth on his face. He carried a medical

bag that was worn and shabby—Francesca suspected he had
gotten it secondhand. Still, he was an extremely attractive
man. Although he looked so much like Bragg, in a way he
reminded her of Hart. Had he not been carrying his satchel,
one might assume him to be a riverboat gambler, returning
after a long and fruitful night.

Evan leaned close. "Now *he* is available, and he is four
years older than you," he whispered fervently in her ear.
"Now, is that not perfect?"

Francesca stabbed her heel on his instep.

He yelped.

Rourke smiled at them both. "It's nice to see that our
family is not alone in behaving like a pack of cats and dogs.
Good morning."

Francesca smiled, but it was brief. "How is she?"

"She is better," he said. "Her fever is down to just under
a hundred. She is sleeping comfortably now."

"That is good news!" Francesca exclaimed.

"Well, it could be worse. Her fever was too high last night
for comfort. Perhaps Finney is right and it is merely a cold.
Fortunately it is not her lungs—I woke her to check them
again. They are clear."

"You feared pneumonia?" Francesca asked with dread.

"She told me her back hurt, and it was my first thought.
In any case, she should rest. And she certainly should not
be burdened with anything right now." He did frown thoughtfully.

"What is it?" Francesca asked.

"Miss Channing has a large bruise on her upper arm. Her
mother has no idea of how she got it."

Francesca blinked. Last night Sarah had been wearing
sleeves. "Surely she must have had an accident."

Rourke turned his amber eyes on her. They were flecked
with light gold. "It looks to me as if someone grabbed her
in an excessively brutal manner."

Francesca was stunned. "Well, there must be a simple explanation; did you ask Sarah?"

"She was sleeping so soundly this morning when I arrived

that I had no wish to awaken her." He glanced at Evan. "You can go up, Cahill, if you wish to sit and hold your fiancée's hand."

"If she's asleep, I shall not disturb her," Evan returned.

Rourke stared at him. It was impossible to read his eyes or fathom his expression. But Francesca felt that there was censure there, somewhere, lurking beneath the surface.

Francesca was surprised when Rourke glanced at her and said, "I stole down to her studio last night. Lucy is right. She is rather brilliant, for such a tiny girl."

"Yes, she is, and I am glad you think so," Francesca said, when Bartolla appeared on the stairs behind them, smiling. She was wearing an extremely fitted royal blue brocade suit and skirt, trimmed with paler blue fox at the cuffs and hem. A trio of sapphires winked from her throat. Her hair had been perfectly waved, with a few auburn tendrils escaping to wisp sensually about her face.

Francesca introduced Rourke. "This is Bragg's brother Rourke, and this is the Countess Benevente."

Bartolla shook her head. "You look so much like your brother! Of course, there is a difference, but it is obvious you are brothers—or twins."

"We only look alike," Rourke assured her with a twinkle in his eye. He lifted her hand to his lips and kissed it gallantly. "Rest assured I am far more clever, far more interesting, and far more amoral."

Bartolla laughed. "Then I am truly delighted to make your acquaintance, as morality is a stiff bore."

"It is indeed," he said, his eyes sparkling with amusement and admiration. "Too bad you did not join us last night."

"I am afraid I had other plans," Bartolla said. In truth, she had not been invited.

"I vow that we shall not exclude you from our next family supper," Rourke declared.

Bartolla laughed again.

Evan stepped over to her, clearing his throat.

She instantly turned, taking his hand, and from the way their gazes met, it was as if everyone else had disappeared.

"How is Sarah this morning?" she asked earnestly.

"Better, fortunately," Evan said, gazing intently at her now. Francesca glanced down and saw him squeeze her hand.

She froze, in that instant wondering if they were lovers. She glanced at Rourke and knew he was wondering the exact same thing.

Bartolla stepped away from Evan and said breezily, "I think I shall buy Sarah a gift. Something to cheer her up. She has been far too distressed ever since she found her studio vandalized. Hmm. I wager an art book would be just the thing to keep an artist preoccupied in bed."

"I can think of better diversions for one confined to a bed," Rourke murmured.

Bartolla glanced at him. "And so can I. But then, I am a widow, while Sarah is not yet a bride."

"Ah, I do offer my condolences, Countess," Rourke said, and it was obvious he hardly regretted the count's death.

"Thank you."

"Bartolla is newly arrived here in the city," Evan said, stepping forward and between them. "I have been showing her the town. With Sarah, of course."

"Of course," Rourke said dryly.

"An art book is a wonderful idea," Francesca cut in. Everyone looked at her. She knew that they could not be lovers. Evan would not abuse his fiancée so, by cuckolding her with her cousin.

Still, she knew firsthand how passion could break free of the bonds of morality and convention. And both Bartolla and Evan were far too experienced in matters of the heart.

"My carriage is outside," Evan said, speaking only to Bartolla. "I can give you a lift downtown, if you like."

"I would love a lift," Bartolla said with an expansive wave of her hand, but she never took her eyes from his face. "And I happen to be ready, as I do have an appointment this morning."

It was not even eleven. Francesca wondered what kind of appointment Bartolla could possibly have on a Sunday morning, especially as she knew that she preferred not to arise, much less leave the house, until eleven. "Bartolla? I need to speak with you for a moment before you go."

Bartolla seemed startled, as if she had forgotten Francesca's presence. "Oh! I hope this isn't about Sarah's studio?"

"It is."

"Don't tell me you still think someone deliberately damaged my portrait—and this is about me?" she exclaimed, clearly amused.

"It's a possibility," Francesca said. "One we must consider. And the portrait was slashed to ribbons—viciously, I might add."

"My dear, I hardly care." She laughed.

"Bartolla." Evan touched her arm. "Maybe you should be worried—maybe the vandal was striking out at you and not at Sarah. I think that is far more likely. I can wait until you have had a chance to speak with Francesca."

"But I do have an appointment," she said lightly. "I must get to midtown. Evan dear, do not worry about me!"

"Of course I worry," he said huskily. "I should hate to see anything ill befall you—or Sarah," he added quickly.

Rourke made an insulting sound.

Evan gave him a very cool look.

"I am leaving," Rourke said. "And as I am going uptown to Hart's, I will not offer the countess a ride. It was a pleasure, madam."

"Please, do call me Bartolla; all of my friends do."

He lifted her hand again. "I am sure our paths shall cross again, Bartolla." He smiled at Francesca. "Good luck, Miss Cahill. Do keep my feckless brother out of harm's way." He chuckled, then nodded at Evan and strode out.

When he was gone, Francesca took Bartolla's hand. "Give me just a moment, please," she said, realizing that with Bartolla being so difficult, she would have to begin the interview alone—and maybe even conclude it that way, too.

"I am running late already," Bartolla said pleasantly, but it was clear she intended to remain as stubborn as a mule.

"Just one moment," Francesca said, feeling pressured to get right to the point. "Do you have enemies?" she asked.

Bartolla seemed amused. "Who does not?"

"Seriously, Bartolla. Please, do take this seriously."

"Yes, Francesca, of course I have enemies."

"Who are they? I need names," Francesca said.

Bartolla sighed. "Do you want the truth?"

She nodded.

"Before I married the count, when I was only sixteen, I came out here in the city. I stole a dozen young men from their sweethearts." Bartolla shook her head. "I was rather a flirt, as a young girl," she said. "And to make matters even worse, I broke too many young male hearts to even count."

"Could any of these women—"

"I don't know," Bartolla said, interrupting. "But if you want to know who really hates me, why, it is the count's family."

Francesca was thinking about the women who might still be in the city hating Bartolla for ruining their prospects. And what about all of those young men whom she had flirted with and left? "But they are all abroad, are they not?"

"His sons live in Paris and Rome. But his daughter lives right here in New York, with her three spoiled brats." Bartolla smiled and it wasn't pleasant.

"What is her name?" Francesca cried eagerly.

"Jane Van Arke," Bartolla said.

Ten

Francesca was about to leave when Bragg stepped past a doorman and into the house. She saw him, not really surprised, and hesitated.

"What is it?" he asked, instantly noting her agitation.

That decided her. She rushed to him. "Bartolla has just left. But I spoke with her," she said breathlessly.

"And I can see that she has given you a lead," he said, his gaze holding hers.

Francesca inhaled and spoke in a rush. "Jane Van Arke lodged a formal complaint against Craddock in April of 1900!" Francesca cried. "But she changed her mind a month later, and the complaint was dismissed."

"And?" He raised both brows.

"Jane Van Arke is Bartolla's stepdaughter—and despises her with a vengeance."

Bragg stared. It was a moment before he spoke. "I seem to be missing something. Are you thinking that Jane Van Arke is behind the vandalism—and that she hired Craddock?"

Francesca wrung her hands. "I don't know what to think. But this is an amazing coincidence."

He was reflective. "Let me back up for a moment. Craddock is a criminal with a record. He is violent, and blackmail is the name of his game. He probably murdered Lester Parridy—but it could not be proved. However, Parridy was another shady sort, and no one really cared."

"You've read the file!"

"I have. Let me continue. Mrs. Van Arke—Bartolla's stepdaughter—was probably a victim of his blackmail. Of course, that is an assumption. She claimed as much initially, then withdrew and claimed she had been mistaken."

"It is rather hard to mistake a blackmailer," Francesca groused.

"I would think so." Briefly he smiled at her.

As briefly, she smiled back.

Now he frowned. "Could it be a coincidence that Craddock was blackmailing Jane Van Arke, who so dislikes Bartolla that she might wish to hurt her, while he is now victimizing my sister?"

"I have no idea," Francesca said. "My mind is still spinning from learning all of this. But I do think we should interview Mrs. Van Arke as soon as possible."

He glanced at his pocket watch. "This is a very good time to try. I doubt she has left the house yet for the day."

Eagerness filled her. "Then let's go."

But he made no move to go. "There is more."

"More?" Francesca had been about to rush out the front door, but she halted.

Bragg was grim. "Lucy's husband was a prisoner at Fort Kendall, in 1890," he said.

Francesca saw Bragg's Daimler parked on the avenue. Beyond it was Central Park, which on this side of the city was mostly deserted, and eerily so. "I simply don't understand," she said.

He had his hand on her back, using a slight pressure to guide her down the walk. "He was erroneously incarcerated, Francesca, but he did do time before he escaped."

"He escaped prison?" She halted, facing him.

Bragg nodded. "He was formally pardoned by the governor in 1899."

She was reeling. "Her husband—"

"His name is Shoz."

"Shoz—this must have something to do with him!"

"I am thinking so," he said gravely. "Shoz is the kind of man to have enemies, and the fact that they were in prison together is simply too coincidental."

They shared a look. Francesca felt as if someone had taken a plywood board and struck her with it. "So maybe this is not about blackmail," she finally said. "Maybe it is about revenge."

He nodded as he opened the side door of the Daimler for her, but she made no move to get in. "It is time for Lucy to come clean," he remarked.

"She won't," Francesca said, feeling certain of it.

He smiled ruefully. "So you have already learned that she is more stubborn than you?"

Francesca almost smiled in return. "It is fairly obvious."

"A trip to Fort Kendall is in order," Bragg said. He gestured at the car. When she slid in, he handed her a pair of goggles and walked around the front of the motorcar.

Disturbed but also excited at the prospect of traveling up to the prison with him, she watched him crank it up. "Shall I try to speak with Lucy, or shall you?"

He glanced up as the engine roared to life. "You might have the opportunity tonight."

She froze.

Guilt must have been written all over her face, because he said, approaching his side of the motorcar, "I am aware of your mother's dinner party tonight."

The one that was on account of Calder Hart, the one he was not invited to. Francesca did not know what to say. Bragg moved around the roadster and climbed into the driver's seat. "Were you going to mention it to me?"

"I hadn't even thought about it," she lied nervously. "Mama refuses to let me off the hook, I must attend, and I do wish you were coming."

"Calder is the catch about town, is he not?"

"Not for me!" she cried earnestly. "You know that!"

He suddenly sighed, the sound heavy. And he looked at her. "You know as well as I that life is hardly sugar candy and rainbows," he said grimly.

Their gazes locked. Francesca recalled every single terrible word they had exchanged the night before. She gripped his hand impulsively. He returned the pressure of her palm but did not speak, and she knew he was also thinking about their conversation of last night.

"I believe in happy endings," she said softly. "I really do."

He smiled a little. "I know you do," he said.

It was brilliantly sunny—and still terribly cold out. Because of the sun, which was shining almost directly in her eyes, Francesca did not instantly recognize the man who stepped out from between two carriages, approaching them. Francesca felt Bragg stiffen, and then, as he paused before her car door, she recognized the man and became rigid, too.

It was Arthur Kurland, the obnoxious reporter from *The Sun.*

Francesca slipped her hand free of Bragg's.

Kurland's eyes seemed to follow her movement. Then he looked up from the stick shift between them and her lap, where her left hand now lay. "My, my. Imagine my surprise at finding you both here, at the Channings'. " He smiled, his hands in his pockets, shivering.

"We were just leaving," Bragg said, pushing the stick into gear.

But Kurland did not move away from the roadster. "Surely you are working on another case. Or is this a social occasion, a pleasant Sunday afternoon drive?"

Francesca was filled with tension. She had the worst feeling that Kurland not only knew that she and Bragg were fond of each other, but he also knew about Bragg's marital state.

"You are losing your ability to sniff out news," Bragg said. "Yes, we are investigating a case. Francesca is with me as Miss Channing is affianced to her brother."

"Did something happen to Miss Channing?" Kurland asked, wide-eyed with interest.

"Her studio was broken into," Bragg said. "Good day, Kurland." He drove away from the curb.

Francesca twisted to watch Kurland, who stood at the curb, scribbling on a notepad. She saw him turn and hurry toward the Channing house.

She was filled with dread. She turned, facing Bragg. "He saw us holding hands."

Bragg was grim. "You are right."

* * *

The Van Arke home was in the Georgian style and probably dated to the first decades after the last turn of the century. Francesca and Bragg hurried up the walk, where he used the door's bell. Francesca studied him and knew he was still disturbed by everything that had transpired last night.

The door was opened, and a manservant stood there. Bragg introduced them both, presenting himself in his official capacity. They were ushered inside and told that Mrs. Van Arke would be told that they were waiting. No mention was made of Mr. Van Arke.

The parlor was pleasant. One glance told Francesca that the Count Benevente's daughter was well-to-do but not wealthy. She was a step above most gentry, not more.

"Isn't Bartolla very wealthy?" Francesca asked Bragg in a whisper.

"It seems so."

"Did the count—Mrs. Van Arke's father—leave her everything?"

"I do not know. Appearances can be deceiving," he returned softly.

She nodded and then turned as steps and rustling silk could be heard behind her.

An attractive woman with olive skin and dark blond hair stood on the threshold, smiling uncertainly and perhaps even anxiously. "Commissioner?"

Bragg hurried forward. "Mrs. Van Arke, thank you very much for taking the time to see myself and Miss Cahill."

She extracted her hand from his and glanced at Francesca, clearly confused. "It is hardly common for me to have the police commissioner of this city in my salon," she said in a husky voice. Although she was an Italian, the only accent that was discernible was a British one, which told Francesca that she had been educated in Great Britain. Francesca thought that she was in her early thirties.

"And I am afraid we are here on official police business," Bragg said.

Mrs. Van Arke smiled, and it was strained. She folded her

arms across her ample bosom but did not move into the room.

When she did not ask what that business was, Bragg glanced at Francesca, then said, "When was the last time you were in contact with Joseph Craddock?"

Her expression did not change. "I beg your pardon?"

He repeated the question while Francesca wondered at her response.

"I am afraid I do not know who you are talking about," she said tersely.

"Perhaps your memory is merely escaping you," Bragg said kindly. Francesca felt certain that not only did Mrs. Van Arke recall Craddock, but she also wasn't all that surprised by their questions about him. "I do believe a Jane Van Arke of Number Two-fifty Fifth Avenue filed a complaint against Joseph Craddock on April the eighth, 1900," he said.

She stared. And then, dropping her eyes, she said, "You are referring to something in my past. I made a mistake."

"Yes, for you dropped the complaint one month later," Bragg said.

Jane Van Arke went to the pale blue silk sofa, which almost matched her dress, where she sat down. "I told you, it was a mistake."

Bragg moved to the sofa. "Mrs. Van Arke, please help us. We are afraid that another woman is currently in a similar predicament."

She paled. "There is another young woman . . . He is blackmailing a young woman?"

"A young woman with three small children," Francesca said gravely, even though they weren't certain. "Worse, he has accosted her."

"I have two sons," Jane Van Arke suddenly said. She stood, wringing her hands. "They are twelve and fourteen now, but then they were two years younger, and he made it very clear he would harm them if I did not simply pay him off and drop my complaint."

Bragg laid his palm on her shoulder. "Thank you, Mrs. Van Arke. Will you give us a complete statement?"

She turned wide eyes upon him. "I don't know."

"It will be classified. He will never know you were the one to give us our information," Bragg said.

She hesitated, darted a look at Francesca, and said, "There is nothing more to say."

Francesca said, "Mrs. Van Arke? You are clearly afraid of Craddock. Does this mean that you have not seen him in two years?"

She hesitated again. Then she shook her head.

"When was the last time you saw him?" Francesca asked softly but persistently.

She sighed and sat abruptly down. "I don't know." She did not look at either of them now.

Francesca met Bragg's stare. The woman was lying—or hiding something.

"It would be very helpful if you could tell us," Bragg said.

"I don't know!" She stood. "He is a terrible man. Evil. He has no conscience. I was afraid for my sons. I do not want him back in my life!"

"Is he still extorting money from you?" Bragg asked.

She stared at him, then shook her head.

Francesca had the awful feeling that he was. "Mrs. Van Arke? Do you know who would want to hurt Bartolla Benevente?"

Jane Van Arke whirled. "I beg your pardon?"

"We think your stepmother might be in danger," Francesca said.

Jane Van Arke flushed. "I see. Craddock is blackmailing her!"

Francesca looked at Bragg. Their gazes locked. Why hadn't they considered this possibility? Francesca went to the Italian woman and put her hand on her arm. "Poor Bartolla," she said, hoping to gain a response from the Italian woman.

Jane Van Arke gave her an incredulous look. "She is merely getting what she deserves."

Francesca almost winced; clearly Bartolla had not exaggerated when she said that her stepdaughter hated her. "Isn't that a bit excessive?" Francesca asked, after she and Bragg shared a look.

"Excessive? That tramp is the worst thing that ever happened to my father! She bled him for every penny he had, then did as she pleased behind his back—and he knew about her lovers! Oh, yes. The count was a brilliant man, until the end, and he knew his little American wife was a whore. That is what she is, a whore," Jane Van Arke cried passionately. "And I hope Craddock takes her for all that he can get."

Well, Francesca thought, at least they knew where Mrs. Van Arke stood as far as Bartolla went.

"Where were you Thursday night, between midnight and five A.M.?" Bragg asked quietly.

She started, as if she had forgotten his presence, and flushed. "Commissioner, excuse me. I did not mean to go on so. It's just that I adored my father, and it hurt me to see her using him the way that she did."

"I understand," Bragg said. "Thursday night, after midnight?" he prompted.

Her brows furrowed. "Why would it matter where I was that night?"

"Would you please answer the question?" he said, his tone extremely mild.

She glanced at Francesca and shrugged. "I was here, at home, asleep."

"Can Mr. Van Arke testify to that?"

"Can . . . what?" She straightened. "My husband is out of the country, Commissioner. He is in London and will not return for another month."

"Thank you," Bragg said.

Jane Van Arke glanced between Francesca and Bragg again, seeming bewildered. "You're welcome."

"I think that is all for now," Bragg said. He thanked her again for her time.

She walked them to the door. "There is one thing I don't understand," she said.

"What is that?"

"Why the two of you are here, asking me the same questions as that other gentleman?"

Francesca halted so quickly that Bragg smashed into her back. They both turned to face their hostess. "What gentleman?" she asked.

"Chief Farr."

SUNDAY, FEBRUARY 16, 1902 — JUST AFTER NOON
Francesca entered the house and heard her mother shouting. She froze.

Julia never shouted. She did not have to. Her will was iron and far too strong for anyone to resist her.

But she *was* shouting. Francesca had just heard her. She turned to look at Francis, the new doorman, who was pale and pretending to be deaf and a statue. "Francis? What is going on?"

He came to life. "Your parents, Miss Cahill. They have forgotten to shut the door."

She looked in the direction he indicated and realized they were in the salon at the opposite end of the hall. She knew instantly what they were arguing about. And that was another thing—her parents rarely argued.

Either Julia allowed Andrew to have his way, or he allowed her to do so.

They had to be arguing about Evan.

Gingerly, Francesca approached the open doors and, pausing on the threshold, saw her father standing with his arms akimbo, his back to a window. Julia confronted him. "This is your entire fault, Andrew," she said harshly, not shouting now. "You have done this. You have chased him out of the house—our house—my house! And I will not allow it!" And then she had shouted again.

"He cannot break off his engagement and leave the company and simply get away with it. It is utter disrespect!" Andrew returned harshly, but keeping his voice lowered. "We agreed on the engagement, Julia. You have been happy that our wayward son will finally have to become a man!" And *his* voice had verged upon a shout.

"I should not have agreed. I told you she was wrong for him. But oh, no, you did insist, and I stupidly let you have your way! I will not let Evan move out! He is my son—our son—how could you do this? *How?*"

Francesca gaped, as her mother seemed on the verge of tears. She never cried. In fact, Francesca had grown up assuming her mother did not have tear ducts.

"He did not give me a choice!" Andrew cried. "He marched into my office and began to threaten me. He threatened me, Julia! I know that you pretend he can do no wrong, but Evan is dissolute. Dissolute! He is the most irresponsible young man I have ever seen! Irresponsible and dissolute!"

"Don't you dare call him dissolute! And if he threatened you—" She stopped. "I am sure he did not mean it!" She was shouting now. "You have always disliked him!" Julia was furious. "You adore Francesca—she can catch a killer with a fry pan, and nothing comes of it! Oh, no, she makes the newspapers, and you are proud of her! And Connie, well, you are vastly fond of her—but then, she never does anything wrong, thank goodness. But Evan, why, as a child, Evan's grades were not high enough, his friends were not good enough, he could not throw a football far enough, and now he does not work hard or long enough. . . . My son is always failing!"

"That is because he is usually wrong. That is because he has no ambition. Good God, how can you be defending him now? Evan has two interests, period. Two vices! Cheap women and gaming. His standards of behavior are less than acceptable," Andrew finally shouted back. "And they always have been less than acceptable to me."

Francesca actually clapped her hands over her ears. "Stop! The two of you, please, stop!"

Neither one heard her. Julia pointed her finger at him. "I warn you, Andrew, if he leaves this house, then I shall, too."

"Mama!" Francesca gasped, rushing forward.

Andrew turned white with shock. And without another

word, he turned his back on his wife. A window faced him. But the draperies were drawn.

Francesca grasped Julia's hands and saw the tears in her mother's eyes. "Mama, come outside. Let's talk," she said, at the same time wanting to rush over to her father and hug him and reassure him that all would be well.

Julia nodded, casting an angry and tearful glance at Andrew's rigid back, and the moment they were in the hall, she collapsed on a tufted settee, set against one wall. "How could he do this? How could Andrew let Evan walk out?" She covered her face with her hands and her small shoulders shook.

And for one moment, Francesca was simply frozen, stunned to see her mother so distraught, in such emotional pain. Then she wrapped her arm around her and held her close. The two women were exactly the same size, with Julia being but a few pounds heavier. "Mama," Francesca said urgently, taking her hands. Julia looked up. "Evan threatened Father. It's true. And of course that wasn't right. But he was desperate to get out of his engagement, and can we truly blame him? When Father would not back down, Evan made good on his threats."

"I do not blame Evan for any of this," Julia said heavily.

"But don't blame Papa, either! He only wants Evan to cease gambling and begin a family."

"I know what your father wants," Julia said. "Your father wants Evan to be exactly like him, a one-woman man, a family man, a success, and a reformer."

Francesca stared.

"Evan is not like your father, Francesca. He is far more . . ." she hesitated, then said, "ebullient than your father ever was. He is young. He is only twenty-four going on twenty-five. This is my fault, too! I should have never agreed to this match." She closed her eyes tightly.

"Do not blame yourself for anything! After all, it is Evan's fault, too, for incurring those terrible debts. But let us look at the bright side," Francesca tried.

Julia opened her eyes. "There is no bright side."

"Yes, there is. I mean, what has happened is truly terrible, but it is certainly for the best that he and Sarah do not wed, even if it had to happen this way."

"I cannot lose him," Julia said, and Francesca knew she meant her son and not Andrew.

"Mama, you will not lose Evan! He loves you so! He even told me that he would never allow this argument to affect your relationship."

"He simply cannot move out, Francesca," Julia said, her eyes wide with fear.

"I tried to talk him out of it. He will not change his mind. I have never seen him so resolute," she said, and did not add "or so angry."

"But what if he never returns?" Julia asked.

Their gazes locked. "Of course he will come back. But for now, he feels he must make a stand. In a way, I am proud of him. Aren't you? He has never gone up against Father before."

"Proud of him? You are proud of him? How can you be proud of him when he has walked out on his familial obligations?" Julia gasped. "He has walked out on us!"

Francesca would not back down. "I am proud of him. Mama? Please, don't fight with Papa over this. He is hurt, too."

Julia seemed to be recovering her near iron composure. "I have just set a terrible example, Francesca. One never argues with one's spouse as I have done. There are other ways to achieve one's objectives."

Francesca blinked.

"One always gains more with honey than with vinegar." Julia appeared grimly worried now.

"Of course," Francesca said.

Julia gave her a look. "Of course, after twenty-four years, it is only human to make a mistake."

Francesca nodded. "And what about Papa?"

"He must go to Evan and tell him that we will end the engagement, but Evan shall agree to find another, suitable, bride."

Francesca stared. "He will never back down. Papa is a benevolent man, but beneath those whiskery cheeks is a will of steel."

"If he wishes for peace in this household, why, that is what he shall do," Julia said firmly, standing.

"He is never going to change his mind," Francesca said with dread.

Suddenly Andrew came out of the salon. He did not look at them as he approached and then passed them. He said, "Francis, my coat, hat, and walking stick."

Julia stood. Her tone was now calm. "Where are you going, Andrew? We have a conversation to finish."

For the first time that Francesca could ever recall, her father did not answer her mother. He stood before the front door, his back to them, patiently waiting for all that he had asked for—as if he had not heard them.

"Papa," Francesca whispered.

"Andrew! Where are you going?" Her tone became strident.

His shoulders tensed. He did not turn. "Out," he said.

Francis handed him his coat and hat and then, after he had donned his coat, his silver-headed cane.

"That is hardly an answer," Julia said, her eyes wide. "I apologize for how I have argued with you but not for what I have said. I must insist that we finish our conversation."

He turned. "There is no such thing as having a conversation with you, Julia, when the children are involved." He turned and walked out of the house.

Francesca was stunned. Had a two-by-four fallen from the sky and smashed down on her head she could not be more stunned. How could this be happening?

Julia whirled to her. "My home is falling apart!"

She fought for composure. "Mama, nothing is falling apart."

"My home, my family, my life is falling apart!" she cried. "Did you see that? He walked out on me! He has never treated me in such a manner."

"He's coming home. He'll be back. And then you can

calmly come to terms," Francesca tried valiantly. But she did not think they would come to terms on this particular subject. And then what?

Julia stared at her as if she had grown two heads. She began to shake. "Oh, dear God. Andrew has walked out on me. Evan has left home. Connie is in her rooms, refusing to come out. And you!" Julia leveled accusing eyes on her. "You fancy yourself in love with the commissioner, who is married. That I have had enough of, Miss Francesca Louise Cahill!"

Francesca dared not speak.

"Oh, I do know you! Once you have convinced yourself of something, there is no arguing with you! It is like taking a bone from a terrier! Well, I do have news for you! Just because you have decided he is 'the one,' that does not mean it is true! He is not 'the one,' obviously, as he has a wife, my dear. So I expect your nonsense to cease!"

Now was not the time to argue. "Mama, I know all about Bragg's wife."

Tears filled her eyes. Clearly she had not heard. "Oh, God. I so love Andrew. What have I done?"

Francesca tugged her hand. "Go after him. Now!"

Julia seemed about to do so, and then she stiffened. "I cannot," she said.

Bartolla entered the hotel lobby, unable to contain the soft thrill of anticipation that washed over her in warm, almost sexual waves. She glanced around and saw the restaurant where she was expected. Smiling, she crossed the parquet floors, which were covered with Persian rugs.

She was aware of heads turning her way as she passed. She knew she left a wake of interested men craning their necks to get a better look at her.

She had dressed with extreme care for her engagement. The royal blue suit exposed her trim waist, her womanly hips, and a larger expanse of bosom than was usual for day. She had found a new lip rouge at the Lord & Taylor store. Instead of the usual crimson, it was a darker, berry-colored stain. It did amazing things to her fair complexion, and it made her green eyes sparkle. But then, she had carefully applied kohl to the rims, and she had used it on the tips of her lashes as well.

A pale blue fox stole completed her look. She knew she looked elegant, sensual, and wealthy, but not in that order. In fact, she had to look twice at a young six-foot-tall bellman who ogled her as she passed. He was a superb male speci-men, all muscle, blond and blue-eyed, his features strong and pleasant. She sent him a soft smile. God, it had been too long!

She wished Evan Cahill were not engaged to her little cousin. But even if he were not, she could not lead him into her bed anyway—the stakes were simply too high. She felt faint now, thinking about him.

They hadn't even kissed.

And then there was all that Cahill money.

She was still smiling as she stepped into the dining room. She was purposefully late, a half an hour late, as she wished to be the one to make the entrance.

But her party was not present. Dismayed and then an-noyed, Bartolla was led to a small table set for two, where she took a seat, ordered a tea, and then tried to appear in-different to the fact that her grand entrance had been denied.

To amuse herself as she waited, she allowed several gen-tlemen to make eye contact with her, in spite of the fact that they were with their wives or sweethearts. One gentleman went so far as to drop his card by her feet as he walked by on his way to the men's cloakroom. Bartolla picked it up and tucked it into her bodice for use on a rainy afternoon.

She straightened.

Every male head in the restaurant turned.

Bartolla looked at Leigh Anne Bragg and sighed. Nothing had changed. The tiny woman remained impossibly beauti-ful—perhaps because she was as small as a child yet as curved as a woman. Or was it the flawless face with the huge green eyes that always seemed to look slightly bewildered and perfectly innocent? Added to those assets was a perfect rosebud mouth, which was perpetually swollen, and Bartolla knew exactly what men thought of when they looked at those lips. She sighed again. In spite of the fact that she was the tall one, the red-haired one, the statuesque one, Leigh Anne always turned more heads when they were together. Bartolla had decided it was her air of innocence that was the most enticing of all her charms.

Leigh Anne Bragg saw her from across the room and waved airily, smiling.

Bartolla smiled back and stood. She knew there was nothing innocent about Leigh Anne Bragg, but that only made her an extremely interesting woman. And the fact that Leigh Anne was so clever that she never confided anything about herself only made their friendship more challenging. Bartolla could never be certain what the other woman was really thinking or feeling, even though they had spent entire afternoons together last summer in the south of France, even though they had briefly run in the same circles in Venice and Florence.

Every man in the room turned to watch as the two extremely beautiful women hugged.

"You are more beautiful than ever!" Leigh Anne exclaimed as she took her seat. She wore a dark green suit that matched her eyes, trimmed with mink, which Bartolla suspected had cost her a small fortune, as the material was clearly Chinese silk and extremely expensive. Had Bartolola been wearing the same suit, she would have worn it with every emerald she owned. Leigh Anne wore a single diamond pendant on a black ribbon, which nestled in the hollow of her throat. Her long jet-black hair, which was thick and straight, fell unfashionably to her shoulder blades, like a cape. She had not one stitch of makeup on. She did not need any. Her lashes were thick and black, her cheeks tinged with pink, her lips ruby red. If Bartolla were less secure, she might hate and envy the other woman.

But Bartolla had never been jealous of another woman. She was simply not jealous by nature.

She saw that Leigh Anne wore her small engagement ring,

the diamond being perhaps a carat and a half. She also wore her wedding band.

"Thank you. Widowhood suits me, I am afraid," Bartolla laughed.

They both laughed.

"And you have not aged a day. You are as lovely as ever," Bartolla said, smiling.

Leigh Anne's face fell. She leaned anxiously forward. Bartolla felt rather certain that she had not one anxious bone in her entire body. "Do you think so? I have been so distressed, Bartolla, so terribly distressed, ever since I heard the news." Her eyes were wide and innocent and fearful all at once. Tears seemed to moisten them.

How delicious this is, Bartolla thought. It was going to be such an interesting winter. "Yes, I am so sorry."

"They say he is dying," Leigh Anne managed. "My father is dying, and my mother is beside herself, as is my sister." She cast her eyes down at the table. "If he dies, I shall be responsible for everyone."

Bartolla hadn't even known there was a sister, and she hadn't realized they were going to discuss Leigh Anne's father. "I am so sorry," she repeated, instantly bored. And then she had a thought. "I am sure your husband will feel some responsibility toward your family, dear."

Leigh Anne smiled brightly. "I do not know what I shall do," she said, looking on the verge of tears. Clearly she had no interest in biting the hook Bartolla had cast. But then she said, "And now there is this woman."

Bartolla straightened, trying to look surprised, inwardly amused. Oh, yes. It would be such an interesting winter, not that she had anything against Francesca Cahill. In fact, she truly liked her, as she was a very independent woman, just like Bartolla.

And just like Leigh Anne. "What woman?" She blinked.

"Why, Cecelia Thornton was the first one to tell me about her—and then you sent me that letter!" Leigh Anne took her hand. "Bartolla, thank you so. For being such a dear friend and for having that letter hand-delivered, or it might have been weeks before I learned of her."

"What else could I do?" Bartolla murmured.

Leigh Anne straightened now, placing both hands, apparently, on her lap. Her demeanor was demure. She murmured, glancing up from under her long lashes, "Now. You must tell me everything there is to know about this Francesca Cahill."

Eleven

Francesca was rigid with tension, which could not possibly be a result of nerves, as their supper guests arrived. Julia was greeting Rathe and Grace Bragg as they stepped into the hall, but Francesca stood at its far end, on the threshold of the salon where they would sip a cocktail before their meal. She had refused to dress with care for her mother's miserable effort at matchmaking; then, at the last moment, when it was far too late to tong her hair, she had had her maid, Bette, help her tear off an old and boring dove gray gown, replacing it with her new turquoise one, which she had worn the night before to the Plaza. She had managed to loosen her chignon and pull a few wisps of hair out so they feathered her face and neck. She had even dabbed rouge lightly on her lips. She knew damn well what she was doing. She wanted Hart to think her beautiful, as foolish as that desire might be.

Julia and Grace were embracing, but not warmly, and their exchange was both cautious and polite. Francesca could imagine why, for what common bond would a wealthy socialite share with a crusading suffragette? Rathe was saying that Hart and Rourke would be there at any moment, as Hart had gone to pick up Lucy at the Plaza and Rourke was checking up on Sarah Channing.

Her father had just come downstairs and he paused beside her. "You are so beautiful tonight, Francesca," he said, but he wasn't smiling. His eyes were sad.

Instantly, Francesca recalled the terrible argument she had witnessed that afternoon. She took his arm and kissed his cheek. "Please make up with Mama. Please."

He said, "This is not your affair, Francesca," quietly, but still, his words were a shock.

And he was wrong. "Papa! It is my affair! You are my parents—and Evan is my brother!"

He patted her shoulder, smiled firmly, and left her standing there. "Rathe! It is so good to see you!"

Rathe strode forward and the two men clasped hands, smiling now, their expressions as warm and friendly as their wives' had been cautious and wary. Suddenly Lucy stepped into the house, devastatingly beautiful in a Persian lamb coat that had been dyed burgundy to match her dress. Hart was behind her.

As she and Julia clasped hands and exchanged greetings, Hart's gaze found Francesca instantly. She felt more tension overcome her and she forgot to breathe.

His gaze found her, slid over her, and then he was smiling at Julia and murmuring a polite and charming greeting. Oddly, Francesca felt her cheeks warming. She quickly turned and stepped into the salon, needing to compose herself.

What was Julia thinking? Why couldn't she leave well enough alone? Why were reputable young women expected to marry and bear and raise children? How could she convince her mother to leave her alone!

Francesca crossed the opulent room, which was a smaller version of the grand salon, and she pushed open the terrace doors. It had remained frigidly cold all day, but she was somewhat numb inside of herself to begin with now, as she had decided not to think too much in order to get through the evening. So what difference would it make if she became numb on the outside as well? She felt a bit like a poor player in an even poorer stage drama. But far worse was the fact that, even with her emotions carefully on hold, she had a feeling of real dread, which she just could not deny. She simply knew that the evening was going to be a terrible fiasco.

She tried not to think about it.

She walked to the edge of the slate-floored terrace and

stared up at a sliver of moon. A million stars danced in the sky overhead—it was far too cold to snow. Which was fine— they'd had a record year for snowfall, anyway, and the winter had just begun.

She closed her eyes, shivering. Bragg was probably in his library at No. 11 Madison Square, alone, a glass of brandy at his elbow, immersed in police paperwork. Thinking about him now caused a hurtful pang in her heart. The girls were probably finishing up dinner in the kitchen, the table and floor a mess, unless Mrs. Flowers, the new nanny, had some- how taught Dot that throwing food was not a form of play. And was Katie still sulking? Had she begun to eat like a normal child? Peter would be at the sink, playing housemaid as well as cook. She smiled at that particular image, picturing him in an apron. How her heart wished that she were there. The scene was such a domestic one.

But she was not his wife, and now, it did not appear that she would ever be his wife.

An image of how she thought his wife looked flashed through her mind. A petite image of dark-haired perfection. She hugged herself harder. Any day now, Leigh Anne might appear in her . . . their . . . his . . . life.

"Are you insane?" Hart breathed against her neck.

His breath had been warm and soft. Francesca jumped, turning to face him, as he settled his black dinner jacket upon her bare shoulders, not even asking her if she wished for it or not. Briefly his large hands lingered as their gazes locked. And for one moment, as she looked into his eyes, she could not speak.

She pulled away. "I do hope not." She could not smile. She was dwarfed by his jacket, and it made her realize how big he was and how small she was in comparison. The satin lining was like silk upon her skin and remained warm from his body. Worse, his jacket smelled distinctly male. A touch of spice, a touch of wood, and some fine Scotch or Irish whiskey.

And something else, she decided, her heart hammering. It was easy to decide what that something was, given Hart's inclination to spend any and all extra time in a paramour's bed.

His eyes were moving over her features slowly, as if mesmerizing each and every one. "It is no more than ten degrees out tonight, Francesca. Why are you brooding outside?"

"I'm not really brooding," she said, a complete lie.

He tilted up her chin. "A book, remember? To me you are an open book, and I know you are out here testing the limits of your ability to perform mental gymnastics. Why not relax and enjoy the evening?"

She almost smiled, then caught herself. "Perhaps I don't wish to relax."

His black gaze was steady. "Do you wish for me to make an excuse and leave?" he asked quietly.

"No!" She hadn't even thought about it, and the vehemence of her reply surprised them both.

He grinned. "I am flattered."

"Don't be. But I do have a request."

His slashing brows lifted.

"Go inside and pour a double scotch. We'll share." That would be the best way to survive this night, she decided.

"Oh, ho," he said with another grin. "This shall be an interesting evening." He gave her a long and lazy look and strolled back into the salon.

Francesca felt frozen. And not from the cold. There had been amusement in his regard, and warmth—so much warmth—and something else. It was extremely hard to define what that something else was; after all, they were only friends and would never be anything more. How could a mere look from Calder Hart be so provocative? He had a way of looking at her that hinted at sexual speculation.

Did he even know what he was doing?

She shivered.

He returned, two glasses in hand. "This will warm you up," he said.

She was happily diverted and truly amazed. "How did you manage this? Did my mother see?" she asked, pleased. This would certainly improve the evening.

"She did, although she pretended not to," Hart said, clearly amused.

"You can do no wrong in her eyes," Francesca said, disbelieving, and then she took a sip. "Yummy," she sighed.

"I see I have thoroughly corrupted you. I am pleased," he laughed, also sipping his drink.

"Aren't you cold?" she asked, after taking a second drink, enjoying the scotch thoroughly.

"How can I be cold when I am under a sky filled with stars with such a beautiful woman beside me?" he asked with a quiet smile, one of contentment.

She felt her smile vanish.

His did, too. Then he sighed. "I am sorry, Francesca, but that kind of flattery, which I am used to giving to women without even a thought, simply formed itself."

"It was rather superficial." She hated being the recipient of the kind of thoughtless charm he directed upon the rest of her sex. "I wish you wouldn't treat me the way you treat other women."

"My dear, I hardly treat you the way I treat the rest of your gender." He gave her a significant look. "That issue we laid to rest on Saturday, I believe."

They had. For if he chose to treat her as he did other women, right now, she would be in his bed and not on the terrace sipping whiskey.

"Actually," he said, appearing a bit surprised and thoughtful, "it is true. I am not cold, and I am in my shirtsleeves," he remarked. As if she did not know. He stood inches from her, and every time he raised his glass, his custom shirt rippled over his chest, arms, and shoulders. She glanced at his chest and shoulders again. "The sky is extraordinary tonight, and frankly, so are you. And I do mean my every word, Francesca."

She backed up. "Hart."

"Do not be a ninny. We are friends, good friends now, I hope, and you know as well as I do that you are unique. One could never find a carbon copy of Francesca Cahill should he search the entire world over." He turned his attention to his scotch, as if he found the liquid in his glass fascinating.

His praise was stunning. Francesca was oddly paralyzed, and then a small thrill began to wash over her, which she was reluctant to feel but helpless to stop.

"Does my praise bother you, Francesca?" he asked softly.

"Yes, no . . . yes."

For a moment he looked at her and did not speak. "If I cannot be honest with you, then we cannot be friends," he said simply.

She took a big gulp of scotch, felt her insides now thoroughly warmed, and said breathlessly, "You are right."

"I am usually right."

She eyed him. They were on safer ground now. "Not always?" It was hard not to smile a little, so she did.

He grinned. He had perfectly spaced, extremely white teeth and one dimple in his right cheek. Still, he did not look boyish when he grinned; he looked more like an archangel sent to tempt the innocent. "Not always, Francesca. And at last, you allow yourself a smile."

"God, that is a relief!" she quipped, ignoring his comment. "You can be so insufferable at times, one might conclude that you are of the mind that you are always in the right."

"Not I. One does not lift one up by his bootstraps, attaining a shipping and insurance company, an enviable art collection, and several stately homes, through arrogance and close-mindedness." He lifted his glass in a salute. Then he sobered. "So? Are you ready to tell me why you were out here alone, frowning with worry, your expression so sad, when I first stepped outside?"

She inhaled, all of her problems tumbling through her mind. How much should she tell him? Should she tell him anything at all?

She realized that she so wanted to confide in him. Standing beside him now, alone in the night, she almost basked in his strength and power. He was strong, smart, and opinionated, she would always respect his advice, and, oddly, she felt that her secrets would be safe with him.

How odd.

But she had attained a warm and fuzzy glow, now, that was exceedingly pleasant. She wasn't drunk, simply . . . relaxed. Perhaps the scotch was the reason she wished to wag her tongue so boldly.

"Francesca? What kind of internal debate are you waging?" He was amused again. His good humor made his near-black eyes sparkle as he regarded her over the rim of his glass.

She watched him sip and swallow. She watched a muscle move in his strong throat. "I have the oddest urge to tell you all. But of course, I dare not make you my confidant," she said.

"But why ever not? Hasn't it occurred to you that I might make a valuable confidant and an even more valuable ally?"

He had said as much once before. She stared.

"I only want to help. But the truth is, I don't think I even have to ask. If you are distressed, there can only be one cause." His humor instantly began to fade.

She stiffened, tore her regard from his—no easy task—and sipped her drink. She was not going to discuss Bragg with him, not when they had been having a perfectly fine time, not when such a discussion would only cause him to lose his temper and her to become upset.

"So now what has he done?" Hart asked, an edge to his tone, his glance dark and even wary.

She had finished half of her drink. She looked up. "Evan has left Father's company and the house. He intends to break off his engagement to Sarah and find new employment and a flat. Mama is heartbroken."

Hart smiled. "Good for him." He raised his glass in a mock salute to her brother.

"You approve?"

"I do. And I would say his stab at independent thinking and behavior is long overdue. Besides, he and Sarah do not suit."

Francesca agreed with him completely, and she was surprised. "You do not think he needs a woman like Sarah to temper his ways?"

"I think he is a grown man who must learn through his own experience. And I think he has every right to marry or not as he chooses. I do not see your brother as being ready for marriage, Francesca. I also sense he is a romantic, just like you."

Francesca could not be more surprised. "He is romantic. He is constantly falling in love—with the Grace Conways and Bartolla Beneventes of the world."

Hart laughed and shook his head. "Give him a bit of advice. He might think to avoid involvement with Bartolla, as she will only hurt him in the end."

Francesca nodded grimly. Then, "If anything happens with the countess, I am sure it will be quite casual."

"Why? She is a widow, and your brother is a catch."

"You think she wishes to marry my brother? But why? She is wealthy and independent now—no, Calder, you are wrong."

He shook his head and laughed again. "Do not come crying to me another time, for I will remind you that this time I was right. So what did your father hold over Evan's head? I assume the engagement was a forced one."

Francesca hesitated, surprised once more at how astute Hart was. She had another odd feeling—that if she asked Hart to help her brother financially, he would. "Evan has incurred a few debts."

One brow rose. "A few?"

She hesitated again.

He patted her shoulder. "I understand. So what is the real reason you are troubled tonight?" His gaze held hers.

She looked away instantly. "Mama and Papa are fighting," she replied. "It is too terrible to describe."

He appeared exasperated. "All married couples fight, Francesca. No one lives happily ever after."

"They don't fight. Ever. And they truly love each other, Calder."

Hart eyed her, the pause a long and tense one now. Tension crept into his voice when he finally spoke. "I know you are brooding about Rick. Who else could cause you such grief?"

"He does not cause me grief," she said, meeting his gaze reluctantly.

"No? How odd. I see it differently; I see you as nothing but distraught ever since you have fallen in so-called love with him."

She eyed him warily but saw no sign of an imminent tempest. "Why does he always come up when we are trying to have a conversation?" she asked.

"Because he is causing you pain and I don't like it," he said flatly.

She turned away. In a way, he was right. But it wasn't Bragg causing her heartache; it was the circumstance in which they found themselves.

She jumped nervously when Hart touched her shoulder, turning to face him.

"Nervous?"

She pulled away. "I am not nervous. It is just that this evening is extremely trying."

"Yes, it is trying," he agreed.

That was not an answer that she had expected. "What does that mean?" she demanded, her heart beating a bit too wildly for comfort.

"I think you know, as we have discussed this matter the other day."

She stared.

He touched her cheek with a fingertip. "I'd like nothing more than to take you in my arms, Francesca, and I know you'd like nothing more, too."

"That's not true!" she cried instantly, and then fell still, horrified because her words were a lie.

For, in a way, she would die to experience one devastating kiss.

His grim smile was a knowing one. They stared at each other. "And now you are feeling utterly disloyal to my brother," he said calmly.

"Disloyal?" she managed. *Deny everything,* she thought with panic. "The one thing I am is loyal," she snapped. "And trustworthy."

He sighed, annoyance crossing over his features. "As if I do not know that! You owe him nothing, Francesca. You certainly do not owe him loyalty—or fidelity—in any form. If you enjoy my company, if you have thought about me in sexual ways, you have no reason to feel disloyal or guilty."

She could not cross her arms, because of the drink she held. She quaffed down as much as she possibly could and began to choke.

"Oh, Christ," he said, his tone amused. He set his glass down on the terrace slates at his feet, then patted her back gently.

And even through his jacket, which she wore, his hand was so distinct. She coughed again and, finally, gasped for air. "Hart . . . I don't think about you . . . that way!" Had she ever told a bigger lie? How many times had she thought about him in bed with both Daisy and Rose? Not to mention his making love to Bartolla? She had even begun to think about him and Connie once!

"You know, Francesca, you are adorable when you lie to yourself, but if you think to lie to me, you are out of your league," he said with a soft smile. He thumped her once again, a bit too hard. "Better?" he asked, still smiling.

"I do not feel disloyal and I do not feel guilty when I am with you," she managed, her tone husky now. She tried to glare and failed.

"Did I mention guilt?" He shook his head. "You can try a man's patience, Francesca. I am completely honest with you, but you are terrified of being honest with yourself and thus with me."

She handed him her scotch and crossed her arms tightly. "Do you want honesty?"

He stared and a terse pause ensued. "It would be a refreshing change," he remarked dryly.

She had a dozen questions; she would only ask two. "Lucy said Leigh Anne broke his heart."

Hart rolled his eyes in annoyance. "And to think I had deluded myself in thinking you might remain on the topic of us."

"He told me it was only lust. Did she break his heart, Calder? Was he in love with her?" Francesca cried, grabbing his sleeve.

"Christ. This is so boring." He placed her drink alongside of his, on the ground by their feet. He gave her a cool look and Francesca knew there would be no mercy now. "Dear, Bragg was head over heels for his little wife. He was smitten at first sight, but then, she is extremely lovely, and she led him around by his nose from the moment that they met. His infatuation was laughable indeed. It took him a very long time to realize that the woman he so loved was disloyal, self-serving, and selfish—not to mention a bit of a whore."

Francesca stared, feeling ill. "Are you trying to hurt me?" she finally whispered.

"No, I am not. I am telling you what half of the world knows. Within weeks he announced that he intended to marry her, and no one, not I, not Rathe, not Rourke, could persuade or reason with him. Everyone begged him to wait. But he refused to heed anyone, and I think it is obvious why he was so eager to tie the knot."

Francesca hugged herself. "You are cruel."

"Are you going to become ill? If so, I would like some warning."

She shook her head, turning away from him. Bragg had been in love, and his lust had led him to marry a woman he hardly knew within months of their meeting. He had wanted her that badly.

Francesca couldn't help drawing a comparison—with her he was the epitome of self-control.

Hart sighed in exasperation.

"Go away," she heard herself say, and there were tears in her voice.

His hands closed over her shoulders. She tensed but did not jerk away; he pulled her backward, and she felt his chest against her back, just for an instant. He turned her gently around and she found herself loosely in his arms. "Stop this, Francesca. What difference does it make if Rick loved another woman four years ago?" His tone was surprisingly soft, gentle, and kind. He pushed some wisps of hair out of her face. "Why are you on the verge of tears? That was four years ago. He was as young, hot-blooded, and naive then as you are now," he continued softly. "He may have been twenty-four, but he was a boy, and now he is a man," he soothed. His fingers brushed her cheek.

She trembled. He hadn't released her. She was acutely aware of his hands, his chest, his face, so close to hers. Mostly, she was aware of his steady gaze. She tried to think clearly, to answer the question, but it was hard, given the proximity between them. "I don't know. I've never loved anyone before. But he has. And . . . he still does." There, she had said it.

He was staring, surprised. "He despises her, Francesca. And honestly, he does love you." He hesitated, grim. Their gazes remained locked. "I think I am jealous of my brother, in this one instance." He released her, retrieved one glass from the slate at their feet, and drank.

What did that mean? She gripped his arm. "What does that mean?" she whispered, stunned.

"God knows. Here's to you." He finished the drink, looking put out and put upon.

She stared. No, it was impossible, she finally decided. He did not mean that he wished she loved him the way she loved Bragg. It was simply absurd.

"Shall we go inside? I think I am finally cold." His gaze had certainly cooled and she could not see what he was thinking now.

"No."

He started. "I beg your pardon?"

Francesca hugged herself. They had come this far. . . . "I am in trouble, Hart."

He started. "What kind of trouble?" His tone remained calm, controlled.

"I'm not sure. But maybe you can tell me." She hesitated,

her heart pounding now, with terrible force. Once she made
him her confidant, there was no turning back. "Can I trust
you? Not to say anything, not to interfere? Merely to ad-
vise?"

"I told you the other day that you can trust me, Francesca.
But what is it you want from me? And why aren't you going
to my brother instead?"

"I want your advice and your opinion," she said breathlessly. No one would understand the situation and be able to
analyze it better than Hart, as he knew all of the players
firsthand. She knew he would be ruthless in his assessment
of her dilemma, but the time had come to face the worst
reality that there was.

"Fire away," he said, but tersely, and he was not smiling.

She nodded and not removing her gaze from his, she slid
her hand into the low bodice of her dress. As she fished
around her bosom, she felt herself flush. He seemed quite
accustomed to women retrieving odds and ends from within
their undergarments, for he did not even blink as she pulled
the folded note out. She handed the tiny square to him.

He gave her an odd look and began unfolding the page.
He gave her another look, turned toward the light spilling
from the house, and read it. "Well, well," he said, facing her.
"So Leigh Anne has heard the news and wishes to meet you."

There was a huge relief in having shared her secret with
him, and she faced him, trembling with anticipation. "What
do you think of this?"

"I think you had better stay away from her; that is what
I think. What does Rick have to say about this?"

She simply looked at him.

"Oh, ho. This is a situation indeed." And he dared to
smile, with real mirth. "You haven't *told* him?"

She shook her head. "I meant to, but—"

"You *meant* to?" He was disbelieving, and now he had
the audacity to laugh. "His wife knows the two of you are
on the verge of an affair—or are having one." He gave her
a quick look, and it was a question. Francesca didn't move.
"She is on her way to New York, she is on her way here,

and you haven't told him?" He laughed again, harder.

"This is not funny!" Francesca shouted.

"Oh, but it is. I am so sorry!" he cried with mirth.

She punched his arm.

He stopped laughing. "I am sorry. I suppose, caught up as you are in this sordid little love triangle, you cannot see the irony of the situation. Do you intend to tell my poor brother that his wife is on her way to town, or do you wish for him to be shocked into a heart attack when he sees her on his doorstep? I mean, they have been separated for four years."

"You think I should tell him," she breathed, never looking away from his dark and handsome face.

He ceased smiling. "You know you should tell him," he said flatly.

She grasped his hands. "I am afraid, Calder. *I am so afraid.*"

His hands closed over hers. He seemed to pull her closer. "Yes, I can understand why you would be afraid."

He never minced words. He never told her what she wished to hear. Francesca felt tears rising. She was so afraid to ask, but she had no choice now. "Does he still love her?"

Hart hesitated. Francesca vaguely realized he clasped her hands against the solid wall of his chest.

"Calder!" she cried, terrified.

He sighed. "He despises her, Francesca, but isn't hatred on the same coin as love? Isn't it merely the flip side? And don't they have unfinished business to conclude? And isn't she legally his wife?"

"You are not reassuring me," she whispered. "You are making it worse."

"I will never lie to you, Francesca," he said firmly. *"Not ever."*

Oddly, she was frightened now, but his words washed over her like a soothing wave.

And he sensed the change in her, as he softened and his tone was gentle when he spoke. "Poor Francesca. Your little fairy tale is going to blow up, isn't it? In a few days, when she comes to town, you will have to face a truly horrid reality."

"Yes, I think so," she whispered.

He pulled her into his embrace, and for one instant she felt every inch of his tall, strong body and his heart beat steadily, powerfully, against her breasts. She felt his cheek on the top of her head. She felt his hand caress the baby-soft hair at her nape. Then he released her, completely. "Do you really want my advice? Other than the advice I have already given you, which is to forget my brother completely and spare yourself any further grief?"

She nodded fearfully, but confusion seemed to reign. Hart's hard chest, his beating heart, his hands . . . Bragg's golden eyes, the warmth there, his perfectly beautiful little wife.

"Stay away from Leigh Anne. Tell Rick promptly about this note, and then avoid her at all costs," Hart said.

"Why?" She was mesmerized by him now, by his stare, his intensity, his words.

"Why? She is clever, Francesca, and, unlike you, has not one moral fiber to her being. She will swallow you whole, then spit you out in tiny, useless, mangled pieces that no one will ever recognize. You cannot fight her and win. You simply cannot."

"This is not a battle," she managed, riveted by him.

"A battle?" His brows lifted. "Darling, this is not a battle. Unless you come to your senses and forget this absurd notion that you love my brother, this is war."

It had become impossible now, with Hart there, inches away from her, reeking sexuality, to really feel the depth of her own emotions, but she knew where her true feelings lay and she said, "I do love him."

He sighed with exasperation and looked up at the stars and said, "Jesus does not help fools."

"What does she want from me, Calder? And why does she intend to confront me?" Francesca asked simply.

He took her arm and pulled her close, but not into his embrace. "Whoever said she wishes to confront you? Listen carefully, Francesca, and I will tell you about women like Mrs. Rick Bragg."

"I don't care about other women, only about her."

He ignored that. "She might not love Rick, but she will never allow another woman, especially someone like you—someone fine and good—to steal his heart away, much less to steal him away. It is classic. She didn't want him—but you cannot have him. Not to mention the fact that her ego is huge and she is vain. She will not be humiliated by having her husband love another woman. And then there are her bills. She has most of what she wants, I believe. So now, if you insist upon clinging to my brother, you will have a huge war to wage, for undoubtedly she will accept the gauntlet. And, Francesca, you are too ethical to ever win such a war."

Francesca wet her lips. Mechanically she asked, "What should I do?"

"What do you really want, Francesca? What do you really want with my brother?"

She backed up, staring at him, unable to look away.

"If you truly want my advice, I suggest you be brutally honest now," he said flatly.

She hesitated, suddenly confused. What did she want? Truly?

Panic assailed her—she knew what she wanted! It was Hart's charismatic presence, that was interfering now with her mind. She shook off the cobwebs of bewilderment. "I want to marry him, have his children, support him in his run for the Senate, grow old with him, and reform the world together with him," she said.

His jaw flexed. "No white picket fence?"

"You asked, Calder. That is what I want." She hugged herself.

"He will not divorce her, and she is in good health. Is that still what you want?" he asked in a no-nonsense tone.

She almost told him that Bragg had considered divorcing Leigh Anne, but as they had now ruled that possibility out, there was no point. "Yes," she said, in a way feeling a bit like a student reciting expected answers.

He folded his arms across his chest. His biceps swelled as he did so. "You know, men have been getting rid of un- wanted wives for centuries," he remarked casually.

"They . . . what?" she gasped in shock.

"I do believe Henry the Eighth beheaded a couple of his wives, did he not? And then there was that earl, Leicester, I believe, whose wife had a convenient accident on the stairs? She did die from the fall. And there is always poison—"

She grabbed his rock-hard arm. "Enough! Are you trying to be funny?"

"I am simply telling you that there is historical precedent for getting rid of an unwanted spouse."

"Are you suggesting that I . . . that I . . ." She simply could not continue.

He stared.

She suddenly realized what he was doing. He was point- ing out that unless she became a murderess, her dreams were entirely hopeless.

"No, Francesca, I am not suggesting that you commit murder," he said softly.

Tears filled her eyes.

He cupped her cheek. "I'm sorry," he said, a rough whis- per.

She closed her eyes and felt the warmth and strength of his hand, turning her face more fully into his palm. Instantly his palm vanished.

Her gaze flew open and they stared at each other.

She bit her lip, tried to breathe normally, failed. Perhaps making him a confidant had been a terrible mistake. But then, she had known the evening would come to this, hadn't she?

"Let's join the others. By now their tongues are wagging."

She did not move.

"What is it?"

She was so confused, she realized. "You really haven't been helpful."

"That's because you are more stubborn than a hundred mules, and you simply do not listen," he said.

She was annoyed. And annoyance was a relief. "Calder. What would you do, if you were me?"

"I am not you."

"That was not helpful, either."

He shrugged.

She hesitated.

"What is it that you wish to ask me? Why are you suddenly tongue-tied?"

Tension filled her. He had raised the subject of murder to teach her a lesson, but his lesson had raised a single, important question—one that was horrifying, one she sensed the answer to. "Would you ever. . . . commit murder?"

He had been avoiding her eyes; now he looked up instantly and their gazes locked. "Yes, I would."

She knew it.

"If someone I loved was in danger, I would commit murder in order to protect that person," he said. "I think we had better go inside," he added, nodding toward the French doors, "as your mother is looking for us."

Francesca whirled and saw Julia standing ten feet away in the doorway of the salon, outside. She was incredulous. Her mother was close enough to have heard Hart's words, yet there was no disapproval on her features. In fact, she was smiling at them. "Do come inside," she said cheerfully. "We are going in to dine." She turned and left.

A touch on Francesca's arm made her flinch. Breathless, she looked at Hart, who had gripped her elbow. "Shall we?"

Her mind jumped with lightning speed. She balked, refusing to go in. "You do not believe in love," she said.

"Did I say love?" His smile was lazy, easy—he had recovered his natural arrogance. "It was an unfortunate slip of the tongue."

They went inside.

Twelve

Even though he did not love Sarah Channing, he felt guilty as he was admitted into the Channing home. Visiting Sarah in order to see how she was faring was a pretext for seeing the countess; he was that badly smitten. They had come to understand each other so well, and when he had mentioned he would stop by in the early evening in order to visit his fiancée, Bartolla had smiled at him, understanding—or so he thought. Now, as his coat was taken, the Channing butler said, "Miss Channing has remained in her rooms all day, sir, but I shall send her your card. Shall I inform Mrs. Channing that you are here?"

"That is not necessary. I would hate to interrupt her Sunday evening," Evan said. He was filled with impatience, and it was hard to remain impassive of expression. He felt like pacing about like a restless caged lion. Had Bartolla understood? Was she present in the house? Would he have a chance to see her, even if it was but for a moment?

And if only Sarah did not stand between them!

Of course, Evan had not changed his mind about ending the engagement, and he felt certain his frustration would soon be at an end. However, he would wait until Sarah was feeling better before he sat down with her to give her the blow.

He did not dread the encounter entirely. Francesca had said Sarah had no wish to marry, and as astonishing as that was, he knew his sister well, and she fervently believed her words. So Sarah would undoubtedly be pleased to be let off the hook. Perhaps, he mused, she had a yearning for someone else. But he doubted it. Sarah was just not terribly interested in men. Her life was her painting, it seemed.

He found it a bit odd.

Of course, if Francesca were somehow wrong, the encounter might become terrible indeed. But Evan could not think about that. He owed too much money to the wrong kinds of people, and planning how to elude and evade them was what preoccupied most of his waking hours.

That and his father.

Evan stood abruptly, his fists clenching, his entire body coursing with anger. Why had it taken him all of these years to finally tell the old man to shove it? One could only be pushed so far, he mused. He had been pushed about by his father his entire life, yet he had always swallowed his anger and he had always been respectful and obedient. He had always done what he had been told to do, yet Andrew had never shown one sign of encouragement, never uttered one word of praise. If he stayed at the office until ten in the evening, his father's response was to ask if he had finished a report. And if he hadn't, while no more was said, the disapproval was there, in his father's eyes.

There was always disapproval in Andrew Cahill's eyes.

And when he did, finally, score a touchdown, in his senior year at Columbia, there had simply been no praise. Brad Lewis had scored eight TDs for the season, and that was what Andrew had been talking about at supper that night.

He could not win. Not ever. And the reason was an astoundingly simple one. Because he was not like his father and he never would be.

He had not been born dirt poor on a farm; he had not worked his fingers to the bone saving every possible penny, while slowly but surely rising to a position of self-made success. It wasn't even fair to be judged by the chart that was Andrew's life, because he had been born in a canopied bed in a Lake Michigan manor.

He almost hated Andrew Cahill now.

Perhaps, in fact, he did.

And the depth of this emotion frightened him. He had

never felt anything like it before. But it was his anger—and
hatred—that had enabled him to stand up to the old man and
finally, after all of these years, tell him off. And of course,
the old man had let him walk out and go.

Because he didn't care enough to beg him to stay.

It was too painful to contemplate—the love Andrew had
for Connie and Francesca, the disgust he had for his own
son. Trembling, Evan faced a window, but blindly. It was
hard to see now.

But he had done the right thing. He cared as much about
his father as his father cared about him. He was not going
to be his whipping boy any longer, oh no. Thank God he
would never have to spend another minute in that office,
poring over slaughterhouse accounts! Thank God he was not
going to have to wed and bed Sarah Channing. From this
moment on, he would live his life as he chose, not as his
father wished.

Of course, he might not live for very much longer if he
did not raise at least $50,000, fast.

Fear pierced through him, arrow-straight. A real father
would come to his son's rescue, he thought bitterly. And he
realized that he had never had a real father and now he did
not have any father at all.

"Evan?" Bartolla murmured from the threshold of the salon.

He turned at the sound of her voice and, shockingly, desire
seared him with sudden, shattering force. Of course he
wanted her. He had from the first moment they had met. It
did not matter, either, that he was experienced enough to
know that the countess was a tease, just as he was experienced enough to know that she would astound him in bed
and he would not be the first or the last of her lovers. It had
been a long time since he had wanted a woman as much as
he wanted her; and now, immobilized by anger and grief and
arousal, he thought about taking her a dozen different ways.

They hadn't even kissed, for crissakes.

Bartolla smiled at him, a seductive, intent smile that
reached her lovely green eyes, as if she knew exactly what

he was thinking. She was clearly dressed for an evening affair in a daring sapphire blue gown; Evan had never seen her demure or ladylike in appearance—her dresses were always figure-hugging and revealing, with an exotic, seductive flair. She had the most amazing body: long legs, full hips, full breasts.

"This is such a surprise," she said in a conversational tone. "You must be here to see Sarah. A few moments ago she was sleeping," she added.

"A pity," he returned evenly. Actually, his tone was rough with need, and he tried to clear it. "I had so hoped she was doing better." He walked toward Bartolla and abruptly closed the door behind her—surprising them both.

"Evan?" Bartolla asked, her eyes wide.

He hesitated for one moment, warring with himself. Then he seized her shoulders and claimed her mouth.

For one instant, she was rigid with surprise, and then she melted against him, her arms going around him, her mouth opening wide and hot for him. He had met her weeks ago, and this moment was long overdue—he moved her against the wall, anchored her head with his hand in her nape, where he grasped a handful of curls, and he used his thigh to spread both of hers. Their tongues mated, the way their bodies were trying to.

He tore his mouth from hers to kiss the soft underside of her throat, muttering, "I need you desperately."

She gripped his head, urging his face lower. "I want you desperately, too."

He moved his mouth back and forth over the edge of her bodice, using his tongue there, while she rode his thigh.

"Oh, God, Evan," she gasped, and he was also experienced enough to know that she was now as fully aroused as he was, and he thought he could quickly bring her to a climax, if only he dared.

He pushed down her dress and a large, erect nipple was bared.

She froze.

He knew she was thinking about Sarah and Mrs. Channing. "You are the loveliest woman I have ever seen," he whispered, and then he drew her nipple into his mouth.

She held his head hard, whimpering in soft, low, sexy tones.

He tugged her nipple with his teeth and she cried out; instantly he gentled. His hands moved over her buttocks, which were soft and round and perfectly plump. He grasped them, separating them.

"Oh, dear God," she whispered, tonguing his ear. "Oh, please!" she cried, licking it.

He straightened and their eyes met and he took her hand and pressed it over the elongated ridge of his arousal. Her eyes heated even more, and she smiled, not looking away.

For one moment he considered doing something absolutely inappropriate, considering his affianced status and the time and place where they stood, and an image of her bending over him, sucking him into her mouth, sucking long and hard, as they stood there in the salon, paralyzed him.

She ran her nails up and down that ridge, still smiling a soft, sexy smile.

He kissed her, hard. Then he tore his mouth from hers and walked to the opposite end of the room, panting and seriously close to losing all control. He stared out of a window that faced the back gardens, blanketed now in snow. He supposed but was not sure that the Hudson River would be visible in the light of day.

If Bartolla was moving, he could not hear a thing. He felt her eyes on his back.

Still highly aroused, he raked his hair with one hand, sighed, and turned. He had been right; she remained with her back against the wall, staring. But she looked exactly as she had when she had first walked in—she must have repaired her hair, and her bodice was back in place.

No, she did not look exactly as she had when she had walked in—she looked like a woman who had been making love.

"I am sorry," he began roughly, meaning it.

"No. You don't have to apologize, not to me." Her smile

was brief but anxious. "We're both adults, and rather experienced ones at that. We both know that this has been brewing from the moment we met."

"Yes, it has." He smiled a little, liking her even more for being so straightforward. "I didn't call here tonight to ravage you."

"I know." She approached him swiftly then and laid her forefinger on his mouth. "Ssh. It's all right. I am feeling what you are feeling." She hesitated. "Perhaps more."

He stared, trying to comprehend her, his heart accelerating. "More? What do you mean?"

She shook her head with a sad little smile. "This can never happen again, Evan. You know that."

He seized her hands. A little voice in his head began to warn him not to speak, but he ignored it. "Can you keep a confidence, Bartolla?" he asked softly.

"You know that I can," she returned, her gaze unwavering upon him.

Because she was breathless, it was difficult not to keep glancing down at her spectacular bosom. He forced himself to concentrate on her face, amazingly aroused again. "I am ending it with Sarah. As soon as she is well enough, I shall tell her."

Bartolla's eyes widened; clearly she was stunned. "But your parents? Mrs. Channing? I mean, I know this was arranged for certain reasons."

"My father does not control me anymore," Evan said flatly. "I have taken a stand, and nothing shall change my mind now."

She stared. Her full bosom moved even more strenuously against the flimsy material of her gown. Her nipples were clearly erect. "Oh dear," she managed finally.

He swallowed hard, sweating now. "I know Sarah is your cousin," he began, suddenly wondering if, in spite of Bartolla's passionate nature, she might not condemn him for his actions, "but I cannot marry a woman I do not care at all for. I may marry one day, but it will be for love."

"No, that is not it," she breathed, gripping his hands as

tightly as he held hers. "The two of you are a terrible mismatch, and Sarah doesn't even want to marry—not ever. She only wants to paint. I just did not expect you to break it off; somehow, I thought Francesca might persuade your father to do so—eventually."

Evan was relieved. "I will tell Sarah as soon as she is well," he murmured.

She nodded, her gaze unwavering on his face.

He told himself that if he kissed her again he would quickly take her on the floor. "I am very wound up tonight," he said flatly, releasing her hands and turning away.

"I know," she murmured.

He whirled and their gazes locked.

A flush covered her cheeks and heat filled her eyes.

And he thought, *One more kiss, I am a man, not a boy.* . . . He seized her and she cried out, but he cut off her cry, tearing at her mouth with his. Her teeth cut his lips; he penetrated her fully with his tongue, thinking about getting down on his knees and using his tongue against her sex, between her legs. Their tongues entwined, their mouths fused. He clasped her buttocks and lifted her up two inches, until she was against his loins. Fire blazed in his mind, only fire.

And he knew that he simply could not wait—he would have to take her now.

She tore away. "Someone's coming!" she cried in a stage whisper.

He was so aroused it was a moment before he understood, but by then it was too late—a knock sounded.

Evan straightened like a shot, hearing another knock now. He adjusted himself, his shirt, his tie. "Your hair," he said grimly, now appalled with himself and his behavior. He was not a free man yet.

And as he stepped quickly forward, tugging up one of her slim shoulder straps, the door slowly opened.

He leaped away from her as she whirled to face the intruder. It was Rourke who stepped through the door.

His face impassive, his amber eyes hooded, Rourke looked from Evan to Bartolla and back again. The man was a rake, for Evan knew a ladies' man when he saw one, so he had to know what had just transpired between them. However, he gave no sign. And whatever his reaction was to the affair, he gave no indication of that, either.

"The butler told me you were here," he said. Now his gaze slid over Bartolla, inch by inch.

She stood straight and still, a smile pasted to her face, letting him take his fill. She did not flush.

Evan's fists closed. He felt like pounding the other man for looking at the countess in such a sexual way.

"I had hoped to see Sarah," Evan said, hoping his voice would not betray him. It did—his tone was rough with need, and he coughed to clear it.

"Oh, yes, I can see that," Rourke said, quite coolly now. The glance he sent Bartolla was a disparaging one.

Evan stiffened. "How is she?" He now noticed that Rourke carried his medical bag.

"She has a fever of one hundred and one again," Rourke said, looking now at Bartolla as if she were a tropical insect that he wished to dispose of. "I am worried, Cahill. She does not have the flu, and although I have checked her lungs, I am going to bring a specialist over to make sure she does not have pneumonia."

Pneumonia was more often deadly than not. Evan started with dread.

Bartolla stepped forward. "I hadn't realized she had a fever again," she whispered, wringing her hands, stricken with worry. "Please, you don't suspect pneumonia, do you?"

"How could you realize anything?" Abruptly—rudely—he turned and walked out.

Evan and Bartolla looked at each other with dismay. Then he turned and hurried after Rourke. "Rourke! Can I go up and see her?"

"No." Rourke was receiving his coat from the houseman and did not even look at Evan as he spoke.

"Now what the hell does that mean?"

"It means she is ill with a high fever and she does not need to be agitated any further."

Evan felt like punching the other man. "Do not judge me," he warned.

"Why not? This is a democracy, the last I heard. And judgments are free." Rourke's eyes burned. "If you think to fuck the countess, at least do it in another house," he said. "At least have that simple decency."

Evan struck, intending to hit Rourke right in the face. The other man's reflexes were a surprise, as he dodged and the blow grazed his high cheekbone. But he straightened swinging. Evan felt a mean blow in the chest. It sent him backward across the hall.

"Stop! The two of you!" Bartolla cried with horror in her tone.

Evan caught himself before falling, balling his fists, wanting to pummel the other man to a pulp. But Rourke stood in a similar stance, clearly wishing for another round.

"Apologize. Not to me. But to the lady," Evan said, and it was a warning.

Rourke flushed. He glanced at Bartolla, then said, "I was rather uncouth. I am sorry."

Bartolla looked at him with huge eyes. "Thank you."

Rourke appeared disgusted and he turned to go.

Bartolla gripped his arm. "Rourke, wait. Please try and understand. We have never—it was a mistake—it just happened and we both love Sarah dearly!"

He faced her, shaking her off. "Please! I am a man of the world! Nothing *just* happened. But Miss Channing deserves more respect than either of you seem capable of giving her. I apologize only for using such ungentlemanly language, but not for the gist of what I have said. The two of you clearly deserve each other." He turned abruptly, angrily. Fortunately, the doorman was listening to their every word and he managed to fling the front door open before Rourke crashed into it as he strode furiously out.

He was right, at least partly. Sarah did deserve respect, and the passion that had erupted in the salon had been untimely and wrong. Evan was grim, glancing at Bartolla. "I had better go."

She nodded, pale. Then, "He is right. I am going to go upstairs and spend the rest of the evening seeing if I can make Sarah more comfortable."

Something melted inside of him. "That is very kind of you."

"She is my cousin," Bartolla returned. "I love her."

Evan hesitated. In that instant, with the utmost certainty he knew that some of the things being whispered about by the likes of his father about Bartolla Benevente were completely wrong. She could not help the fact that she had been born so desirable, and it did not detract one whit from the innate goodness of her heart. "I know you do," he said.

SUNDAY, FEBRUARY 16, 1902 — 8 P.M.

Francesca felt as if she were a freakish display in a circus. The moment she stepped into the salon, all eyes fell upon her. She remained very aware of Hart behind her and now, too late, that she was draped in his black dinner jacket. Somehow, she smiled at the Braggs, but only Rourke was smiling, and there was a knowing light in his eyes. Francesca darted a worried glance at Rathe and Grace Bragg. She wanted to explain to them that she and Hart were only friends and that nothing had happened on the terrace. But Hart was removing his jacket from her shoulders. Francesca flinched at the touch of silk and his fingertips, but she was not given the chance to speak. For Julia was ushering everyone from the salon. "Shall we go in? Supper is being served," Julia announced.

Francesca suddenly realized that her mother and father stood at polar ends of the group gathered in the center of the salon, ignoring each other. Worry swept over her with hurricane force. She could withstand many crises, but a disruption in her parents' relationship, in their marriage, was not one of them.

Andrew held his arm out to Grace. "May I, dear? I do believe you are my dinner partner tonight."

Grace smiled and she became beautiful when she did so,

even though she had chosen to wear a pair of horn-rimmed spectacles, which kept slipping down her nose. "You know I have missed our political debates, Andrew," she said softly. "And I do want your opinion on Rick's efforts with the police department—and his clash with the mayor."

Francesca straightened like a shot. Bragg had clashed with Mayor Lowe? When had this happened? How come he had not told her?

"Lowe cannot afford to alienate the workman's vote—no matter that they are led by the nose through the Tammany machine. He has backed down on the issue of Sunday saloon closings. I do believe your son remains firm in his convictions to uphold the letter of the law."

Oh, no, Francesca thought, seized with more than worry, then fear. She knew Bragg. He had been appointed to reform the police department, and that meant, to him, upholding the law—with no exceptions. Sunday saloon openings were a direct violation of the Blue Laws. In principle, Lowe supported those laws. Clearly he felt that his political future might be threatened now by actually doing so.

Hart leaned close and whispered, "Your knight in shining armor will survive."

Francesca met his dark eyes and saw he was annoyed, so she did not bother to reply.

Rathe had taken Julia's arm, and as they began to file out, Lucy seized Francesca's hand. "I need to talk to you," she said in a low, tense tone. And fear was in her eyes.

Francesca knew that something dire had happened. "The best time shall be after supper," she said as quietly, aware of Hart at her elbow and Rourke lazily moving closer to them. She had no wish to have either man overhear them now.

Lucy whirled. "Hart, Rourke, wait for us in the hall," she ordered tersely.

Hart's brow lifted. "I might be inclined to agree, if such an imperious tone were not used," he said. Then his gaze narrowed. "Is something wrong?"

"Nothing is wrong," Lucy said, far too swiftly.

Rourke stared. "She's worse than that when company is not present. What is wrong?"

Lucy smiled too brightly. "Just leave us to our wicked gossip! Please!" Lucy cried, gripping his arm. She kissed him on the cheek. "Now, go!"

Hart smiled a little but looked at the two women thoughtfully. "Seeing you both together, I shudder. I sense a conspiracy of danger, and no good can come of it."

"There is no conspiracy here!" Lucy cried, her smile brittle.

Francesca touched his arm and smiled. "We will be in momentarily," she assured him.

His gaze locked with hers; any annoyance he had just felt vanished, and he finally nodded. "Very well. Francesca . . ." He hesitated.

Her heart seemed to flutter. "Yes?"

He shook his head rather self-derisively. "I do hope that the two of you are not in any trouble."

"We're not!" Lucy pushed him toward the door. "Now good-bye!"

Francesca could not look away from Hart's dark, piercing eyes until he finally acquiesced and walked out with Rourke. Instantly Lucy slammed the salon door closed and ran to Francesca. "You are right. I lied. I am in trouble and I don't know what to do!"

Francesca gripped her arms. "Craddock?"

For one moment, Lucy did not speak. Then she reached into her bodice and handed Francesca a crumpled note.

Francesca unfolded it and smoothed it out and was faced with crude childish handwriting and many misspellings:

> Five thousand dollars Twosday noon or children
> wont be reel happy.
> Nice children. I like thm real lot.

Andrew had suggested that the men adjourn into the library for cigars and brandies. Connie and Neil had declined and left, Connie seeming very tired though it was not that late in the evening. Hart had sent Francesca an amused look, which clearly said he would rather sip a good scotch with her. But rather pliant, he had gone off with the men.

Julia, Grace, Lucy, and Francesca were left to their own devices in the salon where they had first gathered. Francesca had not had a chance to speak any further with Lucy before supper, for the moment she had read the threatening note, Julia had appeared, demanding that they come into supper. She was determined now to speak to Lucy at length and alone and felt that the determination was mutual. But leaving her mother and Grace Bragg would be more than awkward. The two women had so very little in common.

Julia was politely asking Lucy about her life in Texas and her grandparents, whom she had met twice in Washington at state occasions. Francesca stood before the fire, carefully contemplating Craddock's note. There was no doubt in her mind now that this was a police matter.

"We haven't had a chance to speak," Grace said quietly, at her elbow.

Francesca started, because she had been so engrossed in her speculations that she had not heard the other woman approach. She managed a smile; knowing she had to appear terribly nervous. "No, we haven't."

Grace smiled a little, studying her. "You seem like an unusual young woman. I take it your family does not approve of your interest in criminal investigations?"

Francesca hesitated, but they had kept their voices low. "No, they don't. Mama is very traditional—she wants me to be exactly like Connie."

"Yes, that is obvious. Connie has so fit her bill. She is married to a nobleman, she has two children in the house, and she attends enough charities to assuage any and all guilt. I cannot quite see you following in your sister's footsteps." Her soft smile was a pleasant one.

But Francesca knew an interview when she was in the midst of one. "I am very different from my sister."

"That is rather obvious. I don't think your sister would have tracked down the killer of Hart's father with such courage and conviction. More women should dare to gain a higher education, be politically and socially active, and pursue a profession." She paused. "I understand that, briefly, my son was a suspect. Thank you, Francesca, for all that you did on his behalf."

She flushed. "Calder is a friend. And Bragg—Rick—helped me. We solved the murder together."

Grace studied her.

The silence felt more than awkward, and nervously Francesca said, "And I would do the same for anyone who is the victim of injustice and crime."

"Are you in love with one of my sons?"

Francesca froze. No coherent reply came to mind; there was only panic.

It was sheer and very real.

Grace studied her. "The last thing I wish to see is two of my sons fighting with each other over a woman, even a very unique woman like you."

Francesca inhaled, felt tears rise, and fought for composure. "Mrs. Bragg. Hart and I are friends, that is all—"

"And Rick is married; Calder is not," she said pointedly.

Francesca felt herself blanch.

Grace gave her a long, thoughtful look. "I would not want to be in your position," she said at last. Then she softened visibly and kissed her cheek. "I am tired. There was a very long meeting of the Ladies Republican Club this morning; and this afternoon, the Suffragettes of America. I have not had a moment to sit down." She turned. "Julia? I must retire for the night, but it has been lovely, thank you."

Julia stood and hurried forward. "I am so glad you came," she cried, and as the two women left to retrieve Rathe Bragg, Francesca and Lucy looked at each other.

This time, it was Francesca who rushed to close the salon door. "Lucy, what is happening? Is Craddock blackmailing you?"

"I don't know what is happening!" she cried. "This is the first time he has demanded money!" She was as white as a freshly laundered sheet.

Francesca took her hand. "Let's sit down. You must start from the beginning."

"The beginning?" Lucy looked at her as if she did not understand the definition of the word.

"Yes, the very beginning." Francesca guided her to the sofa and sat down there beside her.

Lucy stared at her as if she had grown two heads.

"Lucy?"

"I first saw him a month ago. He started appearing in town—in Paradise—where I was. I would be picking up a few things at the grocer's or having a fitting at Madame Delfine's, and I'd look up, and there he was, staring at me through the window. Of course, the first time I thought nothing of it!" she cried. "But then I saw him here, Francesca, here—he followed me all the way from Texas to New York City."

"Has he demanded money before?" Francesca asked.

Lucy shook her head. "No." Then, "Five thousand dollars! I don't have that kind of money lying around. Shoz is a rancher. Everything we have is tied up in the ranch."

"You're not paying him," Francesca said firmly.

Lucy grabbed her hand. "He's told me more than once that he is a *friend* of my husband's."

Their gazes locked. "What else did he say?"

She shook her head. "Nothing. But . . . you have to understand, Francesca. When I met my husband, he was a hard, dangerous man. He'd been in prison. Wrongfully, I might add, but what difference does that make? It hardened him even more. He had a life before our marriage, one I do not like to think about—one I do not know very much about." Tears filled her eyes. "We have been so happy," she whispered. "I love him more now than I ever did, and I will do anything to protect him!"

Francesca hesitated. "I saw Craddock's police records. He was in Fort Kendall, Lucy."

Lucy gasped. "That's where Shoz was," she said fearfully.

Francesca did not pretend to be surprised. "I know. Bragg told me."

Lucy shot to her feet. "Rick can't know! No one must know! There are things in Shoz's past, things I have always been afraid of—we simply have to pay off this Craddock and get him to go away!" Tears fell now in a stream down her porcelain cheeks.

Francesca also stood. "I think we had better find out just why Craddock thinks he can blackmail you and your husband."

Lucy shook her head. "I am going to get the five thousand dollars, somehow—Hart will lend it to me!"

"Lucy, he will come back for more. This is a police matter. Please, trust me now," Francesca tried.

"Don't you understand? Rick is a *policeman*. What will he do when he uncovers some terrible secret from Shoz's past?" Her blue eyes were wide, intense.

Francesca stared. She hadn't even considered that Lucy's husband might have a criminal background. Nor had she thought about the position it would place Bragg in, should he learn of it. "Bragg told me Shoz was erroneously incarcerated and that he was later pardoned."

"That's true. But there's so much more." Lucy wet her lips. "When I met him he was running guns illegally, Francesca. To the rebels in Cuba. And that is only the tip of the iceberg, I think." She sat back down and covered her face with her hands. "I knew this was going to happen one day. I have been waiting for his past to blow up in our faces. And what of our children? He loves them so! He is such a good father!"

"Nothing is going to blow up in your face," Francesca said firmly. But now she felt unsure. Maybe it was not a good idea to bring Bragg into this. He *was* the law. And he was passionately committed to upholding it. Yet he was a family man through and through. His moral dilemma would be horrendous. "We have to get to the bottom of whatever it is that Craddock thinks he has on you and Shoz," she finally said. "That is what we must do first."

Lucy looked up, wiping her eyes. "You are forgetting

about the note. He wants five thousand dollars by Tuesday at noon. He has threatened the children!"

"Then we have more than an entire day in which to get our facts," Francesca said decisively. "I am expecting a telegram tomorrow from the warden at Fort Kendall," she said. She prayed his reply would be that timely and did not say that in truth she was hoping for a response to her inquiry.

"What happens if I don't hand the money over to him on Tuesday? He might hurt the children!" Lucy cried frantically.

"Ssh," Francesca said, clapping her hand over Lucy's mouth. "Keep your voice down. Your family has a few very curious and bold snoops in their midst. Let me spend tomorrow trying to get to the bottom of this, before we become hysterical. It is not Tuesday yet."

When she dropped her hand, Lucy said, more quietly, "Hart has money. Tons of it. He could hand me cash tomorrow."

"And what will that accomplish? Lucy! I know you are terrified for Shoz and now for the children. But listen to me. Try to displace the fear so you can think clearly, and hear what I have to say! Caving in to Craddock's blackmail attempt will only encourage him to come back for more—"

"You are right."

"What?"

Lucy stared at her. Her eyes were wide; clearly her mind was spinning. "You are right," she repeated. Her gaze had intensified, almost frighteningly. "We do need Calder."

"What do you mean?" Francesca asked warily. She did not like the look in Lucy's eyes, oh no. It was chilling.

"I am going to Calder. Not for money—for help."

At first Francesca did not understand. "For help? What kind of help? How can—" She stopped.

"Would you ever . . . commit murder?"

"If someone I loved was in danger, I would commit murder to protect that person."

Lucy was staring at her now, her eyes ruthlessly hard. Francesca locked gazes with her. "You want to go to Hart."

"Yes." Her face tightened. It had become almost unattractive.

At first, Francesca couldn't breathe, much less speak. And then a red haze seemed to form over her eyes. She fought it. "I see. Because he will do the kind of dirty work you cannot? That you would not let Shoz or anyone else do?" How calm she sounded to her own ears when, inside of herself, she was hardly calm, as the fury began to build.

"Yes."

Francesca inhaled, trembling. The explosion came. "How dare you!"

"Oh, I dare." Lucy's eyes blazed as she got up.

"You would ask Calder to what? *To get rid of Craddock?* Instead of going to the police, you would go to Calder, have him *remove* Craddock somehow?"

"What other choice do I have?"

"You would have him commit a criminal act—*murder*—for you?" She was shouting, shaking.

"There is no other choice!" Lucy shouted back.

"I will never allow it!" Francesca cried. She could not even think straight; all she knew was that she would never let Lucy use Calder in such a way. In that moment, she hated her new friend.

"I don't believe I need your permission to ask my own brother for anything," Lucy said coldly.

Francesca stared. Could she stop Calder from coming to Lucy's aid—in such a frightful and wrong manner?

In a manner that might backfire, hurting him?

He would be a murderer.

"I take it I am interrupting?"

Francesca whirled as Hart stepped into the room.

Thirteen

His timing was simply uncanny. Francesca looked at him, overcome with dismay.

He stared carefully back and then turned to smile at Lucy. "The two of you are shouting—and causing some concern in the front hall."

Francesca was horrified—had they been overheard? And what had Hart heard? Clearly Lucy was equally worried—frantically so. She ran up to her stepbrother. "Did they hear what we were arguing about?" She practically ripped off his sleeve.

He eyed Francesca again, his composure unshaken—unflappable. "The walls are thick, and no, I don't believe the actual text of your argument was audible. But I did happen to overhear a sentence or two from this doorway. What is it that Francesca will not let you ask me?" His gaze moved to and locked on Francesca again.

She leaped forward, to his side. Had she been able to step directly between him and Lucy, she would have. "Calder, it's so late! Shouldn't you be on your way?" She smiled brightly, desperately, at him. "Isn't Rourke ready to take Lucy back to the hotel?"

"A book, Francesca," he said softly. Then, in a normal tone, "I am taking Lucy back to the Plaza. Rourke has been playing doctor again. He wishes to stop by the Channing residence and will take a cab."

Francesca could only stare, consumed with dismay. Hart and Lucy alone in his carriage? She would beg him for his help, and Francesca would not be there to intervene.

She told herself that Hart would not rush out and murder

Craddock the moment Lucy asked him to. In fact, he would probably hire an assassin.

She was not relieved. Bloody images began to dance through her mind.

"We should go; it is late!" Lucy cried, glancing at Francesca. Her eyes were wild, the eyes of a desperate and frightened woman. In them was a warning that Francesca had better mind her own affairs. So quickly, then, their friendship had evaporated—Lucy was not going to let Francesca get in her way now.

"Francesca?" Hart's silken voice washed over her in cashmere-soft waves.

She gripped his hand. Her mind raced. "What if I told you I wished to share a scotch with you, outside in the moonlight—alone?"

He started. "Are you thinking to seduce me in order to keep me from taking Lucy back?"

Of course he guessed her intentions. She didn't bother to deny it. "Yes."

He stared at her. Then, "That is very tempting, Francesca."

She stared back, speechless.

"I don't know why you are so frightened. But I can guess." His expression changed, hardened. "This is clearly about Rick. Or Leigh Anne. As for what Lucy wishes of me, I have not a clue. Have no fear, Francesca. Your problems are not as overwhelming as you think they are. In the end, life has a way of leveling out the playing field."

She was ready to cry. Now she had an image of Hart holding a smoking gun. It was followed by an image of him standing before a judge in a packed courtroom, the verdict: *guilty*.

"Chin up," he murmured, and he leaned forward, about to kiss her cheek.

She started. He had never done more than kiss her hand; what was he doing?

At the last moment, he changed his mind, smiled with

some degree of self-derision, and about-faced. Lucy gave her
another warning glance and ran out of the room behind him.

It remained horrifically cold. Francesca stepped out of the
drive and onto Fifth Avenue, hugging her fur-lined coat to
her. It did not help. She was shivering madly.

She was not about to go to bed, where she would never
sleep. By now, Lucy had asked Hart to do the unthinkable.
Francesca felt certain he had agreed. When he had told her
he would commit murder for a person he loved, she had
believed him because he had meant it. She had to stop him
from murdering Craddock.

She looked up the avenue for a cab and at this late—or
early—hour saw nothing except two private coaches. She
began to shiver and shake. She would never find a cab, because to make matters worse, it was a Sunday night, which
was a night most people uptown spent at home. She was
going to have to walk.

It was only ten blocks, but ten of the coldest blocks in
her life. A gusting wind from the north did not help matters.
When Francesca paused outside of Hart's door at No. 973
Fifth Avenue, she felt blue. There was no more feeling in
her fingertips and toes.

She estimated it was half past midnight, so that the entire
house should be asleep, except for a doorman. Her knock
was promptly answered by Alfred. "Miss Cahill," he said, as
surprised to see her as she was to see him.

Francesca stepped quickly inside. "You are up late, Alfred."

"I was about to say the same thing about you." Alfred
seemed rather fond of her, and she had stumbled upon Hart
terribly drunk one afternoon and made him lock up all of
his employer's liquor. As Alfred had not been dismissed,
clearly it had worked out. "Dear God, you are blue. Here,
let me take that," he said, reaching for her coat. If he was

shocked that she was calling in the wee hours of the morning, he gave no sign.

"I'll keep it." She hugged her coat to her body. "This is an emergency, Alfred. I must speak with Calder. If he is asleep, I must ask you to rouse him."

Alfred smiled. "Mr. Hart never sleeps until one, sometimes two. Rather amazingly, he is up by five or six. He is in his library doing his paperwork, Miss Cahill."

Francesca was surprised. There was so much she did not know about him, she realized. But she was relieved. Doing paperwork was innocuous enough. "He enjoys his businesses, then?"

"I believe so. There is always a negotiation that is crucial and in progress," Alfred remarked, leading her down the front hall. "He has a meeting over breakfast at the Union Club this morning at seven," he said.

Francesca avoided glancing at the beautiful adolescent girl with the dove as they passed it. "Is anybody else up and about?" she asked carefully.

"Everyone retired some time ago." He seemed about to say more but checked himself.

They turned down a corridor with paintings lining the walls. There was a tapestry that seemed to be ancient, perhaps from the period of the Norman Conquest; she saw a Rembrandt, a Sargent, and an abstract that appeared to be nothing more than childish lines. Above it was a Titian. His collection was truly spectacular. Why would he want a portrait of her?

Alfred knocked on a pair of beautifully finished doors that were ajar. "Mr. Hart, sir," he said quietly.

Francesca had already stepped up behind Alfred, so she could gaze inside. Hart was sitting behind a huge desk that was probably eighty-odd inches long; legs as thick as her torso and beautifully sculpted in swirls supported it. The top was leather, she thought, but as most of the desk was covered with folders, files, and papers, it was hard to say. He had been sitting with his elbows on the desk, hands clasped, forehead on his hands. Francesca knew she was catching him in an extremely private moment—she could imagine what he was contemplating. Oddly, her heart leaped in the most erratic way.

He straightened and looked up. Their gazes locked. He shot to his feet. Papers fell to the floor. "Francesca?"

He was wearing his white dress shirt, which was open to the middle of his chest. The bow tie he'd worn earlier dangled about his collar. He still had on his black evening pants, but he'd removed the cummerbund. She somehow smiled, not the easiest task. "I hope that is an 'I am pleased to see Francesca' 'Francesca?' and not a 'do not disturb me' one." Her smile seemed to fail her. His shirtsleeves were rolled up, revealing strong, muscular forearms. Of course, she already knew that his hands were large and strong. But now, with him dressed so simply, she saw how broad his chest and shoulders were, how lean his waist, how narrow his hips. And she could not help noticing that his thighs, which were very muscular, strained against the expensive wool of his pants.

And he smiled, recovering. "I am always pleased to see you," he said in his lazy drawl—as if he had not just knocked over his papers like an awkward schoolboy. He stepped out from behind his desk, glancing at a huge antique bronze clock, set on another desk, this one small and for show and beneath a window. "It's half past midnight," he said. "The neighbors will talk."

She had to smile, because he had no neighbors.

He smiled back, but his gaze was inordinately watchful now. "Alfred? Bring us two brandies—the Louis Quatorze."

"I won't be that long," she said, oddly nervous now.

He smiled and it filled his dark eyes. "If you like scotch, you will like brandy, especially this brandy, which is from a very private and restricted reserve."

Alfred smiled far too widely for a servant, then backed out of the room, closing the doors behind him. The sound was oddly final.

"I suppose I could experiment with a brandy," Francesca said, more nervous now than before. An hour ago, she could

think of nothing else but convincing Hart not to do the unthinkable. Now, she despaired. Why hadn't she waited until
the early morning to confront him in his den?

He suddenly grinned. "Frankly, I imagine that there shall
come a day when you will wish to experiment in many
ways," he said.

"What does that mean?" She stiffened, suddenly wondering what his master suite was like and, more specifically, his
bed.

"You have been caged up like all proper young women. I
think that you have one wing out of the cage, Francesca, and
nothing will stop you from flying freely now."

She stared. Her heart turned over, hard. "Conventions are
tiresome, and even ridiculous, at times," she agreed. "And
unfair—as women must follow one set of rules, men another."

"I happen to agree with you completely," he murmured,
settling one hip on the edge of his desk.

"Hart. We have to talk," she said, finding his posture far
too provocative.

"So now it is 'Hart.' You do know that whenever you are
angry or upset with me—or nervous—'Calder' gets left by
the wayside and I become 'Hart.'"

"I'm upset," she said. Their gazes held, and she simply
had no wish to look away. "Very upset."

"You were very upset an hour ago," he agreed, his gaze
intent upon her face.

"What happened when you left? Did Lucy . . ." She
stopped. "What did she say?"

He reached out and caught her left hand. "She told me
everything," he said softly, while Francesca stiffened. Then
he reeled her toward him. "You are so worried, Francesca."

She stared at him. With him sitting on his desk while she
stood, they were almost eye-to-eye and nose-to-nose. "Why
are you smiling? What did she tell you? And then what happened!" she cried.

"And to think that last night I assumed it was Rick you

were worried about." He smiled, and he was obviously
pleased.

"Do not be boorish, now!" She tried to shake her hand
free of his, and when she failed, he let it go. She straightened,
asking, "Did she ask you to . . ." She stopped.

Her gaze had moved past his left shoulder. Sitting in the
center of his desk, amid his papers and files, was a gleaming
black gun. *"What's that?"*

He stood, glanced behind him. With no apparent urgency,
he walked around his desk and slipped the gun into a drawer.
She watched him lock it. And he looked up.

His eyes were so dark and so grim—Francesca wasn't
sure she had ever seen him this way. She had been frozen;
now she came to life. She raced around the desk and grabbed
his shirt with her good hand, her bandaged hand on his chest.
"Please. Please do not do this!"

He slid his own palm over her back. "Calm down. The
sky is not falling—yet."

"I can't calm down," she gasped. And even though she
was afraid, terribly so, his gesture felt like a caress. "Why
was that gun on your desk?"

"Francesca, unlike you, I am a very deliberate person. I
never act on impulse. I was considering my options," he said.
He still seemed unshaken, but no trace of his trademark
amusement could be seen. "Lucy is being blackmailed," he
continued calmly. "This fellow Craddock has recently threatened her children. And you and now I are the only ones who
know." He added, "First thing tomorrow, she and the children
are moving into this house, where they will be safe."

"You are so calm," Francesca remarked rigidly. "How can
you be so calm?"

"Calm? A woman I consider my sister is suffering greatly.
My calm is only surface-deep."

She was hardly reassured. And as their eyes held, she
sensed but did not see a huge well of anger within him. It
was so contained, so controlled. "This is out of control," she
whispered. "I begged her on Saturday to go to Bragg."

"I am not sure that going to the police is the best thing

to do," he said. "There may not be any love lost between Rick and me, but even I should pity him were he put in a position of having to arrest his own brother-in-law."

Francesca wet her lips. "So what is the answer?"

"Craddock's demise would help," Hart said as calmly.

"I knew it!" Francesca cried, her fists now clenched. Had she ever been this angry? "She dared to ask you to remove Calder, didn't she? She hasn't told her husband a word—God forbid he should be the one to commit murder—but you, you she does not hesitate to go to!"

"Yes, she asked me to remove Craddock." He could not seem to stop studying her.

"How could she!"

"Easily. We grew up together, Francesca. We share no blood, but we share a family—and a history. In a way, she is my sister, and there are times when I almost forget that we do not share a single drop of blood."

Francesca found herself grabbing his hands. "What did you say? Did you tell her you would do it?"

His hands tightened on hers in return; their gazes held. "Francesca, Lucy is in trouble. Who will help her if I do not? Frankly, she should have told Shoz. He would have ended this little matter before it ever began. But she didn't. And he is in Texas—we are here. If I do not help her, who will?"

"There is still the police. There is still Bragg. The one thing about him, he will see that there is justice—"

"Her husband was wrongfully incarcerated once," Hart said, interrupting. "I know you are a supreme romantic, but justice is a rare and capricious thing, Francesca. I am afraid for Shoz as well. I am afraid that, no matter the record of his life these past twelve years, Lucy may be right. If Craddock is blackmailing Lucy, Shoz has something to hide. Are you telling me that you think Rick would sweep this under the rug ... if Shoz is guilty?"

"I think there would be a way to prove him innocent!"

"As I said, you are a terrible and hopeless romantic," he said softly.

His tone was almost tender, but she could hardly remark

that now. "So the answer is to *murder* Craddock?"

He stared. "That is one answer," he finally said.

"I am begging you, Hart, begging you not to do this! Please, Hart, please, do not compromise yourself this way! What Lucy is asking of you is wrong. It is that simple. Murder is wrong!" she cried.

"So that is the extent of your concern? You wish to protect a convicted and violent felon from an illegal fate? A fate which, I might add, he does deserve?" He watched her carefully now.

"No," she said huskily, watching him as closely, "that is the least of my concerns." And she spoke the truth. Once, not so long ago, she would have been incredulous and disbelieving if anyone had ever suggested she might be thinking in the way that she now was. How strange life was.

He waited.

She breathed hard. "What if you can't get away with it? What if you are the one to be tried and convicted in the end?"

His gaze moved from her eyes, wandered over her face, then came back to her eyes. "I am flattered, Francesca," he said, with no mockery at all.

"This is not about flattery! Do you wish to be a sacrificial lamb?"

His gaze narrowed. It was brilliant with intensity now. "Actually, I have no intention of ever standing trial for any crime, my dear. How much do you care, Francesca?"

"Oh, stop it! Of course I care—or I wouldn't be here! There has to be another way, Calder; there simply has to be!" Oddly, the tears she had refused to allow to well for the past hour suddenly came, blurring her vision. She almost felt as if her own life were at stake.

He pulled her into his arms. "Don't cry."

The tears fell freely now, but she refused to make a sound. It crossed her dazed and stricken mind that she was actually in Calder Hart's arms. Her cheek was actually on his chest. . . . Her heart lurched and her body stilled. The tears stopped.

She was afraid to move. With the one eye she was capable

of using, as her other eye was pressed shut against his now wet shirt, she could see a large swath of dark skin, dusted with pitch-black hair. She could see the hard and muscular swell of the one side of his chest. She became aware of the firm, strong beat of his heart.

He had both hands on her back; even so, he held her rather loosely.

Every fiber of her being was on the highest alert. If she made one movement, she felt like she would snap. Still, she shifted and looked up, slowly pulling away. She saw the notch between his collarbones, the underside of his strong throat, the cleft of his chin.

His hands tightened, and then he released her.

He stood up so quickly that she almost fell face first onto his desk.

Francesca gripped the edge to save herself, for one moment so thoroughly dazed she did not have a coherent thought.

"Were those tears for me?" he asked.

She stared at her white knuckles, and she nodded.

He did not speak and he did not move.

Francesca dared to straighten and turn. "If you care about me at all—if you care about Lucy, Shoz, your family, yourself—you will not *remove* anyone!"

"I believe you already called in your marker, did you not?"

She was relieved he had become his callous self. She had—although she could not recall how and when. "This is not about markers," she said, after a pause. "And you know it."

"Touché." He shoved his hands into his trouser pockets. It only strained the fabric more tightly over his groin. "No one has been removed yet; no murder trial is pending."

"I can't let you do this, Calder," she said heatedly. And she was aware of flushing and forcing her gaze to hold his. "And I mean it."

"God help the man whom you love enough to marry." His brief smile vanished. "I think the first order of business is to interview Craddock. Thus far, he has been toying with a frightened woman; it is time he dares to toy with me."

Relief swamped her. "Thank God! But how will you find him? I have put out a reward, and we have yet to locate him."

He started; then amusement began. "You have offered a reward for him?"

She nodded. "Don't forget, my sidekick can get around the worst wards downtown."

He eyed her. "Have you forgotten that is where I also grew up?" he asked softly.

For a moment, surrounded by his art and his wealth, there alone in his huge house, facing him—a wealthy and powerful man—she had.

He smiled a little at her. "Leave this to me now, Francesca." His tone was patronizing. "I have already hired one fellow whom I have worked with in the past. I am fully confident that he can locate Craddock. We will find him— although perhaps not by Tuesday at noon."

She decided to ignore the fact that he had almost patted her on the head and told her to go home. "So you will confront him Tuesday, then, if you have not already done so?"

"Yes." He nodded approvingly. "That would be step one."

She froze. Comprehension seared her. She stood unsteadily. "And what is step two?"

He stared at her and did not answer.

She did not move. But the words came out, unbidden. "And then you will kill him?"

"Yes."

Fourteen

Bragg was just stepping out the door when Francesca arrived at his town house on Madison Square. He saw her as she stepped out of the cab, his eyes widening with surprise.

She rushed forward, tripping in her haste. He caught her, steadying her. She didn't think she had ever been happier to see anyone, and she clung to him. He would stop Hart from carrying out his mad scheme.

"Francesca? What's wrong?"

She embraced him and, leaning her cheek against the wool of his overcoat, she was aware of how much comfort and relief there was. There was no one she trusted more than this man, and she decided that she was going to make sure she never forgot that—especially around Hart.

She had intended to go to Bragg last night after leaving Hart's mansion. But Hart had insisted he escort her home personally, and she had been effectively waylaid.

His hand found her nape. "Francesca?"

She stepped back a little so their eyes could meet. "There is trouble, Bragg. You have to stop Hart—before he kills."

Bragg's eyes widened in shock. For one moment he did not respond, and then he released her, his face hardening. "I do not like the sound of this."

"I am so afraid," she returned.

"I can see that. I was on my way to headquarters, but let's go inside and you can explain yourself."

His choice of words took her back, but then she decided she was overwrought. She followed him back into the house and heard a woman's raised voice in the kitchen. It had to be the new nanny, Mrs. Flowers.

Guilt seized her. She hadn't seen the children since Thursday, when Bragg had brought them both by to visit her.

"And I have grown tired of your interference. Is that clear, my good man?" the crisp British voice asked.

Francesca looked at Bragg, imagining a tall, thin woman with a ramrod-straight bearing, spectacles, and the character of a marine sergeant. "Poor Peter," she whispered.

"Cats and dogs," he said, remaining terribly grim. "Do you wish to see the girls and meet the nanny your mother hired?"

"Of course," she said, pasting a smile on her face. She moved past him, trying to momentarily shove aside her worries about Hart and what he intended to do. In the light of day, she was very angry at Lucy for placing him in this position, no matter how understanding she tried to be.

Francesca paused in the kitchen doorway. Dot was on the floor, playing in a mess of cooked cereal. Katie was actually eating the very same oatmeal at the table. Both girls saw Francesca at the same time. Katie almost dropped her spoon, her brown eyes going wide. Dot clapped her hands and began to scream at the top of her lungs, "Frack! Frack! Frack come!"

Francesca saw Katie look down and pretend indifference to her arrival. She ate now with care. But at least the six-year-old was eating. The first week with Bragg—which was right after her mother's death—she hadn't eaten at all, and she was as thin as a rail to begin with.

Francesca swooped down on Dot, lifting her into her arms, taking in the scene by the stove. Mrs. Flowers was hardly tall and mean-looking. She was a tiny woman with curly dark hair and quite pretty features, just slightly plump. She did wear spectacles, but they somehow added to her pretty face. She could not be even five foot tall, Francesca saw, hiding a smile, and it was truly absurd for her to be confronting the Swede, who was six feet, six inches. Still, Mrs. Flowers stood facing Peter, her hands on her curved hips. He, of course, towered over her. His expression was one of resignation; no, he appeared to be suffering greatly and resigned to *that*.

"Katie shall go to school today, and that is that. There. Have I made myself clear, Mr. Olsen?"

Peter looked helplessly at Bragg.

Francesca hesitated. Was school a good idea? Of course, Katie should be in school, but the school would be a new one, and she had just lost her mother. Her behavior remained sullen and hostile, as well as aloof.

But before Francesca could speak, Mrs. Flowers faced them. "I have had years of experience, sir. I am fully aware of all that Katie is going through. But she must return to a normal routine. He shows me no respect. I cannot work here if my authority is not absolute, Commissioner."

Bragg said, "It is absolute, Mrs. Flowers. Peter, do you not agree?"

Peter grunted and walked to Katie. "Kat? A bit more?"

Katie shrugged, her gaze darting to Francesca, who was being strangled by Dot. Peter took that as an affirmative, and he took Katie's bowl to the stove to refill it.

"Hello, Mrs. Flowers," Francesca said as Dot began to tug on her hat and laugh as a flower came off in her hand. "I am Francesca Cahill. I believe my mother hired you."

Mrs. Flowers hurried over with the energy of a locomotive. "Yes, she did. And I told her I am used to running the household, as far as the children go. My references are impeccable, Miss Cahill. I cannot tolerate interference!" She huffed and she didn't look at Peter, but it was obvious to whom she referred.

"I am sure Peter has other duties he wishes to attend to," Francesca murmured. Then, "I do think the commissioner and I need to discuss whether Katie should return to school today or perhaps next week."

Mrs. Flowers did not look pleased.

"Ow, Dot, you have stabbed me with a hat pin," Francesca scolded gently while Dot cooed happily at her.

"Frack!" she screamed. It was an ecstatic and ear-splitting sound.

"School will get her mind off of her ordeal," Mrs. Flowers said. "Please put Dot down. She will hurt herself with that hat pin." Mrs. Flowers took the pin away from the child.

Francesca was impressed. At least the new nanny would safeguard the children from harm. She handed the struggling toddler over to Mrs. Flowers; Dot screeched in protest. Wincing, Francesca was about to take her back. "She hasn't seen me in a few days."

"A spoiled child is a troublesome child," Mrs. Flowers said firmly, not releasing Dot. "Dot, do calm down this instant."

From behind her, Peter gave Mrs. Flowers a glance. Clearly he was not about to miss a thing.

And to Francesca's amazement, Dot, who had opened her mouth to scream at the top of her lungs, now shut it. She regarded her nanny carefully.

"That's my sweet, good girl," Mrs. Flowers said, not using baby talk in her tone. "Now, let's get your sister ready for school and after we drop her there, you and I can go for a nice stroll in the park."

Dot hesitated, then smiled. "Park," she said. Then she beamed angelically at Francesca. "Frack!"

Francesca understood. "I'm afraid I have business to attend to, Dot. But we shall go to the park another time, when your sister can join us." She glanced at Katie, who was shoving her oatmeal around now with her spoon, clearly listening to their every word, but not looking up. Maybe it *would* get her mind off of her mother's death if she went to school.

Francesca paused by the small kitchen table where Katie sat. Katie did not look up. "Good morning, Katie. I'm sorry I haven't been by in a few days, but as you can see, I hurt my hand, and I was ordered to remain in bed."

Katie looked up. Then she surprised Francesca by speaking directly to her. "What happened?"

Francesca blinked and saw that Bragg, Peter, and Mrs. Flowers were all as surprised as she was. She quickly recovered and pulled out a chair and sat down beside the dark-haired child. "I burned my hand. Rather badly. I was, ah, trying to remove a log from the fireplace, and it was on fire. I am very lucky I did not set myself on fire. But all is well now, and I do believe the bandages will come off later today."

Katie looked at her, burst into tears, and ran from the room.

Francesca jumped up. "What happened?"

"I don't know, but thank God she is starting to show an interest in her surroundings," Bragg said.

Francesca hardly heard him. She dashed for the door, to follow Katie, but so did Peter and Mrs. Flowers. The big Swede and the nanny were faster than Francesca, and they collided in the doorway. Francesca halted before ramming into them herself.

"I will handle this," Mrs. Flowers said firmly, setting Dot down.

The toddler immediately crawled in a beeline to the kitchen table. She sat under it, grinning.

Peter gave Mrs. Flowers a very dark look, and without a word, he walked out of the kitchen first, using his bulk to do so.

Mrs. Flowers rushed after him. "Mr. Olsen! Olsen! *Olsen!*"

Francesca was about to tell them she would handle Katie when Bragg grabbed her arm. "What is going on, Francesca?" he said tersely.

"Shouldn't I go after Katie?" she asked worriedly.

"Kay Tee!" Dot shouted, crawling out from under the table. She hugged Bragg around the ankles. "Kaytee."

"In a minute. I have a nine o'clock meeting with Farr and several inspectors." He looked down and sighed. "Dot? You should be with your new nanny."

Dot ceased smiling and glared at him while Francesca wondered if Bragg expected Dot to understand his every word and to get up and obey. Dot said slyly, "Pa."

Although Francesca realized he had to leave immediately if he wished to be on time for his meeting, she blinked.

"What did she say?" she gasped, smothering the urge to laugh.

Bragg eyed her. "I have no idea."

"Pa!" Dot used his legs to haul herself up into a standing position. "Pa! Pa!"

Francesca clapped her hand over her mouth, helplessly giggling.

"What is so funny? She is the loudest child I have ever come across, the most demanding, and she piddles where she pleases."

Francesca nodded and said, "Craddock has demanded five thousand dollars. He has indirectly threatened the children. There has been a note and Lucy showed it to me."

"Christ," was his equally swift response. His eyes had turned nearly black. "And how is Calder involved?"

"Lucy went to him for help," she said tersely now. "Knowing his conscience is less than yours, she went to him so he would do her dirty work for her!"

"I see." Bragg seemed amazingly calm. "And Hart decided to remove Craddock from this life?"

"Yes, but first he intends to confront Craddock—when he finds him—in order to discover whatever it is that Craddock has on Shoz and Lucy."

"The picture becomes clear," Bragg commented. "You are very upset, Francesca."

"How can I not be upset? You should be upset as well! Your brother is intending to murder a man, Bragg."

"I am hardly surprised," he said.

She grabbed him. "That is not fair. You know as well as I do that this is entirely unfair. Hart may be many things, but he is not a killer."

His jaw was tight. "I take it Shoz has been left in the dark about this entire affair?"

"Lucy is trying to protect him. He remains in Texas at the ranch, ignorant of all that is happening here."

Bragg gave her a dark look. He walked away from Francesca, stepped in the oatmeal on the floor, and slid. He cursed.

Francesca knew his reaction had nothing to do with the mess on the floor. She hurried to him, avoiding the oatmeal. "Are you all right?" she asked softly. Of course he was upset. Hart was his brother, Lucy his sister, Shoz his brother-in-law.

He didn't turn. "Craddock is a convicted felon, of the worst sort. I have done some investigative work, and it seems likely that he did murder Larry Parridy. He is the kind of hoodlum that need not exist on the face of this earth. When he finishes terrorizing my sister, he will move on and find another victim."

"What are you saying?" she asked fearfully.

"I am saying that another police officer would look the other way and allow Calder to solve the problem. Another police officer would sweep any unsavory remains under the table, then throw away the key to any open doors." He faced her. His golden eyes moved over her face. "That is not the kind of man I am," he said.

"I know," she whispered, shaken. And she did know, but the extent of his personal and professional dilemma was only now beginning to hit her, hard. "What will you do?"

"I don't know," he said.

She stared.

"My brother-in-law has a past. A criminal past," he said. "My sister is happy. She loves her husband. I could never live with myself if I destroyed her marriage, her life, her happiness."

"Oh, God," Francesca whispered, scooping up Dot, who screeched and gripped her with gooey fingers. "Bragg? Shoz needs to know. He needs to know what is going on; he has a right to know! And we need to talk to him. He can tell us what Craddock knows. But there is no time!"

Bragg sighed. "Come with me," he said.

Curious, Francesca followed him out of the kitchen, down the hall, and into the study. He went to his desk and lifted what was clearly a telegram. "What is that?" She set Dot down.

"It's from the warden at Kendall. He was very cooperative," Bragg said. "Dot, the fire is still hot, no!" He rushed over to her and led her away from the fireplace where ashes were still glowing. Dot grinned at him.

"But I sent him a telegram yesterday!" Francesca cried as he let Dot go. She toddled off happily, only to fall to the floor. Undeterred, she managed to get up and start toddling again, making crowing sounds of glee.

"I sent him a telegram on Saturday, as soon as I had read Craddock's file," Bragg said. They both kept one eye on the child.

And Francesca sensed the worst. "What does it say?"

"It says he will meet me himself at the depot near Kendall tomorrow afternoon."

Exhilaration began to course over her. "You do mean he will meet *us* at the depot!"

"Francesca—"

She grabbed his arm. "I am coming, and besides, we work best as a team and you know it." She released him, filled with excitement. "What time do we leave?"

He hesitated. "At noon."

She was already out the door.

MONDAY, FEBRUARY 17, 1902 — 11:00 A.M.
Neil shook hands with the gentleman he had spent the morning doing business with, a smile on his face. But the moment the other man was out the door, the door solidly closed behind him, Neil's smile vanished. He stood in his entry hall, alone except for the doorman, and while his house was filled with people, it felt eerily empty.

Gloom settled over Neal like a heavy, soaking wet cloak. It was not a feeling he was accustomed to, so he did his best to ignore it, shake it off. It remained.

He walked through a large dining room, where their table had, at times, seated sixteen or even eighteen, with the addition of a leaf or two. For larger parties, the table would be removed and numerous round tables would fill up the room, covered with ivory damask cloths, silver, and crystal. In that instant, he could imagine the dining room on just such a festive evening—his wife was brilliant when it came to decor; she was brilliant as a hostess. An unusual flower arrangement would grace each table; the guests would be seated in a clever manner, so that the conversation never ceased. And Connie would not sit all night, not even to eat. She would flit from table to table, a vision in whichever evening gown she had chosen to wear, smiling, happy, loving every moment of the evening—loving him.

The scene vanished before his very eyes. He was shaken—it had been so real.

The gloom returned, heavier now. He dared not think of just when they had last had such an enjoyable evening. Even so, he knew the answer—before his damned stupid affair with Eliza Burton.

He regretted every moment he had ever spent thinking about the other woman, not just being in her arms. There was simply no excuse for his lapse. None. He should have remained faithful. He had not tried hard enough.

Unfortunately, his wife did not really care for relations. Not that she did not respond to him, for she did. He just knew that she preferred to avoid that part of their life. And he had tried so hard to avoid it, too.

As, unfortunately, until his marriage, he had been with a woman each and every night. He was a very virile man.

He entered the kitchen. He had probably never entered the kitchen in his entire life, not here, in his American home, and not in either of his homes in Great Britain. And the moment that he did, he was surprised.

Dozens of people were within. The noise level—all happy conversation punctuated with an Irishwoman's lilting song—was astounding. Added to it was the chopping of a knife on a wood block and the clattering of pots and pans. He could also hear his daughter Charlotte's laughter. His gaze found her at the pine table in the center of the room, where she was helping a kitchen maid mix a batter. Charlotte was eating the dough as much as she was stirring it, and the sight of her broke his heart.

She looked exactly like his wife. Charlotte was the most beautiful child he had ever beheld, just as Connie was the most beautiful woman.

The conversation ceased. The chopping of the knife on wood stopped. Pots banged—and then the silence was absolute.

Dozens of eyes turned to him, each and every one wide and astounded.

He felt himself flush. Before he could speak, Charlotte saw him and screeched, "Papa!" She leapt off the stool, to his amazement, not falling on her face, before Mrs. Partridge could react. Charlotte raced toward him on chubby legs and he caught her in his arms and swept her up against his chest.

"Hello, darling," he said, squeezing her hard.

"Papa, I am baking pie. Apple pie, we shall have it for supper tonight," she announced.

"And I shall love every bite," he said.

Charlotte's smile disappeared. "I am making it for Mama," she said.

He froze. He was afraid of what his little girl might say next.

But she only smiled. "Mama will love it and be happy," she said.

His heart lurched, hard, as if he were having cardiac arrest. "Of course she will love it," he said softly, setting Charlotte down. He looked up, at Mrs. Partridge. He had never paid very much attention to the girl's nanny until recently; now she seemed to be his confidante.

But the innuendos were intimate enough. "Where is Lady Montrose?" he asked quietly.

"She remains in her rooms, my lord," the tall, lanky woman said.

He had thought so. He stared—and the nanny stared back. Their thoughts flowed, melded. Why was Connie doing this? Each day it became worse. The woman he had married was up at six with the children. That woman had more energy than ten women combined. That woman would never remain in bed a bit later and later each and every day. Who was the woman upstairs, who no longer wished to go out and attend parties, who no longer wished to entertain their friends?

Who no longer loved her husband, her family, her life?

"Shall I go up and see if she needs anything?" Mrs. Partridge asked carefully.

"No. Have breakfast sent up." His mind sped. Connie had hardly been eating—he could see that she had lost weight. Her face was taking on gauntness. "An omelette, please, with her usual tea and toast."

"Papa?" Charlotte tugged on his hand. "I want to see Mama, too."

He hesitated. "Another time, sweetheart."

Charlotte's eyes widened, and then her expression changed, becoming set and stubborn, oh yes. In this way, she reminded him not of her mother, but of her Aunt Francesca. "No! I want to see Mama, Papa! I want Mama!" And suddenly tears filled her wide blue eyes. "Mama doesn't play with me anymore! She doesn't play with Lucinda! I want Mama!" She stomped her little foot, hard.

It would be so easy to give in. He lifted her up into his arms, gave Mrs. Partridge a look, which she understood, and left the kitchen. Mrs. Partridge followed. "You may visit Mama when she has her breakfast. I wish to speak to her alone first."

Charlotte hesitated, and he almost smiled, for her mind was racing—she was trying to decide whether or not to accept his offer. Finally, she smiled just a little and nodded. "Can I have breakfast, too? I want an omelette."

"Have you eaten?" he asked.

She nodded.

"Then you shall have to ask Mrs. Partridge," he said. He left the two of them negotiating over the terms of a second breakfast. The gloom was inescapable now. It filled each step as he went upstairs. Outside Connie's closed door he paused, listening intently. But if she was moving about her rooms, he did not hear a thing.

He hesitated, then knocked. There was no reply.

He knocked again, with more insistence. After a long

pause, he reached for the doorknob. As he turned it, he heard her say, "Who is it?"

He froze, the door ajar. "It is I, Connie."

She hesitated now. "One moment, Neil."

Oddly, he did not like the sound of that. Without thinking it through, he pushed open her door and was faced with utter darkness.

He blinked and saw his wife standing before the drawn draperies, about to open them. She was wearing her night-clothes, her hand on the pull cord, looking over her shoulder at him. Not a single light was on.

She came to life, pulling open the curtains, and sunlight filled the sitting room. "I asked you to wait," she said calmly, moving to another set of draperies and opening those, too.

He did not answer. He walked over to the closed door that adjoined her bedroom and opened it. That room was utterly dark, too.

"Neil?" Her tone was terse.

He found a lamp and turned it on. The four-poster bed was mussed, for clearly she had slept there. The rest of the room was as neat as a pin.

"Neil?"

He went to the heavy gold satin draperies and pulled them open. Connie's room was painted a warm buttercup yellow. Her bed was upholstered in shades of beige, gold, and yellow, the pattern floral, with flashes of dark red and burnt orange. Similar colors had been used throughout the room, and rich Persian rugs covered the wood floors. It was a warm, happy, cheerful room, at once elegant and inviting. The same color scheme extended to her sitting room, except that there the walls were a darker gold, and numerous red pillows brightened up the sofa. He turned and found her standing in the sitting room, watching him. The moment he turned, she smiled, but it seemed terribly grim.

"Have you just gotten up?"

"Yes. I don't feel well, today."

"Shall I call Dr. Finney?"

"No, I am sure it will pass."

"Connie." He strode across her bedroom and into the sitting room. It, too, seemed undisturbed. It was as if no one had been there for even a moment. And his wife was not excessively neat. She was hardly indifferent to tidiness, but usually a scarf would be lying on a chair, a purse on a bureau, jewelry by the bedside table. She was an avid reader of fiction, mostly popular romance, and there was always a book lying open somewhere, along with a pair of reading glasses.

And then he realized what was really missing, not just from this room, but from the house. Connie adored flowers. The house was always full of them, and in her own rooms she might have a half a dozen arrangements, from a single rose in a bud vase to a huge and extravagant bouquet. Where were all the flowers?

Where was his wife?

"What is it, Neil? Did you wish to speak to me?"

He stared. Even now, she remained impossibly beautiful; even having just arisen from bed, she could have slipped off her nightclothes and thrown on an evening gown and gone out just that way. Then he had an image of her perfect, naked body. The few times he had dared to admire her, she had been flushing with embarrassment.

He did not want to think about her that way now. Desire was instantaneous. He knew he was always going to want to make love to his wife.

"You are staring," she said rigidly. "I did just get up, Neil. I did ask you to wait."

"Charlotte misses you. I miss you," he said impulsively.

Something flashed in her blue eyes and then she turned her back to him. "Did she say that?"

He hesitated, her heart pounding, a roar in his ears. "Yes. And I am saying it, Connie." He went to her and gently cupped her shoulders from behind.

She stiffened. "I am merely a bit under the weather, Neil. I shall be fine in no time at all," she said in a light, forced tone of voice.

Despair claimed him. "You are not fine. You are slipping

away from me. Please come back," he heard himself say.

She pulled away, walked over to the windows, and stared out at the corner of Madison Avenue and Sixty-first Street. "I am not slipping away, Neil. I have a cold, I think, and a touch of a migraine." She did not turn to him as she spoke.

He closed his eyes, in real despair. How could he win his wife back? How? He tried another tack. "Did you enjoy yourself last night?"

She turned, and he saw relief in her eyes. "Yes, I did."

"I am not pleased with Julia's scheming over Hart and Francesca. That must be stopped."

"Why? He clearly is fond of her, and he does need to wed, eventually."

Neil could not believe his ears. "He will break her heart, Connie." He did not add, "just as he would have broken yours if you dared to continue flirting with him."

"Well, I think we should take a wait-and-see attitude." She smiled at him.

The smile was genuine, if brief; he was thrilled. He rushed to her, but before he could take her hand she pulled away. He froze.

Then she smiled again, and it was forced. "Can you send up the girls?"

"I already have. Charlotte is having a second breakfast with you."

Her smile vanished. "I have no appetite."

"Connie, we have to talk."

"Neil? I am really not up to anything, much less a serious conversation. Which, from your grim expression, I can see is what you have in mind. I didn't sleep well last night. In fact, I haven't been sleeping well all week. I am really tired."

He watched her walk away. "Are you punishing me?"

She halted but did not turn. It was a moment before she spoke. He expected her to deny it politely. She said, "You made your bed and now you shall sleep in it, Neil."

As Francesca and her maid, Bette, began packing a few necessities for an overnight trip, most of which would be spent upon a train, Francesca tried to develop a plausible reason for going out of town for a day. But this was the first investigation that was taking her so far afield, and she was too excited to come up with a single excuse. She really couldn't think of a single thing that she would rather do than travel out of the city with Bragg while trying to solve a crime.

"I think that will do," Francesca said, glancing at the bronzed clock on her desk, which sat catty-corner from her lovely four-poster bed, on a wall before a window. She had packed her best (prettiest) nightgown and robe, slippers, a change of undergarments, a second shirtwaist, and a few items for her personal hygiene. At the last moment she added a pot of lip rouge and a bottle of French perfume. Bette had eyed her a few times as she folded the lacy nightgown, which was hardly a winter garment. "Can you leave the bag downstairs by the front door? Thank you, Bette!"

Francesca ran from the room, down the hall, and to her parents' bedroom. The door was ajar—a maid was within, making the bed and tidying up. "Where is my mother?"

"In her dressing room, Miss Cahill."

Francesca smiled a thank-you and darted through the bedroom and an opulent sitting room with orange marble floors and into a carpeted boudoir with peach-hued walls and matching upholstery in a variety of prints.

Julia was choosing a hat as she ran in. "Francesca? This is a surprise." She was wearing a navy blue dress in an exquisite washed silk, so the dress seemed to catch and then reflect the light every time she moved. "Do you like this hat?" She held up a small pretty dark blue hat with a lace band and several very real-looking roses upon it.

"Yes. Mama, I must go out of town. But I shall be back first thing in the morning!"

"Absolutely not," Julia said calmly.

Francesca smiled brightly. "You have not even asked why. It is a matter of extreme importance to the Bragg family. Actually, I am doing Lucy a huge favor."

Julia had put on the hat and was studying her reflection carefully in the mirror.

"Mama?"

She turned. "What kind of favor, Francesca?"

"It is a very personal one," she said.

"Are you on another investigation?"

Francesca froze.

"I thought so. The way you have been dashing about these past few days, I simply knew it." Julia removed the hat and stared grimly at her.

"Mama, I am helping Lucy. Please try to understand. Do not make me defy your authority!" Francesca cried.

"I don't want you in danger," Julia said.

"I am twenty years old. If I cannot make my own decisions now, when will I ever be able to?"

Julia said, "Many women never make an important decision, not a single one, not once in their life."

"You have made every important decision in this house," Francesca said. She grabbed her mother's hand with her left one. "Mama? Surely you realize I intend to make my own decisions, even if I do marry one day?"

Julia sighed. "Yes, I do know that."

"I am trying to help Lucy, Mama. It is really important. And . . . I am not lying to you."

"Francesca, you are not a liar. You have never been a liar," Julia said with a slight smile.

"But in the past few cases, I had to withhold the truth. I am not doing that now," Francesca said earnestly.

"Where are you going?"

"Upstate."

"Where, exactly?"

"I cannot say."

"And with whom?"

She didn't hesitate. She kept a straight face. "I am going with Bragg—and Hart." And that was a lie. A complete and terrible lie.

"Hart is joining you?" she asked, smiling widely. "And Rick Bragg?"

Francesca bit her lip. If Julia ever found out, she would

never trust her again. But if she had told her the truth, a huge argument would have ensued.

"When do you leave?" Julia asked, her smile not fading.

"Right now."

Julia hugged her. "Andrew may murder me for this." Her smile vanished and her gaze met Francesca's.

Francesca bit her lip. "Can't you and Papa make up?"

Julia pulled away. "I don't know. Evan has moved out. But you already know that, don't you?"

Francesca nodded. "But you and Papa must make up! You cannot quarrel over Evan, as I truly do not think there is anything you can do to make him change his mind."

Julia closed her eyes in despair, then opened them and smiled. "Have a safe trip," she said, and she hugged her. "I will manage your father."

It was a rare day indeed that he was out and about so early, as he was a creature of the night. Evan smiled up at the morning sun, inhaling the cold fresh air. He stood on the steps of the Fifth Avenue Hotel, where he had taken a room.

He had almost taken a suite. But as he was checking in, he thought about his finances—the fact that he had no income and was hugely in debt, but had, currently, good credit, at least with the right people. So he had taken a room instead of a suite, feeling rather pleased with himself as he did so.

He glanced up and down Fifth Avenue. Just across the avenue was Madison Park. To his surprise, quite a few gentlemen and ladies were strolling across it, usually in pairs of the same gender. As it truly was a beautiful morning, he realized it was not that surprising.

He set off, heading downtown. Over breakfast in his room, he had made a list of gentlemen whom he might approach for a job. These were men he knew socially, as did his father. He had crossed off anyone on that list who was a real friend and not just a social acquaintance of Andrew Cahill. He felt confident that he would have a job and an income by that evening. After all, he had been employed in a big business most of his life. He could analyze finances no matter the subject. He realized he was excited to begin using his intellect for something other than slaughterhouse accounts.

He heard himself whistling as he strode down the block. And as he did, it crossed his mind that he hadn't had a chance to say good-bye to Mrs. Kennedy and her children before leaving the house. That fact made him sober a bit. As he had no intention of going back to the house, he decided that he would send her a note. And perhaps he would invite Julia to meet him for lunch or tea later that day, simply to reassure her that all was well and that his leaving was not the end of the world.

A gentleman without a coat was walking ahead of him, but more slowly. As he stopped to regard a shop-front window, Evan shifted slightly so as to avoid bumping into him as he passed. But the man suddenly moved, and Evan was knocked completely off balance, almost to the point of falling.

"Hey!" he exclaimed, regaining his balance and meeting a pair of dark eyes. "I do beg—" He never finished his sentence. Metal flashed in a gloved hand. In that instant, he knew the man was not a gentleman, just as he knew what was going to happen and why it was happening.

But no shot was fired. He was hit in the back of the head. The pain was like lightning, blinding him.

But still he managed to stay upright, panicked. And as he swung his fist to defend himself, he knew this was the end.

His blow glanced off of the other man's chest. And then brass knuckles connected with his cheek, and as his head snapped back, as the impact of the brutal blow filled him with more pain, Evan found his feet knocked out from under him as the man kicked him in the leg. As he went down, an arm went around him, like a vise.

Panic.

God, was this really the end?

And even through the haze of white-hot pain, he felt himself dragged across the street, thrown down. He finally managed to see his assailant's face, and he recognized that man as Charlie, just Charlie, a big brute who guarded a particular moneylender and loan shark. He knew he had to explain; the brass knuckles smashed across his forehead. Evan caught Charlie's wrist.

Charlie laughed, shaking him off, and a booted kick came, right in the ribs.

Evan gasped, blinded, as his ribs cracked and broke.

More kicks followed, each and every one carefully aimed—his stomach, his kidneys, his groin. There were more blows with the brass knuckles. And he lay helpless, a heap of broken bones, choking on his own blood.

And then the whisper came. "Don't worry; you won't die. This is just a warning, Cahill," it said.

Fifteen

The warden had met them at the train depot, which consisted of nothing more than a wood shack with a bolted door and a dilapidated sign that was hanging lopsidedly and read: KEN-DALL. They were the only two passengers to disembark; in another hour and fifteen minutes the train would be stopping in Albany.

"You must be Commissioner Bragg. Read a bit about you, I did. Guess you're the lady detective, Miz Cahill. Decided to come down and meet you folks, as it ain't often I got a big investigation on my hands."

Bragg shook Warden Timbull's hands. The warden was a big man with heavy jowls and a huge belly. He was chewing tobacco and he smelled a bit like cheap whiskey, but he had smiling eyes. "Thanks for meeting us, Warden," Bragg said. "I appreciate it, as time is of the essence. We are taking the twelve-oh-five back to the city tonight."

"Can't say I blame you," Timbull remarked, shifting the wad of tobacco to another cheek. He smiled as he picked up Francesca's bag. "Now that's the prettiest detective I ever did see."

Francesca actually flushed. "Thank you, Warden."

"Nothing of it," he said, leading the way down three oak steps, one with a gaping crack, and onto a boardwalk that was crusted with ice and snow. "Careful. Slippery as anything out here."

As it was a dark, moonless night, it was hard to see, much less to watch her step. One streetlight was glowing perhaps a half a football field away, and as Francesca could see the outlines of a dozen buildings, she assumed that was the heart of the town. She felt Bragg grasp her elbow firmly and she dared to look at him.

He avoided her eyes.

He had been avoiding her all day, it seemed, no easy task, considering that they had been sharing a private compartment together ever since they had boarded the train just before noon. The eight-hour train ride had passed in an awkward manner, as if they were strangers, not a man and a woman in love or even friends. Bragg had hunkered down with more reports and files than any man should ever have to read. He'd merely remarked that this was his chance to catch up on paperwork and then he'd erected a brick wall around himself, which she knew she must not breach. Francesca had been stunned.

She had expected to spend the day in conversation, discussing the case, politics, their life. Apparently Bragg had different ideas.

Fortunately, Francesca had brought both her biology text and Flaubert's *Madame Bovary* with her, and she used the time to catch up on her own studies. The conductor had also come by with various newspapers, and she had taken the *Times, The Sun,* and the *Daily News.* At six Bragg had suggested that they break to dine.

Francesca had carefully folded up the *Times.* "You're ignoring me," she had said quietly. The truth was, she felt crushed.

"I am trying to get through my work," he'd said as quietly.

"I think we need to talk."

"Francesca, I think that is not a good idea. We have a very long evening ahead of us." His gaze was direct.

"Why are you doing this?" She stood up.

He hesitated. Then, "I am afraid to let you come too close—when we are alone like this. It is myself I do not trust," he said, his eyes holding hers.

With her somewhat relieved and somewhat mollified, they'd gone to the dining car. When they began their meal, Bragg told her that he'd sent a telegram to Shoz, advising him to come to New York. "I want to find out from Shoz himself what happened, and then I shall know how to proceed," he had said.

Francesca had reached across the linen-clad table to take his hand. As it was now dark out, nothing could be seen outside of the train's window, with the dining car lit by glass-domed candles. "Then *we* shall know how to proceed, Bragg."

He had smiled a little at her, their eyes meeting, and she'd thought about the sleeper train they would take back to the city, her heart quickening. She knew he was thinking about it, too, for she saw the flare of heat in his eyes before he withdrew his hand, looked away, and picked up his fork, eating his steak with determination.

Now Timbull heaved her small valise into the back of an open buggy. Bragg tossed in his own small duffel. "Sorry I ain't got a better vehicle. Belongs to the prison, you know."

"How far is it from here?" Francesca asked.

"Not far. Maybe thirty minutes." He smiled at her, his teeth stained and yellow.

When they were all seated together on the single front seat and on their way out of town, Timbull said, "Decided to read those files you asked for, in case it jogged the ole brain. Hard to recollect all the way back to '96, much less to 1890."

"And did it help?" Bragg asked.

Francesca was shivering. She sat between the two men, and she inched a bit closer to Bragg, her only wish to become warm.

Timbull saw and eyed her. "Real cold up north, ain't it? Five below, tonight."

"No wonder I can't stop shivering," Francesca said, managing a smile anyway.

Bragg hesitated and their eyes met. Then he put his arm around her. "That coat isn't warm enough."

"No, it is not," Francesca agreed, her teeth chattering. Then, snuggling closer to him and trying to ignore the thrilling tingle of desire, she said, "What did you find, Warden?"

"He sure was a model prisoner. Recall him now, oh yeah.

Kept to himself, stayed out of fights, did as he was told."
Timbull glanced at them both as the gelding trotted along
the snowy country road. They were passing rolling pastures
now, Cranston having been left far behind. Cattle seemed to
dot the countryside.

"Craddock was a model prisoner?" Francesca gasped.

Bragg twisted to look at her. "No, he's talking about Shoz.
Aren't you, Warden?"

"Yeah, Shozkay Savage. The Indian. He was no trouble,
although when he first arrived, there were a few fights. I been
warden here since '89. Once I read those files, it all come
back to me. That Savage fellow ain't the kind of man a
fellow forgets. Strong, silent type. Yeah, I remember him.
Kinda man you don't want to make mad, if you know what
I mean. All them fights was him bein' picked on, tested.
Savage defended himself real good and then he was left
alone. Can't tell you what a big surprise it was, my best-
behavin' prisoner up and escaping." He frowned.

Francesca was still shivering, and she was pleased when
Bragg rubbed her arm lightly, not looking at her. "What
about Craddock?" Bragg asked the warden. "Do you remember him at all?"

"I didn't, not until I read *his* file. Ha!" Timbull snorted.
"Now he was a problem. He was in more fights than you
could count, did solitary two dozen times. He actually
stabbed a fellow inmate with a toothbrush, right in the eye,
blindin' him, the argument over some woman who came to
visit one of them prisoners. He was trouble from day one,"
Timbull said flatly. "An' he didn't think twice about taking
out another man's eye."

Francesca and Bragg exchanged a look.

"That's hardly a surprise," Francesca said. "What about
the relationship between Shoz Savage and Joseph Craddock?"

"Don't know." He grinned at her.

Francesca was disappointed. "Is there anyone at the prison
now who was there in 1890 whom we might speak to?"

"Doubt it," Timbull said cheerfully. " 'Nother five minutes or so. Prison's up on the top of that hill."

Francesca followed his gaze and saw nothing but a series of dark hilly outlines.

Bragg said, "I've had two of my men doing a bit of investigative work, Warden."

Timbull cocked a brow. Francesca looked at Bragg in surprise.

"Apparently there was a big scandal just after you took over Fort Kendall."

Timbull stared. "You must mean the murder," he finally said.

Francesca twisted. "The murder? What murder?"

Timbull sighed. "Just one of the prisoners, ma'am."

"It was never solved," Bragg said quietly. "And Shoz escaped a week later, at the end of February 1890."

Timbull grunted. He shook the reins, urging the horse on.

Francesca could not believe that Bragg had not mentioned this before. Of course, the murder of a fellow inmate just before Shoz's escape might not mean anything. Or it could mean everything.

"Warden? Surely you recall the first and only scandal of your administration of the prison?"

He spat now, almost angrily, over the side of the buggy. "One morning a guard found him strung up in his cell, carved up good, and hanged. Coroner said he died from a broken neck, not loss of blood. Someone did a number on him."

"You mean torture?" Francesca gasped.

"Oh, yeah, he was tortured, all right, Injun style. Long and slow."

Francesca did not want to think about the fact that Lucy's husband was mostly Apache and, to use her own words, extremely hard and dangerous. "Who was he?" she whispered.

"Cooper. Randy Cooper. Cooper had been a big man inside. He ran the show, so to speak. In every prison there's a king and his army. Cooper was king. Big smart fellow, as cold as ice—colder. Anyone who didn't play his game his way got his head busted, sooner or later. You know what I mean." He gave Bragg a significant look. "Wasn't a single witness, if you know what I mean. We're here," he said as they drove past a pair of fortlike gates.

Francesca saw that a long, ugly building lay ahead of them, surrounded by a wood stockade. She shivered—this prison felt terribly unpleasant now.

Bragg faced Timbull. "Any guesses as to why Cooper was tortured and murdered? Any suspicions as to who did it?"

"There was an investigation, but bein' as no one came forward to say a single word about him or the murder, it was dropped. He was a badass—er, a real bully, Commissioner. He had his own army of soldiers; even the guards were afraid of him."

"So any prisoner might have hated Cooper enough to torture and murder him?"

"That's right."

Francesca and Bragg faced each other again. It was a moment before he turned to Timbull. "Any interactions between him and Shoz?" Bragg asked.

"Shoz got his ass kicked a few times, if I recall, by Cooper and his gang of thugs. Everyone did. But he wouldn't join the gang; like I said, he kept to himself. Never said a word, pointed a finger, nuthin'. But generally speaking, they didn't have any business, if you know what I mean."

"An' Craddock?"

Timbull grinned. "He was one of Cooper's top guns. In fact, after Cooper, he was top man. When Cooper bit the bullet, Craddock got the throne." With that, he heaved himself out of the front seat of the buggy.

Francesca met Bragg's glance. "What are you thinking? Where are you going with this?" She asked in a whisper so Warden Timbull would not hear.

He hesitated. "Cooper was the alias Shoz used after escaping prison."

Three hours later, the local train was pulling out of Kendall. Francesca and Bragg had spent the past hours in the warden's

office, reading every word in the files of all three men, as
well as the extremely scant investigative report. They had
learned nothing new, but the warden had told them that Craddock's reign hadn't lasted very long—another felon had been
placed at the prison, someone stronger, smarter, and meaner
than Craddock, who had been demoted to a lieutenant again.

"Lady's compartment," the conductor said, sliding open
her wood door. Two beds were in the small space, one directly above the lower one. "Beds fold in. Table there comes
out," he said, indicating a folded tabletop beside which was
a single small chair. "Dining car opens at six; club car stays
open all night." He turned in the small space of the corridor.
"Your compartment, sir." He slid open the door to an identical cubicle.

"Thank you," Bragg said.

Because it was extremely difficult to move with the three
of them standing in the narrow corridor, Francesca stepped
inside her compartment. The conductor tipped his hat and
walked on down the train.

Francesca looked at Bragg. "We have to meet Shoz. I'm
sure he has quite a bit to say on the subject of prison life—
and some strong opinions about Cooper's murder."

Bragg didn't comment.

She touched his arm; he was so very grim. "Just because
Shoz used Cooper as an alias for seven years doesn't mean
he killed him."

"I'll bet there were quite a few witnesses to Cooper's murder, and I have a hunch that Craddock was one of them."

Francesca started.

"I am going to the club car," Bragg said abruptly. He
smiled, but it was tight. "Good night, Francesca."

She felt her mouth drop open, but he didn't see, as he
was already walking after the conductor, swaying a bit along
with the train.

She was in disbelief. This was their chance to freely discuss the case, and he was simply walking away. And what
was she supposed to do by herself? Sleep? As if she could!

She slammed shut her compartment in a fit of anger, and

it crossed her mind that Calder Hart would never abandon her like this. He'd go to the club car, fetch a pair of whiskeys, and they'd spend the next few hours discussing the world— and his jaded view of it.

Francesca sat down hard on the lower bunk, whacking her head as she did so. Tears filled her eyes.

She was losing him.

She stood, because sitting was impossible without craning her neck in a hurtful position. She told herself that she was not losing him. He was trying to be virtuous. He was trying to protect her virtue—because he loved her. And because being alone with her was simply too difficult, now.

Francesca moved carefully to the chair beside the folding tabletop, and sat down on it. What should she do?

Hart's image came to mind. *Unless you come to your senses and forget this absurd notion that you love my brother, this is war.*

She did not want to think about Leigh Anne now.

Rick is married; Calder is not.

Grace's words dared to echo next. Francesca wanted to clap her hands over her ears. Neither of them knew that Bragg was prepared to divorce his wife for her. Perhaps she was wrong to refuse his marriage proposal. Perhaps their personal happiness was more important than his political future; besides, they could still reform the world even if he wasn't in politics. There were hundreds of causes they could take up, hundreds of societies and unions to join and support, and countless charities to raise money for.

But he was a natural-born leader. His place was in government.

Francesca rubbed her eyes. Suddenly she was exhausted. Nothing was going the way she had hoped, and now, too late, she realized she had packed her sheer, lacy nightgown for a reason, so he could admire her in it—worse—to break his self-control.

But he was stronger than she was. He wasn't going to compromise her, and she loved him even more for it.

But where, dear God, could they go from here?

The answer was chilling. It whispered through her tiny sleeping compartment like a sigh coming from the train's chugging wheels. *Nowhere.*

Francesca left the stool abruptly, curling up on the lower bunk, hugging her pillow. The weight of worry coupled with grief settled upon her like a hundred-pound rock. Perhaps Bragg wasn't her destiny after all; perhaps they were doomed.

Tears moistened her eyes, blurring her vision. The train chugged on, but there was no comfort in the rocking motion or the steady sound. The small light from the lantern danced before her eyes. She saw Bragg and Leigh Anne; she saw Hart.

Suddenly Francesca was awake. The lantern continued to burn brightly, and she realized she had fallen asleep, but obviously not for very long. She strained to hear, for something had awoken her, and then she was rewarded by the sound of his compartment door sliding closed with a loud and resounding click.

She sat up, whacking her head as she did so.

"Ow." Holding her throbbing head, she slipped out from under the top bunk, breathless now. What time was it? Did it matter? She stood unsteadily and fell against one wall as the train veered around a curve. She unlatched the shade to peek outside—it remained pitch-black. She didn't have a clue as to whether she'd been sleeping for an hour or hours.

Her gaze fell upon her small valise. An image danced in her mind, and while she knew she should not, she snatched the valise, opening it. She quickly dug out her lace night-gown and a silk robe trimmed with the same ivory lace.

The garments were nearly weightless and silken in her hands.

Did she dare?

And why was she so afraid?

If they made love now, there was no going back. It would solve their problems—seal their love. And that was what she wanted. That was what she had wanted from the moment they had met.

She refused to entertain doubts now. Francesca unbuttoned and shrugged out of her shirtwaist and camisole. Her nipples hardened from the cold, but she ignored the chill. She slipped off her skirt, petticoat, and drawers. Then she stepped into the nightgown, a sheer sheath held up by two tiny lace straps. Lace trimmed the low bodice and the hem. A small rosebud was in the center of the bodice, which was enticingly sheer.

Her teeth were chattering now. It was probably five below in the compartment, too, she thought, and it was easier dwelling on that notion than on what she intended to do—and what might or might not happen. She slipped on the robe, belting it tightly; then she realized that was not helpful, and she loosened the sash.

She hesitated, then unpinned her hair, shaking out the golden waves. Her hair fell to her shoulder blades.

Rouge.

She dug into the valise, found the pot, and applied a dab to her lips and cheeks. It was hard to feel now. She just knew she could not turn back, as if, in doing so, she might never get back on track.

She had a small hand mirror tucked inside the valise, and she paused to check her reflection. She started, because her eyes were wide with apprehension and anxiety and perhaps even fear.

What could she possibly be afraid of?

Bragg *was* her destiny.

She looked again, but the fear remained in her wide cornflower blue eyes. The rouge, however, was fine. She lowered the glass and hesitated. Her ensemble hid nothing. Her every curve was obvious, the outline of her breasts, her aureoles and nipples, her ribs, her navel, her sex. She could hardly breathe. Could she really do this?

I am throwing myself at a man, she thought, suddenly grim.

A married man.

She was about to sit back down on the bunk, but in the nick of time she recalled hitting her head twice. Instead, she held onto the wall with one hand. But she loved Bragg. And he loved her. He despised his wife, and he'd been separated for four years.

She wasn't soothed. She could hardly breathe.

Just do it, she thought.

But what if it did not solve all of their problems?

Even if you become his lover, there will only be ruin, guilt, and shame.

Are you afraid that the story you have told yourself will blow up in your face?

She refused to heed her fear or Hart's terrible words. Filled with determination, Francesca slid open her compartment door just enough to peek out and make sure that no one was in the corridor. It was empty. She stepped out and knocked on his door. "Bragg!" she cried, almost desperate now.

There was no answer.

She banged again. "Bragg! I'm locked out of my compartment!"

A moment passed, in which she wondered if he had heard her and was being obstinate, or if he was sound asleep. But then his door slid open. "Why don't you call the—" he began, and he stopped.

His gaze slammed to her breasts, her hips, her thighs, and the hot delta in between.

Francesca managed a smile and darted past him, into his compartment. She was trembling now.

He turned slowly. "Your compartment door is open, Francesca," he said calmly.

"I lied. I can't sleep," she said in a rush. Oh, God. What was she doing? *So cling to your damn fairy tale! But there will not be a happy ending, Francesca.* And with his words, Hart's dark, intense, and angry image came to mind.

She did not want to think about him now! Not now!

"You cannot stay here," Bragg said, unmoving.

She met his gaze and stilled. The panic and the fear stilled. The voices in her head stilled. And something else came to life, deep within her, and she recognized it instantly.

She was alone in a tiny sleeping compartment with a gorgeous man, a man she loved, and there was no mistaking the way he was looking at her now. This was what she wanted—wasn't it?

Francesca did not understand herself now. She remained afraid, and there was dread, too, but with her ambivalence there were other sensations that were not ambivalent at all. Her loins were swelling, an involuntary reaction to the man she was with and the night. She recognized the tightening there, the budding urgency, the need.

"You are trying to seduce me," Bragg said roughly.

She nodded. "Yes."

He leaned back against the compartment door, which he'd left ajar. He stared up at the ceiling. She could see his pulse throbbing in his throat.

Her thoughts began to simmer down, to calm. The night was no longer cold, it was warm and vital, alive, and she was on a train, hundreds of miles from the city, with Bragg. *They were alone.* Entirely, completely alone. No one would walk in on them now. No one would ever know what happened in his sleeping compartment, other than her and him.

Her breasts felt swollen, too. Heavy, full. And he was looking at them. Staring at her low bodice, her erect nipples, which were barely covered by the French lace.

"Francesca." Bragg's tone was low, husky . . . seductive. He looked up now, his golden eyes heated. "Please go."

And she hesitated.

Your friendship is more important to me than sex, Hart's voice purred in her mind. *Oh yes, I see the writing on the wall. And I must stand by and watch it all unfold . . .*

Francesca almost hated Hart then. How dare he predict her future? And he was wrong! Wasn't he?

"Last chance," Bragg said so softly she could hardly hear him, and she saw him tremble.

It crossed her mind that she could go, that she should go, that Hart was right. "I'm staying," she heard herself whisper, but not without a terrible accompanying pang of anxiety.

After this moment, there would be no going back.

Bragg's arm whipped out before she had even finished her words, and he caught her, his grip so hard that she gasped. But he did not loosen it, and their gazes collided, locked.

Hunger consumed his eyes, his face.

What was she doing?

He pulled her against him, his mouth covering hers. He was all muscle and bone, a man of steel. And the moment she was against him, her body seemed to explode in greed and pleasure; the moment she was wrapped in his arms, she knew it was right. Francesca wrapped her arms around him as their mouths fused, as his tongue thrust against hers, mating wildly within her mouth. She felt him reach out behind her, abruptly sliding the door closed.

Anxiety stabbed at her again. Should she go through with this?

What if Hart was right?

And then she felt his hands on her buttocks, caressing them, molding them, spreading them wide. Her thighs opened for him instantly as her knees buckled, as intense desire flooded her.

He shoved the weight of his arousal against her sex and she cried out, shocked by his weight, his heat, his hardness. There were no thoughts now. His sex burned; her sex answered, yearned.

He cupped her face with his hands. "I love you. I want you. This is how badly I want you, that I am doing what I have sworn I would not do. I can't even think right now!" he cried urgently.

She could hardly speak; she was insane with the throbbing member between her thighs. "Bragg," she gasped.

He caught her by her buttocks again, lifting her harder, higher, on the ridge of his manhood. Francesca felt the delicious friction and the sparks going off, one by one, quickly, and as he rubbed himself over her, again and again, rhythmically, a masculine demand, the sparks caught fire. He moved harder, faster, sensing where she was going, carrying her there. The explosion took her by surprise. She cried out frantically, he was banging against her, and she was swept up, away, far away, into a black void shattered by a zillion stars, each and every one exploding, fire and light.

When she drifted back to earth, she was in his arms and on the bunk, on her back. His hand was splayed dangerously low on her belly, just inches above her wet, swollen sex. She blinked her eyes open and was met by golden fire. He bent and kissed her long and hard, his tongue thrusting into her mouth.

And when he straightened, he smiled just a little, at her.

Francesca could not smile back. Reality hit her, hard. She was flat on her back on his bunk, in his sleeping compartment, and they had come precariously close to consummating their relationship.

"Are you all right?" he whispered.

She must not think now. She loved him and, more important, she trusted him—he would never hurt her.

"Francesca?"

She nodded and looked down at his hand.

He inched it lower. Her silk robe and gown clung damply to her pubis, and she might as well have been naked. His middle finger had reached the top of her cleft. It pressed there, strong and long, unmoving.

Her body became limp. Lax. His finger pressed lower. If he went just a bit farther, she was going to die all over again, finding God and heaven and release. "Bragg," she whispered. But she had moaned his name, and the moan shocked her. It was a sexual plea, long, low, and deep.

He moved his hand lower and his middle finger began to rub back and forth in an expert circular motion. She cried out, beginning to shake.

"I love you," he said harshly, and he kissed an aching nipple. "Come for me, Francesca."

She managed to meet his gaze, already spiraling along the paths of untamable pleasure, guiltless ecstasy. And he knew.

He bent and began licking and tugging at her nipple, while his finger continued its devastating work. Suddenly her gown was whipped up, his hand now on her naked flesh. She was slick, slippery, wet. He palmed her entire sex, then began to rub her with his thumb.

She exploded, arching off of the bunk, her cries deep, harsh, loud.

When she came back to earth this time, he was holding her tightly in his arms, her face was against his chest, he had one leg wrapped over her, and she felt every inch of his arousal against one thigh. "You have to go," he said. "And I mean it."

It was hard to think clearly. "No." She tried to look up at him, but his eyes were screwed tightly shut. "I love you, too, Bragg." And as her mind began to function, fear began spiraling down her spine.

He gripped her shoulders, straightening. "That's just it," he said. "I'm not sure that you do love me. Because if you did, you would understand that if this goes much further, I will never be able to forgive myself."

She stared.

Because, my dear, I am sick of it, him, the two of you!

I am sorry I will not be at your wedding, the first one to toast the police commissioner and his new, second wife.

Francesca hated Calder Hart then, with all of her being, for daring to come between them then, now.

"What is it?" he asked quickly, sitting and moving away from her.

"Where do we go from here?" she had asked him, not too long ago.

"I don't know."

She slowly sat up. "I do love you," she said. It was the truth. "I have loved you from the moment we first met and engaged in a debate. You have no idea how much I admire you. There is no one I respect more."

Something flitted through his eyes; he did not speak.

Francesca suddenly turned partially away from him. Tears were coming, fast and hard, but why? She had just experienced mind-shattering pleasure in the arms of a man she admired and loved more than anyone. And he loved her enough to try to protect her from ruin. There was no reason for her to be on the edge of grief.

Hart was there in her mind, mocking her.

You want Rick as your husband, but I am the man you want in your bed.

I want to take you to my bed very much. . . . Your friendship is more important to me than sex.

"Francesca? Are you crying?" Bragg's voice was tight with surprise and fear and perhaps even guilt.

"No," she lied, the very first blatant lie she had ever told to him. She began to stand. Calder Hart had nothing to do with this.

It was Leigh Anne. She was the reason Francesca was grief-stricken, because she was the reason they might not find lifelong happiness.

Bragg caught her wrist. "I'm sorry." His tone was agonized. "This is my fault. I should have sent you away—"

"No!" She whirled and put her finger to his lips. "No. Never say you're sorry, not to me. You never have to say you're sorry, not to me." But why was she crying? The tears were streaming down her face.

"What is it?" Bragg asked, his gaze riveted on hers, with real apprehension.

And the truth struck her then. "You're right, Bragg. You've been right all along."

He stood abruptly, his eyes wide, anxious.

"I'm confused," she whispered, shaken to the very depths of her being. "I love you, but . . ."

"But what?"

"But I'm not ready. It's so simple. I'm afraid."

Sixteen

The train was slowing as it entered the Ninety-sixth Street tunnel, and as quickly as one could blink, the morning became the night. Francesca hesitated as she stood, swaying from side to side, in the doorway of her compartment. Had she slept a wink all night? She did not think so. Perhaps it served her right.

She was frightened by her sudden confusion, but she was relieved that she had not gone through with her original intentions. She could still become Bragg's lover, at any time. She still wanted to be his lover. Because she loved him so much. But she was afraid—she was afraid because he was married, because his wife wanted to meet with her, and because once she took that fateful step, there would be no undoing it. How had her life become so complicated?

She felt as if her life were a total shambles. And perhaps it was.

Suddenly his door slid open and their gazes met. She recalled the way he had held her and touched her and she flushed, looking nervously away. Still, those memories were enough to leave her breathless.

"Good morning," he said, his tone noncommittal.

His tone was so carefully modulated that her gaze flew to his. She could tell nothing from his eyes. "Good morning," she said, and she coughed to clear her throat, as she was so hoarse from tension she could hardly get such a simple salutation out.

"Are you all right?" he asked, his gaze never leaving her face.

She hesitated, then smiled too brightly. "I am fine!" Good God, she had sounded like a cheerleader!

He studied her, unsmiling and grim. Her heart lurched with dread. "I am almost fine," she whispered, an amendment.

"I lost all control, Francesca. It won't happen again." His jaw flexed and a steely determination filled his eyes.

She didn't know what she wanted him to say or do now, but telling her that he would never hold her and make love to her again was hardly reassuring. She wanted to protest, and she opened her mouth to do just that. But she was speechless, for she simply did not know what to say.

Worse, she no longer felt that the answers were simple and easy ones. The path of their future seemed to be booby-trapped with pitfalls and land mines, not to mention the specter of his wife.

"Last night was my fault, entirely so," she heard herself say.

Before he could respond, the conductor began to shout, "Grand Central Depot. Last stop, Manhattan. Grand Central Depot! Last stop! Manhattan."

They looked at each other. The train was slowing down vastly now.

As the conductor continued to call out the last stop, Bragg finally smiled slightly, and she knew he meant to be reassuring now. But she was not reassured. How could she be?

He pulled out his pocket watch. "In two hours Hart shall confront Craddock."

A new and different fear gripped her. "Will you stop him now?"

His gaze met hers. "No. Let's see what he can find out."

Francesca could hardly believe her ears. Images of Hart confronting Craddock and the situation escalating into violence filled her mind. "Bragg, don't let him go."

"Hart is usually extremely effective. I will be lurking close enough to the rendezvous to help him—or hinder him, as the case may be."

She was hardly satisfied. The train had come to a halt.

"You will also let him do dirty work you would not deign to do?" She was trembling.

His response was as sharp as the lash of a whip. "No, Francesca. But I am bound by the letter of the law, and he is not." He turned his back on her.

She froze, bewildered and torn, uncertain of what to think and of even what she was feeling. She seized his arm from behind, forcing him to look at her. "I'm sorry. That was unfair of me."

"Yes, it was," he said quietly, and their gazes locked.

And Francesca knew that the one thing she never wished to do was argue with this man. She smiled a little at him, and finally, his expression softened, too.

The platform was visible outside of the window behind Bragg's silhouette, along with the white tiles of the walls, other passengers awaiting a train on the parallel track, and conductors and baggage men in their blue uniforms. "Peter will meet us on Fourth Avenue," Bragg said.

Francesca nodded.

A few moments later, they were hurrying along with the crowd of disembarking passengers, Bragg carrying both her valise and his smaller duffel. They crossed the huge main lobby of the terminal, which had been completed recently. And then they were pushing through swinging glass-and-iron doors. Outside, it was snowing, the skies heavy, threatening and gray.

Francesca saw the Daimler first, sandwiched between two gleaming black carriages. Then she saw Peter, standing by the hood, his hands shoved in the pockets of his baggy black overcoat. Two policemen in uniform stood not far away. Bragg stumbled.

She glanced at him and saw shock on his face; she quickly followed his gaze.

A very small, stunningly beautiful woman stood beside Peter. She had dark hair and fair skin and the face of an angel. "Hello, Rick," his wife said.

Bragg stopped in his tracks, still holding both of their bags.

Francesca also halted, her heart seeming to have stopped. *Oh, my God. It had begun. The ending of everything she treasured, the ending of their love.*

Bragg was starkly white. "Leigh Anne?"

She should have told him, Francesca managed to think. She suddenly knew she had made the worst mistake of her life.

Leigh Anne came forward, smiling. "You seem surprised to see me, Rick. How are you?" She paused before him and Francesca thought she was only five foot tall, a petite perfect china doll with sea-green eyes and thick black lashes. She laid a small gloved hand on his arm and strained up on her tiptoes and somehow planted a soft kiss on his jaw.

Bragg pulled back. "Of course I am surprised." He was flushing now. He wet his lips. "Leigh Anne, this is—"

"I know. This is Miss Cahill." Leigh Anne finally turned to Francesca, her hand extended. "How do you do, Miss Cahill?" she asked politely, her eyes wide and innocent. No accusations seemed to lurk there.

Francesca could not speak, but she finally managed to breathe. It sounded as if she was frantically gulping oxygen, which, perhaps, she was.

"Surely Miss Cahill told you that I was on my way to New York?" Leigh Anne asked, turning her soft smile on Bragg.

"What?" And he finally looked at Francesca.

Leigh Anne said patiently, "I sent Miss Cahill a note. Surely she told you?"

Bragg stared at her, stunned again, while Francesca felt her cheeks blaze with fire. "I . . . I can explain," she gasped.

His stare widened. "You *knew*? She sent you a *note*? You did not say a *word*?"

She could not think of, much less summon up, a coherent reply.

"Please. Do not be angry with Miss Cahill, Rick; I'm sure she intended to mention it. It must have slipped her mind, Rick," Leigh Anne said quickly.

His wife was defending her? Was this really happening?

Or was this a dream? A horrid, ghastly nightmare?

Bragg's gaze slammed back to his wife. "What is this about, Leigh Anne?"

She stared back at him for a long moment, and there was no sign of anger or hatred upon her perfect face. Pain filled Francesca. "It's been four years," Leigh Anne said simply. "Don't you think it's time we spoke?"

He stiffened. He was darkly red, now. "Peter. Hail Miss Cahill a cab."

His words were a bloody blow. "I can hail my own taxi," she heard herself say thickly.

He did not look at her. "I cannot imagine why you wish to speak to me," he said to Leigh Anne.

"You knew I was in Boston. Surely you knew I would come to New York, sooner or later." Her green eyes never wavered from his face. They were direct, searching.

"Actually, I hadn't thought about it at all," he said harshly.

"Well, I can see my timing is poor," she said, with a rueful smile. "I did not come here to upset you, Rick. I went to the house and happened to catch your man as he was leaving to pick you up. I am staying at the Waldorf-Astoria," she said. "If you change your mind about speaking, you may find me there."

Francesca felt tears blur her eyes, and she was horrified. But she could still see the way Leigh Anne stared at him— and the way he stared back. Bragg seemed extremely distressed, while Leigh Anne seemed entirely unruffled. She was a woman of extreme composure, Francesca thought grimly, but then, she had the advantage of surprise.

And a cab was waiting, having pulled up alongside Bragg's motorcar.

Bragg turned, his gaze impossibly hard. "Your cab is here," he said to Francesca.

She hesitated, a dozen responses coming to mind, and in the end, she said nothing. It was in that moment that her heart began breaking. She could not manage this; she simply could not. She had never imagined that it would be so impossibly painful to come face-to-face with his wife.

She tried to take her valise from him, but he did not release it; instead, he set his duffel down, switched her valise to his other hand, and gripped her elbow. He steered her across the curb and in front of the Daimler to the side of the hansom, where Peter stood.

Peter opened the taxi door.

Bragg looked at her.

"I was afraid to tell you," she said, aware of the tears now shimmering in her eyes.

His jaw hardened.

She opened her purse and handed him the note.

He finally released her elbow, unfolded it, and read it. Then he handed it back to her.

"I don't want it," she whispered. "You are so angry."

His expression did not soften. "I am furious. But not with you." And finally, a light she recognized came into his eyes. "I am angry with you, Francesca, but not furious with you. We will most definitely talk about this at another time."

"I am so sorry. As you said, I have the worst judgment." She felt as if she were begging now for his love.

He hesitated, and finally, he softened. "Sometimes that is true. We will talk about this later." His gaze did not waver from her face. He added, "Don't worry."

There was really no relief. She nodded anxiously. "Will you be all right?"

He was incredulous. "The woman I am married to—a woman I despise—suddenly walks back into my life and you ask me if I will be all right?"

She shivered. "How can I help?"

He was too much of a gentleman to point out that she had done enough. "We have an operation to see to, Francesca. Peter will take you directly to Hart, and I will follow." He glanced over his shoulder and so did Francesca; Leigh Anne stood on the sidewalk, motionless, watching them, her hands inside a silver fox muff that matched the huge collar and lapels of her chinchilla coat.

She had to know. "Will you speak to her?"

His face closed. "No."

*   *   *

He did not have time for this.

He did not have time for her.

What did she want?

Bragg got out of a cab, paid the driver through the window, and hurried up the broad front steps of the Waldorf-Astoria Hotel. As he entered the spacious high-ceilinged lobby with its gleaming wood floors and Persian rugs, he faltered.

Leigh Anne stood at the front desk, collecting her key. She smiled, perhaps in thanks, and the clerk appeared smitten. She turned away; the man stared after her helplessly, with longing.

It had always been that way. Nothing had changed. His little wife knew how to manipulate and entrance men, just as she had manipulated and entranced him from the moment they had met.

He was trembling. What did she want? What could she want? Why was she here? They hadn't seen each other in four years, although he had seen her once, that single time when he had gone to Paris to bring her home and had found her instead in the company of another man. *God damn her,* he thought, shaken.

She could still shake him, enrage him, distress him the way no other person could.

And she still had the perfect beauty of a little angel. She could be in one of the religious or mythological paintings hanging in Calder's home. She had not aged a single day. And he could still look at her and wonder if, somehow, he was entirely to blame for it all.

Which was absurd.

She had left him.

After blackmailing him.

She saw him and froze.

He gathered his determination and hatred around him the way one would a heavy cloak in the midst of a freezing day and stalked to her. "I have urgent matters to attend to," he said briskly. "But I can give you ten or fifteen minutes."

"That is terribly kind of you," she said, without any sarcasm at all. Her green eyes held his.

Instantly he looked away. Her eyes hadn't changed, either; they were the color of emeralds, the color unusual, dark and intense. Heavy black lashes fringed them, and they were wide and almond-shaped. When she stared, she had a look of absolute innocence, of extreme naïveté. He was not going to fall into the trap he once had. There was not an innocent bone in her body.

Once, there had been. On their wedding night.

Hot slick memories and images of pale porcelain skin and dusky nipples, heavy black hair, swinging like a cape, hit him hard then. Soft, breathy cries of sheer pleasure echoed in his mind.

She laid her tiny hand on his arm. He jumped away. "My room is on the sixth floor," she said.

He nodded, his heart pounding as if he'd just made love. And following her to the elevator, he refused to think about her body, which had once been as perfect as her face. Small and fragile, but only in appearance; in fact, strong and impossibly flexible, impossibly eager. Why was he recalling the only thing they had ever had in their marriage? Because he was intelligent enough now to know he had married her for sex and not for any other reason.

In the elevator, they were the sole occupants. He stared at the floor indicator as it inched from 1 to 2 to 3 to 4 and then 5. And finally, it stopped on 6, and the light above the arrow's tip lit up. He loosened his tie. He was perspiring.

She had stared at the tips of her shoes the entire time; now, she smiled uncertainly at him and stepped from the elevator after he opened the cage. He ignored her smile and her glance; it was all an act, a perfect act, for she was a perfect actress. For even now, he marveled at her aura of dignity and calm.

What did she want?

His heart lurched and then sped. The note she had sent to Francesca he dismissed. It was irrelevant now; he intended to handle his little wife, and he was not going to allow her

to come close to Francesca and do what damage she might
there. He would protect Francesca from his wife's scheming
and manipulations.

"You have changed, Rick," she said softly, leading him
up the hallway.

"I am the same man you married."

She did smile, and it appeared guileless. "I think I married
a boy. I am definitely walking up this hallway with a man."

He steeled himself—did she intend to flatter him or dis-
parage him? And he did not reply.

But he had not been completely honest with Francesca.
This woman had done more than break his heart. She had
ripped it from his chest, only to tear off pieces and feed them
to the waiting lions.

Callously. Cruelly. Selfishly.

Which was why he so hated her. It was why he could not
stand being near her. It was why he intended to put her on
the next train to Boston.

He had been completely, helplessly, head over heels in
love with his wife. Even when he had spent long nights at
the office, poring over cases, she had always been there with
him, on his mind. Coming home each evening, even when
she was already asleep, had been the best part of his day.
Leaving every morning, usually just after dawn, had been
the hardest.

He realized he was sweating.

The carpeted hallway was empty. As he waited for her to
unlock her door, he took off his coat, detecting her perfume.
It had changed. It was sweeter and spicier. It seemed to en-
velop him; he also could detect her natural scent, the scent
of a sexual woman.

He shifted his weight, hardened his jaw, wondering how
many lovers she had taken in the past four years. For him,
there had been three—a brief fling to assuage his broken
heart and restore his manhood, a mistress he had kept in
Boston, and his last mistress, whom he had kept in Washington. In his own way he had loved both of his mistresses;
he had been genuinely fond of them, for each had been a

strong, intellectual, and beautiful woman. They remained friends. And just a month ago he had found the woman of his dreams—Francesca—and last night he had been desperate to make love to her, but today, standing there in the endless hallway of the elegant hotel, he was acutely, hatefully aware of his wife, who had come to the city to destroy him.

There could be no other reason.

She glanced at him over her shoulder, smiled again, her lips rosebud pink without the aid of any rouge, and stepped inside a pleasant room with a four-poster bed, a small dining table and two chairs, a sofa, an ottoman, and a fireplace. "A suite was too expensive," she murmured, removing her chinchilla coat.

His reflex was automatic, he jumped to take her coat, and as he did so, their hands brushed. He leaped away; she arched an eyebrow at him. "I hardly have leprosy, Rick," she said.

"Forgive me for not welcoming you home with open arms," he muttered, opening the closet and hanging up her coat. He threw his own coat over the back of one of the chairs and folded his arms across his chest.

She glanced at his chest, or was it his arms? Then she glanced lower, at his hips. His resolve hardened. "When are you returning to Boston?"

"In a few days, I suppose," she said, turning away to fiddle with a vase full of flowers. She began to rearrange them and he sensed she was nervous, even though her manner indicated otherwise, and he was viciously pleased.

"Should I send for some refreshments? Have you eaten breakfast?" she asked, not turning.

He caught her wrist and turned her around. "My time is limited," he said harshly. "So let's not beat around the bush."

"You act as if you hate me," she said, her gaze wide and on his. Her glance slipped to his mouth.

He released her and said nothing. He was a gentleman, and he simply would not respond in the manner that he wished to.

She nodded, hurt changing her expression, and for a moment she appeared as vulnerable as a small child, which she was not. "Should I order breakfast?" she asked.

"We ate on the train."

She looked at him and this time he did not look away. Her eyes continued to mirror hurt, but that was simply impossible. "She is very beautiful," Leigh Anne finally said, removing a very elegant hat and placing it carefully on a bureau. She sat down as carefully in a chair—her toes just reached the floor; her heels did not. She clasped her small hands in her lap.

"Yes, she is very beautiful." He did not want to discuss Francesca with her. Sultry images from the night before flashed through his mind. To his amazement, he felt guilt intruding.

"I have heard she is also clever, that she solves crimes," Leigh Anne said quietly.

"Is that what you wish to talk about? Francesca?"

"Do you love her?"

"Yes." He did not hesitate.

She looked down. She did not speak.

He was not going to feel guilty, as if he were the one with the parade of lovers, as if he were the one betraying her and their marriage. "Is that why you have come to the city? To discuss my relationship with Francesca?"

She looked up. Her mouth, which was extremely full, was trembling. "My husband is in love with another woman. Should I merrily go about my business and pretend that naught is amiss?"

"We ended our marriage four years ago!" he cried, and it was an explosion. His fist hit the table. The vase jumped but did not overturn. Leigh Anne paled. "Yes, you should have continued your affairs and pretended nothing was amiss!"

She stared up at him. Her bosom heaved. "We have ended our marriage? Since when? I receive your checks every month. I send you my bills. I have never received divorce papers, Rick."

Divorce. How easily they had segued into the topic he wished to broach. He leaned forward, aware of shaking now. "That can be easily rectified."

She gasped. Then, "Is that what you are thinking? Now you think to divorce me? After all that you have done? *Now* you think to divorce me?" She was on her feet, her mouth quivering, her eyes filling with tears. Her small body was trembling. "My father is at death's door. My mother is incompetent and you know it. And then there is Charlie, my uncle's bastard. She is a hoodlum, Rick, uncontrollable, wild, without any social graces! And I am supposed to find her a husband! She has been left in my household, for me to raise! Now you would divorce me?" The tears finally fell, drop after drop. And to make matters worse, Leigh Anne was as beautiful when she was crying as when she was not.

He grabbed her in sudden fury.

She stiffened.

"Don't even think of starting with me, now," he ground out, almost shaking her. Her shoulders were small and fragile beneath his hands—he felt as if he could crush them into dust if he tried. "I want a divorce. I have made up my mind. I shall marry Francesca, whom I love. And you, you can then do as you please, freely. Fuck the whole world, Leigh Anne, and I shall not care!"

"You're hurting me," she whispered, her eyes filled with fear. *"Stop."*

"I'm hurting you? You walked out on me, my dear, not the other way around." But he eased his grip. He was seeing red now, red and white, for she was impossibly porcelain, impossibly beautiful, and her fear only heightened her beauty.

"You broke every single promise you ever made to me!" she cried with a gasp. "Let me go!"

"I broke promises?" He pulled her off her feet. Her small body could so easily be crushed by his larger one. He felt every inch of her now, against his own anger-wracked frame. "You swore to love and cherish me until death, Leigh Anne. Through better and for worse."

"You also swore to love and cherish me until death, Rick, and you promised me a wonderful life! A wonderful life! You promised me that Georgian mansion with the cast-iron fence, the one we both fell in love with, the one just two blocks from your parents'! There were gong to be family dinners on Sunday nights! And what about the two children we were going to have? There was going to be supper parties, once a week, I do believe. Our first guest list would be your partners at Holt, Holt and Smith! You promised me a home, a family, an entire life—and then you reneged on every single one of your promises," she gasped, the tears falling in a ceaseless stream now. "And you are hurting me. Damn it. Let me go."

He held onto her for one more minute, through the haze of anger and pain, acutely aware of her fragility and femininity, and even her breasts, crushed against his chest. And then he released her, as she had asked, but he made a mistake in doing so, and she slid down his body before her feet hit the floor.

Unfortunately, he was a virile man, one denied the pleasure of the bedroom for the past two months, and his reaction was reflexive and instantaneous.

She felt it, backed away, and became utterly still, freezing in the process of beginning to rub her arms where he had gripped them.

He hated himself.

"You still think I'm beautiful," she whispered.

"I am a man, Leigh Anne, not a eunuch," he said roughly.

"You still want me," she said.

He laughed without mirth and shook his head. "There is only one woman I want, and she is not you."

Leigh Anne stiffened. Her eyes blazed. "That's not what your body says."

"I get hard in my dreams," he ground out. "And what does that mean? It means I have been in public office for well over a month and I have been living like a monk for even longer than that."

"Deny it if it makes you feel better," she whispered. "But you could never take your hands off of me. I don't think anything has changed."

"I don't care what you think," he said, turning away.

When she did not speak, he glanced at her.

"I am not giving you a divorce," she said.

He faced her. "Then we will have a bitter battle on our hands." He did not want to think about the fact that Francesca was against his divorcing as well, but for all the right reasons.

He stared, struck then by the utter and most basic difference between the woman he had once loved and the woman he now loved. Leigh Anne remained selfish to the core; Francesca was selfless. She did not have a single selfish bone in her entire body.

His heart turned over, hard and painfully.

"I understand that you have an excellent reputation," Leigh Anne said softly, staring directly at him. She smiled a little, her gaze intent. "I understand that you are highly thought of and that, in some circles, the talk is that you will be groomed to run for the Senate."

He knew exactly where she intended to go, and he became even more tense, if possible.

"I can help you, Rick," she said.

He stared. What game was this? "I don't want your help."

"No? I can help you win the Senate. While a divorce will end your career—forever. No one in this country would ever forget it—you would be a political pariah. But to run for the Senate, why, you need a gracious and elegant wife at your side. Someone to shake hands with the wealthy who will support your run with their funds, someone to host those fund-raising dinners and even mere political affairs. You need a wife to smile at the gentlemen who will back you and to campaign at your side. You need me, Rick."

"I may not run for the Senate ever," he said.

She shrugged. "I am not giving you a divorce. Not now, not ever. I am sorry you have fallen in love with someone else, but now I am doing what I have to do," she said. "For it would ruin me, too, or have you so coldly forgotten that a divorced woman is a social pariah?"

His heart beat hard. He could see Francesca so clearly now in his mind's eye, smart, beautiful, impossibly determined—mulishly so. When he had thought about her after they had first met, while they were falling in love but blissfully ignorant of it, his thoughts had made him smile, and they had made him want to cheer and laugh. Now, he thought of her and felt like weeping.

He could not let Leigh Anne stand in their way, but hadn't he known, on some level, that Leigh Anne would never complacently let him leave? And hadn't he also known that the pull of his political future was simply irresistible and not to be denied? Because he had so much to achieve; so much remained to do! Cleaning out the hornets in the corrupt nest that was New York's police department was only a beginning.

He gripped the back of a chair. "You will never campaign at my side. We are separated, and that is not going to change."

She smiled, a soft, secret sensual smile, and did not say a word.

His knuckles turned white. "This isn't about my future, is it? This is your way of punishing me. Why? It's been four years. We've both moved on with our lives. Why? Why stand in my way? Why did you really come back?"

Her beautiful green eyes became moist. "Isn't it obvious?" she asked.

"Nothing about you is obvious," he said harshly.

"I still love you, Rick," she said. "And I will not let another woman have you."

Francesca could not concentrate. Her cab had arrived and now sat in the driveway before Calder Hart's huge home. She did not move. She couldn't move. Leigh Anne Bragg's lovely face was engraved on her mind, as was Bragg's furious one.

Grief weighed her down. The sense of loss was acute. The fear was even greater—it felt like panic. Nothing was ever going to be the same again, she thought in terror. Leigh Anne had returned, and her every instinct told Francesca that she meant to stay.

You can let him divorce her, a small voice inside of her head said. *That option remains.*

Francesca covered her face with her hands. They were shaking. She wanted to cry. She would not. And divorce was not an option, because she could not steal him away from his destiny.

But there will not be a happy ending, Francesca.

I will tell you about women like Mrs. Rick Bragg. . . . She didn't want him—but you cannot have him.

Hart's voice was so strong and resonant that she blinked and opened her eyes, expecting to find him standing outside the cab, peering inside. But he wasn't there, of course; no one was there. There was only the bleak and dreary day, the wind and the snow.

It was coming down fast and furious now.

"Miss? That's seventy-five cents," the cabbie said, staring at her over his shoulder.

Francesca tried to smile and handed him a silver dollar. She shook her head when he tried to offer her change, already pushing open her door. How was she going to survive? And what did Leigh Anne really want? Why had she really come to New York?

She wants Bragg, you fool, she heard her mind answer her. What woman would not?

More despondent now, Francesca crossed the drive to Hart's house. The huge stag on the roof seemed to be gazing knowingly down at her. It said, *I told you so!*

As she rang the door's bell, she told herself to forget about Leigh Anne now. There was work to do, a criminal to apprehend. Besides, she was his *wife*.

To her shock, Hart thrust open the door himself. He was in his shirtsleeves and an open vest, looking as if he had just gotten out of bed. He saw her and his eyes widened—and then his face hardened into a barely controlled mask of anger. "Where is my brother?" he demanded.

Francesca had never been greeted so rudely. But the words were hardly out when she knew something was terribly amiss. "I don't know," she began.

Hart grabbed her arm and dragged her inside, slamming the door closed behind her. "I already know he went to Fort Kendall, Francesca," he said dangerously, his black eyes flashing.

She inhaled, hard. She was ready to become undone now, and this was not the time or the place.

"And you have been crying." Now he gripped her by both shoulders. "What's wrong? Didn't the two of you enjoy the night you spent together on that train all by yourselves?"

She could not move. She could hardly speak. Hart was furious—and he was furious with her. "We didn't," she began breathlessly.

He released her. "I hardly care. So spare me the sordid details of your little love affair," he said harshly. But he was looking at her mouth, her hair. His gaze moved into the opening of her coat and over the front of her tightly buttoned jacket. She knew he was searching for signs of recent lovemaking.

Francesca swallowed. "Leigh Anne is here."

He stiffened. And his expression changed.

She would not bawl like a cow. "She met us at the train," she whispered unsteadily. The urge to cry was overwhelming; she choked on a sob instead.

"Poor Francesca," Hart murmured, and he pulled her against his chest. There was no mockery in his tone.

She buried her face there on one hard plane and wept.

He held her, stroking her back. She heard him say, "I am sorry, my dear. I am very, very sorry for you."

She thought that he meant it. She gripped his vest until her knuckles turned numb. She felt his shirt growing wet beneath her cheek. She also felt him stroking her nape beneath her hat.

The tears ceased. Where he was stroking her, her skin tingled. Instantly grief was replaced by something else, something she did not want, something she truly feared. That was when she became acutely aware of his heart, pounding in a rhythm that was strong and insistent, but not at all slow.

His hands moved to her upper arms, holding her in such

a manner that she could not move. For one instant, she felt every inch of his body, a body of strength and power. And then he pushed her an inch, no two, away.

He was staring searchingly at her now, looking so terribly grim. She felt her cheeks flush. How could she deny that she felt a terrible attraction to him? After last night, she had never been more in tune with her body. This man merely had to walk into the room to make her breathless.

"Are you feeling better?" he asked quietly, never moving his gaze from hers.

"Yes." She tried to breathe normally, and failed. "I fear you have been right. Hart! She is so beautiful."

"She is not as beautiful as you," he said quietly.

Francesca stiffened. "You are being kind—"

"I am not a kind man. Wipe your tears. Unless you wish for the entire family to know what has happened in the past twenty-four hours." He seemed about to go. He turned back to her. "Oh. Your mother is furious. Apparently I was not supposed to miss the train."

She flushed.

His gaze remained even. "I covered for you, Francesca. I told Julia a meeting caused me to miss the train and that I was planning to accompany you and Rick."

"Thank you," she managed.

"I shall collect another time. Now where the hell is Rick?" Suddenly his expression changed. "No. I see. He must be with Leigh Anne. Damn it!"

"Hart, what happened?" She grabbed his wrist.

"What happened?" His brows slashed upward; he was incredulous. "One of the twins was abducted, Francesca, right out of her nanny's hands, this morning after breakfast."

Seventeen

Francesca gasped.

"That is right," Hart said grimly. "The nanny takes the twins for a walk every morning after breakfast. She left at nine. She was back before half past. Craddock walked right up to her, grabbed Chrissy from the baby carriage, and leapt into a waiting vehicle."

"Oh, my God." Francesca grabbed him. "Lucy?"

"Is in hysterics," he said. He started down the corridor and Francesca followed, running to keep up with him.

"What about his note? I thought he intended to collect more money, today at noon!" she cried.

"Apparently he changed his mind. The good news is that he wanted money, and I can only assume he still wants money and that murder is the last thing on his mind."

"Calder!" She grabbed the back of his vest.

He whirled so quickly that her nose crashed into the wall of his chest. She backed up. "There was a gruesome murder at Fort Kendall in 1890. It was never solved. Shoz escaped a week later, while Craddock took over this murdered man's position among the inmates. Craddock is extremely dangerous," she said, trying to keep her voice down.

"He will not be dangerous for very much longer," Hart told her. "My private detective is on his tail—we learned where he has been staying until last week. Have no fear—I shall dispose of him the moment he is found—one way or the other."

Their gazes locked and she knew he meant his every word. Somehow, now, she could not blame him. She thought about the beautiful blond twin, and then she thought about Lucy. Anguish filled her.

"What do we do now? Wait for word from your detective? From Craddock himself? Surely there will be a ransom note," Francesca said.

"I guarantee it," Hart said harshly. "The only thing we can do is wait. But we do need Rick now. The one thing he is, is astute."

As he spoke, his front doorbell rang. He stared at her. "That must be my oh-so-virtuous brother." The look he gave her was a dark one, filled with innuendos, and she knew he was thinking about the night she had just spent with Bragg on the train. He whirled and rushed back down the hall.

Francesca set chase and saw Alfred admitting Bragg. Hart did not slow as he entered the front hall; Francesca halted by the reclining nude with the dove, at the hall's far threshold. She trembled and could barely breathe as she set her eyes upon him.

Bragg looked extremely upset. No, he looked grim, horribly so. Whatever had happened after she had left Grand Central Depot, it had not been a pleasant experience. What *had* happened?

"Did you enjoy your journey upstate?" Hart purred.

"Don't even think to begin," Bragg warned unpleasantly. "I am in no mood to spar with you."

"Craddock abducted Chrissy this morning," Hart returned coldly.

Bragg turned white.

"Why else would I leave a message of such urgency with your clerk?" Hart asked.

"Give me all the details. Why didn't you go to the police?"

Hart said, "Considering the bottom line, which is our brother-in-law, I decided this should be kept unofficial. It is a family matter, not a police matter, Rick."

"What happened? Where is Lucy? How is she holding up?" Bragg demanded.

"The nanny took the twins for a stroll at nine this morning. Craddock got out of a waiting coach, snatched Chrissy from her baby carriage, got back in the coach, and drove off. Actually, he had an accomplice, as the coach had a driver. There has been no ransom note, but it had been less than three hours since he took her. I have already hired a private detective to locate him, and the entire family is with Lucy in the library. She is crying," Hart added with a downturn to his mouth.

"I need your phone," Bragg said tersely.

"I will not have the police involved," Hart warned.

"Generally, you are not a foolish man. So why start now?" Bragg asked coolly. "And I am the police, Calder, or have you forgotten? So the police are involved."

Hart clenched his fists, his expression hardening with anger. He looked ready to strike a blow; Bragg also clenched his fists, but he was smiling, extremely unpleasantly now.

"Calder, don't!" Francesca cried.

Bragg started. He looked across the huge hall for the first time and she stepped out from behind the reclining statue. Their gazes met, held, locked. *What had Leigh Anne said to him? What had happened when they were alone? Had he admitted to his wife that he loved Francesca? Had her name even come up?*

Bragg dragged his gaze back to his half brother, who had been watching them both. "I have more resources at my beck and call than the entire Pinkerton Agency," he said, very softly. "And I do not suggest we sit around here twiddling our thumbs while waiting for a ransom note—which may or may not come. I intend to locate Craddock before he ever sends that note."

"He wants money," Hart said coldly. "There will be a note, before nightfall, if I do not miss my guess."

"He is a murderer," Bragg snapped. "And I do not trust him with my niece."

Hart's mouth twisted upward, without any mirth at all. "Ah yes, shove my face in the fact that Chrissy is not really my niece. And when your little investigation gets out of hand? Then what? If Cooper was murdered by Shoz, will you cover it up?"

Bragg looked murderous. "First things first. First we must get Chrissy back—alive. Now get the fuck out of my way, Calder."

"Losing your balls, Rick? Could it be that this is a bad memory come back to life? Jonny Burton was found, alive. We can find Chrissy alive and not send her father to the scaffold. This isn't about Chrissy; this is about you."

"You are the coldest man I know. Chrissy's life is at stake," Bragg said softly, dangerously. "And I am through arguing with you."

She could no longer stand it. She hurried forward, between them. She grasped Hart's fist. "Calder, for now, we could use the resources of the police. I think it is wise to bring the department into what is a criminal act. We can worry about the Cooper murder at another time!"

His eyes turned to her, and they were livid. She recoiled instantly; he shook off her hand. "The two of you deserve each other," he said, and the venom in his tone was a blow.

"Calder!" she began.

As if he had not heard her—which he had—he strode out of the hall with long, hard strides.

Francesca watched him go, unable to move, unable to breathe. It felt like déjà vu. Had it only been a few days ago that he had walked out on her in the exact same manner? And why did it frighten her so?

She wanted to run after him and reassure him, but of what? She did not move.

When he had disappeared into the corridor, she faced Bragg, only to find him staring at her so closely that she stiffened. It was hard now to look him in the eye. She bit her lip and looked down, then dared to meet his gaze. "You're right. Of that I have no doubt. We must find Craddock and get Chrissy back and worry about everything else later." She smiled, but it felt horribly weak and fragile.

"He knows we went to Fort Kendall together, doesn't he?" Bragg asked.

She nodded. "I didn't tell him. He was looking for you—"

"My staff knew where I was. It was hardly a secret."

She gazed in the direction he had disappeared. "He's so angry," she whispered. "And he's angry with me, not you."

"He's jealous," Bragg said flatly.

She faced him, stunned. "No, I think you are very wrong. Why would he be jealous?"

Bragg made a sound. It was disbelieving and disparaging all at once. "You are a beautiful woman, and he wants you. But you do not want him." He stared.

She flushed and could not think of a reply. But her mind went haywire. Could Bragg be right? But Calder was always so cool, so composed! He had admitted he wanted her in his bed, but the way he had said it, it had been as if it was easy for him to ignore any desire he felt. Still, she had seen his jealousy of Bragg in other matters.

"Do you?" Bragg asked abruptly, coolly.

She started. "Do I what?"

"Do you want him?"

She felt her cheeks heating dangerously. She opened her mouth to deny everything, but not a single word came out.

"Are you falling in love with him?"

She was breathing shallowly now. "No! Of course not!" It was hard to speak. It was as if a huge ball of fur were there in her chest. "How can you—after last night—how can you even ask such a thing?" she managed to gasp.

"Very easily." His gaze was hard. "If you are, he will break your heart a hundred times over. Where does he keep the telephone?"

But she already knew that. He was infamous for loving and leaving women. Except he didn't even love them; he only made love to them. "I know," she whispered.

"The phone?"

"The library," she said tightly.

Bragg hurried past her and disappeared down the hall.

Francesca sank down onto a settee against one wall and between two classical busts of Roman emperors. She was so dazed now that she could not think. How could Bragg have asked her such a thing after last night?

He was the brother she loved.

She covered her face with her hands. *Think,* she told herself. *Concentrate! A child's life is at stake!*

"Miss Cahill?" The intonation was kind; it was Alfred.

She looked up and tried to smile. Fortunately, she had wept so hard on Hart's chest that she had no tears left.

"May I somehow be of help?"

She shook her head no.

"Might I offer an opinion?"

She hesitated. They had a crime to solve, a child to find. "Yes, of course, Alfred."

"Do not hold Mr. Hart's harsh words against him. I do believe he cares greatly for this family, and he blames himself for the little girl's disappearance, as she was here in his safekeeping."

Francesca straightened, comprehension searing her. Of course Hart would blame himself; she knew him well enough to know he set high standards and always achieved them. *He was feeling responsible for Chrissy's abduction.* But it was not his fault.

"And I do believe he is rather jealous of Mr. Bragg," Alfred added as someone pounded on the door.

Francesca nodded again. "Thank you, Alfred. I think you are right."

He smiled at her and went to answer the door.

Francesca stood as a tall, dark man stepped into the house. She took one look at his high cheekbones, his bronzed skin, and his jet-black hair, which reached his shoulders, and knew she was looking at Lucy's husband. He had a dangerous uncivilized look about him, and it was not because of the hair, and his expensive custom-made suit did not cloak the man in civility one bit. He looked hard, rough, lawless. He was also extremely attractive, but in a dark and even disturbing way. Then she saw his bright blue lizard cowboy boots with their silver snakeskin tips. Oddly, they were not incongruous with his dark charcoal gray suit.

"Sir?"

"I have been told my wife is here," he said. His gaze
moved over Francesca and dismissed her. "Lucy Savage."

"She is in the library, sir," Alfred said.

Francesca followed Shoz down the corridor. The library
doors were open. Francesca saw at a glance that the entire
family was present.

Grace sat with her arm around Lucy on the large sofa in
the middle of the room. Bragg was on the telephone, standing
by the desk; Hart, Rathe, Rourke, and a very handsome
young man of about eighteen were all clustered a few feet
from him, speaking in low tones.

Lucy saw her husband and stiffened. She was eerily pale
and red-eyed from weeping. "Shoz? What . . . what are you
doing here?"

He took in the scene and rushed forward. "I left for New
York last week. I decided to join you and the children. What
is it? What's happened?" he demanded, lifting her to her feet.

"Someone's taken Chrissy!" Lucy cried, clinging to the
lapels of his jacket.

His silver eyes went wide.

"It's all my fault," Lucy said, bursting into tears. "This is
all my fault!"

"It's not your fault," he said firmly, pulling her into his
arms. He held her there, stroking her hair, which was loose
and rioting down her back. His gaze moved to Rathe. "What
the hell happened?"

"Lucy has been blackmailed," Rathe said, moving to Shoz
and clasping his shoulder. "And at nine this morning Chrissy
was seized while on her way to the park. There has been no
ransom note since then."

Shoz's face was a mask of darkly controlled anger. Francesca shivered, because she had never seen any man look so
hard and so dangerous. It crossed her mind that this man was
capable of hanging a man and then torturing him slowly until
he died, given the right reason.

Bragg joined them. "Shoz, we need to talk. Now. In an unofficial capacity, before the police arrive."

Shoz's mouth curled. "I wish you hadn't called in the police, Rick."

Bragg looked him in the eye. "Are you planning on hanging him and then carving him up?"

Shoz started. Then, his smile chilling, "Maybe."

"Shoz!" Lucy cried. "No!"

He looked at her. "I don't want you here. Grace, take her upstairs. Join the children. Stay there until I say so."

Francesca lifted a brow. He was very imperious.

And Lucy said, her eyes flashing, "I am not going to join the children; I want to help."

"No," he said flatly. Then he softened, and he pulled her close. "I will get Chrissy back. Alive. Trust me," he said.

Lucy's eyes shimmered with tears and she nodded. "I am so sorry," she whispered.

He suddenly seized her chin and kissed her hard. "I will take care of everything," he promised her, as if they were the only two people in the room.

Lucy nodded. "I know you will."

Grace was waiting for her. "Come on. Let's go upstairs and let the men plan their course of action. I think it would be good for Roberto to be with you now. He's very brave and trying to hide it, but I can see how worried he is."

Lucy nodded, but before she left she took her husband's hand and squeezed it. "I love you."

He smiled but did not answer her; still, his silver gaze never left her until she and Grace were out of sight. Then Shoz turned and looked at Francesca, hard.

"This is Francesca Cahill," Bragg said, interpreting the look. "She has helped me solve three major cases; she is a sleuth. She stays."

Francesca would have been thrilled with his matter-of-fact description of her another time, but not now. She smiled a little at Shoz.

His nod was curt. "Who took Chrissy? When did the blackmail start?"

Hart moved past Francesca, closing the door to the library. He did not look at her once, clearly ignoring her now.

"Joseph Craddock."

Shoz absorbed that—and started. "Joe Craddock?"

"I take it you recall him?"

Shoz's straight nose flared. "Hell, yes. A sonuvabitch from the tip of his toes to the top of his head. I'm going to kill him."

Bragg gripped his arm. "Craddock is blackmailing Lucy. He appeared in Paradise a month or so ago. On Sunday he handed her a note threatening the children and demanding five thousand dollars today at noon. Then he abducted Chrissy."

Shoz was trembling. "I should have killed that sonuvabitch a long time ago."

Francesca winced, because he clearly meant it.

"What does Craddock have on you, Shoz?" Bragg asked, his gaze unwavering.

Shoz smiled, and it was hard. "He hates my guts. This isn't about money—this is about revenge."

Francesca shivered. "Why?"

His cold gaze shot to hers, and clearly he did not like or appreciate the question. Francesca forced a smile. "If you don't mind, it is probably important." She felt as if she was making a terrible mistake in even addressing this man. He was not a man to cross.

Someone moved to stand beside her. The gesture was a protective one; Francesca started and managed to tear her gaze from Shoz. She looked up and, although he wasn't looking at her, Hart stood at her side.

Her heart skipped a beat and lurched oddly.

"Let's just say I stole his woman," Shoz drawled. Then he added, "We ran guns together before I met my wife. Back in '96, '97."

Francesca glanced at Bragg. He stepped forward, appearing determined. "Who murdered Randy Cooper?"

Shoz shrugged, his smile hard, mirthless. If he was surprised by the sudden question, one would never know it.

"The prison held seventy-one men. Any one of them—or all of them—could have done it. My guess is it was Craddock and a few of his hoodlum buddies. No one cared that Cooper got it; even the warden was glad to be rid of him. The case was closed before it ever began," he said flatly. "What does this have to do with my daughter?"

"You escaped a week later. And Cooper was tortured before he died, not to mention that you took his name as an alias."

Shoz seemed amused. "You accusing me of something . . . Rick?" he asked, whisper-soft.

Francesca froze, her heart lurching with dread. She looked from one man to the other.

Before Bragg could respond, Rathe stepped between them. "No one is accusing you of anything," he said firmly. "We're wasting time. We need to find Craddock, now."

If Shoz was relieved, it did not show on his impassive face. The man was probably an extraordinary poker player. Francesca had to briefly close her eyes, breathless now. *Shoz was guilty.* She simply knew it.

A heavy, tense silence fell.

There was a knock on the door.

Hart answered it, not looking at her as he turned to do so. "Alfred?"

"The police are here, sir," Alfred said.

Hart hesitated and turned to Bragg, Shoz, and Rathe. Then he sighed and faced Alfred. "Show them in."

Francesca now had a very bad feeling. It was intensified when the chief of police walked in.

Brendan Farr took one look at the cast of players assembled in the room, and said, "I heard the terrible news, Rick. I decided to take over the case personally." And he smiled.

Eighteen

Francesca was stunned; she met Bragg's gaze briefly. He was as surprised; he quickly recovered. He said, "I shall appreciate your help, Chief. Time is of the essence now. We must locate Joe Craddock, and I want every precinct notified. Wardsmen should begin beating the streets. Someone must have seen him recently. I want Craddock found *before* a ransom note arrives."

Farr said, "Craddock took your niece?" His eyes glinted with surprise while his face remained rather impassive. But he glanced at Francesca.

Hart now drifted over to their small huddle. His gaze narrowed on Farr.

"That's right." Bragg looked the chief of police right in the eye. "I believe you have read his file?"

"Oh, yes," Farr said. "But his style isn't abduction and ransom; it is blackmail."

"Apparently his style has changed," Bragg said.

"And the child's parents?"

Shoz stepped forward. "The child's name is Chrissy Savage. She is my daughter; my wife is upstairs." His eyes continued to blaze with anger. His fists were clenched.

Farr studied him. "Any idea of why Craddock wished to pick on you, Mr. Savage? Other than the fact that your daughter is Derek Bragg's great-granddaughter?"

Shoz's mouth curled. "Isn't that a good-enough reason? My father-in-law adores Chrissy. He'd do anything to get her back."

Farr studied him, then said, "When did you marry into

the family? Is this the wedding I read about, the one that took place in Heaven, Texas?"

"It was Paradise, Texas," Bragg said. "Chief, I need men out on the streets, now."

Farr smiled; it was benign. "May I use the telephone?" he asked. Being polite did not suit him. Francesca thought she saw suspicion in his eyes.

Bragg gestured and Farr walked over to Hart's massive desk. He did not sit down as he dialed headquarters and began to instruct the captain there on the wording of the telegram that would be sent to every station house in the city. Francesca quickly stepped over to where Bragg and Hart stood. She spoke in a whisper. "He wants motive, Bragg. This is not good."

His gaze met hers. "I am aware of that. I do not want him interviewing Lucy. Not now, not later, not ever." He turned his hard gaze on Shoz. "And you give him nothing, Shoz. Not one detail of your life. I don't want him figuring out that you served even a day with Craddock."

Shoz's response was a mirthless flash of teeth. "My pardon is an official record, Rick. He'll find it if he digs deep enough."

"I'll worry about that when the time comes."

"He is already suspicious," Hart remarked flatly. His gaze locked with Rick's. "You do not have a loyal subordinate, Rick."

Bragg's jaw flexed. "I am aware of that."

Hart stared; Bragg stared back. "A knife in the back," Calder finally murmured. "We must all watch our backs now."

They exchanged glances, the four of them, absorbing that. Francesca felt that Hart was right. She tugged on Bragg's sleeve. "We need to find J.C. first," she said in a whisper. Then she let go, as she heard Farr hanging up the receiver. He returned to their group. Now they were all conspicuously silent.

Farr looked from Bragg to Francesca, then at Calder, and

finally at Shoz. "I'd like to speak with your wife," he said to Shoz.

"She's sleeping. She's extremely upset and I don't want her disturbed," Shoz returned flatly. He spoke in a way that was not open to debate.

Farr glanced at Bragg. "It would benefit the investigation if she could be awakened."

Bragg said, "I can fill you in. I know every detail of the case. Now is not a good time to speak with Lucy. She is hysterical, Chief."

Farr shrugged. "Very well, then I am going to go back to headquarters," he said. "It will probably be a few hours before we have any rumors to go on."

Bragg nodded and slapped his shoulder. "Thanks, Chief."

Farr met his gaze and nodded at them all, his gaze lingering on Francesca. She did not flinch or flush. He said, "Perhaps we might speak privately, Miss Cahill?"

Alarm filled her.

Bragg said, "Miss Cahill is on her way home."

Farr smiled oddly—clearly aware that he was being thwarted at every turn—and walked out.

Francesca would have fanned herself if she had a fan.

Shoz said, "I'm hitting the streets, too. I am not going to sit around this house waiting for someone else to find my daughter."

"Money buys just about everything," Hart said coolly. Francesca realized he was still ignoring her. He hadn't looked at her since Bragg had arrived at the house. "I think we should split up and begin dispensing large amounts of cash in order to buy what information that we can."

"I agree," Bragg said. "Craddock's last known address was Eighteen Allen Street. No one's seen him there in over a year, but that may be a good place to start."

"Actually, until last week he had taken a room over a saloon on West Tenth and Broadway," Hart said.

"I'll go," Shoz said, his silver eyes glinting with what Francesca was afraid was blood lust.

"I think the rest of us should begin by canvassing this

area. Maybe someone saw the abduction. I want a description of the coach and the driver. I'm going to go to Mrs. Van Arke's. It's a long shot, but maybe she has an idea of where Craddock is or how he can be reached. Everyone should check back at this house in three hours so we can analyze what we have learned."

Francesca had drifted away from the group of men to stare out the window. She was rewarded when she saw Brendan Farr on Fifth Avenue, speaking with two detectives. Her heart lurched with more unease.

If Shoz was guilty, then this man could destroy the Bragg family.

She did not trust him.

"Francesca?" It was Bragg, having moved to come stand beside her. "Farr is going to try to find out why you were interested in Craddock the other day."

"I know. He will have to tear off my fingernails to get any information from me. I am very worried, Bragg."

"I can see that. Care to share why?"

She glanced over her shoulder at the men, but they were making plans and speaking among themselves. "Shoz is guilty. I feel certain of it."

Bragg started and stared. Then he expelled his breath. "God, I pray you are wrong!"

She gripped his hand. "I want to follow Farr, Bragg. He is up to something. Did you see his face when he realized Craddock had abducted Chrissy?"

He looked at her.

She said, "He is not going back to headquarters. He is hailing a cab."

Bragg's gaze shot to the window and the avenue that was across an acre of snowy lawns.

"He is hailing a cab when he has a coach and driver of his own. Now isn't that odd?" Francesca murmured.

Bragg hesitated. "Very. I'm coming with you," he finally said.

*   *   *

"What is he up to?" Bragg breathed in her ear.

His breath was warm and disturbing; it reminded her of his equally disturbing touch the night before. She shifted; they were both seated in the backseat of a cab and parked a few carriage lengths away from the front door of a seedy hotel on Forty-fourth Street and Fourth Avenue. Just a few blocks away was Grand Central Depot. Farr had walked into the hotel a moment ago, with two detectives. "Is it possible that Craddock is here?" she asked with excitement.

He placed his hand on her arm, restraining her. "Let's wait and see," he said.

It was hard to be patient now. She nodded, briefly meeting his gaze; then, as there was no sign of either the chief of police or his two men, she shifted in order to face Bragg. This was hardly the time or the place, but she had to know. "What did Leigh Anne want?"

His eyes widened, and then he sighed heavily, raking a hand through his sun-streaked hair. The gesture was not characteristic of him. "God knows."

That was hardly a satisfactory answer. "She wants you back, doesn't she?" She found it hard to breathe properly as she spoke. But she simply had to know.

He stiffened and their gazes met. "What she does not want is to become a divorcée," he said.

"You told her?" she gasped.

"I despise the woman," he said harshly. "Yes, I told her. I'm not sure what her game is, Francesca. But she can cause me tremendous trouble, and she can hurt you, too." His gaze darkened as their eyes met.

"Don't you dare worry about me," she said, taking his hand and squeezing it.

"I shall always worry about you," he said simply. He was so grim. "Can we discuss my wife another time?"

She nodded, then said, "Did she say anything about me?"

He sighed again. "Yes."

"Bragg!"

He smiled slightly. "I could not resist. She asked if I loved you. I said yes."

Her heart turned over so many times that she lost count of the flips. How had she even thought herself attracted to Calder Hart for even an instant? Love warmed her thoroughly now.

"Why are you staring at me like that? Is this news? Have I not told you how I feel, several times, in fact?"

Tears came to her eyes. She kissed his cheek impulsively. "Yes, but it is different now, isn't it? I mean, with her here in the city."

"The situation is different, yes. But my feelings have not changed." His tone changed. "Farr is coming out," he said tersely.

Francesca twisted and saw Farr standing on the bottom of the three small steps leading up to the Fourth Avenue Hotel. He was speaking to his men. They nodded in compliance to whatever it was that he had said, and then they all split up. Farr got into his waiting cab, and the moment it was out of sight, Bragg threw open his door and they both rushed out of the hansom.

"Wait right there," Bragg shouted as they raced up the three front steps and inside the hotel.

At the front desk, which was no more than two foot long and stained with scars and tobacco, Bragg pounded on a bell. The small lobby, which had a single chair and table and an overflowing ashtray, and was more of a cubicle than anything else, was empty. A very heavy clerk came out of a back room. He yawned at them. "More flies? Ain't here. Checked out yesterday."

Bragg and Francesca turned to gape at each other. Then Bragg faced the clerk, saying, "Joseph Craddock checked out yesterday?"

"That's right, but I already told the other copper that."

Bragg and Francesca looked at each other again. Dread filled her now. "He knew—or thought he knew—that Craddock was here. And he never said a word!" she cried.

"I am aware of that," Bragg said, his jaw hard.

"Why? When a child's life is at stake? Why?"

His gaze was black. "He wants to find something to hold over me, Francesca. It is as simple as that."

"That is hardly simple!" Francesca cried. She faced the big clerk. "Do you have any idea where Craddock has gone? Did he say anything? Leave any word?"

"Nope. He paid his bill and walked out, not even a 'thank you very much.' " The clerk eyed her now with some lascivious interest.

"Show us to his room," Bragg said.

The clerk nodded, and a few minutes later Bragg was unlocking the door to the room Craddock had used for an entire week. The shades were mostly down and the small, square room was cloaked in shadow. Bragg stepped in first and went to the single lamp by the bed. It was a gas lamp; he turned it on and lit it.

Francesca grimaced. The room was small and dirty and it smelled suspiciously like urine. The cot was unmade, the sheets appearing rather dirty. A rag rug that was torn and muddy was in the center of the floor. A few pegs were on one wall, as was a very poor watercolor painting of a vase of flowers. One lopsided bureau with a water pitcher and stained glasses completed the interior.

Bragg walked over to the bureau and began opening drawers. Francesca went to the single window and looked out on a small, black alleyway where a trash can lay on its side. Then she turned to the bed, not particularly wanting to touch anything. She lifted the sheets and looked under the pillows, but nothing was present.

"Come here," Bragg said harshly.

Francesca turned and saw him holding a piece of newspaper. "What is it?"

"It's an article about cattle ranching," Bragg said quietly, reading. "It's about the difficulties ranchers are facing today in the western part of this country, and it's dated August 2, 1901."

That was a half a year ago. "Does it mention your grandfather's ranch? The one where Lucy and Shoz and their children live?"

"It mentions the D and M, all right," Bragg said, looking up. "But only insofar as it is a model for other ranchers to follow. There's a whole paragraph here on Shoz and some of the innovations he's made." Bragg stared at her. "It even mentions that Shoz was a lawyer, but the son of a rancher himself. It does not mention that he was in prison, or that my grandfather began the ranch. This article is about ranching and subsequently about Shoz as a rancher. There is not a word in here about my family," he said, his gaze on hers.

Francesca shivered. "So this is how, after all these years, Craddock found Shoz. Shoz was telling the truth. Craddock hates him. This isn't about money; it's about revenge."

"It most certainly is," Bragg said grimly.

Francesca moved closer to him. "If this isn't about money, what about Chrissy?"

He met her gaze. "I am praying she is alive," he said.

Francesca had to return home at some point—she had been expected earlier that morning, shortly after the arrival of their train. Her intention was to be back at the Hart mansion at three that afternoon, along with the rest of the family.

She prayed that by then someone would have come up with a lead that would take them to Craddock and Chrissy.

Now she entered the marble-floored foyer, gathering up her composure, as surely she would soon face Julia's wrath. She refused to think about the fact that Hart had lied in order to protect her from being caught in her own web of deceit.

The house was oddly silent.

Francesca handed her coat and hat to a houseman. "Wallace, where is everyone?"

"Upstairs in the Blue Suite, Miss Cahill," he said.

Francesca was bewildered. The Blue Suite was used for houseguests, but as it was the most luxurious accommodation they had, only an extremely important visitor was ever placed there—like a duke or an earl or the president of the United States. "Do we have company?"

"It is Master Cahill," he said. "There has been an accident."

She felt her eyes widen and her heart stop. "What?! What kind of accident? Is Evan all right?"

"Dr. Finney has just left," he began.

But Francesca could not wait. If Evan was at home, then something terrible had happened, and she lifted her skirts and ran up the stairs to the third floor. The moment she skidded onto the landing, she heard her mother's voice, followed by Maggie Kennedy's. The door to the Blue Suite was open. She raced down the hall and into the sitting room.

The first thing she saw was her father, seated on the sofa in front of the hearth. He had his head cradled in his hands. The gesture was a despondent one.

"Papa?" She ran to him, but even as she did, she could glimpse into the bedroom, for the door was wide open. Evan lay in bed, his head swathed in a bandage. Maggie and his mother hovered over him. "Papa? What happened?"

He looked up and she saw that his eyes were moist with tears he would not shed. "Your brother has been in a barroom brawl," he said.

"A barroom brawl?" she echoed stupidly.

"He has suffered a concussion, two broken ribs, a fractured wrist, and far too many bruises to count. He almost lost his eye, from a kick, I believe." Andrew stared at her grimly.

Francesca could hardly believe her ears. She ran into the bedroom.

"Mrs. Kennedy, please, do not trouble yourself," Evan was saying in a low, pain-filled voice.

"Ssh. The laudanum makes you dry. Did you not hear Dr. Finney say you must drink plenty of water?" She sat by his hip, holding a glass to his lips.

Evan was propped up on numerous pillows. He had a bandage around the top of his head and one across his eyes. Even so, the left side of his face was horrifically red and purple. His right wrist was in a plaster cast. He wore pajamas, but the nightshirt was open, revealing that his torso was also tightly bandaged.

Francesca was pierced with anguish just looking at him.

Julia stood not far from Maggie. She heard Francesca and turned. The moment she saw her daughter, she burst into tears, although she did not make a sound.

Francesca rushed forward and they clung to each other. "He will be fine, Mama, just fine," Francesca said. But her mind was finally functioning. A barroom brawl? Her brother did not brawl. Hadn't he said something about being worried about his creditors breaking his neck?

Was it possible?

"Thank you, Francesca," Julia whispered, recovering her control and breaking away from the embrace.

Maggie was fussing with the covers now. "There, you should sleep. I heard Dr. Finney say so."

Evan smiled at her. Even black-and-blue and bandaged like a mummy, he was devilishly handsome. "Has anyone ever told you that you are an angel, Mrs. Kennedy?" His tone was somewhat slurred.

"No one has; you are the first," Maggie said cheerfully. "Now close your eyes, Mr. Cahill. Sleep is the best way to get you back on your feet."

His eyes drifted shut, and he was smiling.

Maggie stroked his brow, bandage and all, as if he were one of her children. Then she turned, her eyes wide, horrified. "Who could have done this?" she gasped, staring at Francesca. "I have seen my share of fistfights, but this is almost as if someone wished to kill him!"

Julia began to tremble.

Francesca laid her hand on her mother's shoulder, giving Maggie a warning look. "Come, Mama; come sit down with Papa," she said.

Julia did not protest. Francesca led her into the sitting room, where Andrew sat staring into the fire. The moment Julia sat down beside him, he pulled her into his arms. Julia sobbed soundless while Andrew said, "This is my fault. I chased him out of the house. This is my entire fault."

"This is hardly your fault!" Julia cried. "Oh, God, he is so badly hurt!"

"There, there, he is a strong young man; Finney said so.

Besides a few broken ribs, why, he will be up and about in no time," Andrew soothed.

Francesca was relieved to see them caring for each other again, and she hurried back to the bedroom. Maggie stood at the foot of the bed, apparently watching Evan as he slept. Francesca hurried to stand beside her. "Evan?"

There was no answer.

"Evan?" She walked over to him, but his eyes were closed and unmoving.

"He's asleep, Miss Cahill. Please, do not wake him," Maggie said, sounding very shaken. She was extremely pale now.

Francesca returned to her side and took her hand. "What did Dr. Finney say?"

"That he is young and strong and very lucky. He has been kicked viciously in the kidneys, Miss Cahill. Dr. Finney says it will be some time before he is up and about."

Francesca slid her arm around her, more to comfort herself than Maggie. "Oh, God. Was it a barroom brawl?"

Maggie nodded. "Mr. Cahill said so himself. Claims he was drunk. I don't know. Does your brother drink like that? He seems like such a gentleman!"

"My brother *is* a gentleman," Francesca said, "and he has never been in a fight like this before. I have never seen him drunk, either." Suspicion assailed her. Could Evan be lying? And if so, why? She desperately needed to speak to him. "But he will be all right?"

"In a week he should be up and about," Maggie said, wringing her hands. "But he will be stiff and sore for a month or more." Tears filled her bright blue eyes and she covered her chest with her palm. "This is too terrible for words."

Francesca inhaled deeply. "Yes, it is." She glanced at her sleeping brother. And prayed this was not because of the inordinate sum of money he owed.

Francesca left her brother's room and quickly freshened up and changed her clothes. As she did so, she was startled to find her blue eyes filled with the same anxiety she had seen the night before on the Albany train. She sobered as she pinned a hat on. Images of Bragg and Calder Hart clashed in her mind, followed by a recollection of Leigh Anne, waiting for them outside of Grand Central Depot.

She sighed, as her personal life seemed impossible now, deliberately turning her thoughts to Chrissy and Craddock. At least the little girl was unhurt—Craddock had nothing to gain and everything to lose by harming her. As she went downstairs, she prayed that by the time she arrived back at Calder's, Craddock would have been found.

It was only two and a half hours since they had split up to search for the hoodlum, not three. In all likelihood, all the Braggs would not be back by the time she got to Hart's mansion.

Francesca had almost reached the ground floor when she heard her mother's voice drifting from the smallest of the entry's three salons. She could not make out her words, but clearly they had a guest. And instantly she was filled with dread.

She froze upon the stairs. She simply knew who the caller was—but not why she had come.

Julia stepped out of the salon, clearly having recovered her composure, although there was a somber set to her face. Leigh Anne Bragg was with her.

Francesca looked past her mother, her heart stopping, and her gaze locked with that of Bragg's wife.

Leigh Anne did not smile. Nor did her gaze waver.

"Francesca? You have a caller. Mrs. Bragg," Julia said simply. She did not seem surprised. "I will have refreshments sent in, perhaps a cup of hot tea and some muffins."

Julia walked down the entry hall and disappeared in the corridor, obviously preoccupied. Francesca realized she remained posed upon the stairs, as if a statue. It was hard to breathe.

If only the other woman did not seem so lovely, and not just in appearance. If only she looked like a seductress, a harlot, a villainess.

"Miss Cahill? I do hope this is not an inconvenient time,"

Leigh Anne said. She had a soft, pretty voice. It suited her completely.

Francesca came to life, thinking she would pretend to be her sister, who was the perfect lady, always, and for whom, in elegance and poise, there was simply no rival. And plastering a smile on her face, she glided down the stairs, her head held high, somewhat amazed by her own grace. In fact, a stranger might mistake her for her sister now, she thought with satisfaction. The trick was to pretend one had one's hair in a braid, and then to attempt to have that braid tickle one's waist. Then, on the bottom step, as she was not watching where she was going, as she could not, with her chin so elevated, she tripped.

Leigh Anne rushed forward, "Are you all right, Miss Cahill?"

Francesca straightened, flushing. "I am fine."

"I must say, those stairs are undoubtedly tricky," Leigh Anne said.

Francesca looked into eyes the color of expensive emeralds. She had never seen such green eyes, such thick lashes—or such an expression of pure innocence. *What if Bragg was wrong?*

She shook her head to clear it. Even Hart claimed that this woman was a virtueless viper. "Shall we?" She led the way back into the salon without responding to Leigh Anne's comment about the stairs or waiting for a reply.

Francesca then shut both doors closed behind Leigh Anne. "What can I do for you, Mrs. Bragg?"

Leigh Anne smiled, and it was rueful. "I hope my note did not shock you."

Of course it had shocked her. "Of course not." She brightened her smile. "I have been so looking forward to meeting you."

Leigh Anne smiled. "Likewise."

Oh, this was good indeed. Her sour mood grew. "Bragg speaks so highly of you—and so frequently."

Leigh Anne continued to smile. "Do you love him very much?"

Francesca stiffened as if shot. "I beg your pardon?"

"Should we really play games?" She gave Francesca a sidelong look and wandered now to a cabinet, as if admiring the blue-and-white china collection there.

"Games?" Francesca repeated, as if a dummy who did not understand the meaning of the word.

Leigh Anne turned, continuing to smile in a pleasant manner. "He loves you. He told me so—and I can see it in his eyes when he speaks of you. I suppose I understand. The two of you have a great deal in common. I have heard you are a very active woman politically. I have also heard that you are an accomplished sleuth. I understand why Rick so admires you." Her expression was serious and grave.

How had this woman learned so much about her? Who had been giving her information? "Bragg and I have worked together on several ghastly crimes," she said stiffly. "We are friends."

Leigh Anne's smile was tearful. "Well, he certainly does not consider you a friend, Miss Cahill. I suppose that in a way, this is entirely my fault, for not being with him, at his side, the way a wife should be. I am so sorry that this has happened, Miss Cahill. I really am," she ended softly.

Francesca folded her arms across her chest. The speech was such a perfect one—had she rehearsed it? Surely she did not mean a single word! "Let's dispense with games," she said abruptly, and was pleased to see Leigh Anne start. "You have lived apart from Bragg for four years. Why have you so suddenly returned?"

"Cecelia Thornton," Leigh Anne said simply, no longer smiling, her gaze uncomfortably direct.

"Cecelia Thornton?" Francesca fought to recover a memory on the edge of her recollection.

"She saw you and my husband at the theater and presumed you were both intimate. She lives in Boston and came to me instantly, to warn me of what was happening."

Francesca became even more uncomfortable. Oh, she did remember that moment now, when she and Bragg had been having drinks before the show. They had turned around to find Mrs. Thornton of the Boston Thorntons—a friend of her mother—watching them ever so closely.

"Are you his mistress?" Leigh Anne asked.

Francesca managed to withhold her reflexive urge to gasp. She hesitated, as stiff as any oak board now. Should she lie? If she said yes, would it somehow be to her advantage and to this woman's disadvantage? Should she be honest? Would honesty make Leigh Anne Bragg disappear from their lives?

Francesca did not think that anything she did or said would make the other woman vanish.

"I see," Leigh Anne said coolly. "I do see."

Francesca realized she had taken her silence for acquiescence but did not correct her mistaken assumption. She could always do so at another time. "Why have you returned, Leigh Anne?" She could not utter the words *Mrs. Bragg,* even though a familiar form of address was incorrect now.

Her gaze narrowed. "He is my husband. My husband has fallen in love with another woman. Surely you did not think I would sit by and allow the two of you to carry on here, for all the world to see?"

"You have nothing to gain by remaining in New York," Francesca said firmly. "Bragg does not love you and a marital separation will hurt him politically."

For a moment Leigh Anne did not speak. She finally smiled. "Bragg claims he loves you. I think he does. But, my dear, he still loves me, as well—he simply refuses to admit it to anyone, much less himself."

Francesca flinched. Her heart beat so hard now. Because she suspected as much and she had for some time.

"You see, we have a bond that can never be severed, Miss Cahill, not by you or anyone. It is hard to explain. Even living apart from him for four years, in a way he was always with me, each and every day. I have never been able to escape that bond, and seeing him today, I know he feels it, too."

Francesca felt her cheeks heat. She believed Leigh Anne's every word. In fact, had she not seen, time and again, Bragg's extreme reaction to her mere name? "What are you going to do?" she managed roughly. She had to know.

"I must ask you the same thing," Leigh Anne returned evenly.

Francesca realized she was still hugging herself. She managed to drop her arms, but her fists clenched automatically. "I don't know."

Leigh Anne absorbed that. "What I will not do is allow Rick to attain a divorce and thus destroy himself, his career, and me."

Francesca jerked and met her gaze.

Leigh Anne stared back for a long moment, her gaze uncompromising now. "But then, he would not be the one destroying himself, now would he?"

She felt herself pale. This was a clever little woman indeed.

"You are the problem here, Miss Cahill, you, not I. In fact, should anyone ever see what Mrs. Thornton has seen, should the newsmen of this city ever learn that you and my husband are lovers, he will be finished politically. And I do believe you are intelligent enough to know that."

Touché. She lifted her chin. She said nothing, because Leigh Anne was right.

Connie's words echoed now, loudly, hurtfully. *You are his Achilles' heel, Francesca. . . . You are the one who can destroy him. If you love him, you must let him go!*

"If you really love him you would never think to put him in such a dangerous position," Leigh Anne said softly.

And Francesca thought, with utter despair, *I have lost.* She did not speak.

Leigh Anne came forward and laid her hand on Francesca's back, the gesture one of compassion. "I am sorry," she said softly. "I understand what it's like to love my husband. You see, I have never stopped loving him, not even after all of these years."

Francesca fought not to allow a single tear to moisten her eyes. She shifted so Leigh Anne's hand dropped away from her body. "You want him back."

"I hadn't really understood that, not until I saw him this morning. I only came here to prevent you from destroying him, and us. But when I came face-to-face with him, my real feelings became inescapable," she said. "I married a boy with dreams; today, I have seen a great man. How could I not love him?"

"So you are staying," Francesca whispered. And she heard how thick with tears her own tone was.

"I am staying." Leigh Anne's smile was grim. "And I am going to help Rick achieve all of his dreams, Miss Cahill." Their gazes locked. "Every single one."

Nineteen

Francesca walked Leigh Anne to the door, feeling very much removed from herself, as if she were not even in her own body. Avoiding thought—and feelings—now seemed like a priority. Yet it was so terribly difficult to do.

Because beneath the surface veneer there was turmoil and heartbreak and oh so much sickness.

As Leigh Anne was helped on with her chinchilla-and-fox coat, Francesca smiled. How brittle it felt. Leigh Anne slipped on her gloves. "Have a pleasant afternoon, Miss Cahill," she said sweetly as Francis opened the front door for her. And unfortunately, there was nothing saccharine about her. In fact, compassion seemed to lurk in her green eyes.

How Francesca hated her. Francesca nodded, the smile plastered in place, as Joel Kennedy burst into the foyer, stomping snow off his boots. "Miz Cahill, do I got news!" he cried excitedly.

Leigh Anne looked at the small boy in the ragged coat, patched pants, and leather gloves with surprise.

"Have a good day," Francesca said quickly, sick at heart that she felt physically ill. She closed the door in Leigh Anne's face, having taken the task over from Francis. She turned, inhaling hard, shaking. "Joel?"

He grabbed her hand and dragged her away from the doorman. "I found me a bloke who wanted that reward we been askin' for," he said in a stage whisper. "Craddock's been in a heavy card game for two hours now. Saloon's on Thirty-second; we gotta go!"

"What?" she gasped, instantly diverted from the horrid

drama that was her own life. Francesca stared, her mind doing cartwheels. *"We have found Craddock?"*

"Yep, but how long will he stay put? Where's the fly you like so much?" Joel demanded, glancing around as if expecting Bragg to materialize from the thin air in the foyer.

Where was Bragg? She, of course, had no idea. "It will take twenty minutes, at least, to get downtown," she said quickly. "If we go to Hart's, it will take another ten."

"Or more!" Joe cried impatiently.

"We cannot lose Craddock," she decided. She raced over to a side table and quickly wrote Bragg a note. "Jonathan! Have this sent over to Calder Hart's at Nine-seventy-three Fifth Avenue this instant! It is a matter of life and death!" she cried, opening a closet herself and dragging out her coat. "Joel, run upstairs and get my purse; you know which one!" She gave him a significant look. Excitement filled her now. They had found Craddock!

"The one with . . . ?"

"Yes, that one," she said, knowing he referred to her gun. Joel took off.

"Bring Jenson about," Francesca said. There was no time for cabs now. They would have to use the Cahill coach.

Jonathan was galvanized into action, while Francesca started to calculate the difference between her time of arrival at the saloon and Bragg's, beginning to perspire. She paced. If she was very lucky, he would only be twenty minutes behind her. But in all likelihood, it would be more than that, as he might not even be back at Hart's yet. It did not matter. They would stick to Craddock like fleas to a dog, until he led them to Chrissy Savage.

Francesca was praying that she was unhurt, that she was alive.

Joel skidded down the stairs and across the entry hall's marble floor. "Got it!" he cried triumphantly.

Francesca took the purse. "Let's go."

As Joel had said, Craddock was immersed in a serious game of cards. The saloon had a CLOSED sign on the front door. It was not locked, however, and after peeking in first to make sure no one was about—and not even the proprietor was in sight—they slipped inside. Joel led her to a closed door on the barroom's other side. It was ajar; and peering around it, Francesca quickly saw a single table filled with six men, each and every one smoking a cigar, drinking whiskey, and silently engrossed in stud poker. One of the six men wore the blue serge uniform of a policeman, which sickened her. Of course a police officer was entitled to a game of cards, but not while on duty, and not with ruffians and crooks. And Craddock sat at an angle to the door—to see her and Joel, he would merely have to turn his head an inch or so to his right.

He was studying his hand. The scar on his cheek was livid in the garish pool of light.

And he had a gun tucked into his belt.

They backed away and looked breathlessly at each other with wide eyes. Francesca wished she had not seen Craddock's gun.

"Now what?" Joel whispered.

"We sit and wait outside for Bragg and his family and perhaps the police," Francesca said, the mere idea of waiting anathema to her. "Or we can try to find and rescue Chrissy," she added on impulse.

Joel grinned at her.

Francesca smiled grimly back, then glanced at the narrow stairs that led upstairs. "We have work to do. Come."

"Women," Joel said. "Harlots up them stairs," he added unnecessarily.

"Let's go," Francesca decided.

He followed her as they hurried up the stairs, which creaked and groaned with every step. They glanced down into the barroom several times, but none of the poker players came running out, demanding to know what they were doing. Upstairs they halted, listening for sounds of activity. There were a few breathy moans and masculine groans coming from behind a door at the end of the hall, but other than that, they heard nothing.

Then they heard a child's laughter.

Francesca and Joel gazed at each other; the sound had come from the first door on their right. Thank God!

Francesca moved. She laid her ear against the rough wood door and heard more laughter and a woman's soft singing. Then, "What a pretty baby you are," the woman said with a smile.

Francesca removed her gun from her purse. She now wished it were an average-sized weapon, which looked far more threatening and not like a toy. Holding it in her left hand was simply not to be borne. Suddenly she tucked the gun in her coat pocket and tore the bandage off her right hand. Her palm was pink and a bit raw, her fingers in a similar condition, but it did not matter now. Clearly she was healing and well on the way to recovery. She retrieved the gun, glad to have it securely in her right hand. She nodded at Joel and made a knocking gesture. Then she flattened herself against the wall. Joel nodded and grinned. He was enjoying himself.

He knocked twice, softly, on the door.

The woman stopped speaking. Chrissy stopped laughing.

Joel knocked again once.

Chrissy said, "Door."

Francesca heard a spring on the bed creak. She heard a floor plank groan. She felt sweat pooling in her cleavage, acutely aware of the woman crossing the room and hesitating before the door.

"Joe?"

Joel glanced at Francesca; she grimaced. He said, "Got a dollar?"

Suddenly the door opened. A woman in a short wrapper and curly blond hair with a tired, worn face appeared. "Go away, boy," she began.

Francesca jammed her gun against the woman's head. "Don't move," she said. "Or I shall blow your head off of your body."

The woman was as frozen as a block of ice. "Don't hurt

me! I didn't do nothing! I only followed orders! It's Craddock you want!"

"Joel, grab Chrissy," Francesca ordered, suddenly aware that this was far too easy—and equally aware that Craddock was downstairs and far too close for comfort.

Joel rushed inside and grabbed the beaming little girl. At least she was happy and unhurt. "Let's get out of here," Francesca said. She dashed down the hall, Joel on her heels, saw Craddock, and stopped.

He was coming up the stairs.

He also froze, his expression one of comical disbelief.

"Joel, the other way!" Francesca shouted as her gaze locked with Craddock's.

His eyes had been wide; now he leaped forward looking ready to tear her head off as Francesca turned to flee without even knowing if there was another way out of the saloon. She prayed that there was. She took two steps when he grabbed her coat by the back of the collar. She was yanked backward, and then she was in his viselike grip.

"Joel, run!" she screamed as Craddock's breath feathered her ear, her cheek.

"Now what do I got here? It ain't a Bragg; now look at that. Anyone ever tell you you are one pain in the ass, lady?" he asked roughly.

By craning her neck she was able to just meet his angry blue eyes. His scar stood out in a white arc now on his crimson cheek. He jerked on her harder, enough so, she thought, to crack her ribs. "Drop that fucking gun," he said.

She dropped it.

And saw that Joel had disappeared down a back stairwell. Relief filled her, but when she felt cold steel against her temple it vanished. "You have ruined everything," Craddock said. "Hmm. Wonder what I should do now?"

She twisted and looked him in the eye again.

Cruel pleasure was there. He laughed.

He had never been so angry, but he put his anger far away, beneath resolve and determination. *Why did she always have*

to go off half-cocked on her own? But that was what made
her unique and different from every other woman he had ever
met, he thought, and it was one of the reasons he loved her.

The coach careened around the corner of Forty-second
Street and onto Second Avenue.

"At least we have located Craddock," his father said.
Rathe laid his hand on his knee. "And I am certain Francesca
and this boy will be all right. She seems like a strong, re-
sourceful, and clever young woman, Rick."

Bragg intended to smile; he felt himself grimace instead.
It was clear to him that his entire family knew the depth of
his feelings for Francesca.

There was simply no excuse for her to go after Craddock
alone. When the case was resolved, with Chrissy safely back
in her mother's arms and Craddock behind bars, he would
throttle her—and then make love to her.

Which was what he should have done last night.

An image of Leigh Anne crept into his mind; furious, he
tried to shove it away to some dusty, forgotten place. Her
smiling face simply would not go.

"There is simply no excuse for allowing her to assist in
any criminal investigation," Hart said coolly. "She has you
twisted around her little finger." His black gaze was sim-
mering with fury. It was clear to Bragg that his half brother
had not recovered from the fact that Francesca had spent the
night with him alone on a train.

Bragg looked at Hart as coldly, wishing he might find
another city to go live in. "I think you are the one she has
wrapped around her little finger, Calder."

A gun was cocked, the snapping metallic sound harsh and
jarring. It was Rourke, and he jammed the revolver in his
belt. "This might be a good time for the two of you to lay
your differences aside," he said flatly.

A silence greeted his words. The coach was full. Hart,
Shoz, and Nicholas D'Archand sat on the rear-facing seat,
Shoz with one of Hart's hunting rifles wrapped in an oilskin
raincoat. Bragg, Rathe, and Rourke faced them, facing forward. Nicholas, who was eighteen and in his first year at

Columbia University, finally spoke. "She is an amazing woman. I have never met a woman so brave and fearless," he said, his silver eyes filled with distinctly male admiration.

Bragg sighed. "She is too old for you."

"Says who?" Nicholas gave him a lazy look.

Bragg decided to ignore his cousin. They were a block from their destination. He rapped on the window and Raoul, Hart's disreputable-looking driver who served more as a bodyguard than anything else, twisted to glance at him. He was joined there by Peter, his own man. Both men were armed. "Sir?"

"Drive slowly past the saloon," Bragg ordered.

Raoul braked and the carriage slowed.

Nicholas and Rourke were seated on the side of the carriage closest to the saloon, which was on the west side of Second Avenue. Everyone strained to peer out the window as they passed. There was a CLOSED sign on the door, and the saloon appeared empty. Bragg glanced out of his own window, at the east side of the avenue. A few other saloons, a grocery store, a milliner, and a tenement were all crammed there. "Raoul, go around the block, quickly now. We will go out on the corner of Thirty-second, between Second and Third," he said.

"What's the plan?" Rourke asked calmly.

"We will split into teams of two. You take Nicholas; Shoz and Hart can go together. Father and I will be the ones to approach the saloon, perhaps enter it, and discern the situation. The rest of you stay back, outside and out of sight. You can duck into the doorway of the milliner's and the apartment building. I will wave you on if we should decide to storm the establishment," Bragg said.

"You are not storming anything," Shoz said coolly. "And I am going in—alone."

Bragg met his cold silver eyes and could not help flinching. Still, he understood, and he reached out and laid his hand reassuringly on the other man's leg. "Shoz, you are emotionally involved. It is best that you do not make decisions now."

"I am an Apache, Rick," Shoz said harshly. "I am the one

who can get into the saloon and most successfully find and rescue my daughter. I am the one who is going to cut Craddock's throat." He smiled, and it did not reach his eyes.

Bragg thought about Cooper, hanging by his neck, his body carefully sliced up. "Shoz, my niece is in there. Right now, I would prefer that we assess the situation, carefully, before deciding on any plan of action."

Shoz hesitated. "Five minutes," he said. "That is what I am giving you, Rick, and then I am going in."

Their gazes locked. Bragg felt real dismay, accompanied by the many icy fingers of dread. God damn it. His brother-in-law was a hard man and not a man to be ordered about, much less to be crossed. He understood him now—his precious daughter was in the hands of a killer. But it was not in Chrissy's best interest that Shoz hunt Craddock down. They were not on the West Texas plains, where a man might commit murder and walk away freely. They were in the middle of New York City. Brendan Farr was out there, hunting them.

Shoz was also not a man to change his mind, once it was set. Still, Bragg tried to negotiate. "Ten minutes," he said. "Give me ten minutes, Shoz. Please."

Shoz's jaw flexed.

Bragg hesitated, then said, "Francesca is in there, too." It was his way of saying that he loved her and was as concerned as Shoz about getting Craddock.

Shoz said, "Eight."

Hart rolled his eyes. "Both of you are emotionally involved; neither one of you should be in charge."

"And you are not emotionally involved?" Rourke asked quietly, tearing the words right out from Bragg's heart.

"We are all emotionally involved," Rathe said firmly. "We're here."

The coach rocked to a stop. The doors opened and the six men came pouring out, their weapons concealed beneath their coats. Shoz carried the hunting rifle wrapped in the oilskin raincoat. A knife appeared in his hand; he slipped it up his sleeve. He was still clad in his western-style suit and silver-tipped cowboy boots, and he and Hart were the only ones not wearing overcoats.

Hart suddenly gripped Bragg's shoulder. "I should go in." He smiled. "I've heard there is a good game to be played." His eyes glinted and he lifted the leather valise he held.

In it was cash. Bragg had not asked how much, but he assumed $10,000. His impulse was to refuse. But what better way to get the lay of the land? In his black suit and tie, his white dress shirt, and his gold Mueller pocket watch and Asprey sapphire-and-diamond ring, Hart could easily be mistaken for a gambler. Of course, he was too elegant and wealthy for this kind of place, but then, gamblers often panicked when a game could not be found.

"He's right," Rathe said quietly. "Calder's just come to town and he is looking for a game. Flash the cash. I am sure they will let you in."

"And I can go with him to back him up. I can go as his nephew or cousin," Nicholas said with excitement. "How many times have I been told I look just like Calder?"

It was the perfect plan.

All eyes were on Bragg now.

He hated handing the job over to his brother. But Chrissy was in there—and so was Francesca. "Do it," Bragg said.

There was the slightest trickle of sweat on his temples. Hart brushed them off of his cousin's face. "Calm down," he said outside the saloon. "We merely want some action, Nick. A cheap whiskey, a good cigar, and some fast cash." He smiled, baring even white teeth.

"How can you be so cool?" Nicholas asked, loosening his tie.

How? The calm was born of urgency and even fear. He adored the tiny child who was somewhere in that saloon, just as he adored her mother. And then there was Francesca.

He would move the entire city in order to rescue her now. And he had not a doubt that he could do so, if that was what had to be done.

Besides, money could buy just about anything—if not everything.

"Calder?"

Hart smiled at the younger man. "Experience," he murmured. "Forget the stakes; think of this as a game." But it was hardly a game. He remained acutely aware of the high stakes—Chrissy's life, Francesca's life. However, this was not the time to dwell on the worst possibilities. This was the time to execute.

And he was a man of action. Had he not proved that, time and again?

He met Nicholas's eyes. He saw that his younger cousin had recovered his composure. Especially when Nicholas winked. Hart nodded and opened the saloon door, walking inside, Nicholas on his heels. The barroom was eerily empty. It was dirty and cheap, but then, he had expected that. It brought back terrible memories, memories he had thought were so distant as to be gone forever. But now was not the time to recall running away from Rathe's home at the age of sixteen. Now was not the time to recall the five following years, including failing out of Princeton and slowly but surely wheeling and dealing his way to the top of the first company he had ever owned.

He heard the soft murmur of voices coming from behind a closed door at its far end. "Let's go," he said with a hard smile. He could not wait to get his hands on Craddock. However, he doubted he would have the chance; Shoz would get there first.

Nicholas smiled in return. To his credit, he looked eager now for battle. As anxious as he might be, it did not show. His smile was cool, amused, and even sensual; the boy reminded Hart a bit of himself.

Hart clapped Nicholas's back and knocked on the door once, before opening it.

Men turned in their chairs. Eyes widened and then narrowed. A half a dozen men stared.

"I am sorry for the intrusion," Hart said calmly. He smiled, setting his valise down at his feet. He did so in such a way that everyone glanced at it. "I heard there was a game; we have just come to town, my nephew Nick and I." But even as he spoke, he casually glanced at each of the six men in the room, five of whom were seated at the table, one of whom was standing. He sensed that the tall, bald standing man was the proprietor of the saloon. One chair at the table was empty. A player was gone, and being that no man already seated there fit Craddock's description, he guessed that their quarry was gone. He quelled any disappointment. He was there to obtain information. There was surely information to be had.

"Game's closed," someone grunted.

"Yeah, but where's Joe? He been gone for ten minutes," a heavyset man said with exasperation.

"Said he had to get upstairs."

"Stupid fool." Another one spat tobacco.

"Shut up and play cards."

Craddock was upstairs. "Might I be directed to another establishment?" Hart asked, picking up his valise.

"Let him play," someone groused.

That was the last thing Hart now wanted. But he smiled with interest anyway, as if waiting to be invited to sit. If he was, he would do so, and he and Nicholas would find the opportunity for Nick to leave and tell the others what they had learned. Patience was a virtue. It was one of the few that Hart possessed, and he had it in spades.

And that was when the screams began and a gunshot rang out.

Hart looked at Nicholas; the screams and the shot had come from above. They ran out of the back room, toward the stairs in the saloon, as all of the card-players jumped up.

Joel had disappeared with Chrissy down the back stairs. Francesca was grateful for that.

She stood by the woman's bed, not daring to move, as Craddock cursed and paced. The woman in the small wrapper looked anxious indeed.

"Dumb moll!" Craddock finally shouted, and with the butt

of his gun he struck the blonde across the side of her face. She screamed and went down in a heap.

"This is all your fuckin' fault!" Craddock shouted, and he kicked her in the thigh.

"Stop!" Francesca dashed to the woman, but Craddock caught her by the shoulder and flung her back hard onto the bed.

"You don't move, lady, not one step!"

The blonde was whimpering and crying now.

"Shit!" Craddock cried.

Francesca sat up, instantly looking at the other woman. The blonde was on her side, clutching her face. Blood seeped through her fingers. "She needs help. She needs a doctor!"

"Shut up!" he shouted at her. "Damn it! Who the hell are you? An' give me one good reason not to kill you right now!"

Francesca froze. Her heart went wild, beating with alarm and fear. She inhaled. "Surely one murder is enough?"

He was hardly stupid. "I ain't ever committed murder."

"I beg to differ," she breathed. "Fort Kendall—1890."

He began to smile, widely. He was truly a cruel thug. "I didn't kill Cooper, lady. Ole Shoz Savage did that deed." He leered. "An' I seen him do it."

Francesca slowly stood. At least the blonde had stopped whimpering. She still lay on her side, but she was watching them both now with the kind of fascination reserved for a striking rattlesnake. Francesca had been testing Craddock, and unfortunately, she felt that he was telling her the truth.

"I told you to stay still!"

Francesca said, "I spoke to Warden Timbull. There were no witnesses."

"Oh, there were witnesses all right. There were seventy-one witnesses, not countin' the guards."

She felt her eyes widen. "You mean—the entire prison watched that man being tortured and killed?"

"Even ole Timbull was there, enjoyin' the show," he sneered.

She was ill.

"Don't bother to swoon. Now who the hell are you?"

Francesca debated her options. Her family had money, so the truth might save her life—he could ransom her now, instead of Chrissy. "Francesca Cahill," she said.

"Cahill? As in Arthur Cahill, that butcher fellow?" His gaze was narrowed.

"My father's name is Andrew Cahill, and his company is meatpacking, not butchering," she said.

He began to smile. "Well, well, looks like I done all right after all." He turned to the woman on the floor. "Whaddya think, Lulabelle? I got me a rich prize here." His gaze narrowed. "Maybe I can figure out a way to make Shoz pay after all." He grinned.

Lulabelle sat up. "Can I go?" she whispered.

"No, you can't go," he shouted, reaching for her.

Francesca realized this was his chance. As he bent to lift the woman and do God only knew what to her, she raced past him for the door, screaming for help.

He cursed.

She flung the door open. "Help! Bragg! Help!" She had never run faster than she now ran down the short distance of the corridor to the stairs.

A bullet whistled by her ear.

She stumbled, tripping as she went down the stairs.

He caught her on the third step, pulling her against his body, his arm going around her waist. And he ground the barrel of the gun into her temple. "Don't move, bitch," he said.

Francesca went still, and at the bottom of the stairs she saw Hart and Nicholas.

"Don't move," Hart said calmly. He smiled a little at her as their eyes met. It was meant to be reassuring, and it was. She had the oddest feeling that he would save her now, and that feeling was accompanied by calm.

Nicholas was pointing a gun at Craddock; Hart's hands were empty, although a black leather valise was at his feet. The poker players from the back room had come into the bar and stood in a jagged circle behind Hart and Nicholas. Now the saloon door burst open, and Bragg appeared on the threshold, a gun in his hand. Behind him were Shoz, Rourke, and Rathe, in that order. Almost simultaneously, every single man saw what was happening and froze. Bragg's gaze slammed to Francesca.

"Joel escaped with Chrissy!" Francesca cried.

His eyes widened.

Craddock jabbed the gun so hard into her temple that she became dizzy and watched the room becoming black. "Shut the fuck up."

"If you hurt her, you will get nothing," Hart said in the same calm but oh-so-authoritative voice.

Bragg had come to stand beside Hart. "Craddock, it is over. I am Rick Bragg, and you are surrounded. Release Miss Cahill, release her now, and we will let you walk out of here, unharmed."

Craddock jerked on Francesca. She managed not to whimper. "Like hell. Well, well. If it ain't my old friend and pard, Shoz Savage."

Francesca glanced breathlessly at Shoz. He was staring coolly at Craddock; he did not speak.

"Guess we got an ole score to settle, now don't we?" Craddock said, jerking hurtfully on Francesca.

She refused to gasp. Sweat trickled into her eye.

"Leave Miss Cahill out of this," Shoz said flatly.

"Now why should I do that? Hey, them rich folks of yours, they know you murdered a man in cold blood?" Craddock laughed. "In front of seventy-one witnesses; no, make that seventy-six. Got to include the guards an' bullyboy Timbull."

"If I go down," Shoz said softly, "I am taking you down with me."

For one moment, Craddock stared, and Francesca felt a new tension tightening his body. Then he said baldly, "I don't think so. You see, I got me a ticket here, one to freedom and cash." He jabbed the gun against her to make his point. This time, she did gasp, as her temple was terribly sore now.

Bragg stepped forward. "Miss Cahill has nothing to do

with this. However, there is a carriage outside, with a driver, and you may take that—but only after you release Miss Cahill."

"An' the cash?"

Bragg glanced at Hart. Hart smiled and picked up the valise, opening it. He tossed out a bound wad of bills. And then another—and another. "Five thousand, ten thousand. Fifteen. Here. Now it is twenty. Do tell me when to stop, Mr. Craddock."

Craddock's eyes were popping. "How much do you got in there?"

"It is not how much I have in this satchel," Hart said. "It is how much I have in my safe and my bank accounts, and the answer is, I will pay what you wish, but you must release Miss Cahill . . . now." His gaze moved to Francesca.

Something warmed inside of her. She had the distinct feeling that he would turn over hundreds of thousands of dollars without even thinking twice about it, to ensure that she was unhurt and freed.

Craddock licked his lips. "Thirty," he said hoarsely. "Thirty thousand dollars."

Hart smiled and tossed two more wads of bills at his feet. "Release her," he said softly.

Francesca felt Craddock's grip loosening—and then footsteps sounded and dozens of men in blue uniforms swarmed into the saloon, with Brendan Farr at their head.

"Get out!" Bragg shouted furiously. "Get your men out of here!"

Craddock's grip tightened and he dragged Francesca back up the stairs, screaming, "No police, fuck you, you bastard! No damn police!" And even though she fought him every step of the way, the next thing she knew, he was shoving her face-first into the small room, and slamming the door closed behind them.

Francesca fell onto the wood floor, chin-up. Pain exploded in her head and she saw stars. And she heard the bolt dropping.

Twenty

The timing was simply unbelievable. Bragg rubbed his face with his hands as a police officer directed the policemen out of the saloon. It was hard to think clearly, hard to keep his fear at bay. *He would never survive if anything happened to Francesca.* Then he got a grip and he looked up at Farr. "Make certain every man leaves this block. I do not want any police anywhere in the vicinity of this saloon! Is that clear?"

Farr was slightly flushed, and Bragg knew it was with anger. "Absolutely," he said. "Harry, you heard him."

"I am not done," Bragg interrupted. Clearly, appointing Farr as chief of police had been a mistake. The man was too smart, ambitious, and self-serving for his own good. But who would have ever thought that Lucy would come to New York, bringing so much trouble? Of course, he would have guessed that Francesca would quickly, irrevocably become involved in Lucy's problematic affairs. "Set up roadblocks on Thirty-third and Thirty-first Streets, on both Second and Third Avenue, as we do not know which direction he will go." Bragg watched Nicholas picking up the piles of money on the floor. "Any sign of Joel and Chrissy?"

Farr said, "The boy and little girl are outside with one of my men. They are both fine."

That was a huge relief. Shoz had been standing slightly to the side, with Rathe, Rourke, and Hart. His eyes widened and he dashed from the saloon. From outside, Chrissy's gleeful cry of, "Papa!" could be heard. Bragg almost smiled, except he could not, as he was too acutely aware of Francesca being upstairs with Craddock.

He must not think now of how often hostages were killed by their captors. He simply must not.

"Shall I go up and attempt to convince Craddock to give up Miss Cahill and surrender?" Farr asked.

Bragg felt like murdering him. Instead, he smiled. "No. Have Hart's coach in front of the saloon." He turned to go.

Farr detained him by gripping his arm. "You are going to let him get in that carriage? We may lose him if you do! It is not a good idea!"

"I am going to do what I have to do in order to rescue Miss Cahill," Bragg said coldly. Farr's gaze was too-knowing now. Undoubtedly the man knew what his entire family did— that he was in love with Francesca Cahill. "Get the rest of those civilians out of here," he said, nodding at the six men who had been playing poker in the back room. Several of them seemed about to drool over the last wad of bills, which Nicholas was replacing in Hart's valise.

Shoz suddenly strode into the saloon. He eyed Farr as he approached Bragg, then halted and did not speak.

It was obvious his brother-in-law wished to speak with him. As Francesca remained a hostage, Bragg could only hope that he had an idea with which to capture Craddock and set her free. But Brendan Farr remained a problem. "Where's Chrissy?"

"With the boy."

"Let's get her safely home," Bragg said decisively. "Rathe?"

Rathe stepped forward. "I'd rather stay—"

"I have enough trigger fingers on hand," Bragg said. "Please see Chrissy and Joel safely home. Kennedy belongs to the Cahills," he added wryly. Only Francesca would have found a way to move the entire Kennedy family into her home.

Rathe hesitated and nodded. He gripped Shoz's arm. "Whatever you are thinking, do not do it," he said. "You have a wife waiting for you, a wife who adores you, and three children who dearly need and love their father."

Shoz said nothing. His expression was at once implacable and impossible to read.

Rathe looked at his son. "Rick, don't let him do anything foolish."

"I won't."

Rathe nodded and strode out.

Shoz glanced toward Farr, who was pretending to observe two of his men as they herded the poker players outside; in fact, he was clearly eavesdropping. Bragg took his arm and they stepped closer to the stairs. Bragg couldn't help glancing up them. Of course, Francesca was all right; Craddock wanted two things, money and his freedom. Murder would not help him now.

But he was a vicious criminal, and he had already committed murder at least once. And most important, what he really wanted was revenge.

"Let them come out. I can pick off Craddock when he steps out of the saloon and before he gets into the carriage," Shoz said softly.

"No," Bragg said, in unison with Hart. His half brother had come over to stand with them.

"It's too risky," Bragg said, meaning it.

"You might miss or, worse, hit Francesca," Hart added darkly.

Shoz gave them both a disparaging look. "Why the hell do you think I brought that fancy English rifle of yours? I can position myself across the street, on that little balcony above the milliner's. I won't miss. I never miss."

"No," they said again in unison.

"I simply cannot allow it," Bragg added. "Besides, we are supposed to apprehend and try Craddock, not kill him."

Shoz's expression, already hard, hardened impossibly more. He walked away, pausing beside Rourke and Nicholas.

Hart faced Bragg. "What if he doesn't release Francesca?"

Bragg hated the look in his half brother's eyes. It was the first time he had ever seen fear there, and he supposed it mirrored his own expression exactly. "He has nothing to gain by keeping her."

"She is his ticket to freedom," Hart said harshly. Then, "God damn it."

Bragg laid a hand on his arm. "I need you to stay calm, Calder."

"I am calm. Calm enough to go up there and kill."

"You know that would only get Francesca killed. I am going to try to convince him to release her."

"He won't. He's going to use her to get safely in that coach," Hart said.

Bragg had opened his mouth to speak when a shout came down the stairs. "You got my carriage ready yet?" Craddock yelled.

Bragg strode to the bottom of the stairwell and saw Craddock on the top step, using Francesca as a shield, his gun against her temple. She was very white, but Bragg saw instantly from her eyes that she was basically calm and in complete control of her wits. He tried to send her a signal of encouragement; he was thankful that she was thinking clearly.

She understood, because she smiled a little at him—and then sent a similar smile to Hart.

He must not think of that now. "Your carriage is directly outside of the saloon door," Bragg said.

"The police? They had better be gone! I see one fly and I put a bullet in the pretty lady's arm. An' it'll only be the first!"

Bragg went rigid. He tried to breathe, tried not to imagine Francesca bleeding from one or more wounds. He understood, though; yes, he did. Craddock was too smart to kill her. He intended to keep her alive and use her. Bragg did not doubt that he would shoot her if he had to. "They're gone, Craddock; I sent them away. Now why don't you release Miss Cahill and we will let you go?"

He snorted. "Like hell! Where's the money?"

"It's here, in the bag," Hart said. He reached behind him without removing his gaze from Craddock; Nicholas handed him the valise.

"Open it. Show me it's all there," Craddock demanded.

Hart did so.

Craddock nodded now, with satisfaction, but sweat was mottling his brow. "OK. Things look good. I'm comin' down with the lady. I see anyone reach fer their gun, I take off her arm. You got that, Mr. Policeman?"

So Craddock knew who he was. Bragg nodded.

"But I want him," and he nodded at Hart, "to go ahead of me an' the lady, an' he can put the valise in the carriage before my eyes."

"No problem," Hart said.

Craddock looked at everyone in the barroom—Rourke and Nicholas, just to the right of the stairs, Bragg and Hart, directly below them, and Brendan Farr, standing a bit to the left and behind. "No one moves, except for the banker there, and he only goes when I tell him to," he said. "All of you, now, get your hands up, high, as high as they can go!"

"Understood," Bragg returned, but his pulse was pounding now as he slowly lifted his hands up. Everyone except Hart raised their hands up in a picture of surrender, even Farr. Hart remained as still as a statue, the valise at his feet. Bragg watched Craddock begin to come down the stairs, a step at a time, his gaze darting everywhere, making certain that no one was reaching for his gun, using Francesca as a shield. It was hard to breathe. It was hard to remain calm, composed, in control. It would be so easy to pull out his own gun and try to blow the man's head away so that Francesca could escape.

But in all likelihood she would be hurt or killed, so he did not do so, no matter the primal urge.

Craddock was halfway down the stairs. He was panting. The sound was soft, yet harsh, and very sharp. No, Francesca was the one panting, he realized with a pang. Sweat trickled down her brow, her cheek, disclosing just how frightened she really was.

Hang in there, he told her silently. *You are going to be just fine—we are going to get you out of this.*

He wished he believed his own silent words.

Her eyes locked with his. He saw the fear there now and

a question. She mouthed something, trying to communicate to him.

It looked like she was saying, *"Where Shoz?"*

He jerked. *Where the hell was Shoz?*

Bragg turned and realized that Shoz was not in the saloon, just as Hart also glanced wildly about, apparently realizing at the exact same time that Lucy's husband had disappeared.

I can position myself across the street, on that little balcony above the milliner's. I won't miss . . .

Bragg's gaze locked with Hart's; surprise and fear mingled, mixed. Shoz was out there and he intended to take Craddock down, never mind that Francesca was his human shield.

"Shit," Hart said, his eyes wide and stunned and afraid.

"What the fuck is goin' on?" Craddock cried. "Why are you lookin' around?" He had halted on the bottom step and Francesca gasped as he dug the barrel of the gun into the side of her head.

"Don't hurt her," Bragg said quietly. "Nothing is going on. We were checking to make sure the coach is outside the door."

Craddock stared at him suspiciously when Hart said, "May I?" indicating the valise filled with money.

Bragg knew he intended to distract Craddock. And it worked. Craddock looked at the bag and nodded. A hungry look had come into his eyes.

Hart picked up the valise. Then he turned, giving Craddock his back, and began to cross the saloon, leading the way.

Francesca made a strangled sound.

Bragg knew what it meant. Hart had his back to Craddock, and the man could so easily shift the gun he held and gun Hart down from behind.

He had to hand it to his half brother. He was very brave, and he remained one of the cleverest and most determined men he knew. And clearly Francesca knew it, too. As clearly, she was afraid for him now.

"Let's go," Craddock said, moving onto the floor now,

dragging Francesca with him. "Get those two to the wall, off to my side!" he yelled.

Rourke and Nicholas leaped back against the wall, never dropping their arms.

"Keep them hands up! Everyone, or I'll put my first bullet in the little lady you all are so fond of!"

Bragg had kept his hands up, and he glanced at Farr. The chief of police had seemed to be lowering his hands; now, reluctantly, he lifted them back up.

Hart had paused at the door; he glanced over his shoulder.

"Keep goin', banker!" Craddock screamed at him.

Hart walked outside.

Bragg's heart accelerated wildly. *Shoz was out there, waiting to take a shot at Craddock.* There was simply no other explanation for his disappearance.

Craddock half-dragged and half-pushed Francesca, carrying her with him, passing Bragg, then Farr. He pushed through the door, Francesca against his side.

The city sidewalk was no more than ten feet wide. Craddock took one step, then two. Bragg had his gun out; Craddock turned. "Drop it!" he screamed. "Drop it now before I kill the lady!"

Bragg dropped it; the revolver clattered to the floor.

Craddock began to smile, sweat streaking his face, and he turned; he was only a few feet from the carriage and, possibly, from freedom as well.

The shot rang out.

Craddock's eyes widened, he staggered backward, and Francesca broke free. As he fell backward onto the boardwalk, she rushed away, directly into Hart's arms. Bragg saw him drag her away from the carriage and to the safety of the side of the building as he ran toward Craddock with Farr, who had his gun in hand. He knelt beside the hoodlum and saw instantly that he was dead.

So did Farr. The chief of police rocked back on his heels. "Well, well," he murmured, more to himself.

Bragg did not rise. He shifted and looked toward the saloon and watched Hart holding Francesca in his arms. He was gripping her tightly and speaking to her with urgency. Francesca never took her eyes from his, and finally she nodded.

He could not stand it, and slowly, he stood.

"Are you all right?" Hart asked her, holding her tightly against his chest.

She couldn't breathe and she couldn't speak; her heart had never beaten so hard. And for one moment, she rested her cheek against the plane of his chest and heard his own urgent, answering heartbeat. She felt his palm cradling her head. Her eyes closed and too many vicious images to count assailed her. Craddock striking Lulabelle, Craddock throwing her across the room, Craddock looking at her with cold, merciless eyes as he jammed the gun into the side of her head.

"Are you all right, Francesca?" Hart repeated, gripping her by the shoulders and setting her back a bit so their gazes could meet.

His was almost black and filled with concern. She nodded. "Yes." Her voice was hoarse-sounding to her own ears.

His dark gaze moved over her features one by one and finally settled on her eyes, where it remained, searching the depths there.

She felt some of her strength and composure returning. The fear began to fade; her mind began to function. She inhaled, realizing she continued to tremble. "I'm fine. Really." She saw from his eyes that he hardly believed her. "Chrissy?"

"Rathe took her home. And Kennedy, too."

"Thank God!" She half-turned and saw Bragg and Farr standing over Craddock, who was prone and motionless. Was he dead? And had Shoz been the one to kill him after all?

How could she even wonder? she thought.

And as she stared at the dead man, Bragg, and Farr, she realized Bragg was staring at her. She smiled a little at him, telling him with her eyes that she was not harmed, and he smiled, just a little, back. His intense gaze did not waver.

"Right," Hart muttered tersely.

She glanced at Hart and saw that any softness and concern was now gone. His gaze was cool and dark. He released her.

She rushed over to Bragg; he caught her arms. "Is he dead?"

Bragg turned her away from the dead man, but it was too late; she had seen that he was, most certainly, dead. "Yes." His gaze scanned her from head to toe. "Yes. Are you all right? Did he hurt you?"

"I'm fine, truly, except for a bruise or two," she said with a valiant smile. Actually, her head throbbed like the devil, as Craddock hadn't cared about whether he was hurting her or not, and she suspected her wrist was red from his grip, and it hurt a bit to breathe, as if her ribs were sore.

Bragg eyed her, clearly doubtful.

"Now *that* was a helluva shot," Farr said.

Francesca looked at him. He was smiling, but coldly.

"Went in right above his right ear, clean out the other side of his skull." His gaze narrowed. "Now who could pull off a stunt like that? We don't see that kind of shooting here in the city, no sir, we do not."

Francesca shivered and glanced at Bragg.

"You saw Craddock's file; he has a list of enemies a mile long," Bragg said.

"Yeah, guess he does. Harry! Robinson! Start a door-to-door search; we got a shooter on the run!" Farr ordered with obvious relish.

Francesca looked at Bragg. He shook his head at her in a warning.

Farr faced them, looking from the one to the other, his hands on his hips. "Well, your entire family seems to be accounted for, considering your daddy took the children home—except for Shoz Savage."

A silence fell.

Hart appeared in their midst. "He went home with his daughter and Rathe," he said coolly. "Isn't that right, Raoul?" He glanced at the husky Spaniard who was his driver and remained in the driver's seat of his elegant brougham, along with Peter.

Raoul nodded. "Yes, sir, he did," he said with a heavy Spanish accent.

Farr smiled unpleasantly at everyone. "Harry, put a dozen men on the streets. I want the shooter picked up before he gets too far. And find me the bullet that got this bastard. I have a feeling we'll discover a rifle was used. A fancy rifle, the kind I haven't seen before."

"Yes, sir," the policeman said.

Farr faced Bragg. "I'll handle things here, sir, if you want to leave with the rest of your family and go check on the little girl."

"Thank you, Brendan," Bragg said. He took Francesca's arm. "Are you really all right?" he asked as they walked toward Hart's coach.

"Yes. A bit bruised, I think, but that is all." She smiled at him earnestly. "I am not the one you should be worrying about," she added softly.

Their gazes met. In that moment, everyone around them seemed to fade out of focus completely. He finally smiled, just a little. "I have never been so scared, Francesca. I wish you could solve crimes without putting yourself in harm's way."

"I'm sorry. Actually, I wish I could, too."

"Couldn't you have waited a few minutes more for us to join you before tackling Craddock?"

"I was afraid Craddock would leave the poker game and we would lose him all over again!" she cried earnestly.

He stared and sighed.

She touched his sleeve when what she really wanted to do was sink into his arms.

"I think we might want to get out of here," Rourke said dryly.

Francesca started. She had forgotten, for a moment, where they were and whom they were with. She glanced around and saw policemen combing the sidewalk for the bullet that might very well indict Shoz for murder, while across the street other officers were coming out of the apartment building and the milliner's shouting to Farr that they hadn't found anyone. Then her gaze fell on Hart.

He was studying her with no expression on his usually mobile face. When she met his gaze he turned abruptly and opened the coach door. Francesca hesitated, recalling being swept into his arms when Craddock had been shot. There had been something very right about that moment, she realized with a pang of what could only be fear.

But it was not right. Nothing about Calder Hart was right, not for her.

"Francesca?" Bragg asked.

She started, shot him a smile, and climbed into the coach. Hart followed, as did Rourke and Nicholas. Bragg climbed in last, slamming the door closed.

Hart said, "We shall drop off Miss Cahill first, Raoul."

There was no reply, but the brougham rolled off.

They all looked at one another, and the exchanged glances were followed by a series of sighs. Francesca knew that while everyone was relieved, everyone had the same fear— that Shoz would not be able to elude the police, that he was he going to be picked up . . . and charged with manslaughter.

But at least Craddock was dead. And the truth about Cooper's murder could now be buried with him.

Rourke said, "The man can melt into shadows. I've seen him do it. If anyone can vanish right now, it's him."

"What about the fact that he had a rifle—and Farr is looking for the bullet that killed Craddock?" Francesca asked, hating being so dismal.

A silence ensued.

Then Nicholas grinned. He reached into his pocket, a glint in his eyes, and held out his hand. "I don't think Chief Farr is going to find what he is looking for," he said, opening his palm.

A bullet lay there.

Bragg's eyes widened and he picked up the bullet and let out a shaky laugh. "Good job!"

"Well done." Hart smacked his knee with a grin.

"See? He is good for something other than seducing ladies," Rourke said, dimpling.

Francesca laughed in sheer relief.

Bragg handed Nicholas the bullet. "I have never seen that," he said.

Twenty-one

Their door was ajar, and as he stood outside it, he softened, for the scene inside was such a domestic one.

Lucy sat on the floor with her back against the sofa, her beautiful red hair loose and flowing about her shoulders, her feet in stockings. Chrissy was in her lap, playing with two miniature horses; Jack sat a few feet away, busying himself with crayons and a coloring book. Shoz lay on the sofa, taking up most of it, gazing at his wife and the twins, his hands behind his head, in a pair of dungarees and a plaid flannel shirt. Roberto sat curled up by his feet, immersed in a novel. A fire crackled merrily in the hearth.

His heart tightened. He would do whatever he had to do to protect his family, he realized, when a movement behind him made him start. He turned and met Hart's dark eyes.

"Blood does tell," Hart murmured. "I was going to ask Shoz a few questions." He lifted both brows questioningly.

Bragg backed away from the door. "So was I." He smiled a little, and so did his half brother. Then, impulsively, the afternoon's events flashing through Bragg's mind, he touched Hart's white shirtsleeve. "Thank you for your help this afternoon," he said.

Hart was startled.

"I could not have rescued Francesca without you," Bragg added.

Hart leaned against the wall and folded his arms across his chest. Although he had discarded his suit jacket, he remained in a silver brocade vest. "I doubt that," Hart said quietly. "The one thing you are is a damn good police commissioner."

Bragg was startled by the sincerity with which he uttered his praise. The urge was sudden and overwhelming and accompanied by far too many childhood memories to count, but in each and every one of them Hart was a small, dark, angry child, gripping his older brother's hand. Why were they constantly at odds? Why did they dislike each other so? Wasn't it time to bury the hatchet and heal old wounds?

"You are staring," Hart murmured. "Have I grown horns?"

An image of Francesca in Hart's arms came to mind and it was simply unbearable. Bragg straightened. "I imagine you grew horns a long time ago, Calder."

"Thank you."

"But horns or no, in a crisis I would want you at my side anytime."

Hart's eyes widened. "You are getting soft, Rick," he said. Then, indicating the peaceful scene in the room beyond, "Shall we?"

Bragg nodded. Hart pushed open the door with a small knock on the wall. "May we?"

Shoz regarded them impassively from the couch, unmoving, except for the small turn of his head. Lucy moved Chrissy aside and leaped to her feet with a small, glad shriek. She rushed to them and hugged first Bragg and then Hart. "I love you both!" she cried. "Thank you!"

"I was merely along for the ride. Rick ran the show," Hart said.

"Rick!"

Bragg looked down and smiled at his niece, who was using his trousers to haul herself into a standing position. He swooped her up into his arms, then watched Jack's expression turn to grim determination. He somehow stood and began swaying aggressively toward his uncle and sister. He could not speak a single word yet, but his mood was clear; he was filled with jealousy and hell-bent on reaching his uncle.

Chrissy grasped his face. "Uncle! Uncle!" she cried happily.

Jack fell and howled with rage.

Lucy lifted him up and kissed Bragg's cheek. "I love you."

He was taken aback. While so much love ran so freely in his family, it wasn't spoken of. "Are you all right now?"

She glanced at Shoz, who was finally sitting up with a yawn—as if he did not know why they were there. "My husband is home, safe and sound, and he has forgiven me my utter stupidity." Then she grinned wickedly. "More than forgiven, I must say."

He had the uncomfortable feeling that they had already made love and he didn't really want to know about it. "Shoz? Can you step outside for a moment? Hart and I would like to clear up a few matters," he said as casually as possible.

Lucy's face fell. "What matters!" she cried.

"There is nothing for you to worry about," Bragg said soothingly.

She stared in dismay, clearly not believing him.

Shoz strolled the short distance from the sitting area to the door, barefoot. His dungarees were so old that they were faded to a grayish white. He laid his hand on the small of Lucy's back. "One moment," he told her, looking into her eyes.

Bragg watched them and saw far more than the silent communication; he saw the flow of love and trust, and it was disturbing—it was what he had always wanted for himself. It was what he had, foolishly, expected to have on his wedding day and every day after that.

The three men walked into the hall, closing the door behind them. Shoz leaned on the wall, apparently unconcerned and indifferent. Bragg glanced at Hart—their eyes connected in silent agreement. Shoz's composure was simply astounding.

"Well?" he drawled. Then, with a glance at Hart, "I owe you a rifle."

Bragg started. "Where is it?"

"The river."

Relief flooded him. He did not ask which river, either, as he had no wish to know. Shoz had not been caught fleeing the scene, the gun would never be recovered, and Nicholas had the bullet—or, by now, had gotten rid of it. "How many lives is this?" he asked. It was hard to be stern with a man who was not merely twelve years older than he was, but strong-willed, intelligent, and dedicated to his family life.

Shoz's mouth twisted into what might be an expression of mirth. "Number seven," he said softly. "But as I am not a cat, I don't know if I have two more coming."

"Don't you think it might be wise to change your ways?" Hart asked.

"I have changed my ways," Shoz said, coming off of the wall. "I changed my ways the day I got married. But I do have a past. I guess I always knew it would catch up with me one day." Suddenly his composure was gone. And fear appeared in his silver eyes. "If anything had happened to my daughter or Lucy or the other children, I would have never been able to live with myself," he whispered roughly.

Bragg gripped his arm and their eyes held. "But it didn't. And it's over. Craddock is dead."

Shoz smiled, without mirth.

He kept his hand on Shoz's shoulder. "Did you kill Cooper?" Bragg asked.

"Yes," Shoz said evenly, "and just about the whole world knows it."

Bragg stared into his brother-in-law's unflinching gray eyes and knew that there was far more here than met the eye. Clearly Hart did, too, because Calder said, "What happened?"

Shoz sighed. "Craddock and a few of his boys hung Cooper up and tortured him. One of the boys was half-Comanche and they knew how to make a man die as slow as can be. The whole prison was enjoying the show, even the guards and the warden. It got pretty ugly; even though Cooper deserved to die, no one deserved to die the way they were making him die." He stared at them both. "I put him out of his misery. It was a mercy killing," he said.

WEDNESDAY, FEBRUARY 19TH, 1902—6:00 P.M.
Francesca smiled as Bragg was escorted into the small pink-and-gold salon where she was pacing. She hadn't seen him

since the evening before, when she had been dropped off at home after Craddock's murder. He returned her smile, but he was very somber for a man who had just gotten his brother-in-law off of a blackmailer's hook.

But then, her own smile was fragile and tentative. She could not escape a feeling of dread. She quickly crossed the salon and closed both doors so that they were utterly alone. What she had to say—and do—could only be said and done in the utmost privacy. And acutely aware of the intimacy now prevailing in the room, she returned, leaning breathlessly against one mahogany door. She had not slept at all last night.

Could she really go through with this?

Her pulse raced. So much had happened in the past twenty-four hours, she thought grimly. Not the least of which was Leigh Anne calling upon her.

We have a bond that can never be severed, Miss Cahill . . .

I am staying. And I am going to help Rick achieve all of his dreams. Every single one.

Francesca wished, desperately, that she had never laid eyes on Leigh Anne, that the other woman had remained in Europe forever.

"What is it?" Bragg asked softly. He walked up to her and grasped her gently by both arms, his gaze searching hers.

"Leigh Anne came here yesterday."

His grip tightened, and then he released her, his eyes wide, unhappy.

She laid her palm on his cheek. "Has the Craddock investigation been laid to rest?" she asked unsteadily.

He gave her a look and paced. "It is closed. Farr could not find the rifle or the bullet and the shooter escaped."

"Thank God," Francesca said.

He paused, facing her. "Actually, we have Nicholas and Shoz to thank."

"I thought as much," she said. Clearly Shoz had disposed of the rifle. She was glad. "And Cooper?"

"It was a mercy killing, but you were right! Shoz was the

one to put him out of his misery," Bragg said harshly. "I shall have a long private conversation with Warden Timbull early next week. As he allowed a prisoner to be tortured and murdered, we can easily sweep this one under the rug."

Francesca was relieved. While Shoz Savage seemed like an extremely hard and difficult man, clearly he loved his wife and children and clearly Lucy adored him and was impervious to his darker side. "Will they stay in the city for a while?"

"As they are all here, yes, they'll stay about a month," he said. "We have to talk, don't we?"

She nodded, refusing to allow any tears to well up in her eyes.

He walked to her and pulled her close and she snuggled in his arms, against his chest. In that moment, she knew that the bond they shared was not going to change simply because his wife had decided to return to his side. And then the moment changed: a recollection flashed through her mind, more tactile than anything else. For one instant, she recalled being in Hart's arms outside the Thirty-second Street saloon, with her cheek on his chest, his heart beating powerfully beneath it.

She stiffened and Bragg felt it immediately, as he let her go. She put a few steps between them. "I don't know what to do," she finally whispered, and it was a lie. Because deep within herself, she knew what to do.

You are his Achilles' heel . . . you are the one who can destroy him.

Connie's words had been echoing in her mind all night.

You are the problem here, Miss Cahill, you, not I. . . . If you really love him you would never think to put him in such a dangerous position.

If only Leigh Anne were in Europe!

"What did she say? What did she want?" he asked tersely, taking her hands in his. Then he said, "Is your right hand fully healed?" And he turned it over, glancing at her pink-and-white palm.

"Yes, Finney looked at it this morning. The scars may

eventually fade a bit," she added with desperation. A tear
finally shimmered in her eyes.

"Don't cry. The one thing you will always have is my
heart, Francesca," Bragg said, taking her face in his hands.

His words could not thrill her. She closed her eyes and
felt his mouth brushing hers, at first soft and gently, then
repeatedly, and suddenly urgency and need flared in her
loins, in the delta of her sex. She opened and strained against
him, and what had begun as a chaste kiss meant to comfort
became a monster of passion and grief.

He jerked away, breathing hard.

She was also breathless. "She is your wife. She has every
right; I have none," she whispered hoarsely. She had thought
of nothing else all night.

He held her hands tightly. "Did I not make a choice? Did
I not choose you over her—and over my political future?"

"And did I not tell you that I could never live with myself
if you did not follow your destiny? You have a destiny, Rick,
a huge and great destiny," she whispered, meaning it. "Just
like this country!"

"You never call me Rick," he said with real surprise.

She was also surprised; his given name had just slipped
out. And she had the awful feeling that it was an indication
of the changes they must now make. "If I were truly brave,
truly selfless, I would find a way to stop loving you."

His jaw flexed. "And if I were truly selfless, I would wish
that you could do just that. But a part of me refuses to let
you go," he said unsteadily.

"I have that same part, inside of me," Francesca returned.
A tear finally trickled down her cheek. "I have thought about
us all night. I have come to a conclusion."

He paled. "I pray now, suddenly, that it is not the very
same conclusion I have been tormented with."

She shook her head. "No, I think not. The one thing I
can't do, Bragg, is lose you as a friend. But I can stand aside
and support you in your quest for justice and reform. I can
also stand aside and support your marriage," she somehow
said.

He stared. "You are the bravest, most amazing woman I have ever known," he finally said roughly. "Don't you understand? It is moments like this that make me love you even more."

She smiled through her tears.

"And I have no real marriage for you to support," he added with a flash of black anger.

"Leigh Anne is staying, and as she has pointed out, I am the problem now, not her."

"Have you so quickly forgotten that we have been separated for four years? That she left me? That I despise her? Has it not occurred to you that she sees my star rising and so now she has come forward, for God forbid she should not rise with me on my way to prominence and power?"

Francesca was shaken. "I think she loves you," she heard herself say.

"She loves no one but herself!" he almost shouted. "Do not let her fool you, too!"

She recoiled. Would it always be this way? Would the mere subject of his wife be enough to inflame him? Surely this was a sign of the bond Leigh Anne had spoken of; surely this was a sign of some kind of peculiar but intractable love.

"I do not love her," he said, as always in tune with her thoughts, her mind. "I love you. And if she chooses to remain in the city, I cannot stop her. But I intend to do my best to negotiate a pact between us, one that will satisfy her, one that will send her back to Boston, if not Europe."

Oddly, hope did not flare. "Even if she leaves the city, she is hardly dead, and you are hardly unwed."

His eyes softened. "I am so sorry for doing this to you."

"Never tell me you are sorry for anything!" she cried, moving into his arms. They clung for a long breathless and hurtful moment. "Bragg? She has held the threat of informing the press about us over my head. Not directly, but I am no fool. I cannot be the one to destroy you. I must stand back now, and somehow, we must deny our real feelings and try to be true friends, and nothing more."

He was grim. "Isn't that what we have been doing? Hasn't

it been far too difficult to achieve? Every time I am with you, I want you in my arms!" he cried.

"We must try harder," she said. "The truth is, until I met her myself, it was almost as if I was pretending that she did not exist. But she does exist. Before yesterday, I did not want to deny anything; before yesterday, I was convinced that because we loved each other, our love would prevail." She looked down. "But this is not a fairy tale, now is it?" she whispered, acutely aware of using Hart's words.

"Now, this is hardly a fairy tale where the hero and the heroine are assured a happy-ever-after ending. Let's navigate through this day by day. As I said, I need to sit down and negotiate a compromise with her, as her being here, intending to resume her position as my wife, is simply unacceptable." His eyes were chilling now.

"But what can you offer her?" She knew she wasn't being tactful, but he did not have any disposable wealth—although his family certainly did.

"Leave that to me," he said.

She nodded uncertainly. Another tear crept into her eyes. She knew with her entire being that Leigh Anne no longer wanted money, and while she could not be sure that she had not been lured back by Bragg's new position and power, she felt certain that she still loved him.

Which meant she was staying, as she had claimed she intended to do.

"I have never seen you so glum!" he exclaimed.

"I have never before come face-to-face with the wife of the man I love," she said simply. "You were right and I was wrong. I am ashamed, and I am filled with guilt, but we never intended to fall in love!" she cried.

He swept her into his arms for a fierce moment's embrace. "I know. This is my fault, not yours. I was aware of my feelings instantly; I should have avoided you like the plague."

He released her, but she remained in his arms, loosely. She attempted a smile. "Bragg? At least we can solve crimes together."

He smiled a bit at her. And she was stunned to see moisture in his amber gaze. She dared to use her fingertip to catch a tear. He looked dismayed, but before she could say that it did not matter, she heard a movement from the other side of the salon door. She tensed, turning.

"I cannot imagine investigative work without you at my side," he said. "But we should avoid being alone like this," he said, "as it is too difficult and dangerous. And I am thinking about your welfare, Francesca, not my own. I am afraid I no longer trust myself when I am around you." His expression changed. "What is it?"

She gave him a warning look and rushed over to the door and flung it open. Her mother was standing there, clearly eavesdropping.

"How long have you been spying upon us?" Francesca cried.

Julia looked extremely grim. "Long enough." She nodded at Bragg. "Your wife called yesterday, Commissioner. I can't imagine what she and my daughter talked about." She looked at Francesca. "Calder Hart is here. I suggest the commissioner leave." She walked away, and suddenly Hart was striding down the hallway toward Francesca.

Anxiety filled her. Tension stiffened her. He had the worst timing, always. And what did he want? She had last seen him yesterday, too, when she had been dropped off at the house.

"Francesca?" Bragg said from behind her, his tone low.

She turned.

"I had better go." He hesitated. "May I call you later?"

Speaking on the telephone was hardly the same as being with him, but she nodded unhappily. Bragg was now persona non grata in the house; she felt certain of it.

"Why do I have the distinct impression that I am intruding?" Hart drawled. "I take it love's little melodrama is not going well?" His dark gaze moved between them.

Francesca gave him a dark look.

Bragg confronted him. "What the hell are you doing here?"

"The same thing as you, I believe," Hart replied, unruffled. "I am calling on Francesca." He looked directly at her and her heart skipped numerous beats. "How is your hand?"

"Fine," she managed.

"Has Finney looked at it?"

"Yes."

"And in his opinion it is healing well?"

"Yes," she cried.

He nodded, satisfied, and faced Bragg. "How is Leigh Anne?" His smile did not reach his eyes.

"I know what you are about!" Bragg exploded. "As always, you wish to cause trouble—you wish to come between me and Francesca."

"I had not realized there was a 'you and Francesca,'" he murmured. "Except in a particular fairy tale." He gave her a look.

She folded her arms tightly across her chest. "Don't start now, please."

Her tone had been pleading; his expression softened.

"I want you to stay away from her," Bragg said harshly. "She is too good for the likes of you—and you damn well know it."

Hart looked at his half brother as if he were an annoying mosquito that had dared to appear within his mosquito netting.

Francesca moved closer to them. "Please, stop it. Not now, not today." More tears threatened to rise. "Today I cannot watch the two of you carry on like small jealous boys."

They both ignored her, of course. Hart smiled, more coldly than before, at his brother. "I am well aware of the fact that I am hardly fit for Francesca to wipe her boots upon," he said softly. "But fortunately, she is somewhat fond of me, and we are friends—whether you like it or not."

Bragg became still. He was furious. "And what do you think to gain from your *friendship* with Francesca?" he demanded.

"Far more than you think to gain from your friendship," he said.

Bragg took a swing. Hart ducked. Francesca shouted at them both, "What do the two of you think you are doing?"

"I think you heard him; he hardly has friendship in mind," Bragg gritted.

Hart appeared amused. "I find it interesting, the interpretation you put upon my words."

Francesca touched him; he sighed and backed off. She turned to Bragg. "You should go. Mother is very upset." She gave him a significant we-will-speak-later look. "And don't worry about Calder. We *are* friends, truly."

Bragg managed to tear his gaze from Hart. He was incredulous. "When will you see the truth? When you let go of your utter naïveté? Hart has no scruples, none. And he does not have friends, Francesca." He turned coldly to Hart. "Correct me if I am wrong, Calder?"

Hart was as calm as Bragg was not. "Francesca is the first."

Bragg faced her with an I-told-you-so look. "You are deceiving yourself if you think it is friendship which he wants from you," he said very softly.

Francesca simply could not argue over this subject now. She took his hand and kissed his cheek, her lips lingering and firm. And she gripped his palm tightly, as if it were the line to a life preserver and she were floundering in a tempestuous sea. But then again, that was exactly how she felt. "Don't worry," she said as softly. "Not about Calder."

He softened, understanding her completely—they had their own relationship to unravel, and the advent of his wife into their lives. She knew he was an instant from pulling her close, but he glanced at the door, as did she. It remained wide open.

Hart made a disparaging sound.

Bragg gave him a hard glance. "Stay away from her," he said again. "And if you ever touch a hair on her head, you will be very sorry indeed." He gave Francesca another look and strode out, rather angrily.

Francesca felt all of her strength draining away. She took

a deep breath, looked up, and found Hart studying her intently.

"I take it that your tragic love affair is not going well?" he asked simply, with no mockery and no cruelty.

She shook her head. "You were right. I was wrong. Please do not say I told you so, and please, do not smirk."

"I am too fond of you to gloat," he said, and he reached out with a rueful smile and touched her cheek. Then he dropped his hand.

Her skin tingled where his fingers had grazed it. She walked quickly away.

"You can run, but you cannot hide," he said softly. "Not from me."

She whirled. "What does that mean?" she cried with real panic.

"It means I have not forgotten our discussion of a few days ago, even if you have. It means we both know that there is more here than meets the eye."

"I am not up to this!" she cried. And she had never meant her words more earnestly.

"I take it your love story is taking an unexpected and unscripted turn for the worse?" His brows arched.

She sat down hard on an ottoman. "Leigh Anne came here."

"I see." He strolled closer but did not sit. She hated it when he chose to loom over her, a tower of male strength and power. "Care to talk about it? I am sorry," he added.

"I do not want your pity," she said firmly.

"And you do not have it!" he exclaimed. "Why would anyone, least of all I, pity you?"

She had to smile, just a little. "You know, Calder, sometimes you actually say the right thing."

He grinned. "But not often."

"No, not often," she said, her smile slipping. She looked up at him, careful not to inventory his body. "And that is why we are friends. I can always count on the truth from you, even when it is unpleasant."

He stared.

She felt herself beginning to flush. "What is it?"

His jaw flexed visibly. "Rick is right," he said. And the color above his cheekbones began to change; Francesca thought he might be blushing, but surely, she was mistaken.

But a pink cast now colored his cheeks.

She stood. "Calder?"

He gave her a look that she could not decipher, one so grim and determined that his eyes had turned to forged steel, and he turned and paced back and forth across the salon, twice.

She watched him warily. He reminded her of a wild animal, locked up for far too long in a cage. "Calder? What do you mean?"

He came to stand before her. He made her feel five feet tall. "Rick is right. My intentions are not platonic ones."

His meaning was a blow; her heart stopped; she gasped. "What?"

"I do believe you heard my every word," he said, but he was not wry. His gaze was brilliant with resolve and intensity, and he was frightening her.

Yet every inch of her body was painfully alive. She wet her lips. "You intend to seduce me?"

His gaze widened; he laughed, the sound incredulous but harsh. "I intend to marry you," he said.

She thought she had misheard. *"What?"*

"I intend to marry you." He gave her a strange look. "I intend to make you my wife."

TWO HOURS LATER

There was a knock on the door, but she did not hear it. She was faint. She sat on the sofa, unmoving, although her mind was racing at impossible speeds. The salon was all darkness and shadow except for the single lamp that had been on when she had first walked in, earlier in the evening. *How could this be happening?*

Calder, is this a jest?

I would never joke about this subject, and certainly not with you.

Francesca could not recall the rest of their conversation, if indeed, it had continued at all. He had left shortly afterward, telling her that he would call on her the next day or the day after that—as casually as if he had not just said he wanted to make her his wife. Had he dropped a cannonball in the center of the room, one that had exploded, she could not be more shocked.

Calder Hart intended to marry her. Had he lost his mind?

And what about Bragg? She loved him. She always would. *She loved his brother.*

I intend to marry you.

I am sick of it, him, the two of you*!*

Afraid of the real woman inside of yourself? . . . It is not me you are afraid of.

Francesca clapped her hand over her ears, but that would not stop his soft, sexual voice from invading her thoughts, her mind. How could this be happening? How?

And she recalled the steely look in his eyes, and fear and panic overcame her. She had never seen such determination, and recalling it, she felt powerless, as if she were in the path of a cyclone, and incapable of moving even a single step out of the way.

Marry Calder Hart? It was absurd!

An image flashed in her mind, of her in a wedding dress, in Hart's arms, on his big four-poster bed.

She shuddered and suddenly felt as if she had been propelled, against her will, to the edge of a terrible precipice. Because marrying Calder Hart was no different from crawling to the very edge of a tree's limb as someone began to saw through it. It was only a matter of time before that limb went crashing to the earth, with her on it in all of her bridal finery.

She closed her eyes tightly and faced a terrible truth. He could undo her body with a single word, a single look, but that was not love. When he walked into a room she became breathless and frightened all at once, but that was not love.

The man she loved was married, a man she could never have.

The arithmetic was extraordinarily simple—why hadn't she done the math sooner? She could not marry without love, Bragg was already married; therefore, she was not marrying anyone, not ever, and that included Calder Hart. Because she was the kind of woman to only give her heart away once and forever.

It struck her then that her worries were groundless. Hart was not going to drag her screaming and kicking in protest down the aisle. All she had to do was go to him and explain herself. She would tell him that although Leigh Anne had returned to Bragg, that could not, and would not, change her heart. Her heart would always belong to Bragg, and because of that, she was not ever going to marry anyone. And she would also remind him of the fact that he was dead set against marriage, period. She would remind him of his innate inclination to remain a single and notorious bachelor, in the strongest manner possible. She might even briefly point out that he had had a temporary lapse in sanity. After all, they hardly were suitable as a couple; they had very little in common! In fact, undoubtedly by the time she got to this last point they would be sipping his finest Scotch whiskey and laughing over the absurdity of it all. They would discuss his true nature and her resolve and then they would realize that their friendship was perfect as it was. They would laugh about his sudden peculiar urge to wed her—of all women! And everything would go back to the way it had been until a few hours ago.

Thank God.

She laughed in utter relief.

Tomorrow morning, first thing, she would go to his house and resolve the entire affair!

Francesca started from the salon and bumped into her father in the hall. "Papa?" She sensed he was looking for her. He did not look pleased.

"You have a telephone call, Francesca. It is Rick."

She stiffened, all of her relief vanishing, although she could not think why. Hadn't he said he would telephone her later? But just then, she had been ready to slip up to her room with some hot tea and perhaps a piece of terribly decadent chocolate cake. Crawling into bed seemed the perfect anecdote to the extremely frightful day.

She thanked her father, changed direction, and hurried into the library. The receiver was off the hook, on his desk. She lifted it to her ear. "Bragg?"

"There has been another act of vandalism, Francesca," he said without preamble.

She clutched the receiver. "Another art studio?" she gasped, instantly thinking of the shambles Sarah's studio had been in when she had first seen it. And she kept thinking about all that dark red paint that had looked exactly like blood.

"Yes, and it has been thoroughly destroyed, in a similar manner to Sarah's studio, but in a more extreme way. It gets worse," he added.

"How can it be worse?" she whispered, already sensing what was to come.

"The artist was a young woman, just a few years older than Sarah."

Her heart lurched. "Was?"

There was a pause. "She has been murdered," he said.

Francesca forgot to breathe. "Where are you?"

"At headquarters. Francesca, I need you."

"I'll be right there," she said, and she hung up the telephone. A killer was on the loose, and if her instincts were serving her correctly, Sarah's life might very well be in danger. There was no time now to dwell upon Hart's odd proposal, even if she could not quite get over it.

Suddenly Francesca shuddered. If Bragg ever found out that Hart had proposed, all hell would break loose.

And then her determination and good sense returned. Bragg must *never* find out, and tomorrow she *would* set the record straight with Calder Hart. Oh yes, she would.

But right now, she had a murder to solve.

Deadly Pleasure

The moment she used the door knocker, footsteps could be heard at a rapid pace in the hall beyond. The door was thrust open immediately.

Francesca was greeted with the sight of a buxom woman in her early thirties, her dyed and curled red hair pinned up, clad in a well-made suit, although the jacket had been designed to show off an undue amount of cleavage. The woman was wearing large aquamarine drop earrings, a huge aquamarine-and-diamond pin in the shape of a butterfly, and three rings, all gems. Her face was pretty and quite made up. Instantly, Francesca knew she was not greeting a gentlewoman.

Francesca peered past the woman almost immediately and saw a wood-floored hall beyond the small entry, stairs that led upstairs just behind the woman. The door directly at the end of the hall was closed, but light spilled out beneath it. The hall itself was dimly lit.

"You came! Thank God, Miss Cahill—who's that?" Her tone changed, becoming one of abject suspicion as she stared down at Joel.

"I'm her assistant," Joel announced, slipping beneath the woman's arm as she held open the door and ducking into the entry.

Francesca made another mental note—Joel should know to let her do all the speaking. "Miss de Labouche?"

"Yes, yes, do come in!" the woman cried, indicating that she had indeed been the one to hand Francesca the note, but she faced Joel. "Stop right there, young man," she said sternly.

Joel slid his rag-clad hands into the pockets of his big wool coat and he shrugged. Georgette de Labouche shut the door behind Francesca. "Thank God you have come, but you should have come alone!"

The woman was in a panic. There was no mistaking the signs—panic was in her eyes and in her tone and written all over her face as well.

"Perhaps we should start from the beginning," Francesca said kindly.

"There is no time!"

Francesca began unbuttoning her fur-lined cloak. "Very well. Shall we sit down somewhere and begin?"

Georgette hesitated, glancing at Joel. Then, "We can go in there." She pointed at the closed door at the end of the hall, where light glared out from beneath it. Clearly the room beyond was brilliantly lit. "But the boy stays right here." She glared at Joel. "You don't move, buster. You got that?"

Joel made a funny face. "I got one boss and that's Miss Cahill."

"Don't talk back to me!" Georgette cried.

Francesca put a hand on her arm and smiled reassuringly. "I can see you are upset. We shall speak privately, have no fear." She looked at Joel. "Joel, your job is to assist me— when I need assistance. Right now, please stay here in the entry and wait for me until I ask you to do otherwise."

His gaze was searching. Francesca realized he was trying to decide what her words really meant—as if she were speaking in code.

"Stay right here," Francesca reiterated. She smiled at Georgette, who was wringing her bejeweled hands. The redhead looked close to tears. "He'll be fine," Francesca said, hoping she spoke the truth. While originally the idea of Joel as an assistant had seemed wonderful, Francesca wasn't quite sure she could trust him to do as she asked. Which made him a loose cannon indeed. She did not want to mismanage her first case because of the little boy.

Georgette led the way briskly down the hall.

Francesca asked, speaking to her rigid but small shoulders, "How did you know to contact me, Miss de Labouche?"

She glanced over her shoulder, her hand on the knob of the closed door. "You gave me one of your cards outside of Tiffany's yesterday. It was an unusual card. I tucked it away. But I never thought I'd have need of it, and certainly not a day later!"

Francesca met her dark brown eyes. The woman was crying. "It will be all right," she said softly.

Georgette turned and thrust the door somewhat open, stepping inside. Instinct caused unease to assail Francesca, and she hesitated for a moment before slipping past Georgette, who instantly slammed the door closed behind her—locking it.

But Francesca only flinched at the sound of the lock clicking, because directly in the middle of the room was a man. A gentleman, by the looks of him. He was lying on his abdomen, on the highly polished wood floor, his face turned to one side, in a pool of dark red blood.

Francesca muffled her very own gasp. "Is he . . . ?"

"He's dead," Georgette said flatly. "And I need you to help me get rid of the body."

FRIDAY, JANUARY 31, 1902 — MIDNIGHT

Francesca gasped. Surely she had misheard Georgette de Labouche. "What?"

"We must get rid of the body. You have to help me! And the first thing we must do is send the boy away!" Georgette cried, as if Francesca were a dolt.

Francesca could hardly believe her ears. This was her very first official case. And it was not just any case; it was a homicide, the gravest of crimes. A murder had been committed, and Francesca intended to get to the bottom of it. But this woman was asking her not to solve the crime, but help hide it. The situation might have been comical had a man not been murdered and lying there dead at their feet.

"Didn't you hear a word I said? If the police find him, they will throw me in the cooler for sure!" Georgette stabbed at the air, near hysteria.

Francesca took a deep, calming breath. She glanced once more at the dead man at their feet. Her stomach heaved. She had seen corpses before, of course, but they had been in their Sunday best and carefully arranged on the satin bed of a beautiful coffin. "Miss de Labouche? Who is this man? And . . . did you kill him?"

"See! Even you think I did it!" Georgette whirled, pacing, her bosom heaving.

Francesca tried to peer more closely at the dead man. "Is that a hole I see in the back of his head?" She wondered if she might retch. She must control the urge. "Was he shot? Or beaten with a stick?"

Georgette whirled. "I would never hurt Paul. He was a dear, dear friend."

Francesca was relieved as she faced Georgette, no longer studying the man. But she had seen right away that he was well dressed, right down to the tips of his shiny new Oxford shoes. She had noticed a gold watch fob in a gray vest where his dark wool jacket was open. The suit, the watch, and the shoes were all of a very fine quality indeed. "A dear, dear friend," Francesca repeated. "You are his mistress?"

Georgette did not flush. "Obviously," she snapped. "Will you or will you not help me dispose of the body?"

"So now you wish to *dispose* of the body?" Francesca gaped. "Miss de Labouche, this man is not a mouse in a trap. He is a human being and the victim of a terrible crime. We must inform the police. A man has been murdered. In cold blood, I might add—from the look of things."

"Of course it was in cold blood!" Georgette cried, and she sank down on a red velvet chair, moaning and holding her face with her hands.

Francesca took another glance at the body. He had removed his overcoat and top hat; both items lay on another chair with a silver-tipped cane. She estimated his age as early fifties. Then she walked over to Georgette and laid her palm reassuringly on her plump but narrow shoulder. "I am sorry for your loss," she said softly.

Georgette did not speak. She moaned again and said, "I

am going straight to the Tombs; I can see it now!"

"No one has accused you of any crime, Miss de Labouche. What happened?" Francesca knew she did not have a lot of time in which to ask questions. In fact, if she was a truly honorable citizen, she would rush off to call the police in that instant. But she preferred to ask some questions first— before the police began their investigation.

An image of Bragg flashed through her mind. They had worked quite closely together to solve the abduction of Jonny Burton. Something stirred in her heart. He had even admitted, once, reluctantly, how helpful she had been. She wondered if they would work together again, to solve this newer and even more dastardly crime.

Georgette looked up. "I was in my bath," she finally said. "Paul comes every Tuesday and Friday evening. His full name is Paul Randall," she added. "I heard him come in, or I thought I did. I expected him to come upstairs. I had a surprise waiting for him." Tears filled her eyes.

"A surprise?" Francesca asked, wishing she had a notepad. First thing tomorrow she would begin acquiring the tools of her new trade.

"I was in the bath, Miss Cahill. With champagne and other . . . things."

Francesca stiffened. "Oh." Things? Did she dare ask what those things were? She was dying of curiosity, and then she reminded herself that as a now-professional sleuth, of course she must ask. "What kind of things?"

Georgette blinked. "Toys. Devices. You know."

Francesca thought her heart had slowed. "Toys? You mean like rubber ducks?"

Georgette sighed in exasperation and shook her head, standing. "You gentlewomen are all the same! No wonder men like Paul come to women like me! Not rubber ducks, my dear. Toys. *Sex* toys. You know. Objects that bring extra pleasure. If you'd like, I can show them to you?" She stared rather coyly.

Francesca tried not to gasp as her cheeks flamed. She was stunned. She hadn't known that such objects existed, and in

any case, what could they be and how were they used? She
fought to get a grip. "I see." Her cheeks remained hot. Would
Connie know anything about sex toys? Francesca doubted it,
but she was the only person Francesca dared to ask. "So you
were in the bath and then what happened?" She tried to
sound brisk, professional.

"Many minutes passed as I lingered there, with the toys."
She briefly smiled at Francesca, some kind of insinuation
hanging there. Francesca did not quite know what she meant.
"Of course he would come to find me; I know him so well.
But he did not, and suddenly, I was concerned. And it was
just at that point when I heard a sharp, loud crack. One
sound. A crack. And I knew it was a gunshot."

Francesca had had an image of Georgette alone in the bath
together with different-sized rubber ducks, the best her suddenly infertile imagination could do. She shoved that rather
unwelcome image aside. "And?"

"And? I leaped up, put on a robe, and ran downstairs,
calling for Paul. I was praying that the sound I had heard
meant something else. When I reached the entry, the door
was wide open, so I closed it."

Francesca had a thought. "What about the staff?"

"I have no staff on Tuesday and Friday evenings, for obvious reasons, reasons of privacy."

"Of course," Francesca said.

"After I closed the door I turned, and the parlor door was
wide open and I saw him. Oh, God! It was so horrid; you
just cannot imagine how horrid it was!" She cried out, a
soblike sound, and covered her face with her hands once
again.

Francesca patted the woman's shoulder again. "I am so
sorry."

Georgette looked up at her tearfully. "Are you?"

"Yes," Francesca said quietly, earnestly. "An innocent
man is dead. This is a ghastly crime. I am terribly sorry, and
I promise you, Miss de Labouche, that I will find out who
perpetrated this deadly and foul deed."

Georgette said, "I only want to hide the body. Paul is

dead. Finding whoever did this will not bring him back."
Her mouth trembled again.

"We *must* tell the police," Francesca reiterated firmly. "So
you ran to him? Was he still alive? Did he say anything?"

Georgette shook her head and briefly closed her eyes. "He
was dead. His eyes were wide open, sightless, and there was
so much blood!" She moaned and sank down again, but this
time on the red brocade sofa.

Francesca looked at the dead man. His eyes were closed.
"Did you touch him?"

Georgette nodded and whispered, "I closed his eyes, I just
had to, but that is all."

Francesca nodded, folding her arms. She studied the dead
man, Paul, for another moment, then glanced at Georgette,
who remained motionless on the sofa, hunched over in apparent misery. Francesca glanced around. "The only way to
enter this room is via that single door from the hall?"

Georgette nodded.

"And you are certain you did not see anyone?"

She nodded again.

Francesca glanced at the clock on the mantel. It was a
quarter to midnight. Georgette had accosted her on the street
outside of Madison Square Garden at half past nine, approx-
imately. Perhaps it had even been fifteen or twenty minutes
past the hour. "At what time did the murder occur? At what
time did you enter your bath? How long were you in it before
you heard the shot?"

"It was six-thirty when I began to prepare to bathe. I was
expecting Paul at seven. He is usually prompt. He was probably murdered a few moments past seven."

"Miss Labouche. This is very important. Did Mr. Randall
have any enemies? Can you think of anyone who might want
him dead?"

"Only his wife," the redhead said, her regard sullen.

"I am in earnest," Francesca returned. "Are you?"

Georgette de Labouche grimaced. "He had no real enemies. He was not the type of man to provoke anyone, Miss
Cahill. He had retired from his position as manager of a

textile company five years ago. We met shortly afterward. He was a simple man. His life revolved around his children and his wife, his golf, his club—and me."

Francesca was the one to nod, thoughtfully. Then she sighed. "Well, I may have more questions for you, Miss de Labouche, but for the moment, that is enough. I must call the police. Do you have a telephone?"

Georgette looked at her. "They will think I am the one. A murder like this is always blamed on the mistress."

"I do not think they will think you are the one," Francesca said, meaning it. "We must inform the police. We *must*."

"Fine," Georgette said, appearing very unhappy. "I do not have a telephone. While you go, I shall go upstairs and try to compose myself. Perhaps I shall lie down."

"I think that is a good idea," Francesca said. She hesitated. Bragg's house was only a few blocks away. Should she go out on the street and wave down a roundsman or go over to Bragg's? Eventually he would be informed of the murder anyway.

Of course she must go directly to Bragg. Otherwise there would be pointless questions and delay as she dealt with the patrolmen who would answer her call.

Of course, he had rebuffed her earlier, and she should not be pleased about their sharing another case. And she was not pleased—this was *her* case. She had found it first.

"I will see you to the door," Georgette said abruptly, standing.

There was something in the woman's tone that made Francesca start, and suspicion filled her. Georgette had said at least three times that she wanted to hide the body. Francesca realized she should stay and *guard* the body while sending Joel for help. Even though it was unlikely that the woman could remove and hide the body in the half hour or so that it would take the police commissioner to arrive.

"I am sending Joel round the block to the police commissioner's house," Francesca announced, watching her closely. "He is a personal friend of mine," she added.

Georgette blanched, and without a word—but looking

even unhappier than before—she ran from the room.

As she did so, Joel fell into the room, clearly having had his ear pressed to the closed parlor door the entire time. "Hell!" he cried, eyes wide. "Look it that! Cold as a wagon tire, Miss Cahill, a real stiff for your first crime." He grinned at her. "An' a real to-do gent by the look of him."

"Yes, he appears to be a gentleman." Francesca was stern. "Joel, if you are to be my assistant, eavesdropping is not allowed."

"Eavesdroppin'? Wut the hell is that?"

"It is spying," she said, coming forward. "You spied on a private conversation between myself and Miss de La-bouche."

"I was lookin' out for you, lady," he said fiercely. "That's me job."

She looked into his almost-black eyes and melted. "You were?"

He nodded. Then, "Did you peek in his purse?"

She stiffened. "We are not stealing a dead man's purse!"

"Why not? He's dead. He can't use the spondulicks!"

"Spondulicks?" Sometimes conversing with Joel was like trying to comprehend a foreign language.

"He's dead. He can't spend a dime."

"We are not stealing from the corpse!" Francesca cried, meaning it. "Now listen carefully. Tomorrow we will sit down and go over some rules. Rules of your employment. But right now, I need you to go over to the police commissioner's house and tell him what has happened. If he is not there, tell Peter, his man." She hesitated, glancing behind her at the dead man. God, she would be alone with the corpse while Joel was gone. It was not a comforting thought.

Of course, Georgette was upstairs, so she would not really be alone.

"And you should hurry," Francesca added.

"Right," Joel said, turning to go.

"Wait!" She caught the shoulder of his jacket. "Do you know where you're going?"

Joel grinned at her. "Sure do. Madison and Twenty-fourth Street."

She stared. "How would you know where Bragg lives?"

He shrugged. "Whole world knows. Ain't no secret. Back in a flash." He hurried away.

Francesca stood very still, watching him leave the house. And then she felt truly alone.

She shivered.

The house was so quiet that she could hear the clock ticking on the mantel. It almost felt as if there were eyes trained on her back—the dead man's eyes. But of course, they were closed—and he was dead.

Fortunately, she did not believe in ghosts. Still, Francesca hurried down the dimly lit hall, wishing it were more brightly lit, relieved to leave the room with the corpse. She checked the front door. It was locked. That made her feel a bit better.

She cracked open the only other door on the hall, other than the parlor door, and glanced into a small dining room. It was cast in shadow. She vaguely made out an oak table and four chairs, a floral arrangement, and a sideboard with knickknacks. A kitchen had to be on the other side of the alcove. Francesca hesitated.

If there was a kitchen door that led to a garden out back or the street out front, she wanted to make sure it was locked. She was very nervous now. And why not? She was guarding the corpse of a man who had been murdered less than five hours ago.

Francesca looked up at the dark stairs. "Miss de Labouche?" she called.

There was no answer.

"Georgette?" she tried again, with the same lack of success.

Francesca glanced behind her. The parlor remained so brilliantly lit, and the dead body in the pool of blood remained a grotesquely eye-catching spectacle. Francesca realized just how nervous she was.

That was it. She dashed through the small dining alcove, trying not to consider that the murderer might still be in the house—of course that made no sense—and she found herself in the kitchen. This house did not have electricity, and it was a moment before Francesca turned on one gaslight. There was a back door. It was locked.

She sighed in abject relief.

When she heard something.

Instinct caused Francesca to turn off the light and crouch down beside the doorway to the dining alcove. She had not closed the dining room door, and she could just glimpse the hall beyond.

She heard something again. God damn it, but it was the front door, she was certain of it, being carefully closed.

Francesca ducked completely behind the kitchen doorway, now perspiring madly. Joel had left about five minutes ago. Maybe, maybe, he could run from here to Bragg's in five minutes. But there was just no way that he was already returning, alone or with Bragg, and anyway, they would have to knock.

She trembled and heard a floorboard creak.

Someone had entered the house. Someone was in the hall. Someone who was not announcing himself—someone who had a key.

She heard more soft footsteps.

Francesca went blank. But she had to know who the intruder was. She thought he had walked past the dining room doorway, but she wasn't sure. Keeping on all fours now, she peered around the kitchen doorway and into the dining room.

Just in time to glimpse a man's silhouette as he walked past while in the hall.

Francesca ducked back. She heard the man halt. And there was a very soft, barely audible expletive, followed by absolute silence.

She imagined he had seen the body and that was what had stopped him in his tracks and caused him to curse. Was he staring at it now?

Suddenly she heard brisk footsteps returning. Francesca did not dare peer around the corner again, as much as she wanted to. She held her breath, afraid he might feel her presence, afraid he might change course and discover her hiding in the other room.

The front door opened and closed.

Francesca jumped up and ran into the dining room and shoved aside the draperies to peer onto the street, her pulse racing wildly. A very nice gig was pulling away from the curb, a single man its occupant—the driver. He was too far away for her to make out any features.

Francesca stared. Who in blazes had just walked into Georgette de Labouche's house in order to stare at her dead lover? Who would do such a thing, then turn around without a word and leave?

What in tarnation was going on?

Deadly Affairs

"You have a caller, Francesca."

Francesca halted at the sound of her mother's voice, having just handed her coat, hat, muff, and gloves to a servant. She slowly turned, with dread.

For the voice had been sharp. Now, disapproval covered Julia's attractive face. She was an older image of both daughters: blond, blue-eyed, with classic and fine features. Although over forty, she remained slim and glamorous; many men her own age often eyed her in a covert manner.

"Good day, Mama," Francesca said nervously. She had seen *The Sun*. Francesca would wager her life on it.

Julia Van Wyck Cahill was magnificently attired, clearly dressed for an early evening affair. Her sapphire-blue gown revealed a slim and pleasing figure, while two tiers of sapphires adorned her neck. Before she could answer, Andrew appeared on the stairs, in a white dinner jacket and satin-trimmed black trousers. He took one look at Francesca and his expression became pinched, with disbelief and accusation warring in his eyes.

"I can explain," Francesca whispered.

"What can you explain?" Andrew demanded, halting beside his wife. "That you have made the front page of *The Sun*? That you once again immersed yourself in a dangerous affair? One belonging, I believe, to the police?"

Francesca inhaled. How to begin? Before she could speak, her mother interrupted.

"I am aghast. I am aghast that my daughter would confront a killer and place herself in unspeakable danger. This shall not continue, Francesca. You have gone too far." Julia turned and nodded at a servant, who was holding her magnificent sable coat for her. She allowed him to slip it over her shoulders.

"I am beginning to wonder if my brilliant daughter has truly lost her mind," Andrew said.

Francesca cringed. Papa never spoke to her in such a manner. "I helped the police enormously," Francesca murmured. The fact was, she had solved the case at the eleventh hour.

"You have been up to your ears in police affairs ever since Bragg arrived in town," Julia said sharply. "Do you think I am blind, Francesca? I can see what is happening."

"Nothing is happening," Francesca tried, stealing a glance at her father. He knew about Bragg's married state, she thought suddenly. This was the secret he had been keeping. But why hadn't he told her?

"We are on our way out for the evening, but we shall speak tomorrow morning, Francesca." Julia gave her a look that was filled with warning, and did not look at her again while Andrew donned his coat. But her father met her gaze, shaking his head, looking so terribly grim that Francesca knew she was in a kind of trouble she had never dreamed of. There was no relief when they left the house. But what could they do? She was a grown woman.

Francesca relaxed slightly. She would worry about her parents tomorrow. She turned as Bette handed her a delicately engraved calling card on a small sterling tray. Francesca studied the card for a moment, curiously; she did not believe she had ever met a Mrs. Lincoln Stuart. She thanked Bette and entered the far salon.

It was beautifully appointed, but small, and used for more intimate gatherings, such as a single caller. It was painted a pale, dusky yellow, and most of the furnishings were in various shades of yellow or gold, with several red and navy-blue accents. The moment Francesca entered the room, she saw Mrs. Lincoln Stuart. She had been sitting on a sofa at the room's other end, but upon espying Francesca, she instantly stood. Francesca smiled and approached.

Mrs. Lincoln Stuart twisted her hands.

Francesca saw that she was a few years older than her. She was rather plain in appearance, her features usual and unsurprising. But her hair was a beautiful cascade of chestnut curls, and it was what one noticed first. She was very well-dressed, in a green floral suit and skirt, and she wore a rather large, yellow diamond ring. Her husband was obviously wealthy. And she was nervous and distressed.

"Miss Cahill. I do hope you do not mind me calling like this," Mrs. Stuart said in a husky voice, one filled with tension. Worry was expressed in her eyes.

Francesca smiled warmly, pausing before her. "Of course not," she said politely. "Have we met?"

"No, we have not, but I was given this by a boy the other day." And Mrs. Stuart handed her a card.

Francesca recognized it instantly—how could she not? Tiffany's had printed the cards at her request upon the conclusion of the Burton Affair. It read:

> *Francesca Cahill*
> *Crime-Solver Extraordinaire*
> *No. 810 Fifth Avenue, New York City*
> *All Cases Accepted, No Crime Too Small*

"My assistant, Joel Kennedy, must have handed this to you," Francesca mused, pleased. She had recently assigned him the task of drumming up business for her. She glanced up at Mrs. Stuart. Was she a prospective client? Francesca's heart thudded in anticipation.

"I don't know the boy's name, I only know that I am frightened and I have no one to turn to," Mrs. Stuart cried, her eyes wide. Francesca saw that they were green and lovely. Mrs. Stuart was the kind of woman who had a quiet kind of beauty, one that was not instantly remarkable, she decided.

Francesca also realized that she was on the verge of tears. She took her arm. "Do sit down, and I am sure I can help you, Mrs. Stuart," she said. "No matter what your problem might be." There was no doubt now; Mrs. Stuart had come to her for help. This would be her second official case!

The woman dug a handkerchief out of her velvet purse. It was hunter-green, like the trim on her elegant tea gown. "Please, call me Lydia," she said, dabbing at her eyes. "I saw today's article in *The Sun*, Miss Cahill. You are a heroine, a brave heroine, and when I realized that you are the same woman on this card, I knew it was you to whom I must turn."

"I am hardly a heroine, Lydia," Francesca said, barely containing her excitement. "Excuse me." She rushed to the salon door and closed it, so that no one might overhear the conversation. Her resolve to take a "sabbatical" from sleuthing had vanished. In fact, she forgot all about her studies now. She hurried back to her guest—her *client*—and sat down. What could this woman's problem be? And was she truly going to have, for the very first time, a paying client? In the past, she had offered her services for free. A paying client would truly make her a professional woman.

Lydia managed to smile at her, and she now handed Francesca a small piece of paper, upon which were two names, Rebecca Hopper, and an address, 40 East 30th Street. "What is this?" Francesca asked.

Lydia Stuart's face changed, becoming filled with distaste. "Mrs. Hopper is a widow, and that is where she lives. I believe my husband is having an affair with her, but I want to know the truth."

Francesca stared.

"And I have no doubt that he will be there tonight, as he has said he is working late and he will not be home for supper," Lydia added.

Mrs. Hopper's residence was a corner one, and while all of the lights were on downstairs, only one bedroom upstairs was illuminated. It had been years since Francesca had climbed a tree, and now she was sorry that she had not gone further downtown to locate Joel to do her evening's work for her. He would have been very useful indeed—especially as he did not have cumbersome skirts to deal with.

Huffing and puffing, her hands freezing because she had

stripped off her gloves, she sought another foothold in the huge tree she was climbing, clinging to the trunk.

She had decided to tackle Lydia's case head-on. It was nine P.M., and a quick look at the house had shown her that if she climbed the big tree in the yard, she might very well be able to spy upon the lovers directly. In fact, if Lydia were right, this case might be solved before it was even begun.

Francesca made it to the large, higher branch. She clung to it, one leg atop it, both arms around it. Her skirts were in the way; she had not worn men's clothing for she did not have the psychic ability to know when she would be climbing trees. With great effort, she somehow moved her other leg onto the thick branch, and then she hugged it with all her might, afraid she was going to fall. She glanced down.

She was not sure she liked heights. When she had been on the ground, in the yard, the tree had not seemed so tall. Now, looking down, her cheek upon the rough bark, her hands feeling rather scraped and raw, the ground looked very far away.

She had not a doubt that if she fell, the snow would be rock-hard, as it was solidly frozen. It would not break her fall; she might wind up with a broken arm, or God forbid, a broken neck.

But she was determined to ignore her cowardice now. Very, very carefully, Francesca sat up. When she was astride the branch as if it were a horse, she began to breathe easier. This wasn't too bad. She believed she could manage.

Dismayed, she suddenly realized her eyes were still below the window and she could not see into the bedroom in order to learn what was going on. She was going to have to stand up.

But Francesca realized she was turned around the wrong way—the trunk of the tree was behind her. *Oh dear.* This might be far too dangerous a maneuver, she thought.

She could not see into the bedroom, and she was at a grave risk if she tried to turn around. Now what?

There was no choice. She had to turn herself around. She

simply had to. *Because Lydia Stuart was her first paying client.*

Francesca lifted her right leg up slowly, until she was able to move it up and over the branch. Now she sat with both legs dangling off the same side of the tree, and her position was precarious at best. She failed to breathe now. She had to reverse herself, but she was afraid to move.

That was when she slipped.

Francesca cried out as she lost her balance and started to slide off the branch. Instantly, desperately, she reached out, trying to grasp the branch with her hands, the bark scraping and abrading her palms, and for one moment, she thought she had succeeded in stopping herself. She gripped the tree, but then her hands failed her and suddenly she was falling through space.

She saw the white snow below, racing towards her face, and she thought, *Oh dear, this is it. It is all over now.*

Whomp.

Francesca landed hard on her shoulder and her side, not her face, her head smacking down last. And then she was spitting out snow.

God, she thought, dazed. Was she intact? Had she broken anything?

She began to move. The snow was not as frozen as she had thought it would be; it was not rock-hard, surprisingly. She wiggled her toes and fingers in the snow, moved her hands and legs.

She froze.

Had she just touched something? Something beneath the snow? Something *sticky*? And *solid*?

Francesca sat up shakily, and as she stood, she looked down at her own hands.

One was pale and white in the moonlight, the other was dark and splotched in places.

She had an inkling. She did not move. She recognized those splotches.

Her heart pumped hard now.

And then she rubbed her fingers together. *Oh, no.*

Francesca was on her knees, tearing at the frozen snow. And as she moved the top layer away, she found a piece of garment.

Francesca stared at a patch of brown wool, and the dark, still not thoroughly frozen, stain upon it.

She touched it.

It was no different than what had been on her fingertips; it was blood, and it was fresh.

Someone was buried in the snow, recently, and maybe the person was alive!

Francesca pawed the snow frantically, shoving it away in clumps, and then she saw the woman's face—she saw the open, sightless blue eyes, and they were glazed in terror.

She saw the throat.

She stood, and unable to help herself, she screamed.

For carved in the once-pristine white skin was a perfect and bloody cross.

THE
CHASE

——

BRENDA JOYCE

NEW YORK TIMES BESTSELLING AUTHOR

CLAIRE HAYDEN has no idea that her world is about to be shattered: at the conclusion of her husband's fortieth birthday party, he is found murdered, his throat cut with a WWII thumb knife. He has no enemies, no one seeking revenge, no one who would want him dead. But the mysterious Ian Marshall, an acquaintance of her husband's, seems to know something. Because someone has been killing this way for decades. Someone whose crimes go back to WWII. Someone who has been a hunter...and the hunted. As Claire and Ian team up to find the killer, they can no longer deny the powerful feelings they have for one another. Then Ian makes a shocking revelation: the murderer may be someone close to her...

> **"Joyce excels at creating twists and turns in her characters' personal lives."**
> **—*Publishers Weekly***

ON SALE JULY 2002
FROM ST. MARTIN'S PRESS

GET A $4 REBATE ON
BRENDA JOYCE'S
NEW HARDCOVER!

Send in this coupon, along with your store receipt(s) for the purchase of *Deadly Desire* in paperback and Brenda Joyce's new hardcover, *The Chase*, to receive a $4.00 rebate. (*The Chase* will be available in stores July 2002.)

Claire Hayden has no idea that her world is about to be shattered: at the conclusion of her husband's 40th birthday party, he is found murdered, his throat cut with a weapon that hasn't been used since WWII. He has no enemies, but the mysterious Ian Marshall, an acquaintance of her husband's, seems to know something. Someone has been killing this way for decades. Someone whose crimes go back to WWII. As Claire and Ian team up to find the killer, Ian makes a shocking revelation: the murderer may be someone close to her...

To receive your $4.00 rebate, please send this form, along with your original dated cash register receipt(s) showing the price for purchase of both the paperback edition of *Deadly Desire* and the hardcover edition of *The Chase* to: St. Martin's Press, Dept. AN, Suite 1500, 175 Fifth Avenue, New York, NY 10010.

NAME:
ADDRESS:
CITY:
STATE/ZIP:

Coupon and receipt(s) must be received by December 31, 2002. Purchases may be made separately. One rebate per person, address, or family. U.S. residents only. Allow 6–8 weeks for delivery of your rebate. St. Martin's Press is not responsible for late, lost or misdirected mail. Void where prohibited.

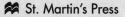 St. Martin's Press